NEW WEBSTER'S SPELLING *AND* PRONUNCIATION GUIDE

edited by
Joseph Yenolam

1996 EDITION

Paradise Press, Inc.

Plantation, Florida

Cover Design 1996 - Carol-Ann McDonald

Printed in U.S.A. All Rights Reserved.

ISBN #1-57657-026-6

30448

A

aardvark... aard'varc
aba... a'ba
abaca... a-ba'ca
aback... a-bac'
abactor... a-bak'tor
abaft... a-baft'
abalone... a-ba'lō-nē
abandon... a-ban'don
abandoned... a-ban'dond
abase... a-bās'
abasement... a-bās'ment
abash... a-bash'
abate... a-bāt'
abatement... a-bāt'ment
abattis... a-b'a-tis
abattoir... a-bat-twar'
abbacy... ab'a-ci
abbe... a-bā'
abbess... a-bas'
abbey... ab'e
abbot... ab'ot
abbreviate... a-brē'vi-āt
abbreviator... a-brē'vi-ā-tėr
abdication... ab-di-cā'shun
abdomen... ab-dō'men
abdominal... ab-dom'in-al
abduce... ab'dus
abduct... ab-duct'
abduction... ab-duc'shun
abe... a'bē
abeam... a-bēm'
aberrant... ab-e'rant
aberration... ab-e-rā'shun
abet... a-bet'
abetment... a-bet'ment
abeyance... a-bā'ans
abhor... ab-hor'
abhorrence... ab-hor'rens
abhorrent... ab-hor'rant
abide... a-bīd
abiding... a-bīd'ing
abietate... a-bē'tāt
ability... a-bil'li-ti
abjoint... ab'joint
abject... ab'ject
abjuration... ab-jū-rā'shun
abjure... ab-jūr'
able... ā'bl
ablution... ab-lū'shun
ably... ā'bli
abnegate... ab'nē-gāt

abnegation... ab-nē-gā'shun
abnormal... ab-norm'al
aboard... a-bōrd'
abode... a-bōd'
abolish... a-bol'ish
abolition... ab-ō-li'shun
abominable... a-bom'in-a-bl
abominably... a-bom'in-a-bli
aboral... a'boōral
abominate... a-bom'in-āt
aborigines... ab-ō-rij'in-ēz
abort... a-bort'
abortion... a-bor'shun
abortive... a-bort'iv
abortively... a-bort'iv-li
abound... a-bound'
abounding... a-bound'ing
about... a-bout'
above... a-bov'
abox... a'bocs
abrase... a'brāz
abrasion... ab-rā'zhun
abreact... abrē'act
abreast... a-brest'
abridge... a-brij'
abroach... a-brōch'
abroad... a-brad'
abrogate... ab'rō-gāt
abrogation... ab-rō-gā'shun
abrood... a'brud
abrupt... a-bropt'
abruptly... a-bropt'li
abruptness... a-bropt'nes
abscess... ab'ces
abscind... ab-cind'
abscond... ab-scond'
abseil... ap'zīl
absence... ab'cens
absent... ab'cent
absent... ab-cent'
absentee... ab-cn-tē'
absenteeism... ab-cn-tē'izm
absently... ab'cnt-li
absolute... ab'sō-lūt
absoluteness... ab'sō-lūt-nes
absolution... ab-sō-lū'shun
absolve... ab-solv'
absorb... ab-sorb'
absorbable... ab-sorb'a-bl
absorbent... ab-sorb'ent
absorption... ab-sorp'shun
abstain... ab-stān'
absterge... ab-stėrg'
abstinence... ab'stin-ense

abstinent... ab'stin-ent
abstinently... ab'stin-ent-li
abstract... ab-stract'
abstract... ab'stract
abstracted... ab-stract'ed
abstractive... ab-stract'iv
abstractly... ab-stract'li
abstruse... ab-strūs'
absurd... ab-sėrd'
absurdity... ab-sėrd'i-ti
absurdly... ab-sėrd'li
abulia... ā'bul'a
abundance... a-bon'dans
abundant... a-bon'dant
abusive... a-būs'iv
abut... a-bot'
abutment... a-bot'ment
abysmal... a-biz'mal
abyss... a-bis'
acacia... a-ca'shi-a
academic... ac-a-dem'ic
academy... a-cad'ē-me
acanthus... a-can'thus
acaridan... a-car'i-dan
accede... ac-sēd'
accelerate... ac-cel'lė-rāt
accelerative... ac-cel'lė-rāt-iv
accent... ac'cent
accented... ac-cent'ed
accentual... ac-cent'ū-al
accentuate... ac-cent'ū-āt
accept... ac-cept'
acceptable... ac-sept'a-bl
acceptably... ac-sept'a-bli
acceptance... ac-sept'ans
acceptation... ac-sep-tā'shun
accepter... ac-sept'ėr
access... ac'ces
accessible... ac-ces'i-bl
accessibly... ac-ces'i-bli
accession... ac-ce'shun
accessory... ac'ces-sō-ri
accidence... ac'si-dens
accident... ac'ci-dent
accidental... ac-ci-dent'al
acclaim... a-clām'
acclimate... a-clī'māt
acclivity... ac-cliv'i-ti
accolade... ac-o-lād'
accompany... a-cum'pa-ni
accomplice... a-com'plis
accomplish... a-com'plish
accomplished... a-com'plisht
accord... a-cord'

accordance... a-cord'ans
accordant... a-cord'ant
according... a-cord'ing
accordingly... a-cord'ing-li
accordion... a-cord'i-on
accost... a-cost'
account... a-count'
accountable... a-count'a-bl
accountant... a-count'ant
accredit... a-cred'it
accredited... a-cred'it-ed
accresce... a-cres'
accretion... a-crē'shun
accretive... a-crēt'iv
accrue... a-cro'
accuracy... ac'cū-rā-si
accurate... ac'cū-rāt
accurately... ac'cū-rāt-li
accursed... a-cėrs'ed
accusable... a-cūz'a-bl
accusation... ac-cū-zā'shun
accusative... ac-cūz'at-iv
accuse... a-cūz'
accused... a-cūzd'
accuser... a-cūz'ėr
accustom... a-cus'tum
accustomed... a-cus'tumd
ace... ās
acerbity... a-sėr'bi-ti
acescent... a-ses'ent
acetic... a-cet'ic
acetify... a-cet'i-fī
achieve... a-chēv
achievement... a-chēv'ment
aching... āc'ing
achromatic... ac-rō-mat'ic
acid... as'id
acidifiable... as-id'i-fī-a-bl
acidifier... as-id'i-fī-ėr
acidity... as-id'i-ti
acidulate... as-id'ū-lāt
acknowledge... ac-nol'lej
acme... ac'mē
acorn... ā'corn
acotyledon... a-cot'il-ē'don
acoustic... a-cous'tic
acoustics... a-cous'tics
acquaint... a-cwānt'
acquaintance... a-cwānt'ans
acquiesce... a-cwi-es'
acquiescence... a-cwi-es'ens
acquiescent... a-cwi-es'ent
acquirable... a-cwīr'a-bl
acquire... a-cwīr'

acquirement... *a-cwīr'ment*
acquisition... *a-cwi-zi'shun*
acquit... *a-cwit'*
acquittal... *a-cwit'al*
acquittance... *a-cwit'ans*
acre... *ā'cėr*
acreage... *ā'cėr-āj*
acred... *ā'cėrd*
acrid... *ac'rid*
acridity... *ac-rid'i-ti*
acrimonious... *ac-ri-mō'ni-us*
acrimony... *ac'ri-mo-ni*
acrobat... *ac'rō-bat*
acrobatic... *ac'rō-bat-ic*
acrogen... *ac'rō-jen*
acrogenous... *a-croj'en-us*
acropolis... *a-crop'o-lis*
across... *a-cros'*
acrostic... *a-cros'tic*
act... *act*
acting... *act'ing*
actinic... *ac-tin'ic*
actinism... *ac'tin-izm*
action... *ac'shun*
actionable... *ac'shun-a-bl*
active... *ac'tiv*
activity... *ac-tiv'i-ti*
actor... *act'ėr*
actress... *act'res*
actual... *ac'tū-al*
actuality... *ac-tū-al'li-ti*
actually... *ac'tū-al-li*
actuary... *ac'tū-a-ri*
actuate... *ac'tū-āt*
acupressure... *ac-ū-pre'shūr*
acute... *a-cūt'*
acutely... *a-cūt'li*
acuteness... *a-cūt'nes*
adage... *ad'āj*
adamant... *ad'a-mant*
adam's-apple... *ad'amz-ap'l*
adapt... *a-dapt'*
adaptability... *a-dapt'a-bil''li-ti*
adaptable... *a-dapt'a-bl*
adaptation... *ad-ap-tā'shun*
add... *ad*
addendum... *ad-den'dom*
addict... *ad-dict'*
addicted... *ad-dict'ed*
addiction... *ad-dic'shun*
additional... *ad-di'shun-al*
additive... *ad'it-iv*
address... *ad-dres'*
addressee... *ad-dres'ē*

adducible... *ad-dūs'i-bl*
adductor... *ad-duct'ėr*
adenoid... *ad'en-oid*
adept... *a-dept'*
adequacy... *ad'ē-cwa-si*
adequate... *ad'ē-cwāt*
adequately... *ad'ē-cwāt-li*
adhere... *ad-hēr'*
adherence... *ad-hēr'ens*
adherent... *ad-hēr'ent*
adhesion... *ad-hē'zhon*
adhesive... *ad-hē'siv*
adhibit... *ad-hib'it*
adhortatory... *ad-hor'ta-tō-ri*
adieu... *a-dū'*
adit... *ad'it*
adjacent... *ad-jā'sent*
adjective... *ad'jec-tiv*
adjoin... *ad-join'*
adjoining... *ad-join'ing*
adjournment... *ad-jėrn'ment*
adjudge... *ad-juj'*
adjudicate... *ad-jōō'di-cāt*
adjunct... *ad'jungct*
adjuration... *ad-jū-rā'shun*
adjure... *ad-jūr'*
adjust... *ad-just'*
adjustable... *ad-just'a-bl*
adjustment... *ad-just'ment*
adjutancy... *ad'jōō-tan-si*
adjutant... *ad'jōō-tant*
admeasure... *ad-me'zhūr*
administer... *ad-min'is-tėr*
admirable... *ad'mi-ra-bl*
admirably... *ad'mi-ra-bli*
admiral... *ad'mi-ral*
admiralty... *ad'mi-ral-ti*
admiration... *ad-mi-rā'shun*
admire... *ad-mīr'*
admirer... *ad-mīr'ėr*
admiringly... *ad-mīr'ing-li*
admissibility... *ad-mis'i-bil''li-ti*
admissible... *ad-mis'i-bl*
admission... *ad-mi'shun*
admittance... *ad-mit'ans*
admonish... *ad-mon'ich*
admonisher... *ad-mon'ich-ėr*
admonition... *ad-mō-ni'shun*
admonitory... *ad-mon'i-tō-ri*
ado... *a-do'*
adobe... *a-dō'be*
adolescence... *ad-ō-les'ans*
adolescent... *ad-ō-les'ant*
adopt... *a-dopt'*

adoption... a-dop'shun
adoptive... a-dopt'iv
adorable... a-dōr'a-bl
adorably... a-dōr'a-bli
adoration... a-dōr-ā'shun
adore... a-dōr'
adoringly... a-dōr'ing-li
adorn... a-dorn'
adrift... a-drift'
adroitly... a-droit'li
adroitness... a-droit'nes
adstriction... ad-stric'shun
adulation... ad-ū-lā'shun
adulatory... ad'ū-lā-tō-ri
adulterate... a-dul'tėr'āt
adulterated... a-dul'tėr-āt-ed
adulterer... a-dul'tėr-ėr
adulteress... a-dul'tėr-es
adulterous... a-dul'tėr-us
adulterously... a-dul'tėr-us-li
adultery... a-dul'tė-ri
advance... ad-vans'
advanced... ad-vanst'
advantage... ad-van'tāj
advantageous... ad-van-tāj'us
advent... ad'vent
adventitious... ad-ven-ti'shi-us
adventure... ad-ven'tūr
adventurer... ad-ven'tūr-ėr
adventuress... ad-ven'tūr-es
adventurous... ad-ven'tūr-us
adverb... ad'vėrb
adverbial... ad-vėrb'i-al
adverbially... ad-vėrb'i-al-li
adversary... ad'vėr-sa-ri
adversative... ad-vėrs'at-iv
adverse... ad'vėrs
adversely... ad-vėrs'li
advert... ad-vėrt'
advertence... ad-vėrt'ens
advertent... ad-vėrt'ant
advertise... ad-vėr-fīz'
advertiser... ad-vėr-fīz'ėr
advertising... ad-vėr-fīz'ing
advice... ad-vīc'
advisable... ad-vīc'a-bl
advise... ad-vīz'
advised... ad-vīzd'
advisedly... ad-vīz'ed-li
adviser... ad-vīz'ėr
advocacy... ad'vō-cā-si
advocate... ad'vō-cāt
aegis... ē'jis
aeolian... ē-ō'li-an

aerate... ā'ėr-āt
aeration... ā-ėr-ā'shun
aerial... ā-ē'ri-al
aerie... ē'rē
aerology... ā-ėr-ol'o-gi
aerometer... ā-ėr-om'et-ėr
aeronaut... ā-ėr-ō-nat
aeronautic... ā'ėr-ō-̈nat''ic
aerostatic... ā'ėr-ō-stät''ic
aerostatics... ā'ėr-ō-stat''ics
aesthetics... ēs-thet'ics, or es-
afar... a-far'
affable... af'fa-bl
affair... af-fār'
affect... af-fect'
affectation... af-fec-tā'shun
affected... af-fect'ed
affectedly... af-fect'ed-li
affecting... af-fect'ing
affectingly... af-fect'ing-li
affection... af-fec'shun
affectionate... af-fec'shun-āt
affectioned... af-fec'shund
affiance... af-fī'ans
affianced... af-fī'anst
affidavit... af-fi-dā'vit
affiliate... af-fil'li-āt
affiliation... af-fil'li-ā''shun
affinity... af-fin'i-ti
affirm... af-fėrm'
affirmable... af-fėrm'a-bl
affirmation... af-fėrm-ā'shun
affirmatively... af-fėrm'at-iv-li
affix... af-fics'
afflict... af-flict'
affluence... af'flū-ans
affluent... af'flū-ant
afflux... af'flucs
afford... af-fōrd'
affray... af-frā'
affront... af-frunt'
afloat... a-flōt'
afoot... a-fut'
aforehand... a-fōr'hand
aforenamed... a-fōr'nāmd
aforesaid... a-fōr'sād
afraid... a-frād'
afresh... a-fresh'
african... af'ric-an
aft... aft
after... aft'ėr
afterbirth... aft'ėr-bėrth
aftermath... aft'ėr-math
aftermost... aft'ėr-most

afternoon... aft'ėr-non
afterpiece... aft'ėr-pēs
again... a-gan'
against... a-ganst'
agape... a-gāp'
agate... ag'āt
age... āj
aged... āj'ed
agency... ā'jen-ci
agenda... a-jen'da
agent... ā'jent
aggrandize... ag'gran-dīz
aggravate... ag'gra-vāt
aggravating... ag'gra-vāt'ing
aggravation... ag-gra-vā'shun
aggregate... ag'grē-gāt
aggregately... ag'grē-gāt-li
aggression... ag-gre'shun
aggressive... ag-gres'iv
aggressor... ag-gres'or
aggrieve... ag-grēv'
aghast... a-gast'
agile... ag'il
agility... a-gil'i-ti
agitate... ag'it-āt
agitated... ag'it-āt-ed
agitator... ag'it-āt-or
aglet... ag'let
agnate... ag'nāt
agnostic... ag-nos'tic
agnosticism... ag-nos'ti-sizm
ago... a-gō
agog... a-gog'
agoing... a-gō'ing
agonize... ag'ō-nīz
agonizing... ag'ō-nīz-ing
agonizingly... ag'ō-nīz-ing-li
agony... ag'ō-ni
agora... ag'o-ra
agree... a-grē'
agreeable... a-grē'a-bl
agreeably... a-grē'a-bli
agreement... a-grē'ment
agricultural... ag-ri-cul'tūr-al
agriculture... ag'ri-cul-tūr
agriculturist... ag-ri-cul'tūr-ist
aground... a-ground'
ague... ā'gū
agued... ā'gūd
aguish... ā'gū-ish
aha... a-ha'
ahead... a-hed'
ahoy... a-hoi'
aid... ād

aiguille... ā'gwil
ail... āl
ailment... āl'ment
aim... ām
aimless... ām'lis
air... ār
aircraft... ār-craft
airgraph... ār'graf
air-gun... ār'gun
airily... ār'i-li
airiness... ār'i-nes
airing... ār'ing
airplane... ār'o-plān
airport... ār'pōrt
air-pump... ār'pump
air-shaft... ār'shaft
air-tight... ār'tīt
airy... ā'ri
aisle... īl
ajar... a-jar'
alabaster... al'a-bas-tėr
alacrity... a-lac'ri-ti
alamode... a-la-mō d'
alarm... a-larm'
alarm clock... a-larm' cloc
alarming... a-larm'ing
alarmingly... a-larm'ing-li
alarmist... a-larm'ist
alas... a-las'
albata... al-bā'ta
albatross... al'ba-tros
albeit... al'bē'it
albino... äl-bī'nō
album... al'bum
albumen... al-bū'men
albuminous... al-bū'min-us
alchemist... al'cem-ist
alchemy... al'ce-mi
alcohol... al'cō-hol
alcoholic... al-cō-hol'ic
alcoholism... al'cō-hol-izm
alcove... al'cov
aldehyde... al'dē-hīd
alder... al'dėr
ale... āl"
alee... a-lē'
alembic... a-lem'bic
alert... a-lėrt'
alertness... a-lėrt'nes
alexandrine... al'legz-an''drin
alga... al'ga
algebra... al'je-bra
alias... ā'li-as
alibi... al'i-bī

alien... āl'yen
alienable... āl'yen-a-bl
alienate... āl'yen-āt
alienation... āl'yen-ā'shun
alight... a-līt'
alike... a-līc'
aliment... al'i-ment
alimental... al-i-ment'al
alimentary... al-i-ment'a-ri
alimony... al'i-mo-ni
aliped... al'i-ped
aliquot... al'i-cwot
alive... a-līv'
alkalescent... al-ca-les'ent
alkaline... al'ca-līn
alkaloid... al'ca-loid
all... al
allah... al'la
allay... al-lā'
allegation... al-lē-gā'shun
allege... al-lej'
allegiance... al-lē'ji-ans
allegorically... al-lē-gor'ic-al-li
allegorist... al'li-gō-rist
allegorize... al'li-gō-rīz
allegory... al'li-gō-ri
alleluiah... al-lē-lū'ya
allergic... a-ler'jic
allergy... al'er-je
alleviate... al-lē'vi-āt
alleviation... al-lē-vi-ā'shun
alley... al'i
alliance... al-lī'ans
allied... al-līd'
alligation... al-li-gā'shun
alligator... al'li-gā-tor
alliteration... al-lit-ėr-ā'shun
alliterative... al-lit'ėr-at-iv
allocation... al-lō-cā'shun
allocution... al-lō-cū'shun
allodium... al-lō'di-um
allopathy... al-lop'a-thi
allot... al-lot'
allotment... al-lot'ment
allotrophy... al-lot'ro-pi
allow... al-lou'
allowable... al-lou'a-bl
allowably... al-lou'a-bli
allowance... al-lou'ans
alloy... al-loi'
all Saints' Day... al'sānts dā
all Souls' Day... ål'sōlz dā
all-spice... al-spīs
allude... al-lūd'

allure... al-lūr'
allurement... al-lūr'ment
alluring... al-lūr'ing
alluringly... al-lūr'ing-li
allusion... al-lū'zhon
alluvial... al-lū'vi-al
alluvion... al-lū'vi-on
ally... al-lī'
almightiness... al-mī'ti-nes
almighty... al-mī'ti
almond... a''mund
almoner... al'mon-ėr
almost... al'most
alms... amz
aloe... al'ō
aloetic... al-ō-et'ic
aloft... a-loft'
alone... a-lōn'
along... a-long'
aloof... a-lof'
aloud... a-loud'
alpaca... al-pac'a
alpha... al'fa
alphabet... al'fa-bet
alphabetical... al-fa-bet'ic-al
alpine... al'pīn
already... al-red'i
also... al'sō
altar... äl'tėr
alter... äl'tėr
alterable... al'tėr-a-bl
alteration... äl-tėr-ā'shun
altercate... äl'tėr-cāt
altercation... al-tėr-cā'shun
alternate... al-tėr'nāt
alternately... al-tėrn'āt-li
alternation... al-tėrn-ā'shun
alternative... al-tėrn'at-iv
alternatively... al-tėrn'at-iv-li
although... al'THō'
altitude... al'ti-tūd
alto... al'tō
altogether... al-to-geTH'ėr
altruism... al'fro-izm
altruistic... al-tro-ist'ic
alum... al'um
alumina... al-ū'min-a
aluminium... al-ū-min'i-um
alumnus... a-lum'nus
always... al'wāz
amalgam... a-mal'gam
amalgamate... a-mal'gam-āt
amaranth... am'a-ranth
amaranthine... am-a-ran'thin

amaryllis... am-a-ril'lis
amass... a-mas'
amatory... am'a-tō-ri
amaze... a-māz'
amazedly... a-māz'ed-li
amazement... a-māz'ment
amazing... a-māz'ing
amazingly... a-māz'ing-li
amazon... am'a-zon
amazonian... am-a-zō'ni-an
ambassador... am-bas'sa-dor
amber... am'bėr
ambergris... am'bėr-grēs
ambient... am'bi-ent
ambiguity... am-bi-gū'i-ti
ambiguous... am-big'ū-us
ambiguously... am-big'ū-us-li
ambit... am'bit
ambition... am-bi'shun
ambitious... am-bi'shus
ambitiously... am-bi'shus-li
amble... am'bl
ambler... am'blėr
ambrosia... am-brō'zhi-a
ambrosial... am-brō'zhi-al
ambulance... am'bū-lans
ambush... am'bush
amen... ā-men'''
amenable... a-mēn'a-bl
amend... a-mend'
amendment... a-mend'ment
amends... a-mendz'
amenity... a-men'i-ti
amerce... a-mėrs'
amercement... a-mėrs'ment
american... a-me'ri-can
amethyst... am'ē-thist
amiability... ā'mi-a-bil'i-ti
amiable... ā'mi-a-bl
amiably... ā'mi-a-bli
amicable... am'ic-a-bl
amicably... am'ic-a-bli
amice... am'is
amidships... a-mid'ships
amiss... a-mis'
ammonia... am-mō'ni-a
ammoniac... am-mō'ni-ac
ammonite... am'mon-īt
ammunition... am-mu-ni'shun
amnesty... am'nes-ti
amoeba... a-mē'ba
amoebean... am-ē-bē'an
amorous... am'or-us
amorously... am'or-us-li

amorphous... a-mor'fus
amount... a-mount'
amour... a-mor'
ampere... am-pār'
amphibian... am-fib'i-an
amphibious... am-fib'i-us
amphibology... am-fi-bol'o-ji
amphibrach... am'fi-brac
ample... am'pl
ampleness... am'pl-nes
amplifier... am'pli-fī-ėr
amplify... am'plif-ī
amplitude... am'pli-tūd
amply... am'pli
amputate... am'pū-tāt
amputation... am-pū-tā'shun
amuck... a-muc'
amulet... am'ū-let
amuse... a-mūz'
amusement... a-mūz'ment
amusingly... a-mūz'ing-li
amyloid... am'il-oid
an... an
anachronism... an-ac'ron-izm
anaconda... an-a-con'da
anagram... an'a-gram
anal... ā'nal
analogical... an-a-loj'ic-al
analogous... an-al'og-us
analysis... an-al'i-sis
analyst... an'a-list
analytically... an-a-lit'ic-al-li
analytics... an-a-lit'ics
analyze... an'a-līz
anapest... an'a-pest
anapestic... an-a-pes'tic
anarchist... an'arc-ist
anarchy... an'ar-ci
anathema... a-nath'e-ma
anatomical... an-a-tom'ic-al
anatomist... a-nat'ō-mist
anatomize... a-nat'ō-mīz
anatomy... a-nat'ō-mi
ancestor... an'ses-tėr
ancestry... an'ses-tri
anchor... ang'cėr
anchorage... ang'cer-āj
anchorite... ang'cō-rīt
anchovy... an-chō'vi
ancient... ān'shent
anciently... ān'shent-li
ancientness... ān'shent-nes
ancillary... an'sil-la-ri
and... and

andante... *an-dan'te*
andiron... *and'ī-ėrn*
anecdote... *an'ec-dōt*
anecdotical... *an-ec-dot'ic-al*
anele... *a-nēl'*
anemia... *a-nē'mi-a*
anemone... *a-nem'o-nē*
anent... *a-nent'*
aneroid... *an'ē-roid*
anesthetic... *an-es-thet'ic*
anew... *a-nū'*
angel... *ān'jel*
angelically... *an-jel'ic-al-li*
anger... *ang'gėr*
angle... *ang'gl*
angle... *ang'gl*
angler... *ang'glėr*
anglicism... *ang'gli-sizm*
anglicize... *ang'gli-sīz*
angrily... *ang'gri-li*
angry... *ang'gri*
anguish... *ang'gwish*
angular... *ang'gū-lėr*
anile... *an'īl*
aniline... *an'i-lin*
anility... *a-nil'i-ti*
animadvert... *an'i-mad-vėrt''*
animal... *an'i-mal*
animalcular... *ani-mal'cūl-ėr*
animalcule... *an-i-mal'cūl*
animalism... *an'i-mal-izm*
animate... *an'i-māt*
animated... *an'i-māt-ed*
animism... *an'i-mizm*
animosity... *an-i-mos'i-ti*
animus... *an'i-mus*
anise... *an'is*
aniseed... *an'i-sēd*
annalist... *an'nal-ist*
annals... *an'nalz*
anneal... *an'nēl'*
annelid... *an'ne-lid*
annex... *an-necs'*
annexation... *an-necs-ā'shun*
annihilable... *an-nī'hil-a-bl*
annihilate... *an-nī'hil-āt*
anniversary... *an-ni-vėrs'a-ri*
annotate... *an'nō-tāt*
annotation... *an-nō-tā'shun*
annotator... *an'nō-tāt-ėr*
announce... *an-nouns'*
annoy... *an-noi'*
annoyance... *an-noi'ans*
annual... *an'nū-al*

annually... *an'nū-al-li*
annuitant... *an-nū'it-ant*
annuity... *an-nū'i-ti*
annual... *annul'*
annular... *an'nū-lėr*
annulment... *an-nul'ment*
annulose... *an'nū-lōs*
anode... *an'ōd*
anointed... *a-noint'ed*
anomalous... *a-nom'a-lus*
anomaly... *a-nom'a-li*
anon... *a-non'*
anonymous... *a-non'im-us*
anonymously... *a-non'im-us-li*
another... *an-uтH'ėr*
anserine... *an'sėr-īn*
answer... *an'sėr*
answerable... *an'sėr-a-bl*
answerably... *an'sėr-a-bli*
ant... *ant*
antagonist... *an-tag'ō-nist*
antarctic... *ant-arc'tic*
antecedent... *an-tē-sē'dent*
antedate... *an'tē-dāt*
antelope... *an'tē-lōp*
antenna... *an-ten'na*
antenuptial... *an-tē-nup'shi-al*
anterior... *an-tē'ri-ėr*
anthem... *an'them*
anther... *an'thėr*
anthological... *an-tho-loj'ic-al*
anthology... *an-thol'o-ji*
anthropoid... *an'thrō-poid*
anti-aircraft... *an'ti-ār-craft*
antic... *an'tic*
antichrist... *an'ti-crīst*
antichristian... *an-ti-cris'ti-an*
anticipate... *an-tis'-i-pāt*
anticipation... *an-tis'i-pā''shun*
anti-climax... *an-ti-clī'macs*
anticlinal... *an-ti-clī'nal*
anticyclone... *an'ti-sī-clōn*
antidote... *an'ti-dōt*
antimonial... *an-ti-mō'ni-al*
antimony... *an'ti-mo-ni*
antinomian... *an-ti-nō'mi-an*
antipathy... *an-tip'a-thi*
antiphon... *an'ti-fōn*
antiphrasis... *an-tif'ra-sis*
antipodes... *an-tip'o-dēz*
antipope... *an'ti-pōp*
antiquarian... *an-ti-cwā'ri-an*
antiquary... *an'ti-cwa-ri*
antiquated... *an'ti-cwāt-ed*

antique... an-tēc'
antiquity... an-tic'wi-ti
antistrophe... an-tis'tro-fi
antitype... an'ti-tīp
antitypical... an-ti-tip'ic-al
antler... ant'lėr
antonym... ant'ō-nim
anus... ā'nus
anvil... an'vil
anxiety... ang-zī'e-ti
anxious... angc'shus
anxiously... angc'shus-li
anxiousness... angc'shus-nes
any... en'i
aorta... ā-ort'a
apace... a-pās'
apart... a-part'
apartment... a-part'ment
apathetic... ap-a-thet'ic
apathy... ap'a-thi
ape... āp
aperient... a-pē'ri-ent
aperture... ap'ėr-tūr
apex... ā'pecs
aphelion... a-fē'li-on
aphorism... af-or-izm
apiece... a-pēs'
apish... āp'ish
aplomb... a-plong
apocalypse... a-poc'a-lips
apocalyptic... a-poc'a-lip''tic
apocope... a-poc'ō-pē
apogee... ap'ō-jē
apologetic... a-pol'ō-jet''ic
apologetics... a-pol'ō-jet''ics
apologist... a-pol'ō-jist
apologize... a-pol'ō-jīz
apologue... ap'o-log
apoplexy... ap'ō-plec'si
apostasy... a-pos'ta-si
apostate... a-pos'tāt
aposteme... ap'os-tēm
apostle... a-pos'l
apostleship... a-pos'l-ship
apostrophe... a-pos'tro-fē
apostrophize... a-pos'trof-īz
apothecary... a-poth'e-ca-ri
apothegm... ap'o-them
appal... ap-pal'
appalling... ap̈-pal'ing
apparel... ap-pa'r̈el
apparent... ap-pā'rent
apparently... ap-pā'rent-li
apparition... ap-pa-ri'shun

appeal... ap-pēl'
appear... ap-pēr'
appearance... ap-pēr'ans
appeasable... ap-pēz'a-bl
appease... ap-pēz'
appellant... ap-pel'ant
appellate... ap-pel'āt
appellation... ap-pel-ā'shun
appellative... ap-pel'at-iv
append... ap-pend'
appendage... ap-pend'āj
appendant... ap-pend'ant
appendix... ap-pen'dics
appetite... ap'pē-fīt
appetize... ap'pē-fīz
appetizer... ap'pē-fīz-ėr
applaud... ap-plad'
applause... ap-plaz'
apple... ap'l
appliance... ap-plī'ans
applicant... ap'pli-cant
application... ap-pli-cā'shun
apply... ap-plī
appoint... ap-point'
appointment... ap-point'ment
apportion... ap-pōr'shun
apportioner... ap-pōr'shun-ėr
apposite... ap'pō-zit
appositely... ap'pō-zit-li
apposition... ap-pō-zi'shun
appraise... ap-prāz'
appraisement... ap-prāz'ment
appraiser... ap-prāz'ėr
appreciable... ap-prē'shi-a-bl
appreciate... ap-prē'shi-āt
apprehend... ap-prē-hend'
apprentice... ap-pren'tis
apprise... ap-prīz'
approach... ap-prōch'
appropriable... ap-prō'pri-a-bl
appropriate... ap-prō'pri-āt
approvable... ap-prov'a-bl
approval... ap-prov'al
approve... ap-prov'
approximate... ap-proc'si-māt
apricot... ā'pri-cot
april... ā'pril
apron... ā'prun
apropos... ap'rō-pō
apsis... ap'sis
apt... apt
aptitude... ap'ti-tūd
aptly... apt'li
aptness... apt'nes

aqua... *ac'wa*
aquafortis... *ac'wa for-tis*
aquarium... *a-cwā'ri-um*
aquarius... *a-cwā'ri-us*
aquatic... *a-cwat'ic*
aquatint... *a'cwa-tint*
aqueduct... *ac'wē-duct*
arab... *a'rab*
arabian... *a-rā'bi-an*
arabic... *a'rab-ic*
arachnida... *a-rac'ni-da*
arbiter... *ar'bit-ėr*
arbitrarily... *ar'bi-tra-ri-li*
arbitrary... *ar'bi-tra-ri*
arbitration... *ar-bi-trā'shun*
arbitrator... *ar'bi-trāt-ėr*
arbor... *ar'bėr*
arboreous... *ar-bō'rē-us*
arboretum... *ar-bo-rē'tum*
arbutus... *ar'bū-tus*
arc... *arc*
arcade... *ar-cād'*
arcadian... *ar-cā'di-an*
arch... *arch*
arch... *arch*
archeologist... *ar-cē-ol'o-jist*
archeology... *ar-cē-ol'o-ji*
archaic... *ar-cā'ic*
archaism... *ar'cā-izm*
archangel... *arc-ān'jel*
archangelic... *arc-an-jel'ic*
archbishop... *arch-bish'up*
archdeacon... *arch-dē'cn*
archer... *arch'ėr*
archery... *arch'ė-ri*
archetype... *ar'cē-fīp*
architect... *ar'ci-tect*
architectural... *ar-ci-tec'tūr-al*
architrave... *ar'ci-trāv*
archive... *ar'cīv*
archly... *arch'li*
archness... *arch'nes*
archway... *arch'wā*
arctic... *arc'tic*
ardency... *ar'den-si*
ardent... *ar'dent*
ardently... *ar'dent-li*
ardor... *ar'dėr*
ardous... *ar'dū-us*
ardously... *ar'dū-us-li*
area... *ā'rē-a*
arena... *a-rē'na*
arenaceous... *a-rē-nā'shus*
argent... *ar'jent*

argil... *ar'jil*
argon... *ar'gon*
argonaut... *ar'go-nạt*
argue... *ar'gū*
argument... *ar'gū-ment*
argus... *ar'gus*
arid... *a'rid*
aridity... *a-rid'i-ti*
aright... *a-rīt'*
arise... *a-rīz'*
aristocracy... *a-ris-toc'ra-si*
aristocrat... *a'ris-to-crat*
aristocratic... *a-ris-to-crat'ic*
arithmetic... *a-rith'met-ic*
arithmetical... *a-rith-met'ic-al*
ark... *ark*
arm... *arm*
armadillo... *ar-ma-dil'lō*
armament... *arm'a-ment*
armenian... *ar-mē'ni-an*
armipotent... *ar-mip'ō-tent*
armorial... *ar-mō'ri-al*
armoric... *ar-mo'ric*
armor... *arm'ėr*
armorer... *arm'ėr-ėr*
armory... *arm'e-ri*
armpit... *arm'pit*
army... *ar'mi*
aroma... *a-rō'ma*
aromatic... *a-rō-mat'ic*
around... *a-round'*
arouse... *a-rouz'*
arraigner... *a-rān'ėr*
arraignment... *a-rān'ment*
arrange... *a-rānj'*
arrangement... *a-rānj'ment*
arrant... *a'rant*
arras... *a'ras*
array... *a-rā'*
arrear... *a-rēr'*
arrest... *a-rest'*
arrival... *a-rīv'al*
arrive... *a-rīv'*
arrogance... *a'rō-gans*
arrogant... *a'rō-gant*
arrogantly... *a'rō-gant-li*
arrogate... *a'rō-gāt*
arrow... *a'rō*
arrow-headed... *a'rō-hed-ed*
arrowroot... *a'rō-rot*
arsenal... *ar'sē-nal*
arsenic... *ar'sen-ic*
arsenical... *ar-sen'ic-al*
arson... *ar'son*

art... *art*
arterial... *ar-tē'ri-al*
artful... *art'ful*
artfully... *art'ful-li*
artfulness... *art'ful-nes*
arthritis... *ar-thrī'tis*
artichoke... *ar'ti-chōk*
article... *ar'ti-cl*
articulate... *ar-tic'ū-lāt*
articulately... *ar-tic'ū-lāt-li*
articulation... *ar-tic'ū-lā''shun*
artifice... *art'i-fis*
artificer... *ar-tif'is-èr*
artificial... *art-i-fi'shal*
artificially... *art-i-fi'shal-li*
artillery... *ar-til'lè-ri*
artisan... *art'i-zan*
artist... *art'ist*
artistic... *ar-tist'ic*
artless... *art'les*
artlessly... *art'les-li*
artlessness... *art'les-nes*
as... *az*
asbestos... *as-bes'tos*
ascend... *as-send'*
ascendant... *as-send'ant*
ascertain... *as-sèr-tān'*
ascetic... *as-set'ic*
ascribable... *as-crī b'a-bl*
ascribe... *as-crī b'*
ascription... *as-crip'shun*
asdic... *as'dic*
aseptic... *a-sep'tic*
ash... *ash*
ashamed... *a-shāmd'*
ashen... *ash'en*
ashes... *ash'ez*
ashore... *a-shōr'*
ashy... *ash'i*
asiatic... *ā-shi-at'ic*
aside... *a-sī d'*
asinine... *as'i-nīn*
ask... *ask*
askew... *a-skū'*
aslant... *a-slant'*
asleep... *a-slēp'*
asp... *asp*
asparagus... *as-pa'ra-gus*
aspect... *as'pect*
aspen... *asp'en*
asperse... *as-pèrs'*
aspersion... *as-pèr'shun*
asphalt... *as-falt'*
asphaltic... *as-falt'ic*

aspirant... *as-pīr'ant*
aspirate... *as'pi-rāt*
aspiration... *as-pi-rā'shun*
aspire... *as-pīr'*
asquint... *a-scwint'*
ass... *as*
assail... *as-sāl'*
assailable... *as-sāl'a-bl*
assailant... *as-sāl'ant*
assassin... *as-sas'sin*
assassinate... *as-sas'sin-āt*
assault... *as-salt'*
assaulter... *as-salt'èr*
assay... *as-sā'*
assayer... *as-sā'èr*
assaying... *as-sā'ing*
assemblage... *as-sem'blāj*
assemble... *as-sem'bl*
assembly... *as-sem'bli*
assent... *as-sent'*
assertion... *as-sèr'shun*
assertive... *as-sèrt'iv*
assess... *as-ses'*
assessable... *as-ses'a-bl*
assessment... *as-ses'ment*
assessor... *as-ses'èr*
assets... *as'sets*
assiduous... *as-sid'ū-us*
assign... *as-sīn'*
assignable... *as-sīn'a-bl*
assignation... *as-sig-nā'shun*
assignee... *as-sī-ne'*
assigner... *as-sīn'èr*
assignment... *as-sīn'ment*
assimilate... *as-sim'il-āt*
assimilation... *as-sim'il-ā''shun*
assist... *as-sist'*
assistance... *as-sist'ans*
assistant... *as-sist'ant*
associable... *as-sō'shi-a-bl*
associate... *as-sō'shi-āt*
association... *as-sō'si-ā''shun*
assoil... *as-soil'*
assonance... *as'sō-nans*
assortment... *as-sort'ment*
assuage... *as-swāj'*
assuagement... *as-swāj'ment*
assume... *as-sūm'*
assuming... *as-sūm'ing*
assumption... *as-sum'shun*
assurance... *a-shor'ans*
assure... *a-shor'*
assuredly... *a-shor'ed-li*
assuredness... *a-shor'ed-nes*

assurer... a-shor'ėr
aster... as'tėr
asterisk... as'tė-risk
astern... a-stėrn'
asteroid... as'tėr-oid
asthma... as'ma or as'thma
asthmatic... as-mat'ic
astir... a-stėr'
astonish... as-ton'ish
astonishing... as-ton'ish-ing
astound... as-tound'
astounding... as-tound'ing
astral... as'tral
astray... a-strā'
astriction... as-tric'shun
astride... a-strīd'
astringency... as-trinj'en-si
astringent... as-trinj'ent
astrolabe... as'trō-lāb
astrologer... as-trol'o-jėr
astrological... as-trō-loj'ic-al
astrology... as-trol'o-ji
astronomer... as-tron'ō-mėr
astronomy... as-tron'o-mi
astrut... a-strut'
astute... as-tūt'
astutely... as-tūt'li
astuteness... as-tūt'nes
asunder... a-sun'dėr
asylum... a-sī'lum
at... at
atheism... ā'thē-izm
atheist... ā'thē-ist
athenaeum... ath-e-nē'um
athenian... a-thēn'i-an
athirst... a-thėrst'
athlete... ath-lēt'
athletic... ath-let'ic
athletics... ath-let'ics
atlantic... at-lan'tic
atlas... at'las
atmosphere... at'mos-fēr
atmospheric... at-mos-fe'ric
atoll... a-tol'
atom... a'tom
atomic... a-tom'ic
atomic bomb... a-tom'ic bom
atomism... at'om-izm
atone... a-tōn'
atonement... a-tōn'ment
atrip... a-trip'
atrocious... a-trō'shus
atrociously... a-trō'shus-li
atrocity... a-tros'i-ti

atrophy... at'rō-fi
attach... at-tach'
attachment... at-tach'ment
attack... at-tac'
attain... at-tān'
attainable... at-tān'a-bl
attainder... at-tān'dėr
attainment... at-tān'ment
attar... at'tar
attemper... at-tem'pėr
attempt... at-temt'
attend... at-tend'
attendance... at-tend'ans
attendant... at-tend'ant
attention... at-ten'shun
attentive... at-tent'iv
attentively... at-tent'iv-li
attentiveness... at-tent'iv-nes
attenuate... at-ten'ū-āt
attest... at-test'
attestation... at-test-ā'shun
attic... at'tic
attire... at-fīr'
attitude... at'ti-tūd
attorney... at-tėr'ni
attract... at-tract'
attractable... at-tract'a-bl
attraction... at-trac'shun
attractive... at-tract'iv
attractively... at-tract'iv-li
attributable... at-trib'ūt-a-bl
attribute... at-trib'ūt
attributive... at-trib'ūt-iv
attrition... at-tri'shun
attune... at-tūn'
auburn... a'bėrn
auction... ac'shun
auctioneer... ac-shun-ēr'
audacious... ạ-dā'shus
audacity... a-das'i-ti
audible... a'di-bl
audibly... ạ'di-bli
audience... a'di-ens
audit... a'dit
auditor... a'dit-ėr
auditorship... a'dit-ėr-ship
auditory... a'dĭ-tō-ri
auger... a'gėr
aught... ạt
augment... ag-ment'
augment... ạg'ment
augmentable... ag-ment'a-bl
augur... a'gėr
august... ạ-gust'

augustan... a̯-gust'an
auk... ak
aurelia... a̯-rē'li-a
auricle... ä'ri-cl
auricula... a̯-ric'ū-la
auricular... a̯-ric'ū-lėr
auriferous... ä-rif'ėr-us
aurist... a̯'rist
aurochs... a̯'rocs
aurora... a̯-rō'ra
auspice... a̯'spis
auspicious... a̯-spi'shus
auspiciously... a̯-spi'shus-li
austere... a̯-stēr'
austerely... a̯-stēr'li
austerity... a̯-ste'ri-ti
austral... as'tral
authentic... a̯-then'tic
authentically... a̯-then'tic-al-li
authenticate... ä-then'ti-cāt
authenticity... a̯-then-tis'i-ti
author... a̯'thėr
authoress... a̯'thėr-es
authoritative... a̯-tho'ri-tā-tiv
authority... a̯-thö'ri-ti
authorize... ä'thor-īz
autocracy... a̯-toc'ra-si
autocrat... a̯'tō-crat
autogiro... ä-tō-jī'rō
autograph... a̯'tō-graf
automaton... ä-tom'a-ton
automobile... ä'tō-mō-bēl''
autonomy... a̯-ton'o-mi
autopsy... a̯'fop-si
autumn... ä'tum
autumnal... a̯-tum'nal
auxiliary... a̯g-zil'i-a-ri
available... ä-vāl'a-bl
avalanche... av'a-lansh
avarice... av'a-ris
avaricious... av-a-ri'shus
avariciously... av-a-ri'shus-li
avast... a-vast'
avatar... av-a-tar'
avaunt... a-vant'
ave... ä'vē
avenge... a-venj'
avenger... a-venj'ėr
avenue... av'e-nū
aver... a-vėr'
averment... a-vėr'ment
averse... a-vėrs'
averseness... a-vėrs'nes
aversion... a-vėr'shun

avert... a-vėrt'
aviary... ā-vi-a-ri
aviation... ā'vi-ā-shun
avidity... a-vid'i-ti
avizandum... av-i-zan'dum
avocation... av-ō-cā'shun
avoid... a-void'
avoidable... a-void'-a-bl
avoidance... a-void'ans
avouch... a-vouch'
avow... a-vou'
avowable... a-vou'a-bl
avowal... a-vou'al
avowedly... a-vou'ed-li
await... a-wāt'
awake... a-wāk'
awaken... a-wāk'n
awakening... a-wāk'n-ing
award... a-ward'
aware... a-wãr'
awe... a
aweary... a-wē'rl
aweigh... a-wā'
awful... a'ful
awfully... a'ful-li
awfulness... ä'ful-nes
awhile... a-whīl'
awkward... ak'wėrd
awkwardly... ak'wėrd-li
awl... al
awn... än
awned... and
awning... än'ing
awry... a-rī'
axe... aks
axial... aks'i-al
axilla... aks-il'la
axiom... aks'i-om
axiomatic... aks'i-ō-mat''ic
axis... aks'is
axle,... aks'l
ay, Aye... ī
ayah... ā'ya
aye... ā
azimuth... az'i-muth
azoic... a-zō'ic
azote... az'ōt
azure... ā'zhūr

B

baa... ba
babbit... 'ba-bet

B

babble... *bab'bl*
babblement... *bab'bl-ment*
babbler... *bab'bl-ėr*
babe... *bāb*
babel... *bā'bel*
baboon... *ba-bōōn'*
baby... *bā'bi*
baccarat... *bac-ca-ra*
bacchante... *ba-cant'*
bachelor... *bach'el-ėr*
bacillus... *ba-sil'us*
back... *bac*
backbite... *bac'bīt*
backbone... *bac'bōn*
back door... *bac'dōr*
backer... *bac'ėr*
background... *bac'ground*
backslider... *bac-slī d'ėr*
backward... *bac'wėrd*
backwardly... *bac'wėrd-li*
backwoods... *bac'wu̇dz*
bacon... *bā'cn*
bacterium... *bac-tē'ri-um*
bade... *bad*
bad... *bad*
badge... *baj*
badger... *baj'ėr*
badly... *bad'li*
badminton... *bad'min-ton*
baffle... *baf'fl*
bag... *bag*
baggage... *bag'āj*
bagging... *bag'ing*
bagpipe... *bag'pīp*
bail... *bāl*
bailable... *bāl'a-bl*
bailiff... *bā'lif*
bait... *bāt*
baize... *bāz*
bake... *bāk*
bakelite... *bāk'l-īt*
bakery... *bāk'ė-ri*
baking... *bāk'ing*
balance... *bal'ans*
balance sheet... *bal'ans-shēt*
balcony... *bal'co-ni*
bald... *bald*
balderdash... *bal'dėr-dash*
baldly... *bald'li*
baldness... *bald'nes*
baldrick... *bald'ric*
bale... *bāl*
baleful... *bāl'ful*
balk... *ba̤k*

ball... *bal*
ballad... *bal'lad*
ballade... *ba-lad'*
ballast... *bal'last*
ballet... *bal'lā*
ballista... *bal-lis'ta*
ballistic... *bal-lis'tik*
balloon... *bal-lon'*
ballot... *bal'lot*
balm... *bam*
balmy... *bam'i*
balsamic... *bal- or bal-sam'ic*
baluster... *bal'us-tėr*
balustrade... *bal-us-trād'*
bamboo... *bam-bo'*
bamboozle... *bam-bo'zl*
ban... *ban*
banal... *ban'al, or ba-nal'*
banana... *ba-na'na*
band... *band*
bandage... *band'āj*
bandbox... *band'bocs*
banded... *band'ed*
bandit... *ban'dit*
bandog... *ban'dog*
bandy... *ban'di*
bane... *bān*
baneful... *bān'ful*
bang... *bang*
bangle... *bang'gl*
banish... *ban'ish*
banishment... *ban'ish-ment*
banister... *ban'is-tėr*
banjo... *ban'jō*
bank... *bangc*
banking... *bangc'ing*
bank note... *bangc'nōt*
bankrupt... *bangc'rupt*
bankruptcy... *bangc'rupt-si*
bank stock... *bangc'stok*
banner... *ban'nėr*
banquet... *bang'kwet*
bantam... *ban'tam*
banter... *ban'tėr*
banyan... *ban'yan*
baptism... *bap'tizm*
baptismal... *bap-tiz'mal*
baptist... *bap'tist*
baptistery... *bap'tis-te-ri*
baptize... *bap-fīz'*
bar... *bar*
barb... *barb*
barbarian... *bar-bā'ri-an*
barbarism... *bar'bar-izm*

barbarity... *bar-ba'ri-ti*
barbarize... *bar'bar-īz*
barbarous... *bar'bar-os*
barbecue... *bar-be-cū*
barbel... *bar'bel*
barberry... *bar'be-ri*
barbette... *bar-bet'*
bard... *bard*
bare... *bār*
barebacked... *bār'bact*
barefaced... *bār'fāst*
barefoot... *bār'fut*
barely... *bār'li*
bargain... *bar'gin*
bargainer... *bar'gin-ėr*
barge... *barj*
bargeman... *barj'man*
baritone... *ba'ri-tōn*
bark... *bark*
barley... *bar'li*
barley corn... *bar'li-corn*
barley sugar... *bar-li-shug'ėr*
barm... *barm*
barmaid... *bar'mād*
barmy... *barm'i*
barn... *barn*
barnacle... *bar'na-kl*
barnacles... *bar'na-klz*
barograph... *ba'rō-graf*
barometric... *ba-rō-met'ric*
barque... *bark*
barrack... *ba'rac*
barrage... *bar'aj*
barrator... *ba'rat-ėr*
barrel... *ba'rel*
barreled... *ba'reld*
barren... *ba'ren*
barrenness... *ba'ren-nes*
barricade... *ba-ri-kād'*
barrier... *ba'ri-ėr*
barrister... *ba'ris-tėr*
barter... *bar'tėr*
bartizan... *bar'ti-zan*
base... *bās*
base born... *bās'born*
baseless... *bās'les*
base line... *bās'līn*
basely... *bās'li*
basement... *bās'ment*
baseness... *bās'nes*
bash... *bash*
bashful... *bash'ful*
bashfully... *bash'ful-li*
basic... *bās'ic*

basil... *baz'll*
basilica... *ba-sil'i-ca*
basin... *bā'sn*
basis... *bās'is*
bask... *bask*
basket... *bas'ket*
bas relief... *bas'rē-lēf, or ba'*
bass... *bas*
basset... *bas'set*
bassinet... *bas'si-net*
bass relief... *bas'rē-lēf*
bast... *bast*
bastard... *bas'tėrd*
bastardize... *bas'tėrd-īz*
bastardy... *bas'tėrd-i*
baste... *bāst*
bastion... *bas'ti-on*
bat... *bat*
batch... *bach*
bate... *bāt*
bath... *bath*
bathe... *bāʈH*
bathometer... *ba-thom'et-ėr*
batman... *bat'man*
baton... *ba'ton*
battalion... *bat-ta'll-on*
batten... *bat'n*
batter... *bat'tėr*
battery... *bat'tė-ri*
battle... *bat'l*
battle axe... *bat'l-acs*
battledore... *bat'l-dōr*
battlement... *bat'l-ment*
bauble... *ba'bl*
bawd... *bäḋ*
bawdy... *ba'di*
bawl... *bal*
bay... *bā*
bayadere... *bā-ya-dēr'*
bayonet... *bā'on-et*
bay window... *bā'win-dō*
bazaar... *ba-zar'*
be... *bē*
beach... *bēch*
beached... *bēcht*
beacon... *bē'cn*
bead... *bēd*
beagle... *bē'gl*
beak... *bēk*
beaked... *bēkt*
beaker... *bēk'ėr*
beam... *bēm*
beaming... *bēm'ing*
beamy... *bēm'i*

bean... *bēn*
bear... *bãr*
bear... *bār*
bearable... *bār'a-bl*
beard... *bērd*
bearded... *bērd'ed*
beardless... *bērd'les*
bearer... *bār'ėr*
bearing... *bār'ing*
bearish... *bār'ish*
beast... *bēst*
beastly... *bēst'li*
beat... *bēt*
beater... *bēt'ėr*
beatific... *bē-a-tif'ic*
beatify... *bē-at'i-fī*
beating... *bēt'ing*
beau... *bō*
beauteous... *bū'tē-us*
beautiful... *bū'ti-ful*
beautifully... *bū'ti-ful-li*
beautify... *bū'ti-fī*
beauty... *bū'ti*
beauty spot... *bū'ti-spot*
beaver... *bē'vėr*
beavered... *bē'vėrd*
becalm... *bē-kam'*
bechamel... *besh'a-mel*
beck... *bek*
beckon... *bek'n*
becloud... *bē-kloud'*
become... *bē-kum'*
becoming... *bē-kum'ing*
becomingly... *bē-kum'ing-li*
bed... *bed*
bedding... *bed'ing*
bedeck... *bē-dec'*
bedew... *bē-dū'*
bedim... *bē-dim'*
bedizen... *bē-dī'zn*
bedlam... *bed'lam*
bedstead... *bed'sted*
bee... *bē*
beech... *bēch*
beechen... *bēch'en*
beef... *bēf*
beef eater... *bēf'ēt-ėr*
beef tea... *bēf'tē*
bee line... *bē'līn*
beer... *bēr*
bees wax... *bēz'waks*
bees wing... *bēz'wing*
beet... *bēt*
beetle... *bē'tl*

beetle browed... *bē'tl-broud*
beeves... *bēvz*
befall... *bē-fal'*
befit... *bē-fit'*
befitting... *bē-fit'ing*
befog... *bē-fog'*
befool... *bē-fol'*
before... *bē-fōr'*
beforehand... *bē-fōr'hand*
befoul... *bē-foul'*
befriend... *bē-frend'*
beget... *bē-get'*
begetter... *bē-get'ėr*
beggar... *beg'gėr*
beggarliness... *beg'gėr-li-nes*
beggarly... *beg'gėr-li*
beggary... *beg'gė-ri*
begin... *bē-gin'*
beginner... *bē-gin'ėr*
beginning... *bē-gin'ing*
begird... *bē-gėrd'*
begone... *bē-gon'*
begonia... *bē-gō'ni-a*
begrudge... *bē-gruj'*
beguile... *bē-gīl'*
beguilement... *bē-gīl'ment*
beguiler... *bē-gīl'ėr*
behalf... *bē-haf'*
behave... *bē-hāv'*
behavior... *bē-hāv'i-ėr*
behead... *bē-hed'*
behind... *bē-hīnd'*
behindhand... *bē-hīnd'hand*
behold... *bē-hōld'*
beholden... *bē-hōld'n*
beige... *bāzh*
being... *bē'ing*
belated... *bē-lāt'ed*
belch... *belch*
beldam... *bel'dam*
beleaguer... *bē-lē'gėr*
belfry... *bel'fri*
belial... *bē'li-al*
belie... *bē-lī'*
believe... *bē-lēv'*
believer... *bē-lēv'ėr*
belittle... *bē-lit'l*
bell... *bel*
belladonna... *bel-la-don'na*
belle... *bel*
bellicose... *bel'li-kōs*
bellied... *bel'lid*
belligerent... *bel-lij'ėr-ent*
bellow... *bel'ō*

bellows... bel'ōz
bell ringer... bel'ring-ėr
bell wether... bel'weŦH-ėr
belly... bel'li
belly band... bel'li-band
belonging... bē-long'ing
beloved... bē-luvd'
below... bē-lō'
belt... belt
belted... belt'ed
beivedere... bei've-dēr
bemoan... bē-mōn'
bemused... bē-mūzd'
bench... bensh
bend... bend
beneath... bē-nēth'
benediction... ben-ē-dik'shun
benefaction... ben-ē-fak'shun
benefactor... ben-ē-fak'tėr
benefactress... ben-ē-fak'tres
benefice... ben'ē-fis
beneficed... ben'ē-fist
beneficence... bē-nef'i-sens
beneficent... bē-nef'i-sent
beneficently... bē-nef'i-sent-li
beneficial... ben-ē-fi'shal
beneficially... ben-ē-fi'shal-li
beneficiary... ben-ē-fi'shi-a-ri
benefit... ben'ē-fit
benight... bē-nīt'
benign... bē-nīn'
benignant... bē-nig'nant
benignantly... bē-nig'nant-li
benignity... bē-nig'ni-ti
benignly... bē-nīn'li
benison... ben'i-zn
benumb... bē-num'
benzene... ben'zēn
bepraise... bē-prāz'
bequeath... bē-kwēŦH'
bequest... bē-kwest'
bereave... bē-rēv'
bereavement... bē-rēv'ment
beret... be'ri
beri beri... ber'i-ber'i
berlin... bėr'lin or bėr-lin'
berry... be'ri
berserker... bėr'sėr-kėr
berth... bėrth
beseech... bē-sēch'
beseechingly... bē-sēch'ing-li
beseem... bē-sēm'
beseeming... bē-sēm'ing
besetting... bē-set'ing

beshrew... bē-shro'
besieger... bē-sēj'ėr
besom... bē'zum
besot... bē-sot'
bespangle... bē-spang'gl
bespread... bē-spred'
besprinkle... bē-spring'kl
best... best
bestead... bē-sted'
bestial... bes'ti-al
bestiality... bes-ti-al'i-ti
bestially... bes'ti-al-li
bestiary... bes'ti-a-ri
bestir... bē-stėr'
bestow... bē-stō'
bestowal... bē-stō'al
bestower... bē-stō'ėr
bestraddle... bē-strad'dl
bestrew... bē-stro'
bestride... bē-strī d'
bet... bet
betake... bē-tāk'
bethink... bē-thingk'
betimes... bē-fīmz'
betoken... bē-tō'kn
betray... bē-trā'
betrayal... bē-trā'al
betrayer... bē-trā'ėr
betroth... bē-trōŦH'
betrothal... bē-trōŦH'al
better... bet'tėr
between... bē-twēn'
betwixt... bē-twikst'
bevel... be'vel
beverage... bev'ėr-āj
bevy... be'vi
beware... bē-wār'
bewilder... bē-wil'dėr
bewitch... bē-wich'
bewitchery... bē-wich'ėr-i
bewitching... bē-wich'ing
bewitchingly... bē-wich'ing-li
bewitchment... bē-wich'ment
bewray... bē-rā'
bey... bā
beyond... bē-yond'
bezel... bez'el
bias... bī'as
biased, biassed... bī'ast
bib... bib
bible... bī'bl
biblical... bib'lik-al
biblically... bib'lik-al-li
biblicist... bib'li-sist

bibliography... *bib-li-og'ra-fi*
bicarbonate... *bī-kar'bon-āt*
bicentenary... *bī-sen'te-na-ri*
biceps... *bī'seps*
bicker... *bik'ėr*
bicycle... *bī'si-kl*
bicyclist... *bī'sik-list*
bid... *bid*
bidding... *bid'ing*
bide... *bīd*
bidet... *bi-det' or bē-dā*
biennial... *bī-en'ni-al*
biennially... *bī-en'ni-al-li*
bifid... *bī'fid*
bifurcate... *bī-fėr'kāt*
big... *big*
bigamist... *big'am-ist*
bigg... *big*
bight... *bīt*
bigness... *big'nes*
bigot... *big'ot*
bigoted... *big'ot-ed*
bigotry... *big'ot-ri*
bijou... *bē-zho'*
bilateral... *bī-lat'ėr-al*
bilboes... *bil'bōz*
bile... *bīl*
biliary... *bil'i-a-ri*
bilingual... *bī-lin'gwal*
bilious... *bil'i-us*
biliteral... *bī-lit'ėr-al*
bilk... *bilk*
bill... *bil*
billiards... *bil'yėrdz*
billion... *bil'yon*
billow... *bil'lō*
billowy... *bil'lō-i*
bimanous... *bī'man-us*
bimonthly... *bī-munth'li*
bin... *bin*
binary... *bī'na-ri*
binder... *bīnd'ėr*
binding... *bīnd'ing*
bing... *bing*
binnacle... *bin'a-kl*
binocular... *bī-nok'ū-lėr*
binomial... *bī-nō'mi-al*
biochemistry... *bī-ō-kem'ist-ri*
biogenesis... *bī-ō-jen'e-sis*
biographer... *bī-og'ra-fėr*
biographical... *bī-ō-graf'ik-al*
biography... *bī-og'ra-fi*
biologist... *bī-ol'o-jist*
biology... *bī-ol'o-ji*

bioplasm... *bī'ō-plazm*
bipartite... *bī-part'īt*
birch... *bėrch*
birch... *bėrch*
bird... *bėrd*
birds-eye... *bėrdz'ī*
bireme... *bī'rēm*
birth... *bėrth*
birthday... *bėrth'dā*
birthplace... *bėrth'plās*
birthright... *bėrth'rīt*
bisect... *bī-sekt'*
bisection... *bī-sek'shun*
bishop... *bish'up*
bismuth... *bis'muth*
bison... *bī'zon*
bisque... *bisc*
bit... *bit*
bitch... *bich*
bite... *bīt*
biting... *bīt'ing*
bitingly... *bīt'ing-li*
bitter... *bit'ėr*
bitterness... *bit'ėr-nes*
bitters... *bit'ėrz*
bitumen... *bi-tū'men*
bituminous... *bi-tū'min-us*
bivouac... *bi'vo-ac*
biweekly... *bī-wēk'li*
bizarre... *bi-zar'*
blab... *blab*
black... *blak*
black-ball... *blak'bal*
blackberry... *blak'bė-ri*
blackbird... *blak'bėrd*
blacken... *blak'n*
blacking... *blak'ing*
black lead... *blak'led*
black letter... *blak'let-tėr*
black list... *blak-list*
black mail... *blak'māl*
black market... *blak-mar'ket*
black out... *blak'out*
black sheep... *blak'shēp*
blacksmith... *blak'smith*
blackthorn... *blak'thorn*
bladder... *blad'ėr*
blade... *blād*
blamable... *blām'a-bl*
blame... *blām*
blameless... *blām'les*
blanch... *blansh*
bland... *bland*
blandish... *bland'ish*

blank... *blangk*
blanket... *blang'ket*
blanketing... *blang'ket-ing*
blankly... *blangk'li*
blank verse... *blangk'vėrs*
blarney... *blar'ni*
blaspheme... *blas-fēm'*
blasphemer... *blas-fēm'ėr*
blasphemous... *blas'fēm-us*
blasphemy... *blas'fēm-i*
blast... *blast*
blatant... *blā'tant*
blaze... *blāz*
blazer... *blāz'ėr*
blazon... *blāz'on*
blazoner... *blāz'on-ėr*
bleach... *blēch*
bleacher... *blēch'ėr*
bleachery... *blēch'ėri-i*
bleak... *blēk*
blear... *blēr*
blear eyed... *blēr'īd*
bleat... *blēt*
bleed... *blēd*
bleeding... *blēd'ing*
blemish... *blem'ish*
blench... *blensh*
blend... *blend*
bless... *bles*
blessedness... *bles'ed-nes*
blessing... *bles'ing*
blest... *blest*
blight... *blīt*
blind... *blīnd*
blindfold... *blīnd'fōld*
blindly... *blīnd'li*
blindness... *blīnd'nes*
blink... *blingk*
blinker... *bling'kėr*
bliss... *blis*
blissful... *blis'ful*
blister... *blis'tėr*
blistery... *blis'tėr-i*
blithe... *blīTH*
blithesome... *blīTH'som*
blitz... *blitz*
blizzard... *bliz'ėrd*
bloat... *blōt*
bloated... *blōt'ed*
bloater... *blōt'ėr*
blob... *blob*
block... *blok*
blockade... *block-ād'*
blockish... *block'ish*

blood... *blud*
blood hound... *blud'hound*
bloodily... *blud'i-li*
bloodiness... *blud'i-nes*
bloodless... *blud'les*
blood money... *blud'mu-ni*
bloodshed... *blud'shed*
blood shot... *blud'shot*
blood stone... *blud'stōn*
blood sucker... *blud'suck-ėr*
bloodthirsty... *blud'thėrs-ti*
blood vessel... *blud'ves-sel*
bloody... *blud'i*
bloom... *blōm*
bloomy... *blom'i*
blossom... *blos'om*
blot... *blot*
blotch... *bloch*
blotchy... *bloch'i*
blotter... *blot'ėr*
blouse... *blouz*
blow... *blō*
blower... *blō'ėr*
blowzy... *blouz'i*
blubber... *blub'bėr*
bludgeon... *blud'jon*
blue... *blu*
bluebell... *blu'bel*
blue book... *blu'buk*
blue jacket... *blu'jäck-et*
blue pill... *blu'pil*
blue rint... *blu'print*
blue stone... *blu'stōn*
bluff... *bluf*
bluish... *blu'ish*
blunder... *blun'dėr*
blunderbuss... *blun'dėr-bus*
blunt... *blunt*
bluntly... *blunt'li*
bluntness... *blunt'nes*
blur... *blėr*
blurb... *blėrb*
blurt... *blėrt*
blush... *blush*
blushing... *blush'ing*
bluster... *blus'tėr*
blusterer... *blus'tėr-ėr*
boa... *bō'a*
boar... *bōr*
board... *bōrd*
boarder... *bōrd'ėr*
boarding... *bōrd'ing*
boarish... *bōr'ish*
boast... *bōst*

boaster... *bōst'ėr*
boastful... *bōst'ful*
boastingly... *bōsťʼing-li*
boat... *bōt*
boatman... *bōt'man*
bob... *bob*
bobbin... *bob'in*
bode... *bōd*
bodice... *bod'is*
bodied... *bo'did*
bodiless... *bo'di-les*
bodily... *bo'di-li*
body... *bo'di*
body guard... *bo'di-gard*
boer... *bor*
bog... *bog*
boggling... *bog'l-ing*
bogie, Bogey... *bō'gi*
bogus... *bō'gus*
bohemian... *bō-hē'mi-an*
boil... *boil*
boiler... *boil'ėr*
boisterous... *bois'tėr-us*
boisterously... *bois'tėr-us-li*
bold... *bōld*
boldly... *bōld'li*
boldness... *bōld'nes*
bolero... *bō-lār'ō*
boll... *bōl*
bolster... *bōl'stėr*
bolt... *bōlt*
bolter... *bōlt'ėr*
bomb... *bom*
bombard... *bom-bard'*
bombardier... *bom-bard-ēr'*
bombardon... *bom-bar'don*
bombast... *bom'bast*
bombastic... *bom-bast'ic*
bona fide... *bō'na fī'dē*
bon bon... *bong-bong*
bond... *bond*
bonded... *bond'ed*
bonder... *bon'dėr*
bond holder... *bond'hōld-ėr*
bondman... *bond'man*
bone... *bōn*
boned... *bōnd*
bonfire... *bon'fīr*
bonne... *bon*
bonnet... *bon'net*
bonny... *bon'ni*
bonus... *bō'nus*
bony... *bōn'i*
bonze... *bonz*

booby... *bo'bi*
book... *buk*
booking office... *buk'ing-of-is*
bookish... *buk'ish*
book keeper... *buk'kēp-ėr*
booklet... *buk'lef*
book maker... *buk'māk-ėr*
bookseller... *buk'sel-ėr*
bookworm... *bŭk'wėrm*
boom... *bom*
boomerang... *bom'e-rang*
boorish... *bor'ish*
boot... *bot*
booted... *bot'ed*
booth... *bofH*
boot jack... *bot'jack*
bootless... *bot'les*
booty... *bo'ti*
boracic... *bō-ras'ic*
borax... *bō'raks*
border... *bor'dėr*
borderer... *bor'dėr-ėr*
bore... *bōr*
boreal... *bō'rē-al*
boreas... *bō'rē-as*
borer... *bōr'ėr*
boric... *bō'ric*
born... *born*
borne... *bōrn*
borough... *bu'ro*
borrow... *bo'rō*
borrower... *bo'rō-ėr*
bosh... *bosh*
bosom... *bo'zum*
boss... *bos*
botanist... *bot'an-ist*
botanize... *bot'an-īz*
botany... *bot'a-ni*
botch... *boch*
botcher... *boch'ėr*
botchy... *boch'i*
both... *bōth*
bother... *bofH'ėr*
bothersome... *bofH'ėr-sum*
bottle... *bot'l*
bottle nose... *bot'l-nōz*
bottom... *bot'tom*
bottomless... *bot'tom-les*
bottomry... *bot'tom-ri*
boudoir... *bo-dwar'*
bough... *bou*
bougie... *bo-zhē*
boulder... *bōl'dėr*
boulevard... *bol-var*

bounce... *bouns*
bouncer... *bouns'ėr*
bouncing... *bouns'ing*
bound... *bound*
boundary... *bound'a-ri*
boundless... *bound'les*
bounteous... *boun'tē-us*
bounteously... *boun'tē-us-li*
bountiful... *boun'ti-ful*
bounty... *boun'ti*
bouquet... *bo-kā'*
bourn... *bōrn*
bout... *bout*
bovine... *bō'vīn*
bow... *bou*
bow... *bō*
bowdlerize... *bō d'lėr-īz*
bowed... *bōd*
bowel... *bou'el*
bower... *bou'ėr*
bowry... *bou'ėr-i*
bowie knife... *bō'i-nīf*
bowl... *bōl*
bow legged... *bō'legd*
bowler... *bōl'ėr*
bowline... *bō'līn*
bowling... *bōl'ing*
bowman... *bō'man*
bowshot... *bō'shot*
bow window... *bō'win-dō*
box... *boks*
boxen... *boks'en*
boxer... *boks'ėr*
boxing... *boks'ing*
boxwood... *boks'wud*
boy... *boi*
boycott... *boi'cot*
boyhood... *boi'hud*
boyish... *boi'ish*
brace... *brās*
bracelet... *brās'let*
bracing... *brās'ing*
bracken... *brack'en*
bracket... *brack'et*
brackish... *brack'ish*
brad... *brad*
brag... *brag*
braggart... *brag'art*
braid... *brād*
braided... *brād'ed*
braille... *brāl*
brainless... *brān'les*
brake... *brāk*
bramble... *bram'bl*

bran... *bran*
branch... *bransh*
branchy... *bransh'i*
brand... *brand*
brandish... *brand'ish*
brandling... *brand'ling*
brandy... *bran'di*
brangle... *brang'gl*
brash... *brash*
brasier... *brā'zhėr*
brass... *bras*
brassy... *bras'i*
brat... *brat*
brattice... *brat'is*
brave... *brāv*
bravely... *brāv'li*
bravery... *brāv'ė-ri*
bravo... *bra'vō*
brawl... *bral*
brawler... *bral'er*
brawling... *bral'ing*
brawn... *bran*
brawny... *bran'i*
braze... *brāz*
brazen... *brāz'n*
brazier... *brā'zi-ėr*
breach... *brēch*
bread... *bred*
bread corn... *bred'corn*
breadstuff... *bred'stuf*
breadth... *bredth*
break... *brāk*
breakage... *brāk'āj*
break down... *brāk'doun*
breaker... *brāk'ėr*
breakfast... *brek'fast*
break up... *brāk'up*
breakwater... *brāk'wa-tėr*
breast... *brest*
breast bone... *brest'bōn*
breastplate... *brest'plāt*
breath... *breth*
breathe... *brēłH*
breathing... *brēłH'ing*
breathless... *breth'les*
bred... *bred*
breech... *brēch*
breed... *brēd*
breeder... *brēd'ėr*
breeding... *brēd'ing*
breeze... *brēz*
breezy... *brēz'i*
brethren... *brełH'ren*
breve... *brēv*

B

brevet... *brev'et*
breviary... *brē'vi-a-ri*
brevier... *brē-vēr'*
brevity... *bre'vi-ti*
brew... *bro*
brewer... *bro'ėr*
brewery... *bro'ė-ri*
brewing... *bro'ing*
briar... *brī'ar*
bribe... *brīb*
briber... *brīb'ėr*
bribery... *brīb'ė-ri*
brick... *brick*
brick field... *brick'fēld*
bricklayer... *brick'lā-ėr*
brickwork... *brick'wėrk*
bridal... *brī'd'al*
brides-cake... *brī dz'cāk*
bridegroom... *brī d'grom*
brides maid... *brī dz'mād*
bridewell... *brī d'wel*
bridge... *brij*
bridle... *brī'dl*
brief... *brēf*
briefless... *brēf'les*
briefly... *brēf'li*
brier... *brī'ėr*
brig... *brig*
brigade... *bri-gād'*
brigadier... *bri-ga-dėr'*
brigand... *bri'gand*
brigantine... *brig'an-fīn*
bright... *brīt*
brighten... *brī't'n*
brightly... *brīt'li*
brill... *bril*
brilliant... *bril'yant*
brilliantly... *bril'yant-li*
brim... *brim*
brimful... *brim'ful*
brimmer... *brim'ėr*
brindled... *brind'ld*
brine... *brīn*
bring... *bring*
brink... *bringk*
briny... *brīn'i*
briquette... *bri-ket'*
brisk... *brisk*
brisket... *brisk'et*
briskly... *brisk'li*
bristle... *bris'l*
bristly... *bris'li*
britannic... *bri-tan'ik*
british... *brit'ish*

briton... *brit'on*
brittle... *brit'l*
broach... *brōch*
broacher... *brōch'ėr*
broad... *brad*
broadcasting... *brad'cast-ing*
broaden... *brad'n*
broadside... *brad'sī d*
brocade... *brō-cād'*
brocaded... *brō-cād'ed*
broccoli... *broc'o-li*
brocc... *brock*
brogue... *brōg*
broider... *broid'ėr*
broil... *broil*
broken... *brōk'n*
broker... *brō'kėr*
brokerage... *bro'kėr-āj*
bronchial... *brong'ke-al*
bronchitis... *brong-kī'tis*
bronze... *bronz*
bronzed... *bronzd*
brooch... *brōch*
brood... *brod*
brook... *bruk*
brooklet... *bruk'let*
broom... *brom*
broomy... *brom'i*
broth... *broth*
brothel... *broth'el*
brother... *bruᴛʜ'ėr*
brow... *brou*
browbeat... *brou'bēt*
brown... *broun*
brownie... *brou'ni*
browse... *brouz*
bruin... *bro'in*
bruise... *broz*
bruiser... *broz'ėr*
bruit... *brot*
brumal... *bro'mal*
brunette... *bro-net'*
brunt... *brunt*
brush... *brush*
brushwood... *brush'wud*
brushy... *brush'i*
brutal... *brot'al*
brutality... *brot-al'i-ti*
brutalize... *brot-al-īz*
brutally... *brot'al-li*
brute... *brot*
brutish... *brot'ish*
bubble... *bub'bl*
bubonic... *bū-bon'ic*

buccaneer... buc-a-nēr'
buck... buck
bucket... buck'et
buckle... buck'l
buckler... buck'lèr
buckthorn... buck'thorn
buckwheat... buck'whēt
bud... bud
buddhism... bud'izm
buddhist... bu'd'ist
budding... büd'ing
budge... buj
budget... buj'et
buff... buf
buffalo... buf'fa-lō
buffer... buf'èr
buffet... buf'et
buffet... buf'et
buffoon... buf-fon'
buffoonery... buf-fon'ė-ri
bug... bug
buggy... bug'i
bugle... bū'gl
bugler... būg'lèr
buhl... bol
build... bild
builder... bild'èr
building... bild'ing
bulb... bulb
bulbul... bul'bul
bulge... būlj
bulk... bulk
bulky... bulk'i
bull... bul
bullace... bul'ās
bull-dog... bul'dog
bulldozer... bul'dōz-èr
bullet... bul'et
bulletin... bul'e-tin
bull-fight... bul'fīt
bullfinch... bul'finsh
bull-frog... bul'frog
bullion... bul'yon
bullock... bul'ock
bull's-eye... bulz'ī
bully... bul'i
bulrush... bul'rush
bulwark... bul'wèrk
bumble-bee... bum'bl-bē
bump... bump
bumper... bump'èr
bumpkin... bump'kin
bun... bun
bunchy... bunsh'i

bundle... bun'dl
bung... bung
bungalow... bung'ga-lō
bungle... bung'gl
bungler... bung'gl-èr
bungling... bung'gl-ing
bunk... bungk
bunker... bung'kèr
bunting... bunt'ing
buoy... boi
buoyancy... boi'an-si
buoyant... boi'ant
burdensome... bèr'dn-sum
burdock... bèr'dock
bureau... bū-rō'
bureaucracy... bū-rō'cra-si
burgeon... bèr'jon
burgess... bèr'jes
burglar... bèrg'lèr
burglarious... bèrg-lā'ri-us
burglary... bèrg'la-ri
burgundy... bèr'gun-di
burial... be'ri-al
burly... bèr'li
burmese... bur'mēz
burn... bèrn
burner... bèrn'èr
burning... bèrn'ing
burning-glass... bèrn'ing-glas
burnish... bèr'nish
burr... bèr
burrow... bu'rō
burst... bèrst
bury... be'ri
bus... bus
busby... buz'bi
bush... bush
bushel... bush'el
bushy... bush'i
busily... bi'zi-li
business... biz'nes
busk... busk
bust... bust
bustard... bus'tèrd
bustle... bus'l
busy... bi'zi
busy-body... bi'zi-bo-di
butcher... buch'èr
butchery... buch'èr-i
butler... but'lèr
butt... but
butter... but'tèr
butter-cup... but'tèr-cup
butterfly... but'tèr-flī

B

buttermilk... *but'ėr-milk*
buttery... *but'tėr-i*
buttock... *but'toc*
button... *but'n*
button-hole... *but'n-hōl*
buttress... *but'tres*
buxom... *buks'um*
buy... *bī*
buyer... *bī'ėr*
buzz... *buz*
buzzard... *buz'ėrd*
by... *bī*
bye... *bī*
by-gone... *bī'gon*
by-play... *bī'plā*
byre... *bīr*
by-stander... *bī'stand-ėr*
by-word... *bī'wėrd*
byzantine... *biz-an'tīn or biz'*

C

cab... *cab*
cabal... *ca-bal'*
caballero... *ca-bal-yā'rō*
cabaret... *cab'a-ret*
cabbage... *cab'āj*
cabby... *cab'i*
caber... *cā'bėr*
cabin... *cab'in*
cabinet... *cab'in-et*
cable... *cā'bl*
cablegram... *cā'bl-gram*
cacao... *ca-cā'ō*
cache... *cash*
cackle... *cac'l*
cactus... *cac'tus*
cad... *cad*
cadaverous... *ca-dav'ėr-us*
caddie... *cad'i*
caddy... *cad'i*
cadence... *cā'dens*
cadet... *ca-det'*
cadmium... *cad'mi-um*
caduceus... *ca-dū'sē-us*
caesura... *sē-zū'ra*
cafe... *caf-ā'*
cafeteria... *caf-e-tēr'i-a*
caffeine... *ca-fē'in*
cage... *cāj*
cairn... *cārn*
cairngorm... *cārn'gorm*

cajole... *ca-jōl'*
cake... *cāk*
calabash... *cal'a-bash*
calamitous... *ca-lam'it-us*
calamity... *ca-lam'i-ti*
calcareous... *cal-cā'rē-us*
calcination... *cal-cin-ā'shun*
calcine... *cal-cīn'*
calculable... *cal'cū-la-bl*
calculate... *cal'cū-lāt*
calculation... *cal-cū-lā'shun*
calculator... *cal'cū-lāt-ėr*
calculus... *cal'cū-lus*
caldron... *cal'dron*
caledonian... *cal-i-dō'ni-an*
calender... *ca'lin-dėr*
calf... *caf*
caliber... *ca'li-bėr*
calico... *ca'li-cō*
calk... *cak*
call... *cal*
calligraphy... *cal-lig'ra-fi*
callipers... *cal'i-pėrz*
callisthenics... *cal-is-then'ics*
callosity... *ca-los'i-ti*
callous... *cal'os*
calm... *cam*
calmly... *cam'li*
calmness... *cam'nes*
caloric... *ca-lo'ric*
calorific... *ca-lo-rif'ic*
calotype... *ca'lō-tīp*
calumet... *cal'ū-met*
calumniate... *ca-lum'ni-āt*
calumniator... *ca-lum'ni-āt-ėr*
calumnious... *ca-lum'ni-us*
calumniously... *ca-lum'ni-us-li*
calvary... *cal'va-ri*
calve... *cav*
calvinist... *cal'vin-ist*
calyx... *cā-lics*
cam... *cam*
camber... *cam'bėr*
cambrian... *cam'bri-an*
cambric... *cām'bric*
camel... *cam'el*
camellia... *ca-mel'i-a*
cameo... *cam'ē-ō*
camera... *cam'ė-ra*
camlet... *cam'let*
camomile... *cam'ō-mīl*
camouflage... *cam-o-flazh*
camp... *camp*
campaign... *cam-pān'*

campaigner... cam-pān'ėr
campanile... cam-pa-nē'lā
camphor... cam'fėr
camphorate... cam'fėr-āt
campion... cam'pi-on
can... can
canal... ca-nal'
canary... ca-nā'ri
cancel... can'cel
cancerous... can'cėr-us
candid... can'did
candidate... can'di-dāt
candied... can'did
candle... can'dl
candlestick... can'dl-stic
candor... can'dėr
candy... can'di
cane... cān
canine... ca'nīn
canister... can'is-tėr
canker... cang'kėr
cankerous... cang'kėr-us
cannibal... can'ni-bal
cannibalism... can'ni-bal-izm
cannon... can'un
cannonade... can-un-ād'
canoe... ca-no'
canon... can'on
canonical... can-on'ic-al
canonicals... can-on'ic-alz
canonist... can'on-ist
canonize... can'on-īz
canopy... can'ō-pi
cantata... can-ta'ta
cantatrice... can-ta-trē'chā
canteen... can-tēn'
canter... can'tėr
canticle... can'ti-cl
cantilever... can'ti-lēv-ėr
cantle... can'tl
canton... can'ton
cantonal... can'ton-al
cantonment... can-ton'ment
canvas... can'vas
canvass... can'vas
canvasser... can'vas-ėr
canzonet... can-zō-net'
cap... cap
capability... cā-pa-bil'i-ti
capable... cā'pa-bl
capacious... ca-pā'shos
capacitate... ca-pas'i-tāt
capacity... ca-pas'i-ti
caparison... ca-pa'ri-son

cape... cāp
caper... cā'pėr
capillary... ca-pil'la-ri,
capitalize... cap'it-al-īz
capitally... cap'it-al-i
capitation... cap-it-ā'shun
capitol... cap'it-ol
capitular... ca-pit'ū-lėr
capitulate... ca-pit'ū-lāt
capon... cā'pon
caprice... ca-prēs'
capricious... ca-pri'shus
capriciously... ca-pri'shus-li
capricorn... ca'pri-corn
capsize... cap-sīz'
capstan... cap'stan
capsular... cap'sūl-ėr
capsule... cap'sūl
captain... cap'tin
captaincy... cap'tin-si
caption... cap'shun
captious... cap'shus
captiously... cap'shus-li
captivate... cap'ti-vāt
captive... cap'tiv
captivity... cap-tiv'i-ti
captor... cap'tėr
capuchin... ca-pū-shēn'
car... car
carafe... ca'raf
caramel... ca'ra-mel
carat... ca'rit
caravan... ca'ra-van
caraway... ca'ra-wā
carbide... car'bīd
carbine... car'bīn
carbolic... car-bol'ic
carbon... car'bon
carbonate... car'bon-āt
carbonic... car-bon'ic
carbonize... car'bon-īz
carbuncle... car'bung-cl
carbureted... car'bū-ret-ed
carburetor... car'bū-ret-ėr
carcass... car'cas
card... card
cardamom... car'da-mum
cardboard... card'bōrd
carder... card'ėr
cardiac... car'di-ac
cardigan... car'di-gan
care... cār
careen... ca-rēn'
career... ca-rēr'

careful... cār'ful	**casern**... ca-zėrn'
carefully... cāār-ful-li	**cash**... cash
carefulness... cāāř'ful-nes	**cashier**... cash-ēr'
careless... cār'les	**cashmere**... cash'mēr
carelessly... cār'les-li	**casing**... cās'ing
carelessness... cār'les-nes	**casino**... ca-sē'nō
caress... ca-res'	**cask**... cask
caret... cā'ret	**casket**... cask'et
care-taker... cār'tā-kėr	**casque**... cask
cargo... car'gō	**casserole**... cas'e-rōl
caricature... ca-ri-ca-tūr'	**cassimere**... cas'si-mēr
caries... cā'ri-ēz	**cassock**... cas'ok
carillon... ca'ril-lon	**cast**... cast
carious... cā'ri-us	**castanet**... cas'ta-net
carminative... car'min-āt-iv	**castaway**... cast'a-wā
carnage... car'nāj	**caster**... cast'ėr
carnal... car'nal	**castigate**... cas'ti-gāt
carnality... car-nal'i-ti	**castigation**... cas-ti-gā'shun
carnally... car'nal-li	**casting**... cast'ing
carnation... car-nā'shun	**cast-iron**... cast'ī-ėrn
carnival... car'ni-val	**castle**... cas'l
carnivorous... car-niv'ō-rus	**castled**... cas'ld
carob... ca'rob	**cast-off**... cast'of
carol... ca'rol	**castor**... cas'tėr
carousal... ca-rouz'al	**castrate**... cas'trāt
carouse... ca-rouz'	**castration**... cas-trā'shun
carp... carp	**casual**... ca'zhū-al
carpenter... car'pen-tėr	**casualty**... ca'zhū-al-ti
carpentry... car'pen-tri	**casuistic**... ca-zū-ist'ic
carpet... car'pet	**casuistry**... ca'zū-is-tri
carpeting... car'pet-ing	**cat**... cat
carriage... ca'rij	**cataclysm**... cat'a-clizm
carrier... ca'ri-ėr	**catacomb**... ca'ta-cōm
carrion... ca'ri-on	**catalogue**... ca'ta-log
carrot... ca'rit	**catamaran**... cat'a-ma-ran''
carry... ca'ri	**cataplasm**... ca'ta-plazm
cart... cart	**catapult**... cat'a-pult
cartage... cart'āj	**cataract**... cat'a-ract
carte... cart	**catarrhal**... ca-tar'al
carte-blanche... cart-blansh	**catch**... cach
cartel... car'tel	**cate**... cāt
carter... cart'ėr	**catechetic**... ca-tē-cet'ic
cartilage... car'ti-lāj	**catechise**... ca'tē-cīz
cartilaginous... car-ti-laj'in-us	**catechism**... ca'tē-cizm
cartography... car-tog'ra-fi	**catechist**... ca'tē-cist
cartridge... car'trij	**categorical**... ca-tē-go'ri-cal
cartulary... car'tū-la-ri	**category**... cat'ē-go-ri
carve... carv	**catenation**... cat-e-nā'shun
carver... carv'ėr	**cater**... cā'tėr
cascade... cas'cād	**caterer**... cā'tėr-ėr
case... cās	**cateress**... cā'tėr-es
casemate... cās'māt	**caterpillar**... cat'ėr-pil-ėr
casement... cās'ment	**cathartic**... ca-thar'tic
caseous... cā'sē-us	**cathedra**... ca-thē'dra

cathedral... ca-thē'dral
catheter... cath'e-tėr
catholic... ca'thol-ic
catholicism... ca-thol'i-sizm
catoptrics... cat-op'trics
cat's-eye... cats'ī
cattle... cat'tl
caucus... ca'cus
caul... cal
caulk... čak
causal... čaz'al
causality... čaz-al'i-ti
causation... čaz-ā'shun
causative... čäz'a-tiv
cause... caz
causeless... caz'les
causeway... cäz'wā
caustic... cas'tic
causticity... cas-tis'i-ti
cautelous... cä'tel-us
cauterize... cä"tėr-īz
caution... ca'shun
cautionary... ca'shun-a-ri
cautious... ca'shus
cautiously... ča'shus-li
cavalcade... čä'val-cād
cavalier... ca-va-lēr'
cavalierly... ca-va-lēr'li
cavalry... ca'val-ri
cave... cāv
caveat... cā'vē-at
cavern... ca'vėrn
cavernous... ca'vėrn-us
caviler... ca'vil-ėr
cavity... ca'vi-ti
cayenne... cā-en'
cease... sēs
ceaseless... sēs'les
cedar... sē'dėr
ceiling... sēl'ing
celandine... sel'an-dīn
celebrant... sel'ē-brant
celebrate... sel'ē-brāt
celebrity... se-leb'ri-ti
celerity... sē-le'ri-ti
celery... se'le-ri
celestial... sē-les'ti-al
celibacy... se'li-ba-si
celibate... se'li-bāt
cell... sel
cellophane... sel'ō-fān
cellular... sel'ū-lėr
celluloid... sel'lū-loid
cellulose... sel'lū-lōs

celtic... selt'ic
cement... sē-ment'
cemetery... se'mē-te-ri
censor... sen'sėr
censorious... sen-sō'ri-us
censorship... sen'sėr-ship
censurable... sen'shūr-a-bl
censurably... sen'shūr-a-bli
censure... sen'shūr
census... sen'sus
cent... sent
centage... sent'āj
cental... sen'tal
centenarian... sen-ten-ā'ri-an
centennial... sen-ten'ni-al
center... sen'tėr
centigrade... sen'ti-grād
centimeter... sen'ti-mē-tėr
centipede... sen'ti-pēd
central... sen'tral
centralize... sen'tral-īz
centrifugal... sen-trif'ū-gal
centuple... sen'tū-pl
centurion... sen-tū'ri-on
century... sen'tū-ri
ceramic... se-ram'ic
cerate... sē'rāt
cerebral... se'rē-bral
cerebration... se-rē-brā'shun
ceremonial... se-rē-mō'ni-al
ceremonious... se-rē-mō'ni-us
ceremony... se'rē-mō-ni
certain... sėr'tān
certainly... sėr'tān-li
certainty... sėr'tān-ti
certificate... sėr-tif'i-cāt
certifier... sėr'ti-fī-ėr
certify... sėr'ti-fī
ceruse... sē'rūz
cervine... sėr'vīn
cess... ses
cessation... ses-ā'shun
cession... se'shun
cesspool... ses'pol
cetaceous... sē-tā'shus
chafe... chāf
chafer... chāf'ėr
chaff... chaf
chagrin... sha-grēn'
chain... chān
chair... chār
chaise... shāz
chalcedony... cal-sed'ō-ni
chaldron... chal'dron

chalice... cha'lis
chalk... chak
chalky... chak'i
challenge... chal'lenj
challengeable... chal'lenj-a-bl
challenger... chal'lenj-ėr
chamber... chăm'bėr
chamberlain... chăm'bėr-lān
chameleon... ca-mē'lē-on
chamfer... cham'fėr
chamomile... ca'mō-mīl
champ... champ
champagne... sham-pān'
champaign... sham'pān
champion... cham'pi-on
chance... chans
chancel... chan'sel
chancellor... chan'sel-lėr
chancery... chan'se-ri
chandelier... shan-dē-lēr'
chandler... chand'lėr
changeable... chānj'a-bl
changeably... chānj'a-bli
changeful... chānj'ful
changeling... chānj'ling
changer... chānj'ėr
channel... chan'nel
channelled... chan'neld
chant... chant
chanter... chant'ėr
chantry... chant'ri
chaos... cā'os
chaotic... cā-ot'ic
chap... chap
chapel... chap'el
chaperon... sha'pe-rōn
chapiter... chap'i-tėr
chaplain... chap'lān
chaplaincy... chap'lān-si
chaplet... chap'let
chapter... chap'tėr
char... char
character... ca'rac-tėr
characterize... ca'rac-tėr-īz
charade... sha-rad'
chare... chār
charge... charj
chargeable... charj'a-bl
charger... charj'ėr
charily... chā'ri-li
chariot... cha'ri-ot
charitable... cha'rit-a-bl
charitably... cha'rit-a-bli
charity... cha'ri-ti

charlatan... shar'la-tan
charm... charm
charmer... charm'ėr
chart... chart
charter... char'tėr
chartered... char'tėrd
chartulary... car'tū-la-ri
chase... chās
chaser... chās'ėr
chasm... cazm
chaste... chāst
chasten... chās'n
chastise... chas-fīz'
chastisement... chas'tiz-ment
chastity... chas'ti-ti
chatter... chat'ėr
chatter-box... chat'ėr-boks
chatterer... chat'ėr-ėr
chatty... chat'i
chauffeur... shō'fėr
chauvinism... shō'vin-izm
cheap... chēp
cheapen... chēp'n
cheaply... chēp'li
cheapness... chēp'nes
cheat... chēt
check... check
checker... check'ėr
checkmate... check'māt
cheddar... ched'ėr
cheek... chēk
cheep... chēp
cheer... chēr
cheerful... chēr'ful
cheerily... chēr'i-li
cheering... chēr'ing
cheerless... chēr'les
cheery... chēr'i
cheese... chēz
chemical... cem'ic-al
chemise... she-mēz'
chemist... cem'ist
chemistry... cem'ist-ri
cherish... che'rish
cherry... che'ri
cherub... che'rub
chess... ches
chess-board... ches'bōrd
chess-man... ches'man
chest... chest
chestnut... ches'nut
chevalier... she'va-lėr
chevron... shev'run
chew... cho

chic... shēc
chick... chick
chicken-pox... chick'en-poks
chicory... chic'o-ri
chide... chīd
chief... chēf
chiefly... chēf'li
chieftain... chēf'tān
child... chīld
childbirth... chīld'bérth
childe... chīld
childhood... chīld'hud
childish... chīld'ish
childless... chīld'les
childlike... chīld'līk
chill... chil
chilly... chil'i
chime... chīm
chimney... chim'nē
chimpanzee... chim'pan-zē
chin... chin
china... chī'na
chinchilla... chin-chil'la
chinese... chī-nēz'
chintz... chints
chip... chip
chirography... cī-rog'ra-fi
chiromancy... cī'rō-man-si
chiropodist... cīr-op'od-ist
chirp... chèrp
chirrup... chi'rup
chisel... chiz'el
chit-chat... chit'chat
chivalry... shi'val-ri
chive... chīv
chloral... clō'ral
chloric... clō'ric
chloride... clō'rid
chlorine... clō'rīn
chlorodyne... clō'rō-dīn
chloroform... clō'rō-form
chlorophyll... clō'rō-fil
chocolate... cho'cō-lāt
choice... chois
choir... cwīr
choke... chōk
cholera... co'lè-ra
choleric... co'lè-ric
choose... choz
chooser... choz'ér
chop... chop
choppy... chop'i
chopsticks... chop'stiks
choral... cō'ral

chorister... co'rist-ér
chorus... cō'rus
chosen... chōz'n
christ... crīst
christen... cris'n
christening... cris'n-ing
christian... cris'ti-an
christianity... cris-ti-an'i-ti
christianize... cris'ti-an-īz
christmas... cris'mas
chromatic... cō-mat'ic
chrome... crōm
chromic... crōm'ic
chronicle... cron'i-cl
chronicler... cron'i-clér
chronologist... cro-nol'o-jist
chronology... cro-nol'o-ji
chronometer... cro-nom'et-ér
chrysalis... chris'a-lis
chub... chub
chubby... chub'i
chuck... chuck
chuckle... chuck'l
chum... chum
chunk... chungk
church... chèrch
churchman... chèrch'man
churl... chèrl
churlish... chèrl'ish
churn... chèrn
cicatrix... si-cā'trics
cicatrize... si'ca-triz
cicely... sis'e-li
cicerone... chi-che-rō'ne
cider... sī'dér
cigar... si-gar'
cigarette... sig-a-ret'
cimmerian... sim-mē'ri-an
cinder... sin'der
cinema... sin'e-ma
cinerary... si'ne-ra-ri
cinnabar... sin'na-bar
cinnamon... sin'na-mon
cipher... sī'fér
circle... sèr'cl
circlet... sèr'clet
circuit... sèr'cit
circuitous... sèr-cū'it-us
circular... sèr'cū-lèr
circulate... sèr'cū-lāt
circulation... sèr-cū-lā'shun
circumflex... sèr'cum-fleks
circumfuse... sèr-cum-fūz'
circumscribe... sèr'cum-scrīb

circumspect... *sėr'cum-spect*
circumstance... *sėr'cum-stans*
circumvent... *sėr-cum-vent'*
circus... *sėr'cus*
cirrus... *sir'rus*
cist... *sist*
citable... *sīt'a-bl*
citadel... *si'ta-del*
citation... *sī-tā'shun*
cite... *sīt*
citizen... *si'ti-zen*
citizenship... *si'ti-zen-ship*
citric... *sit'ric*
citron... *sit'ron*
city... *si'ti*
cive... *sīv*
civic... *si'vic*
civil... *si'vil*
civilian... *si-vil'i-an*
civility... *si-vil'i-ti*
civilization... *si'vil-iz-ā'shun*
claim... *clām*
claimable... *clām'a-bl*
claimant... *clām'ant*
clairvoyance... *clār-voi'ans*
clam... *clam*
clamant... *clam'ant*
clamber... *clam'bėr*
clammy... *clam'i*
clamor... *clam'ėr*
clamp... *clamp*
clan... *clan*
clang... *clang*
clank... *clangk*
clannish... *clan'ish*
clansman... *clanz'man*
clap... *clap*
clapper... *clap'ėr*
claret... *cla'ret*
clarification... *cla'ri-fi-kā''shun*
clarifier... *cla'ri-fī-ėr*
clarify... *cla'ri-fī*
clarion... *cla'ri-on*
clarionet... *cla'ri-on-et*
clash... *clash*
class... *clas*
classic... *clas'ic*
classical... *clas'ic-al*
classicism... *clas'i-sizm*
classicist... *clas'i-sist*
classify... *clas'i-fī*
clatter... *clat'tėr*
clause... *claz*
clavicle... *clav'i-cl*

clavier... *clav'i-ėr*
claw... *cla*
clay... *clā*
clean... *clēn*
cleanliness... *clen'li-nes*
cleanse... *clenz*
cleanser... *clenz'ėr*
clear... *clēr*
clearance... *clēr'ans*
clearer... *clēr'ėr*
clear-headed... *clēr'hed-ed*
clearly... *clēr'li*
cleavable... *clēv'a-bl*
cleavage... *clēv'āj*
cleave... *clēv*
cleft... *cleft*
clematis... *clem'a-tis*
clement... *cle'ment*
clench... *clensh*
clergy... *clėr'ji*
clergyman... *clėr'ji-man*
cleric... *cle'ric*
clerical... *cle'ric-al*
clerc... *clarc*
clercship... *clarc'ship*
clever... *cle'vėr*
cleverness... *cle'vėr-nes*
click... *clīk*
client... *clī'ent*
clientele... *clī'en-tēl*
cliff... *clif*
climacteric... *cli-mac-te'ric*
climate... *clī'māt*
climatic... *clī-mat'ic*
climax... *clī'maks*
climb... *clīm*
climber... *clīm'ėr*
clime... *clīm*
clinch... *clinsh*
cling... *cling*
clinic... *clin'ic*
clink... *clingk*
clinker... *clingk'ėr*
clinometer... *clīn-om'et-ėr*
clip... *clip*
clipper... *clip'ėr*
clique... *clēk*
cloak... *klōk*
clock... *klok*
clod... *klod*
clog... *klog*
cloister... *klois'tėr*
close... *klōz*
close-fisted... *klōs'fist-ed*

closely... *klōs'li*
closet... *kloz'et*
closure... *klōz'ūr*
clot... *klot*
cloth... *kloth*
clothe... *klōŦH*
clothes... *klōŦHz*
clothier... *klōŦH'i-ėr*
cloud... *kloud*
cloudless... *kloud'les*
cloudy... *kloud'i*
clout... *klout*
clove... *klōv*
clover... *klō'vėr*
clown... *kloun*
clownish... *kloun'ish*
club... *klub*
club-house... *klub'hous*
club-room... *klub'rom*
cluck... *kluk*
clue... *klo*
clump... *klump*
clumsily... *klum'zi-li*
clumsiness... *klum'zi-nes*
clumsy... *klum'zi*
cluster... *klus'tėr*
clutch... *kluch*
clutter... *klut'tėr*
coach... *kōch*
coachman... *kōch'man*
coagent... *kō-ā'jent*
coagulable... *kō-ag'ū-la-bl*
coagulate... *kō-ag'ū-lāt*
coalescent... *kō-al-es'ent*
coalition... *kō-al-i'shun*
coal-mine... *kōl'mīn*
coarse... *kōrs*
coarsely... *kōrs'li*
coast... *kōst*
coat... *kōt*
coating... *kōt'ing*
coax... *kōks*
coaxer... *kōks'ėr*
cob... *kob*
cobalt... *kō'balt*
cobble... *kob'l*
cobbler... *kob'l-ėr*
coble... *kō'bl*
cobweb... *kob'web*
coca... *kō'ka*
cocaine... *kō'ka-in*
cochineal... *ko'chi-nēl*
cockatoo... *kok-a-to'*
cockroach... *kok'roch*

coco... *kō'kō*
cocoa... *kō'kō*
coco-nut... *kō'kō-nut*
cod... *kod*
coddle... *kod'l*
code... *kōd*
codicil... *ko'di-sil*
codify... *kōd'i-fī*
cod-liver oil... *kod'li-vėr oil*
coefficient... *kō-ef-fi'shent*
coequal... *kō-ē'kwal*
coerce... *kō-ėrs'*
coercion... *kō-ėr'shun*
coercive... *kō-ėrs'iv*
coessential... *kō-es-sen'shal*
coeternal... *kō-ē-tėr'nal*
coexecutor... *kō-eks-ek'ū-tėr*
coexist... *kō-egz-ist'*
coextend... *kō-eks-tend'*
coextensive... *kō-eks-ten'siv*
coffee... *kof'i*
coffer... *kof'ėr*
coffin... *kof'fin*
cogency... *kō'jen-si*
cogent... *kō'jent*
cogently... *kō'jent-li*
cogitate... *ko'jit-āt*
cogitative... *ko'jit-āt-iv*
cognac... *kō'nyak*
cognate... *kog'nāt*
cognition... *kog-ni'shun*
cognizable... *kog'niz-a-bl*
cohabit... *kō-hab'it*
coheir... *kō-ār'*
coheiress... *kō-ār'es*
cohere... *kō-hēr'*
coherent... *kō-hēr'ent*
coherently... *kō-hēr'ent-li*
cohesion... *kō-hē'zhon*
cohesive... *kō-hē'siv*
cohort... *kō'hort*
coif... *koif*
coiffure... *koif'ūr*
coil... *koil*
coin... *koin*
coinage... *koin'āj*
coincide... *kō-in-sī'd'*
coincidence... *kō-in'si-dens*
coincident... *kō-in'si-dent*
coition... *kō-i'shun*
cola... *kō'la*
cold... *kōld*
cold-blooded... *kōld'blud-ed*
coldish... *kōld'ish*

coldly . . . kōld'li
coldness . . . kōld'nes
cole . . . kōl
colic . . . kol'ik
colitis . . . kō-lī'tis
collaborator . . . kol-la'bo-rāt-ėr
collapse . . . kol-laps'
collar . . . kol'ėr
collar-bone . . . kol'ėr-bōn
collate . . . kol-lāt'
collateral . . . kol-lat'ėr-al
collation . . . kol-lā'shun
collator . . . ko-lāt'ėr
colleague . . . kol'lēg
collect . . . kol-lekt'
collectedly . . . kol-kekt'ed-li
collection . . . kol-kek'shun
collective . . . kol-lekt'iv
collectively . . . kol-lekt'iv-li
collectivism . . . kol-lek'tiv-izm
collector . . . kol-lekt'ėr
collegian . . . kol-lē'ji-an
collegiate . . . kol-lē'ji-āt
collide . . . kol-līd'
collie . . . kol'i
collier . . . kol'yėr
collision . . . kol-li'zhon
collodion . . . kol-lō'di-on
colloquial . . . kol-lō'kwi-al
colloquy . . . kol'lō-kwi
collude . . . 'kol-lūd'
collusion . . . kol-lū'zhon
collusive . . . kol-lū'siv
colon . . . kō'lon
colonial . . . ko-lō'ni-al
colonialism . . . ko-lō'ni-al-izm
colonist . . . ko'lon-ist
colonize . . . ko'lon-īz
colonnade . . . ko-lon-ād'
colony . . . ko'lō-ni
color . . . kul'ėr
colorable . . . kul'ėr-a-bl
colored . . . kul'ėrd
coloring . . . kul'ėr-ing
colorist . . . kul'ėr-ist
colossal . . . kō-los'al
colossus . . . kō-los'us
colt . . . kōlt
columbine . . . ko'lum-bīn
columbium . . . kō-lum'bi-um
column . . . ko'lum
columnar . . . ko-lum'nėr
colure . . . kō-lūr'
coma . . . kō'ma

comatose . . . kō'ma-tōs
comb . . . kōm
combat . . . kom'bat
combatable . . . kom-bat'a-bl
combatant . . . kom'bat-ant
combative . . . kom'bat-iv
combinable . . . kom-bīn'a-bl
combine . . . kom-bīn'
combined . . . kom-bīnd'
combustible . . . kom-bust'i-bl
combustion . . . kom-bust'shun
come . . . kum
comedian . . . ko-mē'di-an
comedy . . . ko'mē-di
comeliness . . . kum'li-nes
comet . . . kom'et
cometary . . . kom'et-a-ri
comfort . . . kum'fėrt
comfortable . . . kum'fėrt-a-bl
comfortably . . . kum'fėrt-a-bli
comforter . . . kum'fėrt-ėr
comfortless . . . kum'fėrt-les
comic . . . kom'ik
comical . . . kom'ik-al
comically . . . kom'ik-al-li
coming . . . kum'ing
comity . . . ko'mi-ti
comma . . . kom'ma
command . . . kom-mand'
commence . . . kom-mens'
commend . . . kom-mend'
comment . . . kom-ment'
commentary . . . kom'ment-a-ri
commerce . . . kom'mėrs
commercial . . . kom-mėr'shal
commiserate . . . kom-miz'é-rāt
commissary . . . kom'mis-sa-ri
commission . . . kom-mi'shun
commissure . . . kom'mis-sūr
commitment . . . kom'mit'ment
committal . . . kom-mit'al
committee . . . kom-mit'tē
commix . . . kom-miks'
commixture . . . kom-miks'tūr
commode . . . kom-mōd'
commodious . . . kom-mō'di-us
commodity . . . kom-mo'di-ti
commodore . . . kom'mo-dōr
common . . . kom'mon
commonage . . . kom'mon-āj
commonly . . . kom'mon-li
commotion . . . kom-mō'shun
commune . . . kom-mūn'
communion . . . kom-mūn'yon

communism... kom'mūn-izm
communist... kom'mūn-ist
community... kom-mū'ni-ti
commutable... kom-mūt'a-bl
commute... kom-mūt'
compact... kom-pakt'
compactly... kom-pakt'li
companion... kom-pan'yon
company... kum'pa-ni
comparably... kom'pa-ra-bli
comparative... kom-pa'ra-tiv
compare... kom-pār'
comparison... kom-pa'ri-son
compass... kum'pas
compassion... kom-pa'shun
compatible... kom-pat'i-bl
compatibly... kom-pat'i-bli
compel... kom-pel'
compellable... kom-pel'a-bl
compensate... kom-pens'āt
compete... kom-pēt'
competent... kom'pē-tent
competently... kom'pē-tent-li
competition... kom-pē-ti'shun
competitive... kom-pet'it-iv
competitor... kom-pet'it-ėr
compilation... kom-pi-lā'shun
compile... kom-pīl'
complacent... kom-plā'sent
complain... kom-plān'
complainant... kom-plān'ant
complaint... kom-plānt'
complaisance... kom'plā-zans
complement... kom'plē-ment
complete... kom-plēt'
completely... kom-plēt'li
completeness... kom-plēt'nes
completion... kom-plē'shun
complex... kom'pleks
complexion... kom-plek'shun
complexity... kom-pleks'i-ti
compliance... kom-plī'ans
compliant... kom-plī'ant
complicacy... kom'pli-ka-si
complicate... kom'pli-kāt
complicity... kom-plis'i-ti
compliment... kom'pli-ment
comply... kom-plī'
component... kom-pōn'ent
compose... kom-pōz'
composer... kom-pōz'ėr
composite... kom'po-zīt or -zit
composition... kom-pō-zi'shun
compost... kom'pōst

composure... kom-pō'zhūr
compound... kom-pound'
compress... kom-pres'
compression... kom-pre'shun
comprise... kom-prīz'
compromise... kom'prō-mīz
comptroller... kon-trōl'ėr
compulsion... kom-pul'shun
compulsive... kom-pul'siv
compulsory... kom-pul'so-ri
computable... kom-pūt'a-bl
compute... kom-pūt'
comrade... kom'rād
con... kon
concave... kon'kāv
concavity... kon-kav'i-ti
conceal... kon-sēl'
concealable... kon-sēl'a-bl
concealment... kon-sēl'ment
concede... kon-sēd'
conceit... kon-sēt'
conceivable... kon-sēv'a-bl
conceivably... kon-sēv'a-bli
conceive... kon-sēv'
concentrate... kon'sen-trāt
concentric... kon-sen'trik
concept... kon'sept
concern... kon-sėrn'
concerning... kon-sėrn'ing
concert... kon-sėrt'
concerto... kon-chār'tō
concession... kon-se'shun
concessive... kon-ses'iv
conch... kongk
conciliate... kon-si'li-āt
conciliation... kon-si'li-ā''shun
concise... kon-sīs'
concisely... kon-sīs'li
conciseness... kon-sīs'nes
concision... kon-si'zhon
conclave... kon'klāv
conclude... kon-klūd'
conclusion... kon-klū'zhon
conclusive... kon-klū'siv
concoct... kon-kokt'
concoction... kon-kok'shun
concomitant... kon-kom'it-ant
concord... kong'kord
concordance... kon-kord'ans
concordant... kon-kord'ant
concourse... kong'kōrs
concretion... kon-krē'shun
concur... kon-kėr'
concurrence... kon-ku'rens

concurrent... *kon-ku'rent*
concussion... *kon-ku'shun*
concussive... *kon-kus'iv*
condemn... *kon-dem'*
condensable... *kon-dens'a-bl*
condense... *kon-dens'*
condescend... *kon-dē-send'*
condign... *kon-dīn'*
condiment... *kon'di-ment*
condition... *kon-di'shun*
conditional... *kon-di'shun-al*
conditioned... *kon-di'shund*
condole... *kon-dōl'*
condolement... *kon-dōl'ment*
condolence... *kon-dōl'ens*
condone... *kon-dōn'*
condor... *kon'dor*
conduce... *kon-dūs'*
conducive... *kon-dūs'iv*
conduct... *kon'dukt*
conductible... *kon-dukt'i-bl*
conductive... *kon-dukt'iv*
conductor... *kon-dukt'ėr*
conduit... *kon'dit* or *kun'dit*
cone... *kōn*
confection... *kon-fek'shun*
confederate... *kon-fe'de-rāt*
confer... *kon-fėr'*
conference... *kon'fėr-ens*
confess... *kon-fes'*
confessedly... *kon-fes'ed-li*
confession... *kon-fe'shun*
confessional... *kon-fe'shun-al*
confessor... *kon-fes'ėr*
confetti... *kon-fet'i*
confidant... *kon'fi-dant*
confide... *kon-fīd'*
confidence... *kon'fi-dens*
confident... *kon'fi-dent*
confidential... *kon-fi-den'shal*
confidently... *kon'fi-dent-li*
confiding... *kon-fīd'ing*
confine... *kon'fīn*
confinement... *kon-fīn'ment*
confirm... *kon-fėrm'*
confiscable... *kon-fis'ka-bl*
confiscate... *kon'fis-kāt*
confiscation... *kon-fis-kā'shun*
conflict... *kon'flikt*
confluence... *kon'flū-ens*
confluent... *kon'flū-ent*
conflux... *kon'fluks*
conform... *kon-form'*
conformable... *kon-for'ma-bl*

conformably... *kon-for'ma-bli*
conformist... *kon-for'mist*
conformity... *kon-for'mi-ti*
confound... *kon-found'*
confraternity... *kon-fra-tėr'ni-ti*
confront... *kon-frunt'*
confuse... *kon-fūz'*
confused... *kon-fūzd'*
confusion... *kon-fū'zhon*
confutable... *kon-fūt'a-bl*
confutation... *kon-fūt-ā'shun*
confute... *kon-fūt'*
congeal... *kon-jēl'*
congelation... *kon-jēl-ā'shun*
congenial... *kon-jē'ni-al*
congenital... *kon-jen'it-al*
conger... *kong'gėr*
congestion... *kon-jest'shun*
conglobate... *kon-glōb'āt*
congratulate... *kon-grat'ū-lāt*
congregate... *kong'grē-gāt*
congress... *kong'gres*
congreve... *kong'grēv*
congruent... *kong'gru-ent*
congruity... *kon-gru'ï-ti*
congruous... *kong'gru-us*
coniferous... *kōn-if'ėr-us*
conjectural... *kon-jek'tūr-al*
conjecture... *kon-jek'tūr*
conjoint... *kon-joint'*
conjointly... *kon-joint'li*
conjugal... *kon'jū-gal*
conjugate... *kon'jū-gāt*
conjugation... *kon-jū-gā'shun*
conjunct... *kon-jungkt'*
conjunction... *kon-jungk'shun*
conjuctive... *kon-jungk'tiv*
conjuncture... *kon-jungk'tūr*
conjuration... *kon-jū-rā'shun*
connate... *kon'nāt*
connatural... *kon-na'tūr-al*
connect... *kon-nekt'*
connectedly... *kon-nekt'ed-li*
connection... *kon-nek'shun*
connective... *kon-nekt'iv*
connector... *kon-nekt'ėr*
connive... *kon-nīv'*
conniver... *kon-nīv'ėr*
connoisseur... *kon'i-sūr*
connotation... *kon-ō-tā'shun*
connote... *kon-nōt'*
conquer... *kong'kėr*
conquerable... *kong'kėr-a-bl*
conqueror... *kong'kėr-ėr*

conquest... *kong'kwest*
conscience... *kon'shens*
conscious... *kon'shus*
consciously... *kon'shus-li*
consciousness... *kon'shus-nes*
consent... *kon-sent'*
consequence... *kon'sē-kwens*
conservative... *kon-sėrv'at-iv*
conservator... *kon-sėrv-āt-ėr*
consider... *kon-si'dėr*
considerable... *kon-si'dėr-a-bl*
considerably... *kon-si'dėr-a-bli*
considerate... *kon-si'dėr-āt*
considering... *kon-si'dėr-ing*
consign... *kon-sīn'*
consignee... *kon-sīn-ē'*
consignment... *kon-sīn'ment*
consignor... *kon-sī'nor*
consist... *kon-sist'*
consistent... *kon-sis'tent*
consistorial... *kon-sis-tō'ri-al*
consistory... *kon'sis-to-ri*
consolable... *kon-sōl'a-bl*
consolation... *kon-sōl-ā'shun*
consolatory... *kon-sol'a-to-ri*
console... *kon-sōl'*
consolidate... *kon-sol'id-āt*
consonance... *kon'sō-nans*
consonant... *kon'sō-nant*
consort... *kon'sort*
conspectus... *kon-spek'tus*
conspicuous... *kon-spik'ū-us*
conspiracy... *kon-spi'ra-si*
conspire... *kon-spīr'*
constable... *kun'sta-bl*
constancy... *kon'stan-si*
constant... *kon'stant*
constantly... *kon'stant-li*
constipate... *kon'sti-pāt*
constipation... *kon-sti-pā'shun*
constituency... *kon-stit'ū-en-si*
constituent... *kon-stit'ū-ent*
constitute... *kon'sti-tūt*
constitution... *kon-sti-tū'shun*
constitutive... *kon'sti-tūt-iv*
constrain... *kon-strān'*
constrainable... *kon-strān'a-bl*
constrained... *kon-strānd'*
constraint... *kon-strānt'*
constrict... *kon-strikt'*
constriction... *kon-strik'shun*
constrictive... *kon-strik'tiv*
constrictor... *kon-strik'tėr*
construct... *kon-strukt'*

construction... *kon-struk'shun*
constructive... *kon-strukt'iv*
construe... *kon'strū*
consular... *kon'sūl-ėr*
consulate... *kon'sūl-āt*
consulship... *kon'sul-ship*
consult... *kon-sult'*
consultation... *kon-sult-ā'shun*
consulter... *kon-sult'ėr*
consulting... *kon-sult'ing*
consumable... *kon-sūm'a-bl*
consume... *kon-sūm'*
consumer... *kon-sūm'ėr*
consummate... *kon'sum-āt*
consummately... *kon-sum'āt-li*
consumption... *kon-sum'shun*
consumptive... *kon-sum'tiv*
contact... *kon'takt*
contagion... *kon-tā'jon*
contagious... *kon-tā'jus*
contagiously... *kon-tā'jus-li*
contain... *kon-tān'*
containable... *kon-tān'a-bl*
container... *kon-tā'nėr*
contaminate... *kon-tam'in-āt*
contemn... *kon-tem'*
contemner... *kon-tem'ėr*
contempt... *kon-temt'*
contemptible... *kon-tem'ti-bl*
contend... *kon-tend'*
contender... *kon-tend'ėr*
content... *kon-tent'*
contented... *kon-tent'ed*
contentedly... *kon-tent'ed-li*
contention... *kon-ten'shun*
contentious... *kon-ten'shus*
contentment... *kon-tent'ment*
contest... *kon-test'*
contestable... *kon-test'a-bl*
context... *kon'tekst*
contexture... *kon-teks'tur*
contiguity... *kon-ti-gū'i-ti*
continence... *kon'ti-nens*
continent... *kon'ti-nent*
continental... *kon-ti-nent'al*
continently... *kon'ti-nent-li*
contingent... *kon-tin'jent*
contingently... *kon-ten'jent-li*
continual... *kon-tin'ū-al*
continually... *kon-tin'ū-al-li*
continue... *kon-tin'ū*
continuous... *kon-tin'ū-us*
continuously... *kon-tin'ū-us-li*
contort... *kon-tort'*

contortion... *kon-tor'shun*
contortionist... *kon-tor'shun-ist*
contour... *kontor'*
contraband... *kon'tra-band*
contract... *kon-trakt'*
contracted... *kon-trakt'ed*
contractedly... *kon-trakt'ed-li*
contractible... *kon-trakt'i-bl*
contractile... *kon-trakt'īl*
contractor... *kon-trakt'ér*
contradict... *kon-tra-dikt'*
contrapuntal... *kon-tra-punt'al*
contrapuntist... *kon-tra-punt'ist*
contrariety... *kon-tra-rī'e-ti*
contrarily... *kon'tra-ri-li*
contrary... *kon'tra-ri*
contrast... *kon-trast'*
contravene... *kon-tra-vēn'*
contribute... *kon-trib'ūt*
contribution... *kon-tri-bū'shun*
contributive... *kon-trib'ūt-iv*
contributory... *kon-trib'ū-to-ri*
contrite... *kon'trīt*
contrition... *kon-tri'shun*
contrivable... *kon-trīv'a-bl*
contrivance... *kon-trīv'ans*
contrive... *kon-trīv'*
contriver... *kon-trīv'ér*
control... *kon-trōl'*
controllable... *kon-trōl'a-bl*
controller... *kon-trōl'ér*
controlment... *kon-trōl'ment*
controversy... *kon'trō-vér-si*
controvert... *kon'trō-vért*
contumely... *kon'tū-me-li*
contuse... *kon-tūz'*
contusion... *kon-tū'zhon*
convalesce... *kon-va-les'*
convalescent... *kon-va-les'ent*
convenable... *kon-vēn'-bl*
convene... *kon-vēn'*
convener... *kon-vēn'ér*
convenient... *kon-vè'ni-ent*
convent... *kon'vent*
conventicle... *kon-ven'ti-kl*
conventual... *kon-ven'tū-al*
converge... *kon-vérj'*
convergent... *kon-vérj'ent*
conversant... *kon'vérs-ant*
converse... *kon-vérs'*
conversely... *kon'vérs-li*
conversion... *kon-vér'shun*
convert... *kon-vért'*
convertible... *kon-vért'i-bl*

convertibly... *kon-vért'i-bli*
convey... *kon-vā*
conveyable... *kon-vā'a-bl*
conveyance... *kon-vā'ans*
conveyancer... *kon-vā'ans-ér*
conveyer... *kon-vā'ér*
convict... *kon-vikt'*
conviction... *kon-vik'shun*
convince... *kon-vins'*
convincingly... *kon-vins'ing-li*
convivial... *kon-vi'vi-al*
conviviality... *kon-vi'vi-al'i-ti*
convoke... *kon-vōk'*
convolution... *kon-vō-lū'shun*
convolve... *kon-volv'*
convulse... *kon-vuls'*
convulsion... *kon-vul'shun*
convulsive... *kon-vuls'iv*
coo... *ko*
cook... *kuk*
cookery... *kuk'é-ri*
cool... *kol*
cooler... *kol'ér*
cool-headed... *kol'hed-ed*
coolness... *kol'nes*
coop... *kop*
co-operate... *kō-op'ér-āt*
co-operative... *kō-op'ér-āt-iv*
co-operator... *kō-op'ér-āt-ér*
co-ordinate... *kō-or'din-āt*
copal... *kō-pal'*
coparcener... *kō-par'sen-ér*
copartner... *kō-part'nér*
cope... *kōp*
copernican... *kō-pér'ni-kan*
copestone... *kōp'stōn*
copier... *ko'pi-ér*
coping... *kōp'ing*
copious... *kō'pi-us*
copper... *kop'ér*
copperas... *kop'ér-as*
copperplate... *kop'ér-plāt*
coppery... *kop-ér-i*
coptic... *kop'tik*
copula... *kop'ū-la*
copulate... *kop'ū-lāt*
copulation... *kop-ū-lā'shun*
copulative... *kop'ū-lāt-iv*
copy... *ko'pl*
copyist... *ko'pi-ist*
copyright... *kop'i-rīt*
coquetry... *kō'ket-ri*
coquette... *kō-ket'*
coquettish... *kō-ket'ish*

coracle... *kor'a-kl*
coral... *ko'ral*
corbel... *kor'bel*
cord... *kord*
cordage... *kord'āj*
cordate... *kor'dāt*
cordelier... *kord'el-ēr*
cordial... *kor'di-al*
cordiality... *kor-di-al'i-ti*
cordite... *kor'dīt*
cordon... *kor'don*
cordovan... *kor'dō-van*
corduroy... *kor-dė-roi'*
core... *kōr*
coriander... *ko-ri-an'dėr*
corinthian... *ko-rin'thi-an*
cork... *kork*
corked... *korkt*
corky... *kork'i*
cormorant... *kor'mō-rant*
corn... *korn*
cornea... *kor'nē-a*
corned... *korned*
corneous... *kor'nē-us*
corner... *kor'nėr*
corner-stone... *kor'nėr-stōn*
cornet... *kor'net*
cornice... *kor'nis*
cornish... *korn'ish*
cornucopia... *kor-nū-kō'pi-a*
cornuted... *kor-nūt'ed*
corny... *kor'ni*
coronal... *ko'rō-nal*
coroner... *ko'rō-nėr*
coronet... *ko'rō-net*
corporal... *kor'po-ral*
corporally... *kor'po-ral-li*
corporate... *kor'po-rāt*
corporately... *kor'po-rāt-li*
corporation... *kor-po-rā'shun*
corporeal... *kor-pō'rē-al*
corporeally... *kor-pō'rē-al-li*
corps... *kōr*
corpse... *korps*
corpulent... *kor'pū-lent*
corpuscle... *kor'pus-l*
corpuscular... *kor-pus'kū-lėr*
corral... *kor-ral'*
correct... *ko-rekt'*
correction... *ko-rek'shun*
correctional... *ko-rek'shun-al*
corrective... *ko-rekt'iv*
correctly... *ko-rekt'li*
correctness... *ko-rekt'nes*

corrector... *ko-rekt'ėr*
correlate... *kor'ē-lāt*
correlation... *ko-rē-lā'shun*
correspond... *ko-rē-spond'*
corridor... *ko'ri-dor*
corrigible... *ko'ri-ji-bl*
corrival... *ko-rī'val*
corroborant... *ko-rob'ō-rant*
corroborate... *ko-rob'ō-rāt*
corrode... *ko-rōd'*
corrodent... *ko-rō'dent*
corrodible... *ko-rō'd'i-bl*
corrosion... *ko-rō'zhon*
corrosive... *ko-rōs'iv*
corrugate... *ko'rū-gāt*
corrugated... *ko'rū-gāt-ed*
corrugation... *ko-rū-gā'shun*
corrupt... *ko-rupt'*
corrupter... *ko-rupt'ėr*
corruptibility... *ko-rupt'i-bil'i-ti*
corruptible... *ko-rupt'i-bl*
corruptibly... *ko-rupt'i-bli*
corruption... *ko-rup'shun*
corruptive... *ko-rupt'iv*
corruptly... *ko-rupt'li*
corsair... *kor'sār*
corset... *kor'set*
cortex... *kor'teks*
cortical... *kor'tik-al*
coruscant... *ko-rus'kant*
coruscate... *ko-rus'kāt*
coruscation... *ko-rus-kā'shun*
corvette... *kor-vet'*
corvine... *kor'vīn*
coryphaeus... *ko-ri-fē'us*
cosmetic... *koz-met'ik*
cosmic... *koz'mik*
cosmic rays... *koz-mik rāz'*
cosmogony... *koz-mog'on-i*
cosmography... *koz-mog'ra-fi*
cosmology... *koz-mol'o-ji*
cosmos... *koz'mos*
cost... *kost*
costal... *kos'tal*
costive... *kos'tiv*
costliness... *kost'li-nes*
costly... *kost'li*
costume... *kos'tūm*
costumier... *kos-tū'mi-ėr*
co-surety... *kō-shūr'ti*
cot... *kot*
coterie... *kō'te-rē*
cotidal... *kō-tī'd'al*
cotillion... *ko-til'yon*

C

cottage... *kot'tāj*
cottager... *kot-tāj-èr*
cotton... *kot'tn*
cotton-wood... *kot'tn-wụd*
cottony... *kot'tn-i*
cotyledon... *kot-i-lē'don*
couch... *kouch*
couchant... *kouch'ant*
cougar... *ko'gar*
cough... *kof*
could... *kụd*
coulter... *kōl'tèr*
council... *koun'sil*
counsel... *koun'sel*
counsellor... *koun'sel-èr*
count... *kount*
countable... *kount'a-bl*
countenance... *koun'ten-ans*
counter... *kount'èr*
counteract... *koun-tèr-akt'*
counterfeit... *koun'tèr-fit*
countermark... *koun'tèr-mark*
counterpoint... *koun'tèr-point*
counterpoise... *koun'tèr-poiz*
counterseal... *koun-tèr-sēl'*
countersign... *koun-tèr-sīn'*
countervail... *koun-tèr-vāl'*
counterwork... *koun-tèr-wèrk'*
countess... *kount'es*
countless... *kount'les*
country... *kun'tri*
country-dance... *kun'tri-dans*
countryman... *kun'tri-man*
country-side... *kun'tri-sīd*
county... *koun'ti*
couple... *ku'pl*
couplet... *kup'let*
coupling... *kup'ling*
coupon... *ko'pon*
courage... *ku'rij*
courageously... *ku-rā'jē-us-li*
courier... *ko'rē-èr*
course... *kōrs*
courser... *kōrs'èr*
coursing... *kōrs'ing*
court-day... *kōrt'dā*
courteous... *kōrt'ē-us*
courteously... *kōrt'ē-us-li*
courter... *kōrt'èr*
courtesy... *kōrt'e-sī*
courthand... *kōrt'hand*
courthouse... *kōrt'hous*
courtier... *kōrt'i-èr*
courtliness... *kōrt'li-nes*

courtly... *kōrt'li*
court-martial... *kōrt'mar'shal*
courtship... *kōrt'ship*
courtyard... *kōrt'yard*
cousin... *kuz'n*
cove... *kōv*
covenant... *kuv'en-ant*
covenanter... *kuv'en-ant-èr*
cover... *kuv'èr*
covering... *kuv'èr-ing*
coverlet... *kuv'èr-let*
covert... *kuv'èrt*
coverture... *kuv'èrt-ūr*
covet... *kuv'et*
covetable... *kuv'et-a-bl*
covetously... *kuv'et-us-li*
covetousness... *kuv'et-us-nes*
covey... *kuv'i*
cow... *kou*
coward... *kou'èrd*
cowardice... *kou'èrd-is*
cowardliness... *kou'èrd-li-nes*
cowardly... *kou'èrd-li*
cower... *kou'èr*
cowherd... *kou'hèrd*
cowl... *koul*
cowled... *kould*
cow-pox... *kou'poks*
cowry... *kou'ri*
coy... *koi*
coyly... *koi'li*
coyness... *koi'nes*
coz... *koz*
cozen... *kuz'n*
cozenage... *kuz'n-āj*
cozener... *kuz'n-èr*
crab... *krab*
crabbed... *krab'ed*
crabbedly... *krab'ed-li*
cracked... *krakt*
cracker... *krak'èr*
crackle... *krak'l*
crackling... *krak'ling*
cracknel... *krak'nel*
cradle... *krā'dl*
craft... *kraft*
craftily... *kraf'ti-li*
craftiness... *kraf'ti-nes*
craftsman... *krafts'man*
crafty... *kraf'ti*
crag... *krag*
cragged... *krag'ed*
craggy... *krag'i*
cram... *kram*

cramp... *kramp*
cramped... *krampt*
cranberry... *kran'be-ri*
crane... *krān*
crane's-bill... *krānz'bil*
cranial... *krā'ni-al*
craniology... *krā-ni-ol'o-ji*
cranium... *krā'ni-um*
crank... *krangk*
crannied... *kran'id*
cranny... *kran'ni*
crape... *krāp*
crapulence... *krap'ū-lens*
crash... *krash*
crass... *kras*
crate... *krāt*
crater... *krā'tėr*
cravat... *kra-vat'*
crave... *krāv*
craven... *krā'vn*
craver... *krāv'ėr*
craving... *krāv'ing*
craw... *kra*
crawfish... *krа'fish*
crawl... *kral*
crawler... *kral'ėr*
crayfish... *krā'fish*
crayon... *krā'on*
craze... *krāz*
crazed... *krāzd*
crazy... *krāz'i*
creak... *krēk*
cream... *krēm*
creamy... *krēm'i*
crease... *krēs*
create... *krē-āt'*
creation... *krē-ā'shun*
creative... *krē-āt'iv*
creator... *krē-āt'ėr*
creature... *krē'tūr*
credence... *krē'dens*
credential... *krē-den'shi-al*
credibility... *kred-i-bil'i-ti*
credible... *kred'i-bl*
credit... *kred'it*
creditable... *kred'it-a-bl*
creditably... *kred'it-a-bli*
creditor... *kred'it-ėr*
credulity... *kred-dū'li-ti*
credulous... *kred'ū-lus*
creed... *krēd*
creek... *krēk*
creep... *krēp*
creeper... *krēp'ėr*

creepy... *krēp-i*
cremate... *krē-māt'*
cremation... *krē-mā'shun*
crenelle... *kre-nel'*
creole... *krē'ōl*
creosote... *krē'ō-sōt*
crepitate... *krep'i-tāt*
crepitation... *krep-it-ā'shun*
crepuscular... *krē-pus'kūl-ėr*
crescent... *kres'ent*
cress... *kres*
cresset... *kres'et*
crest... *krest*
crested... *krest'ed*
cretaceous... *krē-tā'shus*
cretin... *krē'tin*
cretinism... *krē'tin-izm*
cretonne... *kre-ton'*
crevice... *kre'vis*
crew... *kro*
crewel... *kro'el*
crib... *krib*
cribbage... *krib'āj*
cribble... *krib'l*
crick... *krik*
cricket... *krik'et*
cricketer... *krik'et-ėr*
crime... *krīm*
criminal... *krim'in-al*
criminality... *krim-in-al'i-ti*
criminally... *krim'in-al-li*
criminate... *krim'in-āt*
crimination... *krim-in-ā'shun*
criminous... *krim'in-us*
crimp... *krimp*
crimple... *krimp'l*
crimson... *krim'zn*
cringe... *krinj*
cringle... *kring'gl*
crinkle... *kring'kl*
crinoline... *krin'o-līn*
cripple... *krip'l*
crisis... *krī'sis*
crisp... *krisp*
crisper... *krisp-ėr*
crisply... *krisp'li*
crispy... *krisp'i*
cristate... *kris'tāt*
criterion... *krī-tē'ri-un*
critic... *kri'tik*
critical... *kri'tik-al*
criticism... *kri'ti-sizm*
criticize... *kri'ti-sīz*
critique... *kri-tēk'*

C

croak... *krōk*
croaking... *krōk'ing*
crochet... *krō'shā*
crock... *krok*
crockery... *krok'ė-ri*
crocodile... *kro'kō-dīl*
crocus... *krō'kus*
croft... *kroft*
crofter... *krof'tėr*
crone... *krōn*
crony... *krō'ni*
crook... *krok*
crooked... *krok'ed*
crop... *krop*
crop-eared... *krop'ērd*
cropper... *krop'ėr*
croquet... *krō'kā*
cross... *kros*
cross-bones... *kros'bōnz*
crossbow... *kros'bō*
cross-breed... *kros'brēd*
crossing... *kros'ing*
crossly... *kros'li*
crosswise... *kros'wīz*
crotch... *kroch*
crotchet... *kroch'et*
crotchety... *kroch'et-i*
croton... *krō'ton*
crouch... *krouch*
croup... *krop*
croupier... *kro'pē-ėr*
crow... *krō*
crowbar... *krō'bar*
crowd... *kroud*
crowded... *kroud'ed*
crow-flower... *krō'flou-ėr*
crowfoot... *krō'fut*
crown... *kroun*
crowned... *kround*
crowning... *kroun'ing*
crown-prince... *kroun'prins*
crow's-feet... *krōz'fēt*
crucial... *kro'shi-al*
crucible... *kro'si-bl*
cruciferous... *kro-sif'ėr-us*
crucifixion... *kro-si-fik'shun*
cruciform... *kro'si-form*
crucify... *kro'si-fī*
crude... *krod*
crudely... *krod'li*
crudity... *krod'i-ti*
cruel... *kro'el*
cruelly... *kro'el-li*
cruelty... *kro'el-ti*

cruet... *kro'et*
cruise... *kroz*
cruiser... *kroz'ėr*
crumb... *krum*
crumble... *krum'bl*
crumby... *krum'i*
crump... *krump*
crumpet... *krum'pet*
crumple... *krum'pl*
crumpled... *krum'pld*
crunch... *krunch*
crupper... *krup'ėr*
crural... *kror'al*
crusade... *kro-sād'*
crusader... *kro-sād'ėr*
crush... *krush*
crushing... *krush'ing*
crust... *krust*
crustacea... *krus-tā'shē-a*
crustacean... *krus-tā'shė-an*
crustaceous... *krus-tā'shus*
crustily... *krust'i-li*
crusty... *krust'i*
crutch... *kruch*
crutched... *krucht*
cry... *krī*
crying... *krī'ing*
crypt... *kript*
cryptic... *krip'tik*
cryptogam... *krip'tō-gam*
cryptogamy... *krip-tog'a-mi*
cryptography... *krip-tog'ra-fi*
crystal... *kris'tal*
crystalline... *kris'tal-īn*
crystallize... *kris'tal-īz*
cub... *kub*
cube... *kūb*
cubic... *kūb'ik*
cubicle... *kū'bi-kl*
cuckoo... *ku'ko*
cucumber... *kū'kum-bėr*
cud... *kud*
cuddle... *kud'dl*
cudgel... *kuj'el*
cue... *kū*
cuff... *kuf*
cuirass... *kwi-ras'*
cuirassier... *kwi-ras-sēr'*
cuisine... *kwē-zēn'*
cul-de-sac... *kol'de-sak*
culinary... *kū'lin-a-ri*
cull... *kul*
cullender... *kul'en-dėr*
cullion... *kul'i-un*

cully... *kul'li*
culm... *kulm*
culminate... *kul'min-āt*
culmination... *kul-min-ā'shun*
culpability... *kulp-a-bil'i-ti*
culpable... *kulp'a-bl*
culpably... *kulp'a-bli*
culprit... *kul'prit*
cult... *kult*
cultivate... *kul'ti-vāt*
cultivation... *kul-ti-vā'shun*
cultivator... *kul'ti-vāt-ėr*
culture... *kul'tūr*
cultured... *kul'tūrd*
culverin... *kul'vėr-in*
culvert... *kul'vėrt*
cumber... *kum'bėr*
cumbersome... *kum'bėr-sum*
cumbrous... *kum'brus*
cumin... *kum'in*
cummer-bund... *kum'ėr-bund*
cumulate... *kū-mū-lāt*
cumulation... *kū-mū-lā'shun*
cumulative... *kū-mū-lāt-iv*
cumulus... *kū'mū-lus*
cunning... *kun'ing*
cunningly... *kun'ing-li*
cup... *kup*
cupboard... *kup'bōrd*
cupel... *kū'pel*
cupellation... *kū-pel-lā'shun*
cupid... *kū'pid*
cupidity... *kū-pid'i-ti*
cupping... *kup'ing*
cupreous... *kū-prē-us*
cur... *kėr*
curable... *kūr'a-bl*
curate... *kū'rāt*
curative... *kū'rāt-iv*
curator... *kū-rāt'ėr*
curb... *kėrb*
curb-stone... *kėrb'stōn*
curd... *kėrd*
curdle... *kėrd'l*
cure... *kūr*
cure... *kū-rā*
cureless... *kūr'les*
curer... *kūr'ėr*
curfew... *kėr'fū*
curio... *kū'ri-ō*
curiosity... *kū-ri-os'i-ti*
curious... *kū'ri-us*
curiously... *kū'ri-us-li*
curl... *kėrl*

curler... *kėr'lėr*
curlew... *kėr'lū*
curling... *kėrl'ing*
curmudgeon... *kėr-muj'on*
currant... *ku'rant*
currency... *ku'ren-si*
current... *ku'rent*
currently... *ku'rent-li*
curricle... *ku'ri-kl*
curriculum... *ku-rik'ū-lum*
currier... *ku'ri-ėr*
currish... *kėr'ish*
curry... *ku'ri*
curse... *kėrs*
cursed... *kėrs'ed*
cursedly... *kėrs'ed-li*
cursing... *kėrs'ing*
cursive... *kėr'siv*
cursores... *kėr-sō'rēz*
cursorily... *kėr'sō-ri-li*
cursory... *kėr'so-ri*
curt... *kėrt*
curtail... *kėr-tāl'*
curtain... *kėr'tan*
curtly... *kėrt'li*
curtsy... *kėrt'si*
curvature... *kėrv'a-tūr*
curvet... *kėr-vet'*
curvirostral... *kėrv-i-ros'tral*
cushion... *kush'on*
cusp... *kusp*
custard... *kus'tėrd*
custodial... *kus-tō'di-al*
custodian... *kus-tō'di-an*
custodier... *kus-tō'di-ėr*
custody... *kus'tō-di*
custom... *kus'tum*
customable... *kus'tum-a-bl*
customarily... *kus'tum-a-ri-li*
customary... *kus'tum-a-ri*
customer... *kus'tum-ėr*
custom-house... *kus'tum-hous*
cut... *kut*
cutaneous... *kū-tā'nē-us*
cuticle... *kū'ti-kl*
cutlass... *kut'las*
cutler... *kut'lėr*
cutlery... *kut'lė-ri*
cutlet... *kut'let*
cutter... *kut'ėr*
cut-throat... *kut'thrōt*
cuttle... *kut'tl*
cyanean... *sī-ā'nē-an*
cyanide... *sī'an-id*

C

cyanogen... sī-an'ō-jen
cycle... sī'kl
cyclic... sī'klik
cyclist... sī'k'list
cycloid... sī'kloid
cyclone... sī'klōn
cyclopean... sī-klō-pē'an
cyclops... sī'klops
cylinder... sī'lin-dėr
cymbal... sim'bal
cymric... kim'rik
cynic... sin'ik
cynic... sin'ik
cynicism... sin'i-sizm
cynosure... sī'nō-zhor
cypher... sī'fėr
cypress... sī'pres
cyst... sist
cytherean... sith-e-rē'an
czar... tsar or zar
czech... chek

D

dab... dab,
dabble... dab'bl
dachshund... daks'hunt
dacron... 'dācron
dad... dad
daffodil... daf'fō-dil
dagger... dag'ėr
daggle... dag'gl
dahlia... da'li-a
daily... dā'li
daintily... dān'ti-li
dainty... dān'ti
dairy... dā'ri
dais... dā'is
daisy... dā'ci
dale... dāl
dalliance... dal'yans
dally... dal'li
dalmatic... dal-mat'ic
daltonism... dal'ton-izm
dam... dam
damage... dam'āj
damageable... dam'āj-a-bl
dame... dām
damn... dam
damp... damp
dampen... dam'pin
damper... dam'pėr

dampish... damp'ish
dampness... damp'nes
damsel... dam'zel
dance... dans
dancer... dans'ėr
dandelion... dan'di-lī-un
dandruff... dan'druff
dandy... dan'di
dandyish... dan'di-ish
dandyism... dan'di-izm
danger... dān'jėr
dangerous... dān'jėr-os
dangerously... dān'jėr-os-li
dangle... dang'gl
dangler... dang'gl-ėr
dapper... dap'ėr
dapple... dap'l
dappled... dap'pld
dare... dār
daring... dār'ing
daringly... dār'ing-li
dark... dark
darken... dark'n
darkish... dark'ish
darkly... dark'li
darkness... dark'nes
darksome... dark'som
darling... dar'ling
darn... darn
dart... dart
darter... dart'ėr
darwinism... dar'win-ism
dash... dash
dash-board... dash'bōrd
dashing... dash'ing
dastard... das'tėrd
dastardly... das'tėrd-li
data... dā'ta
date... dāt
datum... dā'tom
daub... dab
dauber... dab'ėr
dauby... dab'i
daughterly... da'tėr-li
daunt... dant
dauntless... dant'lis
dauphin... da'fin
davenport... dav'in-port
daw... da
dawdle... da'dl
dawn... dan
dawning... dan'ing
day... dā
day-book... dā'buk

daybreak... dā'brāk
day-dream... dā'drēm
daylight... dā'līt
dayspring... dā'spring
day-star... dā'star
daytime... dā'tīm
daze... dāz
dazzle... daz'zl
deacon... dē'con
deaconess... dē'con-es
deaconhood... dē'con-hu̧d
dead... ded
deaden... ded'n
dead-letter... ded'let-tėr
dead-light... ded'līt
dead-lock... ded'loc
deadly... ded'li
dead-set... ded'set
dead-weight... ded'wāt
deaf... def
deafening... def'n-ing
deaf-mute... def'mūt
deal... dēl
dealing... dēl'ing
dean... dēn
deanery... dēn'ė-ri
deanship... dēn'ship
dear... dēr
dearly... dēr'li
dearth... dėrth
death... deth
death-bed... deth'bed
deathless... deth'lis
deathlike... deth'līk
deathly... deth'li
death-rate... deth'rāt
debacle... de-bak'l
debark... dē-bark'
debase... dē-bās'
debased... dē-bāst'
debasement... dē-bās'ment
debatable... dē-bāt'a-bl
debate... dē-bāt'
debater... dē-bāt'ėr
debauch... dē-bach'
debauched... dē-bacht'
debauchee... deb-ö-shē'
debaucher... dē-bach'ėr
debauchery... dē-bach'ė-ri
debenture... dē-ben'tūr
debilitate... dē-bil'i-tāt
debility... dē-bil'i-ti
debit... deb'it
debonair... de-bō-nār'

debouch... dē-bosh'
debris... dē-brē'
debt... det
debtor... det'ėr
decade... de'kād
decahedron... de-ka-hē'dron
decalogue... de'ka-log
decant... dē-kant'
decanter... dē-kant'ėr
decapitate... dē-kap'it-āt
decapod... dek'a-pod
decay... dē-kā'
decease... dē-sēs'
deceased... dē-sēst'
deceit... dē-sēt'
deceivable... dē-sēv'a-bl
deceive... dē-sēv'
deceiver... dē-sēv'ėr
december... dē-sem'bėr
decemvir... dē-sem'vėr
decency... dē'sen-ci
decennial... dē-sen'ni-al
decent... dē'sent
decently... dē'sent-li
decentralize... dē-sen'tral-īz
deception... dē-sep'shun
deceptive... dē-sep'tiv
decidable... dē-sī'd'a-bl
decide... dē-sī'd'
decided... dē-sī'd'ed
decidely... dē-sī'd'ed-li
decimal... de'si-mal
decimate... de'si-māt
decimation... de-si-mā'shun
decipher... dē-sī'fėr
decipherable... dē-sī'fėr-a-bl
decipherer... dē-sī'fėr-ėr
decision... dē-si'shun
decisive... dē-sī'siv
decisively... dē-sī'siv-li
deck... dec
decker... dec'ėr
declaim... dē-klām'
declaimer... dē-klām'ėr
declarable... dē-klār'a-bl
declaration... de-kla-rā'shun
declaratory... dē-kla'ra-to-ri
declare... dē-klār'
declared... dē-klārd'
declension... dē-klen'shun
declinable... dē-klīn'a-bl
declination... dē-klin-ā'shun
decline... dē-klīn'
declivity... dē-kli'vi-ti

D

decoct... dē-koct'
decollate... dē-kol'āt
decompose... dē-kom-pōz
decorate... dek'ō-rāt
decoration... dek'ō-rā'shun
decorative... dek'ō-rāt-iv
decorator... dek'ō-rāt-ėr
decorous... dē-kō'ros
decorum... dē-kō'rum
decoy... dē-koi'
decrease... dē-krēs'
decree... dē-krē'
decrement... de'krē-ment
decrepit... dē-krep'it
decrepitate... dē-krep'it-āt
decrepitude... dē-krep'it-ūd
decretal... dē-krēt'al
decretive... dē-krēt'iv
decretory... de'krē-to-ri
decrial... dē-krī-al
decry... dē-krī'
decumbent... dē-kum'bent
decussate... dē-kus'āt
dedicate... ded'i-kāt
dedication... ded-i-kā'shun
dedicatory... ded'i-kā-to-ri
deduce... dē-dūs'
deducible... dē-dūs'i-bl
deduct... dē-dukt'
deduction... dē-duk'shun
deductive... dē-duk'tiv
deductively... dē-duk'tiv-li
deed... dēd
deem... dēm
deemster... dēm'stėr
deep... dēp
deepen... dēp'n
deep-laid... dēp'lād
deeply... dēp'li
deer... dēr
deface... dē-'fās'
defacement... dē-fās'ment
defalcate... dē-fal'kāt
defalcation... dē-fal-kā'shun
defalcator... def'al-kāt-ėr
defamation... de-fa-mā'shun
defamatory... dē-fam'a-to-ri
defame... dē-fām'
defamer... dē-fām'ėr
defaulter... dē-falt'ėr
defeat... dē-fēt'
defecate... de'fē-kāt
defecation... de-fē-kā'shun
defect... dē-fekt'

defection... dē-fek'shun
defective... dē-fekt'iv
defectively... dē-fekt'iv-li
defend... dē-fend'
defendant... dē-fen'dant
defender... dē-fend'ėr
defense... dē-fens'
defenseless... dē-fens'les
defensible... dē-fens'i-bl
defensive... dē-fens'iv
defensory... dē-fens'o-ri
defer... dē-fėr'
deference... de'fėr-ens
deferential... de-fėr-en'shal
deferment... dē-fėr-ment
defiance... dē-fī'ans
defiant... dē-fī'ant
deficient... de-fi'shent
deficit... de'fi-sit
defilement... dē-fīl'ment
defiler... dē-fīl'ėr
definable... dē-fīn'a-bl
define... dē-fīn'
definite... de'fin-it
definitely... de'fin-it-li
definition... de-fi-ni'shun
definitive... dē-fin'it-iv
definitively... dē-fin'it-iv-li
deflagrate... de'flā-grāt
deflagration... dē-flā-grā'shun
deflect... dē-flekt'
defloration... dē-flōr-ā'shun
defluxion... dē-fluk'shun
defoliation... dē-fō'li-ā''shun
deform... dē-form'
deformed... dē-formd'
deformity... dē-form'i-ti
defraud... dē-frad'
defray... dē-frā''
deft... deft
deftly... deft'li
defunct... dē-fungkt'
defy... dē-fī'
degenerate... dē-jen'ė-rat
deglutition... dē-glū-ti'shun
degrade... dē-grād'
degree... dē-grē'
dehort... dē-hort'
dehydration... dē-hī-drā'shun
deiform... dē'i-form
deify... dē'i-fī
deign... dān
deism... dē'izm
deist... dē'ist

deity... dē'i-ti
deject... dē-jekt'
dejected... dē-jekt'ed
dejection... dē-jek'shun
delay... dē-lā'
delectable... dē-lekt'a-bl
delectation... dē-lek-tā'shun
delegate... de'lē-gāt
delegation... de-lē-gā'shun
delete... dē-lēt'
deleterious... de-lē-te'ri-us
deletion... dē-lē'shun
delf... delf
delicacy... de'li-ka-si
delicate... de'li-kāt
delicately... de'li-kāt-li
delicious... dē-li'shus
delight... dē-līt'
delighted... dē-līt'ed
delightful... dē-līt'ful
delimit... dē-lim'it
delineate... dē-lin'ē-āt
delineator... dē-lin'ē-āt-ėr
delinquency... dē-lin'kwen-si
delinquent... dē-lin'kwent
delirious... dē-li'ri-us
delirium... dē-li'ri-um
deliver... dē-liv'ėr
deliverance... dē-liv'ėr-ans
deliverer... dē-liv'ėr-ėr
delivery... dē-liv'ė-ri
dell... del
delta... del'ta
delude... dē-lūd'
deluge... del'ūj
delusion... dē-lū'zhon
delusive... dē-lū'siv
delve... delv
delver... delv'ėr
demagogue... dem'a-gog
demand... dē-mand'
demandable... dē-mand'a-bl
demandant... dē-man'dant
demean... dē-mēn'
demeanor... dē-mēn'ėr
demented... dē-ment'ed
demerit... dē-me'rit
demesne... de-mān'
demisable... dē-mīz'a-bl
demise... dē-mīz'
demission... dē-mi'shun
demit... dē-mit'
demobilize... dē-mō'bil-īz
democracy... dē-mok'ra-si

democrat... dem'ō-krat
demoiselle... dem-wa-zel'
demolish... dē-mol'ish
demolition... dē-mō-li'shun
demon... dē'mon
demonetize... dē-mon'e-fīz
demoniac... dē-mō'ni-ak
demonize... dē'mon-īz
demonology... dē-mon-ol'o-ji
demonstrate... de-mon'strāt
demoralize... dē-mo'ral-īz
demos... dē'mos
demotic... dē-mot'ik
demulcent... dē-mul'sent
demur... dē-mėr
demure... dē-mūr'
demurrage... dē-mu'rāj
demurrer... dē-mėr'ėr
demy... dē-mī'
den... den
denary... dē-na-ri
denial... dē-nī'al
denim... den'im
denizen... de'ni-zn
denominate... dē-nom'in-āt
denotable... dē-nōt'a-bl
denote... dē-nōt'
denounce... dē-nouns'
dense... dens
density... dens'i-ti
dent... dent
dentate... den'tāt
denticle... den'ti-kl
dentiform... den'ti-form
dentrifrice... den'ti-fris
dentist... den'tist
dentition... den-ti'shun
denture... den'tūr
denude... dē-nūd'
denunciator... dē-nun'si-āt-ėr
deny... dē-nī'
deodorize... dē-ō'dėr-īz
depart... dē-part'
department... dē-part'ment
departure... dē-part'ūr
depend... dē-pend'
dependency... dē-pend'en-si
depict... dē-pikt'
depilate... dep'i-lāt
depilatory... dē-pī'l'ā-to-ri
deplete... dē-plēt'
depletion... dē-plē'shun
deplorable... dē-plōr'a-bl
deplorably... dē-plōr'a-bli

D

deplore... *dē-plōr'*
deplume... *dē-plūm'*
depolarize... *dē-pō'lar-īz*
depone... *dē-pōn'*
deponent... *dē-pōn'ent*
depopulate... *dē-po'pū-lāt*
deport... *dē-pōrt'*
deportation... *dē-pōrt-ā'shun*
deportment... *dē-pōrt'ment*
deposable... *dē-pōz'a-bl*
depose... *dē-pōz'*
deposit... *dē-poz'it*
depositary... *dē-poz'it-a-ri*
deposition... *dē-pō-zi'shun*
depositor... *dē-poz'it-ėr*
depository... *dē-poz'it-o-ri*
depot... *dep'ō*
depravation... *de-pra-vā'shun*
deprave... *dē-prāv'*
depraved... *dē-prāvd'*
depravity... *dē-prav'i-ti*
deprecate... *de'prē-kāt*
depreciate... *dē'prē'shi-āt*
depredate... *de'prē-dāt*
depredator... *de'prē-dāt-ėr*
depressed... *dē-prest'*
depression... *dē-pre'shun*
depressive... *dē-pres'iv*
deprivation... *de-pri-vā'shun*
deprive... *dē-prīv'*
depth... *depth*
deputy... *de'pū-ti*
deracinate... *dē-ras'in-āt*
derange... *dē-rānj'*
deranged... *dē-rānjd'*
derangement... *dē-rānj'ment*
derelict... *de're-likt*
dereliction... *de-re-lik'shun*
deride... *dē-rī d'*
derider... *dē-rī d'ėr*
deridingly... *dē-rī d'ing-li*
derision... *dē-ri'zhon*
derisive... *dē-rī s'iv*
derivable... *dē-rī v'a-bl*
derivably... *dē-rī v'a-bli*
derivation... *de-ri-vā'shun*
derivative... *de-riv'āt-iv*
derivatively... *de-riv'āt-iv-li*
derive... *de-rī v'*
dermatology... *dėr-ma-tol'o-ji*
derogate... *de'rō-gāt*
derogation... *de-rō-gā'shun*
derogatory... *dē-rog'ā-to-ri*
descant... *des'kant*

descend... *dē-send'*
descendant... *dē-send'ant*
descendent... *dē-send'ent*
descendible... *dē-send'i-bl*
descending... *dē-send'ing*
descent... *dē-sent'*
describable... *dē-skrī b'a-bl*
describe... *dē-skrī b'*
description... *dē-skrip'shun*
descriptive... *dē-skrip'tiv*
descry... *dē-skrī '*
desecrate... *de'sē-krāt*
desecration... *de-sē-krā'shun*
desert... *de'zėrt*
desert... *dē-zėrt'*
deserter... *dē-zėrt'ėr*
desertion... *dē-zėr'shun*
deserve... *dē-zėrv'*
deservedly... *dē-zėrv'ed-li*
desiccate... *dē-sik'āt*
desiderate... *dē-sid'ėr-āt*
desiderative... *dē-sid'ėr-āt-iv*
design... *dē-sī n'*
designate... *de'sig-nāt*
designation... *de-sig-nā'shun*
designedly... *dē-sī n'ed-li*
designer... *dē-sī n'ėr*
designing... *dē-sī n'ing*
desirability... *dē-zīr'a-bil''i-ti*
desirable... *dē-zīr'a-bl*
desirably... *dē-zīr'a-bli*
desire... *dē-zīr'*
desirous... *dē-zīr'us*
desist... *dē-sist'*
desk... *desk*
desolate... *de'sō-lāt*
desolately... *de'sō-lāt-li*
desolation... *de-sō-lā'shun*
despair... *dē-spār'*
desperado... *des-pė-rā'dō*
desperate... *des'pė-rāt*
desperately... *des'pė-rāt-li*
desperation... *des-pė-rā'shun*
despicably... *des'pik-a-bli*
despisable... *dē-spīz'a-bl*
despise... *dē-spīz'*
despiser... *dē-spīz'ėr*
despite... *dē-spīt'*
despiteful... *dē-spīt'ful*
despoil... *dē-spoil'*
despond... *dē-spond'*
despondent... *dē-spond'ent*
despot... *des'pot*
despotic... *des-pot'ik*

dessert... dē-zèrt'
destination... des-tin-ā'shun
destine... des'tin
destiny... des'ti-ni
destitute... des'ti-tūt
destitution... des-ti-tū'shun
destroy... dē-stroi'
destroyer... dē-stroi'èr
destructible... dē-strukt'i-bl
destruction... dē-struk'shun
destructive... dē-strukt'iv
destructively... dē-strukt'iv-li
detach... dē-tach'
detachment... dē-tach'ment
detail... dē-tāl
detailed... dē-tāld'
detain... dē-tān'
detainer... dē-tān'èr
detainment... dē-tān'ment
detect... dē-tekt'
detection... dē-tek'shun
detective... dē-tek'tiv
detent... dē-tent'
detention... dē-ten'shun
deter... dē-tèr'
deterge... dē-tèrj'
detergent... dē-tèrj'ent
deteriorate... dē-tē'ri-ō-rāt
determent... dē-tèr'ment
determine... dē-tèr'min
determined... dē-tèr'mind
deterrent... dē-tèr'ent
detest... dē-test'
detestable... dē-test'a-bl
detestably... dē-test'a-bli
detestation... dē-test-ā'shun
dethrone... dē-thrōn'
detonation... dē-tō-nā'shun
detonator... det'ō-nā-tèr
detract... dē-trakt'
detraction... dē-trak'shun
detractor... dē-trakt'èr
detrimental... de-tri-ment'al
detritus... dē-trīt'us
detruncate... dē-trung'kāt
deuce... dūs
devastate... de'vas-tāt
devastation... de-vas-tā'shun
develop... dē-vel'up
deviate... dē'vi-āt
deviation... dē-vi-ā'shun
device... dē-vīs'
devil... de'vil
devilish... de'vil-ish

devilment... de'vil-ment
devilry... de'vil-ri
devious... dē'vi-us
devisable... dē-vīz'a-bl
devise... dē-vīz'
deviser... de-vīz'èr
devisor... de-vīz'èr
devoir... de-vwar'
devote... dē-vōt'
devoted... dē-vōt'ed
devotee... dev-o-tē'
devotion... dē-vō'shun
devotional... dē-vō'shun-al
devour... dē-vour'
devout... dē-vout'
devoutly... dē-vout'li
dew... dū
dewiness... dū'i-nes
dew-point... dū'point
dewy... dū'i
dexter... deks'tèr
dexterity... deks-te'ri-ti
dexterous... deks'tèr-us
dexterously... deks'tèr-us-li
dextrine... deks'trin
dextrose... deks'tros
diabetes... dī-a-bē'tēz
diabolically... dī-a-bol'ik-al-li
diaconal... dī-ak'on-al
diaconate... dī-ak'on-āt
diacoustics... dī-a-kous'tiks
diadem... dī'a-dem
diagnose... dī-ag-nōs'
diagnosis... dī-ag-nō'sis
diagnostic... dī-ag-nōs'tik
diagonal... dī-ag'on-al
diagonally... dī-ag'on-al-li
diagram... dī'a-gram
dial... dī'al
dialect... dī'a-lekt
dialectal... dī-a-lek'tal
dialectician... dī'a-lek-ti''shan
dialectics... dī-a-lek'tiks
dialling... dī'al-ing
dialogue... dī'a-log
diameter... dī-am'et-èr
diamond... dī'a-mond
diapason... dī-a-pā'zon
diaper... dī'a-pèr
diaphanous... dī-af'an-us
diaphragm... dī'a-fram
diarrhea... dī-a-rē'a
diary... dī'a-ri
diatomic... dī-a-tom'ik

D

diatonic... *dī-a-ton'ik*
dice... *dīs*
dichotomous... *dī-kot'o-mus*
dicotyledon... *dī'kot-i-lē''don*
dictaphone... *dik'ta-fōn*
dictate... *dik'tāt*
dictation... *dik-tā'shun*
dictator... *dik-tāt'ėr*
dictatorial... *dik-ta-tō'ri-al*
dictatorship... *dik-tāt'ėr-ship*
diction... *dik'shun*
dictionary... *dik'shun-a-ri*
dictum... *dik'tum*
did... *did*
diddle... *did'l*
die... *dī*
die... *dī*
dielectric... *dī-ē-lek'trik*
diesel... *dēs'el*
diet... *dī'et*
dietary... *dī'et-a-ri*
dietetics... *dī-et-et'iks*
differ... *dif'ėr*
difference... *dif'ėr-ens*
different... *dif'ėr-ent*
differentiate... *dif-ėr-en'shi-āt*
differently... *dif-ėr-ent-li*
difficult... *dif'fi-kult*
difficulty... *dif'fi-kul-ti*
diffidence... *dif'fi-dens*
diffident... *dif'fi-dent*
diffidently... *dif'fi-dent-li*
diffract... *dif-frakt'*
diffraction... *dif-frak'shun*
diffuse... *dif-fūz'*
diffusely... *dif-fūs'li*
diffusible... *dif-fūz'i-bl*
diffusion... *dif-fū'zhon*
diffusive... *dif-fūs'iv*
diffusively... *dif-fūs'iv-li*
dig... *dig*
digest... *di-jest'*
digester... *di-jest'ėr*
digestible... *di-jest'i-bl*
digestion... *di-jest'yon*
digestive... *di-jest'iv*
digging... *dig'ing*
digit... *di'jit*
digital... *di'jit-al*
dignify... *dig'ni-fī*
dignitary... *dig'ni-ta-ri*
dignity... *dig'ni-ti*
digress... *di-gres' or dī'gres*
digression... *di-gre'shun or dī-*

dilacerate... *dī-la'sė-rāt*
dilapidate... *di-la'pi-dāt*
dilapidated... *di-la'pi-dāt-ed*
dilatability... *dī-lāt'a-bil''i-ti*
dilatable... *dī-lāt'a-bl*
dilate... *dī-lāt'*
dilatorily... *di'la-to-ri-li*
dilatory... *di'la-tō-ri*
dilemma... *di-lem'ma*
diligence... *di'li-jens*
diligent... *di'li-jent*
diluent... *dil'ū-ent*
dilute... *di-lūt'*
dilution... *di-lū'shun*
diluvium... *di-lū'vi-um*
dim... *dim*
dime... *dīm*
dimension... *di-men'shun*
diminish... *di-min'ish*
diminutive... *di-min'ūt-iv*
dimissory... *di-mis'so-ri*
dimity... *di'mi-ti*
dimly... *dim'li*
dimmish... *dim'ish*
dimple... *dim'pl*
dimpled... *dim'pld*
dine... *dīn*
dinghy... *ding'gi*
dingy... *din'ji*
dinner... *din'nėr*
diocesan... *dī-os'es-an*
diocese... *dī'ō-sēs*
dioptrics... *dī-op-triks*
diorama... *dī-ō-ra'ma*
dioramic... *dī-ō-ram'ik*
dip... *dip*
diphtheria... *dif-thē'ri-a*
diploma... *di-plō-ma*
diplomacy... *di-plō'ma-si*
diplomat... *dip'lō-mat*
diplomatics... *dip-lō-mat'iks*
diplomatist... *di-plō'mat-ist*
dipper... *dip'ėr*
dire... *dīr*
direct... *di-rekt'*
direction... *di-rek'shun*
directive... *di-rekt'iv*
directly... *di-rekt'li*
director... *di-rekt'ėr*
directorate... *di-rek'tėr-āt*
directorship... *di-rek'tėr-ship*
directory... *di-rek'to-ri*
direful... *dīr'ful*
direfully... *dīr'ful-li*

dirk . . . *dėrk*
dirt . . . *dėrt*
dirtily . . . *dėrt'i-li*
dirty . . . *dėrt'i*
disability . . . *dis-a-bil'i-ti*
disable . . . *dis-ā'bl*
disabuse . . . *dis-a-būz'*
disadvantage . . . *dis-ad-van'tāj*
disaffect . . . *dis-af-fekt'*
disaffected . . . *dis-af-fek'ted*
disaffection . . . *dis-af-fek'shun*
disaffirm . . . *dis-af-fėrm'*
disagree . . . *dis-a-grē'*
disagreeably . . . *dis-a-grē'a-bli*
disallow . . . *dis-al-lou'*
disallowable . . . *dis-al-lou'a-bl*
disannul . . . *dis-an-nul'*
disappear . . . *dis-ap-pēr'*
disappoint . . . *dis-ap-point'*
disapproval . . . *dis-ap-prov'al*
disapprove . . . *dis-ap-prov'*
disarm . . . *dis-arm'*
disarrange . . . *dis-a-rānj'*
disarray . . . *dis-a-rā'*
disaster . . . *diz-as'tėr*
disastrous . . . *diz-as'trus*
disavouch . . . *dis-a-vouch'*
disavow . . . *dis-a-vou'*
disavowal . . . *dis-a-vou'al*
disband . . . *dis-band'*
disbar . . . *dis-bar'*
disbelief . . . *dis-bē-lēf'*
disbelieve . . . *dis-bē-lēv'*
disburden . . . *dis-bėr'dn*
disburse . . . *dis-bėrs'*
disbursement . . . *dis-bėrs'ment*
disburthen . . . *dis-bėr'ŧHen*
discard . . . *dis-kard'*
discern . . . *dis-sėrn' or di-zėrn'*
discerner . . . *dis-sėrn'ėr*
discernible . . . *dis-sėrn'i-bl*
discerning . . . *dis-sėrn'ing*
discerningly . . . *dis-sėrn'ing-li*
discernment . . . *dis-sėrn'ment*
discharge . . . *dis-charj'*
disciple . . . *dis-sī'pl*
discipleship . . . *dis-sī'pl-ship*
disciplinable . . . *dis'si-plin-a-bl*
disciplinary . . . *dis'si-plin-a-ri*
discipline . . . *dis'si-plin*
disclaim . . . *dis-klām'*
disclaimer . . . *dis-klām'ėr*
disclose . . . *dis-klōz'*
disclosure . . . *dis-klō'zhūr*

discolor . . . *dis-kul'ėr*
discomfit . . . *dis-kom'fit*
discomfort . . . *dis-kum'fėrt*
discompose . . . *dis-kom-pōz'*
disconcert . . . *dis-kon-sėrt'*
disconnect . . . *dis-kon-nekt'*
disconsolate . . . *dis-kon'sō-lāt*
discontinue . . . *dis-kon-tin'ū*
discord . . . *dis'kord*
discordant . . . *dis-kord'ant*
discount . . . *dis'kount*
discountable . . . *dis-kount'a-bl*
discounter . . . *dis'kount-ėr*
discourage . . . *dis-ku'rāj*
discouraging . . . *dis-ku'rāj-ing*
discourse . . . *dis-kōrs'*
discourteous . . . *dis-kōr'tē-us*
discourtesy . . . *dis-kōr'te-si*
discover . . . *dis-kuv'ėr*
discoverable . . . *dis-kuv'ėr-a-bl*
discoverer . . . *dis-kuv'ėr-ėr*
discovery . . . *dis-kuv'ė-ri*
discredit . . . *dis-kred'it*
discreditable . . . *dis-kred'it-a-bl*
discreet . . . *dis-krēt*
discrete . . . *dis'krēt*
discretive . . . *dis-krēt'iv*
discriminate . . . *dis-krim'in-āt*
discursive . . . *dis-kėrs'iv*
discuss . . . *dis-kus'*
discussion . . . *dis-ku'shun*
disdainful . . . *dis-dān'ful*
disdainfully . . . *dis-dān'ful-li*
disease . . . *diz-ēz'*
disembark . . . *dis-em-bark'*
disembarrass . . . *dis-em-ba'ras*
disembody . . . *dis-em-bo'di*
disembowel . . . *dis-em-bou'el*
disembroil . . . *dis-em-broil'*
disenchant . . . *dis-en-chant'*
disengage . . . *dis-en-gāj'*
disengaged . . . *dis-en-gājd'*
disentail . . . *dis-en-tāl'*
disentangle . . . *dis-en-tang'gl*
disenthrall . . . *dis-en-thral'*
disentitle . . . *dis-en-fī'tl*
disestablish . . . *dis-es-tab'lish*
disesteem . . . *dis-es-tēm'*
disfavor . . . *dis-fā'vėr*
disfigure . . . *dis-fi'gūr*
disfranchise . . . *dis-fran'chīz*
disgorge . . . *dis-gorj'*
disgrace . . . *dis-grās'*
disgraceful . . . *dis-grās'ful*

D

disguise... *dis-gīz'*
disgustful... *dis-gust'ful*
disgusting... *dis-gust'ĭng*
dish... *dish*
dishearten... *dis-hart'n*
dishevel... *di-she'vel*
dishunest... *dis-on'est*
dishunesty... *dis-on'est-i*
dishunor... *dis-on'ėr*
dishunorable... *dis-on'ėr-a-bl*
disillusionize... *dis-il-lū'zhon-īz*
disincline... *dis-in-klīn'*
disinfect... *dis-in-fekt'*
disinfectant... *dis-in-fek'tant*
disinfection... *dis-in-fek'shun*
disingenuous... *dis-in-jen'ū-us*
disinherit... *dis-in-he'rit*
disintegrable... *dis-in'tē-gra-bl*
disintegrate... *dis-in'tē-grāt*
disinterment... *dis-in-tėr'ment*
disinthrall... *dis-in-thral'*
disjoin... *dis-join'*
disjoint... *dis-joint'*
disjointed... *dis-joint'ed*
disjunct... *dis-jungkt'*
disjunctive... *dis-jungk'tiv*
disk... *disk*
dislike... *dis-līk'*
dislocate... *dis'lō-kāt*
dislocation... *dis-lō-kā'shun*
dislodge... *dis-loj'*
dislodgment... *dis-loj'ment*
disloyal... *dis-loi'al*
disloyally... *dis-loi'al-li*
disloyalty... *dis-loi'al-ti*
dismal... *diz'mal*
dismally... *diz'mal-li*
dismantle... *dis-man'tl*
dismask... *dis-mask'*
dismast... *dis-mast'*
dismay... *dis-mā'*
dismember... *dis-mem'bėr*
dismiss... *dis-mis'*
dismissal... *dis-mis'al*
dismission... *dis-mi'shun*
dismount... *dis-mount'*
disobedient... *dis-ō-bē'di-ent*
disobey... *dis-ō-bā'*
disorder... *dis-or'dėr*
disorderly... *dis-or'dėr'li*
disorganize... *dis-or'gan-īz*
disown... *dis-ōn'*
disparage... *dis-pa'rāj*
disparate... *dis'pa-rāt*

disparity... *dis-pa'ri-ti*
dispassionate... *dis-pa'shun-āt*
dispatch... *dis-pach'*
dispeace... *dis-pēs'*
dispel... *dis-pel'*
dispensable... *dis-pens'a-bl*
dispensary... *dis-pens'a-ri*
dispensatory... *dis-pens'a-to-ri*
dispense... *dis-pens'*
dispenser... *dis-pens'ėr*
dispensing... *dis-pens'ing*
dispeople... *dis-pē'pl*
disperse... *dis-pėrs'*
dispersion... *dis-pėr'shun*
dispirit... *dis-pi'rit*
dispirited... *dis-pi'rit-ed*
dispiriting... *dis-pi'rit-ing*
displace... *dis-plās'*
displacement... *dis-plās'ment*
display... *dis-plā'*
displease... *dis-plēz*
displeased... *dis-plēzd'*
displeasing... *dis-plēz'ing*
displeasure... *dis-ple'zhŭr*
disposable... *dis-pōz'a-bl*
disposal... *dis-pōz'al*
dispose... *dis-pōz'*
disposed... *dis-pōzd'*
disposer... *dis-pōz'ėr*
disposition... *dis-pō-zi'shun*
dispossess... *dis-poz-zes'*
dispraise... *dis-prāz'*
disproof... *dis-prof'*
disprove... *dis-prov'*
disputant... *dis-pūt-ant*
disputation... *dis-pūt-ā'shun*
disputatious... *dis-pūt-ā'shus*
disputative... *dis-pūt'at-iv*
dispute... *dis-pūt'*
disputer... *dis-pūt'ėr*
disqualify... *dis-kwo'li-fī*
disquiet... *dis-kwī'et*
disquieting... *dis-kwī'et-ing*
disquisition... *dis-kwi-zi'shun*
disregard... *dis-rē-gard'*
disregardful... *dis-rē-gard'ful*
disrepair... *dis-rē-pār'*
disreputable... *dis-re'pūt-a-bl*
disrepute... *dis-rē-pūt'*
disrespect... *dis-rē-spekt'*
disrespectful... *dis-rē-spekt'ful*
disrobe... *dis-rōb'*
disruption... *dis-rup'shun*
disruptive... *dis-rupt'iv*

dissatisfied... *dis-sa'tis-fī d*
dissatisfy... *dis-sa'tis-fī*
dissect... *dis-sekt'*
dissecting... *dis-sekt'ing*
dissection... *dis-sek'shun*
dissector... *dis-sekt'ĕr*
dissemble... *dis-sem'bl*
dissembler... *dis-sem'bl-ĕr*
disseminate... *dis-se'min-āt*
dissension... *dis-sen'shun*
dissent... *dis-sent'*
dissenter... *dis-sent'ĕr*
dissentient... *dis-sen'shi-ent*
dissertation... *dis-sĕr-tā'shun*
disservice... *dis-sĕr'vis*
dissident... *dis'si-dent*
dissilient... *dis-si'li-ent*
dissimilar... *dis-si'mi-lĕr*
dissimilarity... *dis-si'mi-la''ri-ti*
dissimilitude... *dis-si-mil''i-tū d*
dissimulate... *dis-sim'ū-lāt*
dissipate... *dis'si-pāt*
dissipated... *dis'si-pāt'ed*
dissipation... *dis-si-pā'shun*
dissolubility... *dis-so'lū-bil''i-ti*
dissoluble... *dis'so-lū-bl*
dissolute... *dis'sō-lūt*
dissolution... *dis-sō-lū'shun*
dissolvable... *diz-zolv'a-bl*
dissolve... *diz-zolv'*
dissolvent... *diz-zolv'ent*
dissolver... *diz-zolv'ĕr*
dissonance... *dis'sō-nans*
dissonant... *dis'sō-nant*
dissuasion... *dis-swā'zhon*
dissuasive... *dis-swā'siv*
dissuasively... *dis-swā'siv-li*
distain... *dis-tān'*
distance... *dis'tans*
distant... *dis'tant*
distantly... *dis'tant-li*
distaste... *dis-tāst'*
distasteful... *dis-tāst'ful*
distemper... *dis-tem'pĕr*
distempered... *dis-tem'pĕrd*
distend... *dis-tend'*
distensible... *dis-tens'i-bl*
distention... *dis-ten'shun*
distil... *dis'til'*
distillation... *dis-til-ā'shun*
distillatory... *dis-til''ā-to-ri*
distiller... *dis-til'ĕr*
distillery... *dis-til'ĕ-ri*
distinct... *dis-tingkt'*

distinction... *dis-tingk'shun*
distinctive... *dis-tingkt'iv*
distinctively... *dis-tingkt'iv-li*
distinctly... *dis-tingkt'li*
distinctness... *dis-tingkt'nes*
distinguish... *dis-ting'gwish*
distort... *dis-tort'*
distract... *dis-trakt'*
distracted... *dis-trakt'ed*
distractedly... *dis-trakt'ed-li*
distracting... *dis-trakt'ing*
distraction... *dis-trak'shun*
distrain... *dis-trān'*
distrainable... *dis-trān'a-bl*
distraint... *dis-trānt*
distraught... *dis-trat'*
distress... *dis-tres'*
distressed... *dis-trest'*
distressful... *dis-tres'ful*
distressfully... *dis-tres'ful-li*
distressing... *dis-tres'ing*
distributable... *dis-tri'būt-a-bl*
distribute... *dis-tri'būt*
distributer... *dis-tri'būt'ĕr*
distribution... *dis-tri-bū'shun*
distributive... *dis-tri'būt-iv*
distributively... *dis-tri'būt-iv-li*
district... *dis'trikt*
distrust... *dis-trust'*
distrustful... *dis-trust'ful*
disturb... *dis-tĕrb'*
disturber... *dis-tĕrb'ĕr*
ditch... *dich*
ditcher... *dich'ĕr*
ditto... *dit'tō*
diuretic... *dī-ū-rē t'ik*
diurnal... *dī-ĕrn'al*
diurnally... *dī-ĕrn'al-li*
divagation... *dī-va-gā'shun*
divan... *di-van'*
divaricate... *dī-va'ri-kāt*
dive... *dīv*
diver... *dīv'ĕr*
diverge... *di-vĕrj'*
divergent... *di-vĕrj'ent*
divers... *dī'vĕrz*
diverse... *di-vĕrs'*
diversely... *di-vĕrs'li*
diversifiable... *di-vĕrs'i-fī-a-bl*
diversified... *di-vĕrs'i-fī d*
diversify... *di-vĕrs'i-fī*
diversion... *di-vĕr'shun*
diversity... *di-vĕrs'i-ti*
divert... *di-vĕrt'*

D

diverting... *di-vėrt'ing*
dividable... *di-vī d'a-bl*
divide... *di-vī d'*
dividend... *di'vi-dend*
divider... *di-vī d'ėr*
divination... *di-vin-ā'shun*
divine... *di-vīn'*
diviner... *di-vīn'ėr*
divinity... *di-vin'i-ti*
divisibility... *di-viz'i-bil''i-ti*
divisible... *di-viz'i-bl*
division... *di-vi'zhon*
divisional... *di-vizh'on-al*
divisive... *di-vīz'iv*
divisor... *di-vīz'or*
divorce... *di-vōrs'*
divorcement... *di-vōrs'ment*
divot... *div'ot*
divulge... *di-vulj'*
divulsion... *di-vul'shun*
dizziness... *diz'zi-nes*
dizzy... *diz'zi*
do... *do*
docile... *dō'sīl*
docility... *dō-si'li-ti*
dockage... *dok'āj*
docket... *dok'et*
dockyard... *dok'yard*
doctor... *dok'tėr*
doctorate... *dok'tėr-āt*
doctrinaire... *dok-tri-nār'*
doctrinal... *dok'trin-al*
doctrine... *dok'trin*
document... *do'kū-ment*
dodge... *doj*
doe... *dō*
doer... *do'ėr*
doeskin... *dō 'skin*
dog... *dog*
doge... *dōj*
dogged... *dog'ed*
doggedly... *dog'ed-li*
dogger... *dog'ėr*
doggerel... *dog'ė-rel*
doggish... *dog'ish*
dogma... *dog'ma*
dogmatics... *dog-mat'iks*
dogmatism... *dog'mat-izm*
dogmatist... *dog'mat-ist*
doily... *doi'li*
doings... *do'ingz*
doit... *doit*
dole... *dōl*
doleful... *dōl'ful*

dolefully... *dōl'ful-li*
doll... *dol*
dollar... *dol'lėr*
dolman... *dol'man*
dolmen... *dol'men*
dolomite... *dol'o-mīt*
dolphin... *dol'fin*
doltish... *dōlt'ish*
domain... *dō-mān'*
dome... *dōm*
domestic... *dō-mes'tik*
domesticate... *dō-mes'tik-āt*
domicile... *do'mi-sīl*
domiciliary... *do-mi-si'li-a-ri*
dominant... *dom'in-ant*
dominate... *dom'in-āt*
domination... *dom-in-ā'shun*
domineer... *dom-in-ēr'*
domineering... *dom-in-ēr'ing*
dominican... *dō-min'ik-an*
dominion... *dō-min'i-on*
domino... *do'mi-nō*
donate... *dō'nāt*
donation... *dō-nā'shun*
donative... *don'at-iv*
donee... *dō-nē'*
donkey... *dong'ki*
donor... *dō'nėr*
doom... *dom*
doomed... *domd*
doomsday... *domz'dā*
door... *dōr*
dormancy... *dor'man-si*
dormant... *dor'mant*
dormitory... *dor'mi-to-ri*
dormouse... *dor'mous*
dormy... *dor'mi*
dorsal... *dor'sal*
dose... *dōs*
dossier... *dos'ē-ā*
dot... *dot*
dotage... *dōt'āj*
dotal... *dōt'al*
dote... *dōt*
doting... *dōt'ing*
double... *du'bl*
doublet... *du'blet*
doubling... *du'bl-ing*
doubly... *du'bli*
doubt... *dout*
doubter... *dout'ėr*
doubtful... *dout'ful*
doubtfully... *dout'ful-li*
doubtless... *dout'les*

doubtlessly... *dout'les-li*
douceur... *do-sėr'*
douche... *dosh*
dough... *dō*
doughtily... *dou'ti-li*
doughty... *dou'ti*
doughy... *dō'i*
douse... *dous*
dove... *duv*
dovetail... *duv'tāl*
dowager... *dou'ā-jėr*
dowdy... *dou'di*
dowel... *dou'el*
down... *doun*
downcast... *doun'kast*
downfall... *foun'fal*
downhill... *doun'hil*
downpour... *doun'pōr*
downright... *doun'rīt*
downstairs... *doun'stārz*
downward
downy... *doun'i*
dowry... *dou'ri*
doze... *dōz*
dozen... *du'zn*
dozy... *dōz'i*
drab... *drab*
draff... *draf*
draft... *draft*
draftsman... *drafts'man*
drag... *drag*
draggle... *drag'gl*
drag-net... *drag'net*
dragon... *dra'gon*
dragonet... *dra'gon-et*
dragon-fly... *dra'gon-flī*
dragoon... *dra-gon'*
drainage... *drān'āj*
drainer... *drān'ėr*
drake... *drāk*
drama... *dra'ma*
dramatic... *dra-mat'ik*
dramatist... *dra'mat-ist*
dramatize... *dra'mat-īz*
dramaturgy... *dram'a-tėr-ji*
drape... *drāp*
draper... *drāp'ėr*
drapery... *drāp'ė-ri*
drastic... *dras'tik*
draught... *draft*
draughty... *draf'ti*
draw... *dra*
drawback... *dra'bak*
drawbridge... *dra̤'brij*

drawer... *dra'ėr*
drawing... *dra̤'ing*
drawl... *dral*
dray... *drā̤*
dread... *dred*
dreadful... *dred'ful*
dreadfully... *dred'ful-li*
dreadnought... *dred̤'nat*
dream... *drēm*
dreamer... *drēm'ėr*
dreamless... *drēm'les*
dreamy... *drēm'i*
drear... *drēr*
drearily... *drē'ri-li*
dreary... *drē'ri*
dredge... *drej*
dredger... *drej'ėr*
dregs... *dregz*
drench... *drensh*
dress... *dres*
dresser... *dres'ėr*
dressing... *dres'ing*
dressing-room... *dres'ing-rom*
dressy... *dres'i*
dribble... *drib'l*
driblet... *drib'let*
drift... *drift*
driftless... *drift'les*
drill... *dril*
drill... *dril*
drink... *dringk*
drinker... *dringk'ėr*
drip... *drip*
dripping... *drip'ing*
drive... *drīv*
driver... *drīv'ėr*
drizzle... *driz'l*
drizzly... *driz'li*
droll... *drōl*
drollery... *drōl'ė-ri*
drone... *drōn*
dronish... *drōn'ish*
droop... *drop*
drop... *drop*
dropping... *drop'ing*
dropsical... *drop'sik-al*
dropsy... *drop'si*
dross... *dros*
drossy... *dros'i*
drought... *drout*
droughty... *drout'i*
drove... *drōv*
drover... *drōv'ėr*
drown... *droun*

D

drowse... *drouz*
drowsy... *drou'zi*
drubbing... *drub'ing*
drudge... *druj*
drudgery... *druj'è-ri*
drug... *drug*
druggist... *drug'ist*
druid... *drū'id*
druidism... *drū'id-izm*
drum... *drum*
drumhead... *drum'hed*
drum-major... *drum'mā-jèr*
drummer... *drum'èr*
drunk... *drungk*
drunkard... *drungk'èrd*
drunken... *drungk'en*
drunkenness... *drungk'en-nes*
dry... *drī*
dryer... *drī'èr*
dryly... *drī'li*
dryness... *drī'nes*
dry-rot... *drī'rot*
dual... *dū'al*
dualism... *dū'al-izm*
dualist... *dū'al-ist*
dub... *dub*
dubiety... *dū-bī'e-ti*
dubious... *dū'bi-us*
dubiously... *dū'bi-us-li*
ducal... *dūk'al*
ducally... *dūk'al-li*
ducat... *duk'at*
duchess... *duch'es*
duchy... *duch'i*
duck... *duk*
duckling... *duk'ling*
duct... *dukt*
ductile... *duk'tīl*
ductility... *duk-til'i-ti*
dud... *dud*
dude... *dūd*
dudgeon... *du'jon*
due... *dū*
duel... *dū'el*
duellist... *dū'el-ist*
duet... *dū'et*
dug... *dug*
dug-out... *dug out*
duke... *dūk*
dulcimer... *dul'si-mèr*
dull... *dul*
dullard... *dul'èrd*
dully... *dul'li*
dulness... *dul'nes*

duly... *dū'li*
dumb... *dum*
dumb-bell... *dum'bel*
dumbly... *dum'li*
dumfound... *dum-found'*
dummy... *dum'i*
dump... *dump*
dump... *dump*
dumpish... *dump'ish*
dumpling... *dump'ling*
dumpy... *dump'i*
dunce... *duns*
dune... *dūn*
dungeon... *dun'jon*
dunnage... *dun'āj*
dupe... *dūp*
duplex... *dū'pleks*
duplicate... *dū'pli-kāt*
duplication... *dū-pli-kā'shun*
durability... *dūr-a-bil'i-ti*
durable... *dūr'a-bl*
durably... *dūr'a-bli*
durance... *dūr'ans*
duration... *dūr-ā'shun*
duress... *dūr'es*
during... *dūr'ing*
dusk... *dusk*
duskish... *dusk'ish*
dusky... *dusk'i*
dust... *dust*
duster... *dust'èr*
dusty... *dust'i*
dutch... *duch*
duteous... *dū'tē-us*
dutiful... *dū'ti-ful*
duty... *dū'ti*
dwarf... *dwarf*
dwarfish... *dwarf'ish*
dwell... *dwel*
dweller... *dwel'èr*
dwelling... *dwel'ing*
dwindle... *dwin'dl*
dye... *dī*
dying... *dī'ing*
dynamics... *dī-nam'iks*
dynamite... *din'a-mīt*
dynamo... *dī'na-mō*
dynasty... *di'nas-ti*

E

each... *ēch*
eager... *ē'gèr*

eagerly . . . ē-gėr-li
eagerness . . . ē'gėr-nes
eagle . . . ē'gl
eaglet . . . ē'gl-et
ear . . . ēr
ear-ache . . . ēr'āk
ear-drum . . . ēr'drum
earless . . . ēr'les
earn . . . ėrn
earnest . . . ėrn'est
earnestly . . . ėrn'est-li
earnings . . . ėrn'ingz
ear-ring . . . ēr'ring
ear-shot . . . ēr'shot
earth . . . ėrth
earthen . . . ėrth'en
earthling . . . ėrth'ling
earthly . . . ėrth'li
earthquake . . . ėrth'kwāk
earthward . . . ėrth'wėrd
earth-worm . . . ėrth'wėrm
earthy . . . ėrth'i
ease . . . ēz
easel . . . ēz'el
easement . . . ēz'ment
easily . . . ēz'i-li
east . . . ēst
easter . . . ēs'tėr
easterling . . . ēst'ėr-ling
easterly . . . ēst'ėr-li
eastern . . . ēst'ėrn
eastertide . . . ēst'ėr-fīd
eastward . . . ēst'wėrd
easy . . . ēz'i
easy-chair . . . ēz'i-chār
eat . . . ēt
eatable . . . ēt'a-bl
eating . . . ēt'ing
eaves . . . ēvz
eavesdrop . . . ēvz'drop
ebb . . . eb
ebon . . . eb'on
ebonite . . . eb'o-nīt
ebonize . . . eb'o-nīz
ebony . . . eb'on-i
ebriety . . . ē-brī'e-ti
eccentric . . . ek-sen'trik
eccentrically . . . ek-sen'trik-al-li
eccentricity . . . ek-sen-tris'i-ti
ecclesiastic . . . ek-klē'zi-as-tik
echelon . . . esh'e-lon
echo . . . e'kō
eclat . . . e-kla'
eclectic . . . ek-lek'tik

eclecticism . . . ek-lek'ti-sizm
eclipse . . . ē-klips'
ecliptic . . . ē-klip'tik
eclogue . . . ek'log
economics . . . ē-kon-om'iks
economist . . . ē-kon'om-ist
economize . . . ē-kon'om-īz
economy . . . ē-kon'o-mi
ecstasy . . . ek'sta-si
ecstatic . . . ek-stat'ik
edacious . . . ē-dā'shus
eden . . . ē'den
edge . . . ej
edged . . . ejd
edgeways . . . ej'wāz
edging . . . ej'ing
edible . . . ed'i-bl
edict . . . ē'dikt
edification . . . ed'i-fi-kā''shun
edifice . . . ed'i-fis
edify . . . ed'i-fī
edifying . . . ed'i-fī-ing
edit . . . ed'it
edition . . . ē-di'shun
editor . . . ed'it-ėr
editorial . . . ed-i-tō'ri-al
editorship . . . ed'it-ėr-ship
educate . . . ed'ū-kāt
education . . . ed-ū-kā'shun
educative . . . ed'ū-kāt-iv
educator . . . ed'ū-kāt-ėr
eduction . . . ē-duk'shun
eel . . . ēl
eerie . . . ē'ri
effacement . . . ef-fās'ment
effect . . . ef-fekt'
effective . . . ef-fekt'iv
effectively . . . ef-fekt'iv-li
effectual . . . ef-fek'tū-al
effectuate . . . ef-fek'tū-āt
effeminacy . . . ef-fem'in-a-si
effeminate . . . ef-fem'in-āt
effeminately . . . ef-fem'in-āt-li
effervesce . . . ef-fėr-ves'
effervescent . . . ef-fėr-ves'ent
effete . . . ef-fēt'
efficacious . . . ef-fi-kā'shus
efficacy . . . ef'fi-ka-si
efficiency . . . ef-fi'shen-si
efficient . . . ef-fi'shent
effigy . . . ef'fi-ji
effloresce . . . ef-flo-res'
efflorescence . . . ef-flo-res'ens
efflorescent . . . ef-flo-res'ent

E

effluence... ef'flu-ens
effluent... ef'flu-ënt
effluvial... ef-flū'vi-al
effluvium... ef-flū'vi-um
effluxion... ef-fluk'shun
effort... ef'fōrt
effulgence... ef-fulj'ens
effulgent... ef-fulj'ent
effuse... ef-fūz'
effusion... ef-fū'zhon
effusive... ef-fūs'iv
eft... eft
egg... eg
egoism... eg'ō-izm or ē'
egoist... eg'ō-ist or ē'
egotism... eg'ot-izm or ē'
egotist... eg'ot-ist or ē'
egotize... eg'ot-īz or ē'
egregious... e-grē'jus
egress... ē'gres
egret... eg'ret or ē'gret
egyptian... ē-jip'shun
egyptology... ē-jip-tol'o-ji
eight... āt
eighteen... āt'ēn
eighteenth... āt'ēnth
eighth... ātth
eighthly... ātth'li
eighty... āt'i
either... ē'ᵀHėr or ī'ᵀHėr
ejaculate... ē-jak'ū-lāt
ejaculation... ē-jak'ū-lā''shun
ejaculatory... ē-jak'ū-la-to-ri
eject... ē'jekt
ejection... ē-jek'shun
ejectment... ē-jekt'ment
ejector... ē-jekt'or
elaborate... ē-lab'o-rāt
elaborately... ē-lab'o-rāt-li
elaboration... ē-lab'o-rā''shun
eland... ē'land
elapse... ē-laps'
elastic... ē-las'tik
elastically... ē-las'tik-al-li
elasticity... ē-las-tis'i-ti
elate... ē-lāt'
elated... ē-lāt'ed
elation... ē-lā'shun
elbow... el'bō
elder... eld'ėr
elderly... eld'ėr-li
eldest... eld'est
election... ē-lek'shun
electioneer... ē-lek'shun-ēr''

elective... ē-lekt'iv
elector... ē-lekt'ėr
electoral... ē-lekt'ėr-al
electorate... ē-lekt'ėr-āt
electrically... ē-lek'tri-kal-li
electrician... ē-lek-trish'an
electricity... ē-lek-tris'i-ti
electrifiable... ē-lek'tri-fī-a-bl
electrify... ē-lek'tri-fī
electro... ē-lek'trō
electrocute... ē-lek'trō-kūt
electrode... ē-lek'trōd
electrolysis... ē-lek-trol'i-sis
electrolyte... ē-lek'trō-līt
electron... ē-lek'tron
electroplate... ē-lek'trō-plāt
electrotype... ē-lek'trō-fīp
elegant... el'ē-gant
element... el'ē-ment
elemental... el-ē-ment'al
elementary... el-ē-ment'ar-i
elephant... el'ē-fant
elevate... el'ē-vāt
elevation... el-ē-vā'shun
elevator... el'ē-vāt-ėr
eleven... ē-lev'n
eleventh... ē-lev'nth
elf... elf
elicit... ē-lis'it
elide... ē-līd'
eligibility... el'i-ji-bil''i-ti
eligible... el'i-ji-bl
eligibly... el'i-ji-bli
eliminate... ē-lim'in-āt
elimination... ē-lim'in-ā''shun
elision... ē-li'zhon
elite... ā-lēt'
elixir... ē-lik'sėr
elk... elk
ellipse... el-lips'
ellipsis... el-lips'is
elm... elm
elocution... e-lō-kū'shun
elocutionist... e-lō-kū'shun-ist
elogium... ē-lō'ji-um
elongate... ē-long'gāt
elope... ē-lōp'
elopement... ē-lōp'ment
eloquence... e'lō-kwens
eloquent... e'lō-kwent
eloquently... e'lō-kwent-li
else... els
elsewhere... els'whār
elucidate... ē-lū'sid-āt

E

elude... ē-lūd'
elusion... ē-lū'zhon
elusive... ē-lū'siv
elusory... ē-lū'so-ri
elysian... ē-li'zhi-an
elysium... ē-li'zhi-um
elytron... el'i-tron
emaciate... ē-mā'shi-āt
emanant... em'a-nant
emanate... em'a-nāt
emanation... em-a-nā-shun
emancipate... ē-man'si-pāt
emasculate... ē-mas'kū-lāt
embalm... em-bam'
embank... em-bangk'
embargo... em-bar'gō
embarrass... em-ba'ras
embarrassed... em-ba'rast
embassy... em'bas-si
embattle... em-bat'l
embay... em-bā'
embellish... em-bel'lish
ember... em'bėr
embezzle... em-bez'l
embezzler... em-bez'l-ėr
embitter... em-bit'ėr
emblaze... em-blāz'
emblazon... em-blā'zon
emblazoner... em-blā'zon-ėr
emblazonry... em-blā'zn-ri
emblem... em'blem
embody... em-bo'di
embogue... em-bōg'
embolden... em-bōld'en
embolism... em'bol-izm
emboss... em-bos'
embossment... em-bos'ment
embowel... em-bou'el
embrace... em-brās'
embrasure... em-brā'zhūr
embroider... em-broi'dėr
embroidery... em-broi'de-ri
embroil... em-broil'
embroilment... em-broil'ment
embryo... em'bri-ō
embryology... em-bri-ol'o-ji
embryonic... em-bri-on'ik
emend... ē-mend'
emendator... ē-mend'āt-ėr
emendatory... ē-mend'a-to-ri
emerald... e'me-rald
emerge... ē-mėrj'
emergence... ė-mėrj'ens
emergency... ē-mėrj'en-si

emergent... ē-mėrj'ent
emeritus... ė-mer'i-tus
emersion... ē-mėr'shun
emery... e'me-ri
emigrant... em'i-grant
emigrate... em'i-grāt
emigration... em-i-grā'shun
eminence... em'in-ens
eminent... em'in-ent
eminently... em'in-ent-li
emissive... ē-mis'iv
emissory... ē-mis'o-ri
emit... ē-mit'
emollient... ē-mol'li-ent
emolument... ē-mol'ū-ment
emotion... ē-mō'shun
emotional... ē-mō'shun-al
empale... em-pāl'
emperor... em'pėr-ėr
emphasis... em'fa-sis
emphasize... em'fa-sīz
emphatic... em-fat'ik
emphatically... em-fat'ik-al-li
empire... em'pīr
empiric... em-pi'rik
empirical... em-pi'rik-al
empiricism... em-pi'ri-sizm
employ... em-ploi'
employee... em-ploi'ē
employer... em-ploi'ėr
employment... em-ploi'ment
emporium... em-pō'ri-um
empower... em-pou'ėr
empress... em'pres
emulate... em'ū-lāt
emulation... em-ū-lā'shun
emulative... em'ū-lāt-iv
emulator... em'ū-lāt-ėr
emulous... em'ū-lus
emulsion... ē-mul'shun
emulsive... ē-muls'iv
enable... en-ā'bl
enact... en-akt'
enactive... en-akt'iv
enactment... en-akt'ment
enactor... en-akt'ėr
enamel... en-am'el
enamor... en-am'ėr
encage... en-kāj'
encamp... en-kamp'
encaustic... en-kas'tik
encave... en-kāv'
enceinte... ang-sangt'
encephalon... en-sef'a-lon

enchain... en-chān'
enchant... en-chant'
enchanted... en-chant'ed
enchanter... en-chant'ėr
enchase... en-chās'
enchorial... en-kō'ri-al
encircle... en-sėr'kl
enclasp... en-klasp'
enclose... en-klōz'
enclosure... en-klō'zhūr
encomiast... en-kō'mi-ast
encomium... en-kō'mi-um
encompass... en-kum'pas
encounter... en-koun'tėr
encourage... en-ku'rāj
encourager... en-ku'rāj-ėr
encouraging... en-ku'rāj-ing
encrimson... en-krim'zn
encroach... en-krōch'
encroacher... en-krōch'ėr
encrust... en-krust'
encumber... en-kum'bėr
end... end
endanger... en-dān'jėr
endear... en-dēr'
endearing... en-dēr'ing
endearment... en-dēr'ment
endeavor... en-dev'ėr
endive... en'div
endless... end'les
endlessly... end'les-li
endlong... end'long
endorse... en-dors'
endorsement... en-dors'ment
endow... en-dou'
endowment... en-dou'ment
endurable... en-dūr'a-bl
endurance... en-dūr'ans
endure... en-dūr'
enduring... en-dūr'ing
endwise... end'wiz
enema... en'e-ma
enemy... en'e-mi
energize... en'ėr-jīz
energy... en'ėr-ji
enervation... en-ėr-vā'shun
enfilade... en-fi-lād
enforce... en-fōrs'
enforcement... en-fōrs'ment
enfranchise... en-fran'chīz
engage... en-gāj'
engaged... en-gājd'
engaging... en-gāj'ing
engine... en'jin

engineer... en-ji-nēr'
engineering... en-ji-nēr'ing
engird... en-gėrd'
english... ing'glish
englishry... ing'glish-ri
engrail... en-grāl'
engrain... en-grān'
engrave... en-grāv'
engraver... en-grāv'ėr
engraving... en-grāv'ing
engross... en-grōs'
engrosser... en-gros'ėr
engrossment... en-grōs'ment
engulf... en-gulf'
enhance... en-hans'
enigma... ē-nig'ma
enigmatist... ē-nig'mat-ist
enjoin... en-join'
enjoy... en-joi'
enjoyable... en-joi'a-bl
enjoyment... en-joi'ment
enlarge... en-larj'
enlargement... en-larj'ment
enlighten... en-lī't'en
enlightened... en-lī't'end
enlist... en-list'
enlistment... en-list'ment
enliven... en-lī'v'en
enlivener... en-lī'v'en-ėr
enmity... en'mi-ti
enormity... ē-nor'mi-ti
enormous... ė-nor'mus
enormously... ē-nor'mus-li
enough... ē-nuf'
enrage... en-rāj'
enrapture... en-rap'tūr
enrich... en-rich'
enrichment... en-rich'ment
enrobe... en-rōb'
enroll, Enrol... en-rōl'
enrolment... en-rōl'ment
ensconce... en-skons'
ensemble... ong-sam-bl
enshrine... en-shrīn'
enshroud... en-shroud'
ensign... en'sīn
enslave... en-slāv'
enslavement... en-slāv'ment
enslaver... en-slāv'ėr
ensnare... en-snār
ensue... en-sū'
ensure... en-shor'
entail... en-tāl'
entailment... en-tāl'ment

entangle... en-tang'gl
enter... en'tėr
enteric... en-ter'ik
enterprise... en'tėr-prīz
enterprising... en'tėr-prīz-ing
entertain... en-tėr-tān'
entertaining... en-tėr-tān'ing
enthrone... en-thrōn
enthusiasm... en-thū'zi-azm
enthusiast... en-thū'zi-ast
enthusiastic... en-thū'zi-as''tik
entice... en-tīs'
enticement... en-tīs'ment
enticing... en-tīs'ing
entire... en-tīr'
entirely... entīr'li
entity... en'ti-ti
entomb... en-tom'
entombment... en-tom'ment
entrail... en'trāl
entrain... en-trān'
entrance... en'trans
entrance... en-trans'
entrant... en'trant
entrap... en-trap'
entreat... en-trēt'
entreaty... en-trēt'i
entremets... ang-tr-mā
entrench... en-trensh'
entry... en'tri
entwine... en-twīn'
entwist... en-twist'
enumerate... ē-nū'me-rāt
enunciate... ē-nun'si-āt
enunciatory... ē-nun'si-a-to-ri
envelop... en-vel'op
envelope... en'vel-ōp
enviable... en'vi-a-bl
envious... en'vi-us
environ... en-vī'ron
envoy... en'voi
envy... en'vi
enwrap... en-rap'
eozoic... ē-ō-zō'ik
epact... ē'pakt
ephemera... e-fem'e-ra
ephemeral... e-fē'me-ral
ephemeris... e-fem'e-ris
ephod... e'fod
epic... ep'ik
epicarp... ep'i-karp
epicure... ep'i-kūr
epicurean... ep'i-kū-rē''an
epicurism... ep'i-kūr-izm

epidemic... ep-i-dem'ik
epidermis... ep-i-dėr'mis
epigram... ep'i-gram
epigraph... ep'i-graf
epilepsy... ep'i-lep-si
epileptic... ep-i-lep'tik
epilogue... ep'i-log
epiphany... ē-pif'a-ni
epiphyte... ep'i-fīt
episcopacy... ē-pis'kō-pa-si
episode... ep'i-sōd
episodic... ep-i-sod'ik
epistle... ē-pis'l
epitaph... ep'i-taf
epithet... ep'i-thet
epitome... e-pit'o-mi
epitomize... e-pit'om-īz
epoch... ē'pok
epode... ep'ōd
eponym... ep'o-nim
epsom-salt... ep'sum-salt
equability... ē-kwa-bil'i-ti
equable... ē-kwa-bl
equably... ē'kwa-bli
equal... ē'kwal
equality... ē-kwal'i-ti
equalize... ē-kwal-īz
equally... ē'kwal-li
equate... ē-kwāt
equation... ē-kwā'shun
equator... ē-kwā'tėr
equatorial... ē-kwa-tō'ri-al
equestrian... ē-kwes'tri-an
equilibrist... ē-kwil'i-brist or ek-
equip... ē-kwip'
equipment... ē-kwip'ment
equipose... ē'kwi-poiz or ek'
equitable... ek'wit-a-bl
equitably... ek'wit-a-bl
equity... ek'wi-ti
equivalent... ē-kwiv'a-lent
equivocal... ē-kwiv'ō-kal
equivocate... ē-kwiv'ō-kāt
era... ē'ra
eradicate... ē-rad'i-kāt
eradication... ē-rad'i-kā''shun
erase... ē-rās'
erasement... ē-rās'ment
eraser... ē-rās'ėr
erastian... ē-ras'ti-an
erastianism... ē-ras'ti-an-izm
erasure... ē-rā'zhūr
ere... ār
erect... ē-rekt'

E

erection... ē-rek'shun
eremite... e'rē-mīt
ergo... ėr'gō
ergot... ėr'got
erode... ē-rōd'
erosion... ē-rō'zhon
erotic... ē-rot'ik
err... er
errand... e'rand
errant... e'rant
erratic... e-rat'ik
erratum... e-rā'tum
erroneous... e-rō'nē-us
error... e'rėr
erse... ėrs
erst... ėrst
erubescent... e-rū-bes'ent
eructate... ē-rukt'āt
eructation... ē-ruk-tā'shun
erudite... e'rū-dīt
erudition... e-rū-di'shun
erupt... ē-rupt'
eruption... ē-rup'shun
eruptive... ē-rup'tiv
escalade... es-ka-lād'
escalator... es'ka-lā-tėr
escapade... es-ka-pād'
escape... es-kāp'
escarp... es-karp'
escarpment... es-karp'ment
escheat... es-chēt'
eschew... es-cho'
escort... es'kort
esculent... es'kū-lent
escutcheon... es-kuch'on
esophagus... ē-sof'a-gus
esoteric... es-ō-te'rik
espalier... es-pa'li-ėr
especial... es-pe'shal
especially... es-pe'shal-li
espial... es-pī'al
espionage... es'pi-on-āj
esplanade... es-pla-nād'
espousal... es-pouz'al
espouse... es-pouz'
espouser... es-pouz'ėr
esprit... es-prē
espy... es-pī'
esquire... es-kwīr'
essay... es-sā'
essayist... es'sā-ist
essence... es'sens
essentiality... es-sen'shi-al''i-ti
establish... es-tab'lish

established... es-tab'lisht
estate... es-tāt'
esteem... es-tēm'
estimable... es'tim-a-bl
estimate... es'tim-āt
estimation... es-tim-ā'shun
estrange... es-trānj'
estrangement... es-trānj'ment
estray... es-trā'
estreat... es-trēt'
estuary... es'tū-a-ri
etch... ech
etcher... ech'ėr
etching... ech'ing
eternal... ē-tėrn'al
eternally... ē-tėrn'al-li
eternity... ē-tėrn'i-ti
eternize... ē-tėrn'īz
ether... ē'thėr
ethic... eth'ik
ethically... eth'ik-al-li
ethics... eth'iks
ethnic... eth'nik
ethnologist... eth-nol'o-jist
ethnology... eth-nol'o-ji
ethology... eth-ol'o-ji
etiquet... et-i-ket'
etruscan... ē-trus'kan
etymon... e'ti-mon
eucalyptus... ū-ka-lip'tus
eucharist... ū'ka-rist
eugenics... ū-jen'iks
eulogist... ū'lo-jist
eulogistic... ū-lo-jis'tik
eulogium... ū-lō'ji-um
eulogize... ū'lo-jiz
eulogy... ū'lo-ji
eunuch... ū'nuk
eupeptic... ū-pep'tik
euphemism... ū'fem-izm
euphemistic... ū-fem-is'tik
euphony... ū'fo-ni
euphuism... ū'fū-izm
eurasian... ū-rā'shi-an
european... ū-rō-pē'an
euthanasia... ū-tha-nā'zi-a
evacuee... ē-vak'ū-ē
evade... ē-vād'
evaluate... ē-val'ū-āt
evanescence... ev-an-es'ens
evanescent... ev-an-es'ent
evangel... ē-van'jel
evangelist... ē-van'jel-ist
evangelize... ē-van'jel-īz

evaporable... ē-va′pėr-a-bl
evaporate... ē-va′pėr-āt
evasion... ē-vā′zhon
evasive... ē-vā′siv
eve... ēv
even... ē′vn
evening... ē′vn-ing
event... ē′vent′
eventful... ē-vent′ful
eventual... ē-vent′ū-al
eventuality... ē-vent′ū-al′′i-ti
eventuate... ē-vent′ū-āt
ever... ev′ėr
evergreen... ev′ėr-grēn
everlasting... ev-ėr-last′ing
everlastingly... ev-ėr-last′ing-li
every... ev′ri
everybody... ev′ri-bod-i
everyday... ev′ri-dā
everyone... ev′ri-wun
everywhere... ev′ri-whār
evict... ē-vikt′
eviction... ē-vik′shun
evidence... ev′i-dens
evident... ev′i-dent
evidential... ev-i-den′shal
evil... ē′vil
evocation... ev-ō-kā′shun
evoke... ē-vōk′
evolution... ev-o-lū′shun
evolutionist... ev-o-lū′shun-ist
evolve... ē-volv′
evulsion... ē-vul′shun
exacerbate... eks-as′ėr-bāt
exact... egz-akt′
exacting... egz-akt′ing
exaction... egz-ak′shun
exactitude... egz-ak′ti-tūd
exactly... egs-akt′li
exactor... egz-akt′ėr
exalt... egz-alt′
exaltation... ëgz-alt-ā′shun
examine... egz-am′in
examiner... egz-am′in-ėr
examining... egz-am′in-ing
example... egz-am′pl
exasperate... egz-as′pė-rāt
excavate... eks′ka-vāt
excavation... eks-ka-vā′shun
exceed... ek-sēd′
exceeding... ek-sēd′ing
exceedingly... ek-sēd′ing-li
excel... ek-sel′
excellent... ek′sel-lent

except... ek-sept′
excepting... ek-sept′ing
exception... ek-sep′shun
exceptional... ek-sep′shun-al
excerpt... ek-sėrpt′
excess... ek-ses′
excessive... ek-ses′iv
excessively... ek-ses′iv-li
exchange... eks-chānj′
exchanger... eks-chānj-ėr
excise... ek-sīz′
excision... ek-si′zhon
excitability... ek-sī t′a-bil′′i-ti
excitable... ek-sīt′a-bl
excite... ek-sīt′
excitement... ek-sīt′ment
exciting... ek-sīt′ing
exclaim... eks-klām′
exclamatory... eks-klam′a-to-ri
exclude... eks-klūd′
exclusion... eks-klū′zhon
exclusionist... eks-klū′zhon-ist
exclusive... eks-klū′siv
excoriate... eks-kō′ri-āt
excrement... eks′krē-ment
excrescence... eks-kres′ens
excrescent... eks-kres′ent
excrete... eks-krēt′
excretion... eks-krē′shun
excruciate... eks-kro′shi-āt
exculpatory... eks-kul′pa-to-ri
excursion... eks-kėr′shun
excursionist... eks-kėr′shun-ist
excusable... eks-kūz′a-bl
excuser... eks-kūz′ėr
execrate... ek′sē-krāt
execration... ek-sē-krā′shun
executant... eks-ek′ū-tant
execute... ek′sē-kūt
execution... ek-sē-kū′shun
executor... egz-ek′ūt-ėr
executory... egz-ek′ū-to-ri
executrix... egz-ek′ū-triks
exegesis... eks-ē-jē′sis
exegetics... eks-ē-jet′iks
exemplar... egz-em′plėr
exemplarily... egz′em-pla-ri-li
exemplary... egz′em-pla-ri
exemplify... egz-em′pli-fī
exempt... egz-emt′
exemption... egz-em′shun
exercise... eks′ėr-sīz
exert... egz-ėrt
exertion... egz-ėr′shun

E

exfoliate... *eks-fō'li-āt*
exhalation... *egz-hāl-ā'shun*
exhale... *egz-hāl'*
exhaust... *egz-ast'*
exhibit... *egz-ib'it*
exhibiter... *egz-ib'it-ėr*
exhibition... *eks-i-bi'shun*
exhibitioner... *eks-i-bi'shun-ėr*
exhibitory... *egz-ib'i-to-ri*
exhilarate... *egz-il'a-rāt*
exhilaration... *egz-il'a-rā''shun*
exhort... *egz-hort'*
exhortation... *egz-hor-tā'shun*
exhortatory... *egz-hor'ta-to-ri*
exhorter... *egz-hort'ėr*
exhume... *eks'hūm*
exigent... *eks'i-jent*
exigible... *eks'i-ji-bl*
exiguous... *ek-sig'ū-us*
exile... *eks'īl or egz'īl*
exist... *egz-ist'*
existence... *egz-ist'ens*
existent... *egz-ist'ent*
exit... *eks'it*
exodus... *eks'ō-dus*
exogen... *eks'o-jen*
exogenous... *eks-oj'en-us*
exonerate... *egz-on'ē-rāt*
exorable... *eks'ōr-a-bl*
exorbitant... *egz-or'bit-ant*
exorbitantly... *egz-or'bit-ant-li*
exorcise... *eks'or-sīz*
exorcism... *eks'or-sism*
exorcist... *eks'or-sist*
exordium... *egz-or'di-um*
exosmose... *ek'sos-mōs*
exotic... *egz-ot'ik*
expand... *ek-spand'*
expanse... *ek-spans'*
expansible... *ek-spans'i-bl*
expansile... *ek-spans'īl*
expansion... *ek-span'shun*
expansive... *ek-spans'iv*
ex-parte... *eks-par'te*
expatiate... *ek-spā'shi-āt*
expatriate... *eks-pā'tri-āt*
expect... *ek-spekt'*
expectant... *ek-spek'tant*
expectorant... *eks-pek'tō-rant*
expectorate... *eks-pek'tō-rāt*
expedient... *eks-pē'di-ent*
expediently... *eks-pē'di-ent-li*
expedition... *eks-pē-di'shun*
expeditious... *eks-pē-di'shus*

expel... *eks-pel'*
expend... *ek-spend'*
expenditure... *ek-spend'i-tūr*
expense... *ek-spens'*
expensive... *ek-spens'iv*
expensively... *ek-spens'iv-li*
experience... *eks-pē'ri-ens*
experienced... *eks-pē'ri-enst*
experiment... *eks-pe'ri-ment*
expert... *eks-pėrt'*
expertly... *eks-pėrt'li*
expiable... *eks'pi-a-bl*
expiate... *eks'pi-āt*
expiation... *eks-pi-ā'shun*
expiator... *eks'pi-āt-ėr*
expiatory... *eks'pi-a-to-ri*
expiration... *eks-pīr-ā'shun*
expiratory... *eks-pīr'-to-ri*
expire... *eks-pīr'*
expiry... *eks'pi-ri*
explain... *eks-plān'*
explanation... *eks-pla-nā'shun*
expletive... *eks'plēt-iv*
expletory... *eks'ple-to-ri*
explicable... *eks'pli-ka-bl*
explicate... *eks'pli-kāt*
explication... *eks-pli-kā'shun*
explicit... *eks-plis'it*
explicitly... *eks-plis'it-li*
explode... *eks-plō d'*
exploit... *eks-ploit'*
exploitation... *eks-ploi-tā'shun*
exploration... *eks-plō-rā'shun*
explore... *eks-plōr'*
explorer... *eks-plōr'ėr*
explosion... *eks-plō'zhon*
explosive... *eks-plō'siv*
exponent... *eks-pō'nent*
export... *eks-pōrt'*
exportable... *eks-pōrt'a-bli*
exportation... *eks-pōr-tā'shun*
exporter... *eks-pōrt'ėr*
expose... *eks-pōz'*
expose... *eks-po-zā*
exposed... *eks-pōzd'*
exposition... *eks-pō-zi'shun*
expository... *eks-poz'i-to-ri*
expostulate... *eks-pos'tū-lāt*
exposure... *eks-pō-zhūr*
expound... *eks-pound'*
expounder... *eks-pound'ėr*
express... *eks-pres'*
expressible... *eks-pres'i-bl*
expression... *eks-pre'shun*

expressive... *eks-pres'iv*
expressively... *eks-pres'iv-li*
expressly... *eks-pres'li*
expropriate... *eks-prō'pri-āt*
expulsion... *eks-pul'shun*
expulsive... *eks-puls'iv*
expunge... *ek spunj'*
expurgatory... *eks-pėr'ga-to-ri*
exquisite... *eks'kwi-zit*
exscind... *ek-sind'*
extant... *eks'tant*
extempore... *eks-tem'po-rē*
extemporize... *eks-tem'pō-rīz*
extend... *eks-tend'*
extensibility... *eks-ten'si-bil''i-ti*
extensible... *eks-ten'si-bl*
extension... *eks-ten'shun*
extensive... *eks-ten'siv*
extensor... *eks-ten'sėr*
extent... *eks-tent'*
extenuate... *eks-ten'ū-āt*
exterior... *eks-tē'ri-ėr*
exterminate... *eks-tėr'min-āt*
external... *eks-tėr'nal*
externals... *eks-tėr'nalz*
exterritorial... *eks-ter'i-tō''ri-al*
extinct... *ek-stingkt'*
extinction... *ek-stingk'shun*
extinguish... *ek-sting'gwish*
extirpate... *eks-tėrp'āt*
extirpation... *eks-tėrp-ā'shun*
extol... *eks-tol'*
extort... *eks-tort'*
extortion... *eks-tor'shun*
extortionate... *eks-tor'shun-āt*
extra... *eks'tra*
extract... *eks-trakt'*
extraction... *eks-trak'shun*
extractive... *eks-trakt'iv*
extradite... *eks'tra-dīt*
extrados... *eks-trā'dos*
extramural... *eks-tra-mūr'al*
extraneous... *eks-trā'nē-us*
extravasate... *eks-trav'a-sāt*
extreme... *eks-trēm'*
extremely... *eks-trēm'li*
extremist... *eks-trēm'ist*
extremity... *eks-trem'i-ti*
extricable... *eks'tri-ka-bl*
extricate... *eks'tri-kāt*
extrication... *eks-tri-kā'shun*
extrude... *eks-trod'*
extrusion... *eks-tro'zhon*
exuberant... *eks-ū-bė-rant*

exudation... *eks-ūd-ā'shun*
exude... *eks-ūd*
exulcerate... *eg-zul'sėr-āt*
exult... *egz-ult'*
exuviae... *egz-ū'vi-ē*
exuviate... *egz-ū'vi-āt*
eyalet... *ī'a-let*
eyas... *ī'as*
eye... *ī*
eyot... *īot*
eyrie, Eyry... *ī'ri*

F

tabaceous... *fā-ba'shus*
fabian... *fā'bi-an*
fable... *fā'bl*
fabled... *fā'bld*
fabric... *fab'rik*
fabricate... *fab'rik-āt*
fabrication... *fab-rik-ā'shun*
fabricator... *fab'rik-āt-ėr*
fabulist... *fa'bū-list*
fabulous... *fa'bū-lus*
face... *fās*
facet... *fas'et*
facetious... *fa-sē'shus*
facial... *fā'shi-al*
facile... *fa'sil*
facilitate... *fa-sil'it-āt*
facility... *fa-sil'i-ti*
facing... *fās'ing*
facsimile... *fak-sim'i-lē*
fact... *fakt*
faction... *fak'shun*
factionary... *fak'shun-a-ri*
factious... *fak'shus*
factitious... *fak-ti'shus*
factitive... *fak'ti-tiv*
factor... *fak'tėr*
factorage... *fak'tėr-āj*
factory... *fak'to-ri*
factotum... *fak-tō'tum*
facula... *fak'ū-lē*
facultative... *fak'ul-tāt-iv*
faculty... *fak'ul-ti*
fad... *fad*
faddist... *fad'ist*
fade... *fād*
fading... *fād'ing*
fag... *fag*
fahrenheit... *fa'ren-hīt*
faience... *fa-yangs*

fail... fāl
failing... fāl'ing
failure... fāl'ūr
fain... fān
faint... fānt
faint-hearted... fānt'hart-ed
faintly... fānt'li
fairing... fār'ing
fairish... fār'ish
fairly... fār'li
fair-spoken... fār'spōk-en
fairy... fā'ri
faith... fāth
faithful... fāth'ful
faithfully... fāth'ful-li
faithless... fāth'lës
fake... fāk
falange... fal-an'gi
falchion... fal'shun
falcon... fa'kn, or fal'kon
falconer... fa'kn-ėr
falconry... fä'kn-ri
fall... fal
fallaciöus... fal-lā'shus
fallacy... fal'la-si
fallibility... fal-i-bil'i-ti
fallible... fal'i-bl
fallow... fal'ō
false... fals
false-hearted... fals'hart-ed
falsehood... fals'ñod
falsetto... fal-set'tō
falsification... fals'i-fi-kā''shun
falsifier... fals'i-fī-ėr
falsify... fals'i-fī
falsity... fäls'i-ti
falter... fäl'tėr
faltering... fal'tėr-ing
fame... fām
famed... fāmd
fameless... fām'les
familiar... fa-mil'i-ėr
familiarity... fa-mil'i-a''ri-ti
familiarize... fa-mil'i-ėr-īz
family... fam'i-li
famine... fam'in
famish... fam'ish
famous... fām'us
famously... fām'us-li
fan... fan
fanatic... fa-nat'ik
fanatically... fa-nat'ik-al-li
fanaticism... fa-nat'i-sizm
fancied... fan'sid

fancier... fan'si-ėr
fancy... fan'si
fancy-free... fan'si-frē
fandango... fan-dang'gō
fane... fān
fanfare... fan'fār
fanfaron... fan'fa-ron
fanfaronade... fan'fa-ron-ād
fang... fang
fanged... fangd
fanner... fan'ėr
fantail... fan'tāl
fantasia... fan-ta'zē-a
fantasy... fan'ta-si
far... far
farad... far'ad
farce... fars
farcical... fars'ik-al
fardel... far'del
fare... fār
farewell... far'wel
far-fetched... fėr'fect
farina... fa-rī'na
farinaceous... fa-rin-ā'shus
farm... farm
farming... farm'ing
farmost... far'most
farrier... fa'ri-ėr
farriery... fa'ri-ė-ri
farthermost... far'TH ėr-mōst
farthest... far'TH est
farthing... far'TH ing
fascia... fash'i-a
fascicle... fas'si-kl
fascinate... fas'si-nāt
fascinating... fas'si-nāt-ing
fascination... fas-si-nā'shun
fascine... fas-sēn'
fascist... fash'ist
fashion... fa'shun
fashionable... fa'shun-a-bl
fast... fast
fasten... fas'n
fastener... fas'n-ėr
fastening... fas'n-ing
fastidious... fas-tid'i-us
fastness... fast'nes
fat... fat
fatal... fāt'al
fatalist... fāt'al-ist
fatality... fa-tal'i-ti
fatally... fāt'al-li
fate... fāt
fated... fāt'ed

fateful... *fāt'ful*	federalize... *fed'ĕr-al-īz*
father... *fa'THĕr*	federate... *fed'ĕr-āt*
fathom... *faTH'um*	federation... *fed-ĕr-ā'shun*
fatigue... *fa-tēg'*	federative... *fed'ĕr-āt-iv*
fatling... *fat'ling*	fee... *fē*
fatness... *fat'nes*	feeble... *fē'bl*
fatten... *fat'n*	feebly... *fē'bli*
fatty... *fat'i*	feed... *fēd*
fatuity... *fa-tū'i-ti*	feeder... *fēd'ĕr*
fatuous... *fa'tū-us*	feeding... *fēd'ing*
fauces... *fa'sēz*	feel... *fēl*
faucet... *fä'set*	feeler... *fēl'ĕr*
fault... *falf*	feeling... *fēl'ing*
faultily... *falt'i-li*	feet... *fēt*
faultless... *falt'les*	feign... *fān*
faulty... *falt'i*	feigned... *fānd*
faun... *fañ*	feint... *fānt*
fauna... *fa'na*	felicitation... *fē-lis'it-ā''shun*
fauteuil... *fō-tĕ-yė*	felicitous... *fē-lis'it-us*
favorable... *fā'vĕr-a-bl*	felicity... *fē-lis'i-ti*
favored... *fā'vĕrd*	feline... *fē'līn*
favorer... *fā'vĕr-ĕr*	fell... *fel*
favorite... *fā'vĕr-it*	fellow... *fel'ō*
favoritism... *fā'vĕr-it-izm*	fellowship... *fel'ō-ship*
favose... *fa-vōs'*	felon... *fe'lon*
fawn... *fan*	felonious... *fe-lō'ni-us*
fawningly... *fan'ing-li*	felony... *fe'lon-i*
fay... *fā*	felt... *felt*
fealty... *fē'al-ti*	felting... *felt'ing*
fear... *fār*	female... *fē'māl*
fearful... *fēr'ful*	feminine... *fem'in-in*
fearless... *fēr'les*	femur... *fē'mĕr*
feasibility... *fēz-i-bil'i-ti*	fence... *fens*
feasible... *fēz-i-bl*	fencer... *fens'ĕr*
feasibly... *fēz'bli*	fencible... *fen'si-bl*
feast... *fēst*	fencing... *fens'ing*
feat... *fēt*	fend... *fend*
feather... *feTH'ĕr*	fenestration... *fen-es-trā'shun*
feathery... *feTH'ĕr-i*	feracious... *fē-rā'shus*
feature... *fē'tūr*	ferine... *fē'rin*
featured... *fē'tūrd*	ferment... *fĕr'ment*
featureless... *fē'tūr-les*	fermentative... *fĕr-ment'a-tiv*
feaze... *fēz*	fern... *fĕrn*
febrile... *fē'bril*	fernery... *fĕr'nĕr-i*
feces... *fē'sēz*	ferocious... *fē-rō'shus*
feculence... *fe'kū-lens*	ferocity... *fē-ros'i-ti*
feculent... *fe'kū-lent*	ferreous... *fe'rē-us*
fecund... *fē'kund*	ferret... *fe'ret*
fecundate... *fē'kund-āt*	ferriferous... *fe-rif'ĕr-us*
fecundation... *fē-kund-ā'shun*	ferruginous... *fe-rū'jin-us*
fecundity... *fē-kund'i-ti*	ferrule... *fe'rūl*
federal... *fed'ĕr-al*	ferry... *fe'ri*
federalism... *fed'ĕr-al-izm*	field... *fēld*
federalist... *fed'ĕr-al-ist*	field-marshal... *fēld-mar'shal*

F

field-officer... fēld'of-fis-ėr
fiend... fēnd
fiendish... fēnd'ish
fierce... fērs
fiercely... fērs'li
flerily... fī'ė-ri-li
fiery... fī'ė-ri
fifteenth... fif'tēnth
fifth... fifth
fifthly... fifth'li
fiftieth... fif'ti-eth
fifty... fif'ti
fig... fig
fight... fit
fighter... fīt'ėr
fighting... fīt'ing
figment... fig'ment
figurant... fig'ūr-ant
figurate... fig'ūr-āt
figuration... fig-ūr-ā'shun
figurative... fig'ūr-āt-iv
figure... fig'ūr
figured... fig'ūrd
figuring... fig'ūr-ing
filaceous... fil-ā'shus
filament... fil'a-ment
filatory... fil'a-to-ri
filature... fil'a-tūr
filbert... fil'bėrt
filch... filsh or filch
filcher... filsh'ėr
filiate... fil'i-āt
filiation... fil-i-ā'shun
filibuster... fil'i-bus-tėr
filigree... fil'i-grē
filings... fil'ingz
fill... fil
filler... fil'ėr
fillet... fil'et
filling... fil'ing
filly... fil'i
film... film
filmy... film'i
filter... fil'tėr
filth... filth
filthily... filth'i-li
filthy... filth'i
filtrate... fil'trāt
filtration... fil-trā'shun
fin... fin
finable... fīn'a-bl
final... fīn'al
finale... fē-na'lā
finality... fī-nal'i-ti

finally... fīn'al-li
financial... fi-nan'shal
financier... fi-nan'sēr
finch... finsh
find... fīnd
finding... fīnd'ing
fine... fīn
finely... fīn'li
finer... fīn'ėr
finery... fīn'ė-ri
finesse... fi-nes'
finger... fing'gėr
fingered... fing'gėrd
fingering... fing'gėr-ing
finical... fin'i-kal
fining... fīn'ing
finis... fī'nis
finish... fin'ish
finite... fī'nīt
finitely... fī'nīt-li
finless... fin'les
finn... fin
finnish... fin'ish
fiord, Fjord... fyord
fir... fėr
firearm... fīr'arm
fire-engine... fīr'en-jin
fire-escape... fīr'es-kāp
fire-fly... fīr'flī
fireman... fīr'man
fire-proof... fīr'prof
fire-side... fīr'sī d
fire-watcher... fīr-woch'ėr
firework... fīr'wėrk
firing... fīr'ing
firm... fėrm
firmament... fėrm'a-ment
firmly... fėrm'li
first... fėrst
first-born... fėrst'born
first-class... fėrst'klas
first-hand... fėrst'hand
firstling... fėrst'ling
firstly... fėrst'li
first-rate... fėrst'rāt
firth... fėrth
fiscal... fis'kal
fish... fish
fisher... fish'ėr
fishery... fish'ė-ri
fishing... fish'ing
fishmonger... fish'mung-gėr
fishy... fish'i
fissile... fis'sī l

fission... fi'shun
fissure... fi'shūr
fist... fist
fistic... fis'tik
fistula... fis'tū-la
fistular... fis'tū-lèr
fit... fit
fitful... fit'ful
fitly... fit'li
fitter... fit'èr
fitting... fit'ing
fittingly... fit'ing-li
five... fīv
fix... fiks
fixation... fiks-ā'shun
fixative... fiks'a-tiv
fixed... fikst
fixture... fiks'tūr
flabbergast... flab'èr-gast
flaccid... flak'sid
flaccidity... flak-sid'i-ti
flag... flag
flagellant... fla'jel-lant
flagellate... fla'jel-lāt
flagellation... fla-jel-lā'shun
flageolet... fla'jel-et
flagging... flag'ing
flaggy... flag'i
flagitious... fla-ji'shus
flagon... fla'gon
flagrancy... flā'gran-si
flagrant... flā'grant
flagrantly... flā'grant-li
flail... flāl
flake... flāk
flaky... flāk'i
flambeau... flam'bō
flamboyant... flam-boi'ant
flame... flām
flaming... flām'ing
flamingly... flām'ing-li
flamingo... fla-ming'gō
flange... flanj
flannel... flan'el
flap... flap
flap-jack... flap'jak
flapper... flap'èr
flare... flār
flaring... flār'ing
flash... flash
flashily... flash'i-li
flashy... flash'i
flask... flask
flat... flat

flatly... flat'li
flatten... flat'n
flatter... flat'èr
flatterer... flat'èr-èr
flattering... flat'èr-ing
flattery... flat'è-ri
flatulent... flat'ū-lent
flatwise... flat'wīz
flaunt... flant
flavor... flā'vèr
flaw... fla
flawless... fla'les
flax... flaks
flaxy... flaks'i
flea... flē
flea-bite... flē'bī
fleck... flek
flection... flek'shun
fledge... flej
fledgling... flej'ling
flee... flē
fleece... flēs
fleecy... flēs'i
fleer... flēr
fleet... flēt
fleeting... flēt'ing
fleetly... flēt'li
fleming... flem'ing
flemish... flem'ish
flesh... flesh
fleshed... flesht
flesher... flesh'èr
fleshings... flesh'ingz
fleshly... flesh'li
flesh-wound... flesh'wond
fleshy... flesh'i
flex... fleks
flexible... fleks'i-bl
flexile... fleks'īl
flexion... flek'shun
flexure... fleks'ūr
flick... flik
flicker... flik'èr
flight... flīt
flighty... flīt'i
flimsy... flim'zi
flinch... flinsh
fling... fling
flint... flint
flinty... flint'i
flip... flip
flippancy... flip'an-si
flippant... flip'ant
flipper... flip'èr

F

flirt . . . flèrt
flirtation . . . flèrt-ā'shun
float . . . flōt
floatage . . . flōt'āj
floating . . . flōt'ing
flock . . . flok
flood . . . flud
flood-tide . . . flud'tīd
floor . . . flōr
flooring . . . flōr'ing
flop . . . flop
flora . . . flō'ra
floral . . . flō'ral
florescence . . . flō-res'ens
floret . . . flō'ret
floriculture . . . flō'ri-kul-tūr
floriculturist . . . flō'ri-kul-tūr-ist
florist . . . flo'rist
floscule . . . flos'kūl
floss . . . flos
flossy . . . flos'i
flotation . . . flōt-ā'shun
flounce . . . flouns
flounder . . . floun'dèr
flour . . . flour
flourish . . . flu'rish
flourishing . . . flu'rish-ing
flow . . . flō
flower . . . flou'èr
floweret . . . flou'èr-et
flowering . . . flou'èr-ing
flowing . . . flō'ing
fluctuate . . . fluk'tū-āt
fluctuating . . . fluk'tū-āt-ing
fluctuation . . . fluk-tū-ā'shun
fluency . . . flu'en-si
fluent . . . flu'ënt
fluently . . . flu'ent-li
fluff . . . fluf
fluid . . . flu'id
fluidity . . . flu-id'i-tl
fluke . . . flok
flurry . . . flu'ri
flush . . . flush
fluster . . . flus'tèr
flute . . . flot
fluted . . . flot'ed
fluting . . . flot'ing
flutist . . . flot'ist
flutter . . . flut'èr
fluty . . . flot'l
fluvial . . . flo'vi-al
fluviatile . . . flo'vi-a-fīl
flux . . . fluks

fluxion . . . fluk'shun
fly-paper . . . flī'pā-pèr
fly-wheel . . . flī'whèl
foam . . . fōm
foamy . . . fōm'i
focal . . . fō'kal
focus . . . fō'kus
foe . . . fō
foeman . . . fō'man
fog . . . fog
fogey . . . fō'gi
foggage . . . fog'āj
foggy . . . fog'i
foil . . . foil
fold . . . fōld
folder . . . fōld'èr
foliage . . . fō'li-āj
foliate . . . fō'li-āt
foliated . . . fō'li-āt-ed
foliation . . . fō-li'ā'shun
folio . . . fō'li-ō
folk . . . fōk
folk-lore . . . fōk'lōr
follicle . . . fol'li-kl
follow . . . fol'ō
following . . . fol'ō-ing
folly . . . fol'i
foment . . . fō-ment'
fomentation . . . fō-ment-ā'shun
fomenter . . . fō-ment'èr
fond . . . fond
fondle . . . fon'dl
fondly . . . fond'li
fondness . . . fond'nes
font . . . font
food . . . fod
fool . . . fol
foolery . . . fol'è-ri
foolhardy . . . fol'har-di
foolish . . . fol'ish
foolishly . . . fol'ish-li
foot . . . fut
football . . . fut'bal
foothold . . . fut'hōld
footing . . . fut'ing
footprint . . . fut'print
footstep . . . fut'step
footstool . . . fut'stol
for . . . for
forager . . . fo'rāj-èr
forasmuch . . . for-az-much'
foray . . . fo'rā
forbear . . . for-bār'
forbearance . . . for-bār'ans

forbearing... *for-bār'ing*
forbid... *for-bid'*
forbidden... *for-bid'n*
forbidding... *for-bid'ing*
force... *fōrs*
forced... *fōrst*
forceful... *fōrs'ful*
forceless... *fōrs'les*
forceps... *for'seps*
forcible... *fōrs'i-bl*
forcing... *fōrs'ing*
ford... *fōrd*
fordable... *fōrd'a-bl*
fore... *fōr*
fore-and-aft... *fōr'and-aft*
forearm... *fōr'arm'*
forebode... *fōr-bōd'*
forecast... *fōr-kast'*
foreclose... *fōr-klōz'*
forefather... *fōr'fa-ᖶHèr*
forefinger... *fōr'fing-gèr*
forefront... *fōr'frunt*
forego... *fōr-gō'*
foregone... *fōr-gon'*
foreground... *fōr'ground*
forehand... *fōr'hand*
forehanded... *fōr'hand-ed*
forehead... *fōr'hed or fo'red*
foreign... *fo'rin*
foreigner... *fo'rin-èr*
forejudge... *fōr-juj'*
foreknowledge... *fōr-nol'ej*
foreman... *fōr'man*
foremost... *fōr'mōst*
forenoon... *fōr'non*
forensic... *fō-ren'sik*
forepart... *fōr'part*
forerun... *fōr-run'*
foresaid... *fōr'sed*
foresail... *fōr'sāl*
foresee... *fōr-sē'*
foreshadow... *fōr-sha'dō*
foreshore... *fōr'shōr*
forest... *fo'rest*
forestall... *fōr-stal'*
forester... *fo'rest-èr*
forestry... *fo'rest-ri*
foretell... *fōr-tel'*
forethought... *fōr'that*
foretoken... *fōr-tō'kn*
foretop... *fōr'top*
forever... *for-ev'èr*
forewarn... *fōr-warn'*
foreword... *fōr'wèrd*

forfeit... *for'fit*
forfeitable... *for'fit-a-bl*
forfeiture... *for'fit-ūr*
forge... *fōrj*
forger... *fōrj'èr*
forgery... *fōrj'è-ri*
forget... *for-get'*
forgetful... *for-get'ful*
forgetfulness... *for-get'ful-nes*
forging... *fōrj'ing*
forgive... *for-giv'*
forgiveness... *for-giv'nes*
forgiving... *for-giv'ing*
fork... *fork*
forked... *forkt*
forlorn... *for-lorn'*
form... *form*
formal... *form'al*
formalism... *form'al-izm*
formalist... *form'al-ist*
formality... *form-al'i-ti*
formally... *form'al-li*
format... *for'ma*
formation... *form-ā'shun*
formative... *form'at-iv*
former... *form'èr*
formerly... *form'èr-li*
formic... *for'mik*
formicary... *for'mi-ka-ri*
formidable... *for'mid-a-bl*
formless... *form'les*
formula... *for'mū-la*
formulary... *for'mū-la-ri*
formulate... *for'mū-lāt*
fornicate... *for'ni-kāt*
fornication... *for-ni-kā'shun*
fornicator... *for'ni-kāt-èr*
forswear... *for-swār'*
fort... *fōrt*
forte... *fōr'tā*
forte... *fōrt*
forth... *fōrth*
forthcoming... *fōrth-kum'ing*
forthright... *forth'rīt*
forthwith... *fōrth-with'*
fortification... *for'ti-fi-kā''shun*
fortify... *for'ti-fī*
fortitude... *for'ti-tūd*
fortress... *fort'res*
fortuitous... *for-tū'it-us*
fortunate... *for'tū-nāt*
fortunately... *for'tū-nāt-li*
fortune... *for'tūn*
fortune-teller... *for'tūn-tel-èr*

F

forty . . . for'tl
forum . . . fō'rum
forward . . . for'wėrd
forwardly . . . for'wėrd-li
forwardness . . . for'wėrd-nes
forwards . . . for'wėrdz
fossil . . . fos'sil
fossilize . . . fos'sil-īz
fossorial . . . fos-sō'ri-al
foster . . . fos'tėr
foster-child . . . fos'tėr-chīld
foul . . . foul
foul-mouthed . . . foul'mouℸHd
found . . . found
foundation . . . found-ā'shun
founder . . . found'ėr
foundery . . . found'ė-ri
foundling . . . found'ling
foundry . . . found'ri
fount . . . fount
fountain . . . fount'ān
fountainhead . . . fount'ān-hed
fountain-pen . . . fount'ān-pēn
four . . . fōr
fourfold . . . fōr'fōld
fourscore . . . fōr'skōr
fourteen . . . fōr'tēn
fourteenth . . . fōr'tēnth
fourth . . . fōrth
fowl . . . foul
fowler . . . foul'ėr
fox-hound . . . foks'hound
fox-trot . . . foks-trot
foxy . . . foks'i
fraction . . . frak'shun
fractional . . . frak'shun-al
fractious . . . frak'shus
fracture . . . frak'tūr
fragment . . . frag'ment
fragmentary . . . frag'ment-a-ri
fragrant . . . frā'grant
frail . . . frāl
frailty . . . frāl'tl
frame . . . frām
framework . . . frām'wėrk
framing . . . frām'ing
franc . . . frangk
franchise . . . fran'chīz
franciscan . . . fran-sis'kan
francolin . . . frang'ko-lin
frangibility . . . fran-ji-bil'i-ti
frangible . . . fran'ji-bl
frank . . . frangk'
frank . . . frangk

frankincense . . . frangk'in-sens
frantic . . . fran'tik
fraternal . . . fra-tėr'nal
fraternity . . . fra-tėr'ni-ti
fraternize . . . frat'ėr-nīz
fratricidal . . . fra-tri-sī d'al
fratricide . . . fra'tri-sīd
fraud . . . frad
fraudful . . . frad'ful
fraudfully . . . frad'ful-li
fraudulent . . . frad'ū-lent
fraudulently . . . frad'ū-lent-li
fraught . . . frat
fray . . . frā
freak . . . frēk
freakish . . . frēk'ish
freckle . . . frek'l
freckly . . . frek'li
free . . . frē
freeborn . . . frē'born
freedom . . . frē'dum
freehand . . . frē'hand
freehanded . . . frē'hand-ed
freehold . . . frē'hōld
freeholder . . . frē'hōld-ėr
freely . . . frē'li
freeman . . . frē'man
freemason . . . frē'mā-sn
freemasonry . . . frē'mā-sn-ri
freeness . . . frē'nes
free-will . . . frē'wil
freeze . . . frēz
freezing . . . frēz'ing
freight . . . frāt
freightage . . . frāt'āj
freighter . . . frāt'ėr
french . . . frensh
frenetic . . . fre-net'ik
frenzied . . . fren'zid
frenzy . . . fren'zi
frequency . . . frē'kwen-si
frequent . . . frē'kwent
frequently . . . frē'kwent-li
fresh . . . fresh
freshen . . . fresh'n
freshly . . . fresh'li
freshman . . . fresh'man
fret . . . fret
fretful . . . fret'ful
friar . . . frī'ėr
fricassee . . . fri-kas-sē'
friction . . . frik'shun
friend . . . frend
friendless . . . frend'les

friendliness... *frend'li-nes*
friendly... *frend'li*
friendship... *frend'ship*
frieze... *frēz*
friezed... *frēzd*
frigate... *fri'gāt*
fright... *frīt*
frighten... *frīt'n*
frightful... *frīt'ful*
frightfully... *frīt'ful-li*
frigid... *fri'jid*
frigidity... *fri-jid'i-ti*
frigidly... *frij'id-li*
frill... *fril*
frilling... *fril'ing*
fringe... *frinj*
fringed... *frinjd*
frisk... *frisk*
frisket... *fris'ket*
fritter... *frit'ėr*
frivolity... *fri-vol'i-ti*
frivolous... *fri'vol-us*
frizz... *friz*
frizzle... *friz'l*
fro... *frō*
frock... *frok*
frog... *frog*
frolic... *fro'lik*
frolicsome... *fro'lik-sum*
from... *from*
frond... *frond*
frondescence... *frond-es'ens*
front... *frunt*
frontage... *frunt'āj*
frontal... *frunt'al*
fronted... *frunt'ed*
frontier... *fron'tēr*
frontless... *frunt'les*
frost... *frost*
frost-bite... *frost'bīt*
frostily... *frost'i-li*
frosting... *frost'ing*
frosty... *frost'i*
frothy... *froth'i*
frounce... *frouns*
froward... *frō'wėrd*
frown... *froun*
frozen... *frōz'en*
fructescence... *fruk-tes'ens*
fructiferous... *fruk-tif'ėr-us*
fructify... *fruk'ti-fī*
frugal... *fro'gal*
frugality... *fro-gal'i-ti*
frugally... *fro'gal-li*

frugiferous... *fro-jif'ėr-us*
fruit... *frot*
fruitage... *frot'āj*
fruiterer... *frot'ėr-ėr*
fruitfully... *frot'ful-li*
fruition... *fro-i'shun*
fruitless... *frot'les*
fruity... *fro'ti*
frustrate... *frus'trāt*
frustration... *frus-trā'shun*
fry... *fri*
fuchsia... *fū'shi-a*
fudge... *fuj*
fugacious... *fū-gā'shus*
fugacity... *fū-gas'i-ti*
fugitive... *fū-jit-iv*
fugue... *fūg*
fulcrum... *ful'krum*
fulfill... *ful-fil'*
fulfillment... *ful-fil'ment*
fulgency... *ful'jen-si*
fulgent... *ful'jent*
fuliginous... *fū-lij'in-us*
full... *ful*
full-blown... *ful'blōn*
fuller... *ful'ėr*
fulling... *ful'ing*
fully... *ful'li*
fulmar... *ful'mar*
fulminate... *ful'min-āt*
fulmination... *ful-min-ā'shun*
fulness... *ful'nes*
fumble... *fŭm'bli*
fume... *fūm*
fumigate... *fūm'i-gāt*
fumigation... *fūm-i-gā'shun*
fumy... *fūm-'i*
function... *fungk'shun*
functional... *fungk'shun-al*
functionary... *fungk'shun-a-ri*
fund... *fund*
fundament... *fun'da-ment*
fundamental... *fun-da-ment'al*
funeral... *fū'nė-ral*
funereal... *fū-nē'rė-al*
fungous... *fung'gus*
fungus... *fung'gus*
funicle... *fū'ni-kl*
funicular... *fū-nik'ū-lėr*
funnel... *fun'el*
funnily... *fun'i-li*
funny... *fun'i*
fur... *fėr*
furbish... *fėr'bish*

furbisher... fėr'bish-ėr
furious... fū'ri-us
furiously... fū'ri-us-li
furl... fėrl
furlong... fėr'long
furlough... fėr'lō
furnace... fėr'nās
furniture... fėr'ni-tūr
furrier... fu'ri-ėr
furriery... fu'ri-ė-ri
furrow... fu'rō
furrowy... fu'rō-i
furry... fėr'i
further... fėr'ᵀHėr
furtive... fėr'tiv
furtively... fėr'tiv-li
fury... fū'ri
fuscous... fus'kus
fuse... fūz
fuse... fūz
fuselage... fū'sel-āj
fusel-oil... fū'zel-oil
fusible... fūz'i-bl
fusil... fū'sil
fusilier... fū-sil-ēr'
fusillade... fū'zi-lād
fusion... fū'zhon
fuss... fus
fussily... fus'i-li
fussy... fus'i
fustic... fus'tik
future... fū'tūr
futurity... fū-tūr'i-ti
fuzz... fuz
fuzzy... fuz'i

G

gab... gab
gabble... gab'l
gabion... gā'bi-on
gable... gā'bl
gaby... gā'bi
gad... gad
gadder... gad'ėr
gadget... gad'jet
gadhelic... gad'e-lik
gael... gāl
gaelic... gāl'ik
gaff... gaf
gaffer... gaf'ėr
gag... gag

gage... gāj
gaiety... gā'e-ti
gaily... gā'li
gain... gān
gainful... gān'ful
gainless... gān'les
gainsay... gān'sā
gainsayer... gān'sā-ėr
gait... gāt
gaiter... gā'tėr
gala... gal'a
galantine... gal-an-tēn'
galaxy... ga'lak-si
gale... gāl
galena... ga-lē'na
gall... gal
gallant... gal'ant
gallantly... gal'ant-li
gallantry... gal'ant-ri
galleon... gal'ē-un
gallery... gal'ė-ri
galley... gal'i
gallic... gal'ik
gallic... gal'ik
gallicism... gal'i-sizm
gallinaceous... gal-li-nā'shus
galling... gal'ing
gallipot... gal'li-pot
gallon... gal'lun
gallop... gal'up
gallopade... gal-up-ād'
galloper... gal'up-ėr
gallows... gal'ōz
galop... ga-lop'
galore... ga-lōr,'
galvanic... gal-van'ik
galvanism... gal'van-izm
galvanist... gal'van-ist
galvanize... gal'van-īz
gambit... gam'bit
gamble... gam'bl
gambler... gam'bl-ėr
gambling... gam'bl-ing
gamboge... gam-bōj'
gambol... gam'bol
gambrel... gam'brel
game... gām
gamekeeper... gām'kēp-ėr
gamesome... gām'sum
gamester... gām'stėr
gamin... gam'in
gaming... gām'ing
gammer... gam'ėr
gamut... gam'ut

gander... gan'dèr
gang... gang
gangliated... gang'gli-āt-ed
ganglion... gang'gli-on
ganglionic... gang-gli-on'ik
gangrene... gang'grēn
gangrenous... gang'grēn-us
gangster... gang'stėr
gangway... gang'wā
gannet... gan'et
ganoid... gan'oid
gaol... jāl
gap... gap
gape... gāp
garage... gar'aj
garb... garb
garbage... garb'āj
garble... gar'bl
garden... gar'dn
gardener... gar'dn-ėr
gardening... gar'dn-ing
gargle... gar'gl
gargoyle... gar'goil
garland... gar'land
garlic... gar'lik
garment... gar'ment
garner... gar'nėr
garnet... gar'net
garnish... gar'nish
garniture... gar'ni-tūr
garret... ga'ret
garrison... ga'ri-sn
garrotte... ga-rot'
garrotter... ga-rot'ėr
garrulity... ga-rū'li-ti
garrulous... ga'rū-lus
garter... gar'tėr
gas... gas
gascon... gas'kon
gasconade... gas-kon-ād'
gaseous... gā'sē-us
gas-fitter... gas'fit-ėr
gash... gash
gasholder... gas'hōld-ėr
gasification... gas'i-fi-kā''shun
gasify... gas'i-fī
gasket... gas'ket
gasogene... gas'o-jēn
gasometer... gaz-om'et-ėr
gasp... gasp
gastric... gas'trik
gastronomy... gas-tron'o-mi
gate... gāt
gate-crasher... gāt-krash'ėr

gateway... gāt'wā
gather... gaꞮH'ėr
gathering... gaꞮH'ėr-ing
gaucherie... gōsh-rē
gaucho... gou'chō
gaud... gad
gaudily... gad'i-li
gaudy... gad'i
gauge... gāj
gaul... gal
gaunt... gänt
gauntlet... gant'let
gauze... gaz̈
gauzy... gäz'i
gavotte... ga-vot'
gawky... gak'i
gay... gā̈
gazelle... ga-zel'
gazette... ga-zet'
gazetteer... ga-zet-tēr'
gazing-stock... gēz'ing-stok
gear... gēr
gearing... gēr'ing
geese... gēs
gelatine... jel'a-tin
gelatinous... je-lat'in-us
geld... geld
gelding... geld'ing
gelid... je'lid
gem... jem
geminate... jem'i-nāt
gemini... jem'i-nī
gemma... jem'a
gemmation... jem'ē'shun
gemmeous... jem'ē-us
gemmy... jem'i
gendarme... zhang-darm
gender... jen'dėr
genalogist... jen-ē-al'o-jist
genealogy... jen-ē-al'o-ji
genera... jen'è-ra
general... jen'è-ral
generality... jen-è-ral'i-ti
generalize... jen'è-ral-īz
generally... jen'è-ral-li
generate... jen'è-rāt
generation... jen-è-rā'shun
generative... jen'è-rāt-iv
generator... jen'è-rāt-ėr
generically... jē-ne'rik-al-li
generosity... jen-è-ros'i-ti
generous... jen'è-rus
generously... jen'è-rus-li
genesis... jen'e-sis

geneva... je-nē'va
genial... jē'ni-al
geniality... jē-ni-al'i-ti
genially... jē'ni-al-li
genital... jen'it-al
genitals... jen'it-alz
genitive... jen'it-iv
genius... je'ni-us
genteel... jen-tēl
genteelly... jen-tēl'li
gentian... jen'shan
gentility... jen-til'i-ti
gentle... jen'tl
gentleman... jen'tl-man
gentleness... jen'tl-nes
gently... jen'tli
gentry... jen'tri
genuflection... jen-ū-flek'shun
genuine... jen'ū-in
genus... jē'nus
geodesy... jē-od'e-si
geographer... jē-og'ra-fėr
geography... jē-og'ra-fi
geological... jē-o-loj'ik-al
geologist... jē-ol'o-jist
geology... jē-ol'o-ji
geomancy... jē'o-man-si
geometer... jē-om'et-ėr
geometry... jē-om'e-tri
georgic... jorj'ik
geothermic... jē-o-thėr'mik
geranium... jė-rā'ni-um
germ... jėrm
german... jėr'man
german... jėr'man
germanic... jėr-man'ik
germinal... jėrm'in-al
germinate... jėrm'in-āt
gerund... je'rund
gerundial... je-run'di-al
gestapo... ges-ta'pō
gestation... jest-ā'shun
gesticulate... jes-tik'ū-lāt
gesture... jes'tūr
get... get
get-up... get'up
geyser... gī'zėr
ghastly... gast'li
ghee... gē
gherkin... gėr'kin
ghetto... get'to
ghost... gōst
ghostly... gōst'li
ghoul... gol

giant... jī'ant
giaour... jour
gibberish... gib'bėr-ish
gibbet... jib'bet
gibbon... gib'on
gibe... jīb
giber... jī'b'ėr
gibingly... jī'b'ing-li
giblet... jib'let
giddy... gid'i
gift... gift
gifted... gift'ed
gig... gig
gigantic... jī-gan'tik
giggle... gig'l
giglet... gig'let
gigot... jig'ot
gilbertian... gil-bėr'shan
gild... gild
gild... gild
gilder... gild'ėr
gilding... gild'ing
gill... gil
gill... jil
gimbals... jim'balz
gimlet... gim'let
gimp... gimp
gin... jin
ginger... jin'jėr
gingham... ging'am
ginseng... jin'seng
gipsy... jip'si
giraffe... ji-raf'
gird... gėrd
girder... gėrd'ėr
girdle... gėr'dl
girl... gėrl
girlhood... gėrl'hud
girlish... gėrl'ish
girt... gėrt
girth... gėrth
gist... jist
give... giv
giver... giv'ėr
gizzard... giz'ėrd
glacial... glā'shi-al
glacier... glā'shi-ėr
glacis... glā'sis
glad... glad
gladden... glad'n
glade... glād
gladiator... glad'i-ā-tėr
gladiatorial... glad'i-a-tō''ri-al
gladly... glad'li

gladsome... glad'sum
glair... glār
glamor... glam'ėr
glance... glans
gland... gland
glanders... glan'dėrz
glandular... gland'ū-lėr
glandule... gland'ūl
glare... glār
glaring... glār'ing
glaringly... glār'ing-li
glass... glas
glass-work... glas'wėrk
glass... glas'i
glaucous... gla̤'kus
glaze... glāz
glazer... glā'zėr
glazier... glā'zhėr
glazing... glāz'ing
gleam... glēm
gleamy... glēm'i
glean... glēn
gleaner... glēn'ėr
glede... glēd
glee... glē
gleeful... glē'fṳl
glen... glen
glide... glīd
glider... glīd'ėr
glimmer... glim'ėr
glimmering... glim'ėr-ing
glimpse... glimps
glint... glint
glisten... glis'n
glister... glis'tėr
glitter... glit'ėr
gloaming... glōm'ing
gloat... glōt
globe... glōb
globular... glob'ū-lėr
globule... glob'ūl
globulin... glob'ū-lin
glomerate... glom'ė-rāt
glomeration... glom-ė-rā'shun
gloom... glom
gloomily... glom-i-li
gloomy... glom'i
glorify... glō'ri-fī
gloriole... glō'ri-ōl
glorious... glō'ri-us
gloriously... glō'ri-us-li
glory... glō'ri
gloss... glos
glossarial... glos-sā'ri-al

glossary... glos'a-ri
glosser... glos'ėr
glossy... glos'i
glottis... glot'is
glove... gluv
glover... gluv'ėr
glow... glō
glowing... glō'ing
glucose... glo'kōs
glue... glo
gluey... glo'i
glum... glum
glume... glom
glut... glut
gluten... glo'ten
glutinate... glo'tin-āt
glutinous... glo'tin-us
gluttonize... glut'n-īz
gluttonous... glut'n-us
gluttony... glut'n-i
glycerine... glis'ėr-in
glyphic... glif'ik
glyptic... glip'tik
glyptography... glip-tog'ra-fi
gnarl... narl
gnarled... narld
gnash... nash
gnat... nat
gnaw... na
gnome... nōm
gnomic... nō'mik
gnomon... nō'mon
gnostic... nos'tik
gnosticism... nos'ti-sizm
gnu... nū
go... gō
goad... gōd
goal... gōl
goat... gōt
goatish... gōt'ish
goat-skin... gōt'skin
gobble... gob'l
gobbler... gob'lėr
go-between... gō'bē-twēn
goblet... gob'let
goblin... gob'lin
goby... gō'bi
go-by... gō-bī'
god... god
goddess... god'es
godfather... god'fa-ᴛHėr
godless... god'les
godlike... god'līk
godliness... god'li-nes

G

godly... *god'li*
godsend... *god'send*
godship... *god'ship*
god-speed... *god'spēd*
godwit... *god'wit*
goer... *gō'ėr*
goffer... *gof'ėr*
goggle... *gog'l*
going... *gō'ing*
goiter... *goi'tėr*
gold... *gōld*
golden... *gōld'n*
gold-field... *gōld'fēld*
goldfinch... *gōld'finsh*
gold-fish... *gōld'fish*
gold-leaf... *gōld'lēf*
goldsmith... *gōld'smith*
goldylocks... *gōld'i-loks*
golf... *golf*
golfer... *gol'fėr*
golfing... *golf'ing*
gondola... *gon'dō-la*
gondolier... *gon-dō-lēr'*
gong... *gong*
goniometer... *gō-ni-om'et-ėr*
good... *gud*
good-bye... *gud-bī'*
good-day... *gud-dā'*
good-humor... *gud-hū'mėr*
goodly... *gud'li*
good-nature... *gud-nā'tūr*
goodness... *gud'nes*
good-night... *gud-nīt'*
good-sense... *gud-sens'*
good-will... *gud-wil'*
goose... *gos*
gooseberry... *gos'be-ri*
goosery... *gos'ė-ri*
gopher... *gō'fėr*
gore... *gōr*
gorge... *gorj*
gorgeous... *gor'jus*
gorget... *gor'jet*
gorgon... *gor'gon*
gorgonzola... *gor-gon-zō'la*
gorilla... *gor-il'la*
gormand... *gor'mand*
gorse... *gors*
gory... *gō'ri*
goshawk... *gos'hak*
gosling... *goz'ling*
gospel... *gos'pel*
gospeller... *gos'pel-ėr*
gossamer... *gos'a-mėr*

gossip... *gos'ip*
gossipry... *gos'ip-ri*
gossipy... *gos'ip-i*
goth... *goth*
gothic... *goth'ik*
gouda... *gou'da*
gouge... *gouj, goj*
gourd... *gord*
gourmand... *gor'mand*
gourmandize... *gor'mand-īz*
gourmet... *gor-mā or gor'met*
gout... *gout*
gout... *go*
gouty... *gout'i*
govern... *gu'vėrn*
governable... *gu'vėrn-a-bl*
governance... *gu'vėrn-ans*
governess... *gu'vėrn-es*
government... *gu'vėrn-ment*
governor... *gu'vėrn-ėr*
gown... *goun*
grab... *grab*
grace... *grās*
graceful... *grās'ful*
gracefully... *grās'ful-li*
graceless... *grās'les*
gracile... *gras'īl*
gracious... *grā'shus*
graciously... *grā'shus-li*
gradatory... *grā'da-to-ri*
grade... *grād*
gradient... *grā'di-ent*
gradual... *grad'ū-al*
gradually... *grad'ū-al-li*
graduate... *grad'ū-āt*
graduation... *grad-ū-ā'shun*
graft... *graft*
grain... *grān*
grained... *grānd*
graining... *grān'ing*
grallatorial... *gral-a-tō'ri-al*
gram... *gram*
grammar... *gram'ėr*
grammarian... *gram-mā'ri-an*
grampus... *gram'pus*
granary... *grā'na-ri*
grand... *grand*
grandam... *gran'dam*
grandchild... *grand'chīld*
grandee... *gran-dē'*
grandeur... *grand'yūr*
grandfather... *grand'fa-ŦHėr*
grandiose... *gran'di-ōs*
grandsire... *grand'sīr*

grandson... *grand'sun*
grand-stand... *grand'stand*
grange... *grānj*
granite... *gran'ĭt*
granitic... *gran-ĭt'ĭk*
grant... *grant*
grantor... *grant'or*
granular... *gran'ū-lėr*
granulate... *gran'ū-lāt*
granulation... *gran-ū-lā'shun*
granule... *gran'ūl*
grape... *grāp*
grapefruit... *grāp'frot*
graph... *graf*
graphic... *graf'ik*
graphically... *graf'ik-al-li*
graphite... *graf'īt*
grapnel... *grap'nel*
grapple... *grap'l*
graphy... *grāp'i*
grasp... *grasp*
grasping... *grasp'ing*
grass... *gras*
grate... *grāt*
gratify... *grat'i-fī*
gratifying... *grat'i-fī-ing*
grating... *grāt'ing*
gratis... *grā'tis*
gratitude... *grat'i-tūd*
gratuitous... *gra-tū'it-us*
gratuitously... *gra-tū'it-us-li*
gratuity... *gra-tū'i-ti*
gratulate... *grat'ū-lāt*
gratulation... *grat-ū-lā'shun*
gratulatory... *grat'ū-la-to-ri*
grave... *grāv*
grave-digger... *grāv'dig-ėr*
gravel... *gra'vel*
gravelly... *gra'vel-i*
gravely... *grāv'li*
graver... *grāv'ėr*
gravid... *grav'id*
gravitate... *grav'i-tāt*
gravitation... *grav-i-tā'shun*
gravity... *grav'i-ti*
gravy... *grā'vi*
gray... *grā*
grayish... *grā'ish*
grayling... *grā'ling*
grazier... *grā'zhėr*
grazing... *grāz'ing*
grease... *grēs*
greasy... *grēz'i*
great... *grāt*

great-hearted... *grāt'hart-ed*
greatly... *grāt'li*
greatness... *grāt'nes*
greave... *grēv*
grecian... *grē'shan*
greed... *grēd*
greedily... *grēd'i-li*
greedy... *grēd'i*
greek... *grēk*
green... *grēn*
greenhorn... *grēn'horn*
greenhouse... *grēn'hous*
greenish... *grēn'ish*
greenness... *grēn'nes*
green-room... *grēn'rom*
greet... *grēt*
greeting... *grēt'ing*
gregorian... *gre-gō'ri-an*
grenade... *gre-nād'*
grenadier... *gren-a-dēr'*
grey... *grā*
greyhound... *grā'hound*
grice... *grīs*
griddle... *grid'l*
gride... *grīd*
gridiron... *grid'ī-ėrn*
grief... *grēf*
grievance... *grēv'ans*
grieve... *grēv*
grievous... *grēv'us*
grill... *gril*
grim... *grim*
grimace... *gri-mās'*
grime... *grīm*
grimly... *grim'li*
grimy... *grīm'i*
grin... *grin*
grind... *grīnd*
grinder... *grīnd'ėr*
grindstone... *grīnd'stōn*
grip... *grip*
griping... *grīp'ing*
grisette... *gri-zet'*
grisly... *griz'li*
grist... *grist*
gristle... *gris'l*
gristly... *gris'li*
grit... *grit*
gritty... *grit'i*
grizzle... *griz'l*
grizzled... *griz'ld*
grizzly... *griz'li*
groan... *grōn*
groat... *grōt*

G

groats... grōts
grocer... grō'sėr
grocery... grō'sė-ri
grog... grog
groggy... grog'i
groin... groin
groined... groind
groom... grom
groove... grov
grope... grōp
gropingly... grōp'ing-li
grossly... grōs'li
grot... grot
grotesque... grō-tesk'
grotto... grot'tō
ground... ground
ground-floor... ground'flōr
groundless... ground'les
groundling... ground'ling
groundsel... ground'sel
ground-swell... ground'swel
groundwork... ground'wėrk
group... grop
grouping... grop'ing
grouse... grous
grout... grout
grove... grōv
grovel... gro'vel
groveller... gro'vel-ėr
grovelling... gro'vel-ing
grow... grō
grower... grō'ėr
growl... groul
growler... groul'ėr
grown... grōn
groyne... groin
grub... grub
grubber... grub'ėr
grudge... gruj
grudgingly... gruj'ing-li
gruel... grū'el
gruesome... gro'sum
gruff... gruf
gruffly... gruf'li
grum... grum
grumble... grum'bl
grumbler... grum'bl-ėr
grume... grom
grunt... grunt
grunter... grunt'ėr
guarantee... ga-ran-tē'
guarantor... gar-an-tor'
guard... gard
guardedly... gard'ed-li

guardian... gard'i-an
guardianship... gard'i-an-ship
guardsman... gardz'man
gudgeon... gu'jon
guerdon... gėrdon
guess... ges
guess-work... ges'wėrk
guest... gest
guggle... gug'l
guidance... gīd'ans
guide... gīd
guide-book... gīd'buk
guide-post... gīd'pōst
guild... gild
guilder... gil'der
guile... gīl
guileful... gīl'ful
guileless... gīl'les
guillotine... gil-ō-tēn'
guilt... gilt
guiltily... gilt'i-li
guiltless... gilt'les
guilty... gilt'i
guinea... gin'ē
guinea-pig... gin'ē-pig
guipure... gē-pūr'
guise... gīz
guitar... gi-tar'
gulch... gulch
gull... gul
gullet... gul'et
gullible... gul'i-bl
gully... gul'i
gulp... gulp
gum... gum
gumption... gum'shun
gun... gun
gunman... gun'man
gunner... gun'ėr
gunnery... gun'ė-ri
gunpowder... gun'pou-dėr
gunshot... gun'shot
gurgle... gėr'gl
gush... gush
gusset... gus'et
gust... gust
gut... gut
gutter... gut'ėr
guy... gī
guzzle... guz'l
gymnasium... jim-n'zi-um
gymnast... jim'nast
gymnastic... jim-nast'ik
gyneolatry... jin-ē-ol'a-tri

gypseous... *jip'sē-us*
gypsy... *jip'si*
gyrate... *jī'rāt*
gyration... *jī-rā'shun*
gyre... *jīr*

H

habiliment... *ha-bil'i-ment*
habilitate... *ha-bil'i-tāt*
habit... *ha'bit*
habitable... *ha'bit-a-bl*
habitat... *ha'bit-at*
habitation... *ha-bit-ā'shon*
habited... *ha'bit-ed*
habitual... *ha-bit'ū-al*
habitually... *ha-bit'ū-al-li*
habituate... *ha-bit'ū-āt*
habitude... *ha'bit-ūd*
hack... *hak*
hackery... *hak'ėr-i*
hacking... *hak'ing*
hackle... *hak'l*
hackney... *hak'ni*
hackneyed... *hak'nid*
hades... *hā'dēz*
haft... *haft*
hag... *hag*
haggard... *hag'ard*
haggis... *hag'is*
haggish... *hag'ish*
haggle... *hag'l*
ha-ha... *ha'ha*
hail... *hāl*
hailstone... *hāl'stōn*
hair... *hār*
hair-dresser... *hār'dres-ėr*
hairless... *hār'les*
hair-splitting... *hār'split-ing*
hairy... *hār'i*
halberdier... *hal-bėrd-ēr'*
halcyon... *hal'si-on*
hale... *hāl*
half... *haf*
half-back... *haf-bak*
half-brother... *haf'bruᵗH-ėr*
half-dead... *haf-ded'*
half-hearted... *haf-hart'ed*
half-length... *haf'length*
half-sister... *haf'sis-tėr*
half-witted... *haf-wit'ed*
halibut... *ha'li-but*

hall... *hal*
halleluiah... *hal-lē-lu'ya*
hall-mark... *hal'mark*
hallo... *ha-lō'*
hallow... *hal'ō*
halo... *hā'lō*
halt... *halt*
halter... *hal'tėr*
halve... *häv*
ham... *ham*
hamlet... *ham'let*
hammer... *ham'ėr*
hammock... *ham'ok*
hamper... *ham'pėr*
hamstring... *ham'string*
hand... *hand*
handbill... *hand'bil*
handbook... *hand'buk*
handbreadth... *hand'bredth*
handcuff... *hand'kuf*
handed... *hand'ed*
handicap... *hand'i-kap*
handicraft... *hand'i-kraft*
handily... *hand'i-li*
handiwork... *hand'i-wėrk*
handkerchief... *hand'kėr-chif*
handle... *hand'dl*
handmaid... *hand'mād*
handrail... *hand'rāl*
handsome... *hand'sum*
handsomely... *hand'sum-li*
handwriting... *hand-rīt'ing*
handy... *hand'i*
hang... *hang*
hangar... *hang'ar*
hanger... *hang'ėr*
hanger-on... *hang'ėr-on'*
hanging... *hang'ing*
hank... *hangk*
hanker... *hang'kėr*
hap... *hap*
haphazard... *hap-ha'zėrd*
hapless... *hap'les*
haply... *hap'li*
happen... *hap'n*
happiness... *hap'i-nes*
happy... *hap'i*
harass... *ha'ras*
harassing... *ha'ras-ing*
harbinger... *har'bin-jėr*
harbor... *har'bėr*
hard... *hard*
harden... *hard'n*
hardened... *hard'nd*

hard-fisted... hard'fist-ed
hard-headed... hard'hed-ed
hard-hearted... hard'hart-ed
hardily... hard'i-li
hardish... hard'ish
hardly... hard'li
hardness... hard'nes
hards... hardz
hardship... hard'ship
hardware... hard'wār
hardy... hard'i
hare... hār
hare-brained... hār'brānd
harelip... hār'lip
harem... hā'rem
harlequin... har'le-kwin
harlot... har'lot
harlotry... har'lot-ri
harm... harm
harmful... harm'ful
harmless... harm'les
harmlessly... harm'les-li
harmonica... har-mon'i-ka
harmonicon... har-mon'i-kon
harmonious... har-mō'ni-us
harmonist... har'mon-ist
harmonize... har'mon-iz
harmony... har'mo-ni
harness... har'nes
harp... harp
harper... harp'ėr
harpoon... har-pon'
harpooner... har-pon'ėr
harpischord... harp'si-kord
harpy... har'pi
harrow... ha'rō
harrowing... ha'rō-ing
harsh... harsh
harshly... harsh'li
harvest... har'vest
harvester... har'vest-ėr
hash... hash
hashish... hash'ēsh
hasp... hasp
hassock... has'ok
haste... hāst
hasten... hās'n
hastily... hāst'i-li
hasty... hāst'i
hat... hat
hatch... hach
hatchel... hach'el
hatchet... hach'et
hatchment... hach'ment

hatchway... hach'wā
hate... hāt
hateful... hāt'ful
hatefully... hāt'ful-li
hatred... hāt'red
haugh... hah
haughty... hạt'l
haul... hạl
haulage... hạl'āj
haunt... hant
haunted... hant'ed
hauteur... ō-tėr'
have... hav
haven... hā'vn
haversack... hav'ėr-sak
having... hav'ing
havoc... hav'ok
haw... hạ
hawhaw... hạ'hạ
hawk... hak
hawker... hak'ėr
hawking... hak'ing
hawse... has
hawser... hä'sėr
hawthorn... hạ'thorn
hay... hā
haymaker... hā'māk-ėr
haymaking... hā'māk-ing
hazard... ha'zėrd
hazardous... ha'zėrd-us
haze... hāz
hazel... hā'zl
hazy... hāz'i
head... hed
headache... hed'āk
head-gear... hed'gėr
headily... hed'i-li
heading... hed'ing
headland... hed'land
headless... hed'les
headlong... hed'long
headmost... hed'mōst
head-piece... hed'pēs
headship... hed'ship
headsman... hedz'man
head-stone... hed'stōn
headstrong... hed'strong
headway... hed'wā
head-wind... hed'wind
head-work... hed'wėrk
heady... hed'i
heal... hēl
healing... hēl'ing
health... helth

healthful... helth'ful
healthily... helth'i-lĭ
healthy... helth'i
hear... hēr
hearer... hēr'ėr
hearing... hėr'ing
hearken... hark'n
hearsay... hēr'sā
hearse... hėrs
heart... hart
heartache... hart'āk
heart-broken... hart'brōk-n
heartburn... hart'bėrn
heart-burning... hart'bėrn-ing
hearten... hart'n
heartfelt... hart'felt
hearth... harth
hearthstone... harth'stōn
heartily... hart'i-li
heartless... hart'les
heart-rending... hart'rend-ing
heart-sick... hart'sik
heart-whole... hart'hōl
hearty... hart'i
heat... hēt
heater... hēt'ėr
heath... hēth
heathendom... hē'THen-dum
heathenish... hē'THen-ish
heathenism... hē'THen-izm
heather... heTH'ėr
heating... hēt'ing
heave... hēv
heaven... hev'n
heavenly... hev'n-li
heaver... hēv'ėr
heavily... he'vi-li
heaviness... he'vi-nes
heavy... he'vi
hebetate... heb'ē-tāt
hebetude... heb'ē-tūd
hebraist... hē'brā-ist
hebrew... hē'bro
heckle... hek'l
hectare... hek'tār
hectic... hek'tik
hedge... hej
hedgehog... hej'hog
hedger... hej'ėr
hedgerow... hej'rō
hedonic... hē-don'ik
hedonist... hē'don-ist
heed... hēd
heedful... hēd'ful

heedless... hēd'les
heel... hēl
heel-tap... hēl'tap
heft... heft
hegelian... he-gē'li-an
hegelianism... he-gē'li-an-izm
hegemony... hē-jem'o-ni
heifer... hef'ėr
height... hīt
heighten... hīt'n
heinous... hān'us
heir... ār
heiress... ār'es
heirloom... ār'lom
heirship... ār'ship
helicopter... hel-i-kop'tėr
heliocentric... hē'li-o-sen''trik
heliotrope... hē'li-o-trōp
heliotype... hē'li-o-ffp
helium... hē'li-um
helix... hē'liks
hellenic... hel-len'ik
hellenism... hel'len-izm
hellenist... hel'len-ist
hellish... hel'ish
helm... helm
helmet... hel'met
helmsman... helmz'man
help... help
helper... help'ėr
helpful... help'ful
helpless... help'les
helpmate... help'māt
helter-skelter... hel'tėr-skel'tėr
helve... helv
hem... hem
hematite... he'ma-tīt
hemisphere... he'mi-sfēr
hemistich... he'mi-stik
hemlock... hem'lok
hemorrhage... he'mor-āj
hemorrhoids... he'mor-oidz
hemp... hemp
hempen... hemp'n
hen... hen
henceforth... hens-fōrth'
henchman... hensh'man
henpeck... hen'pek
hepatic... hē-pat'ik
heptagon... hep'ta-gon
heptamerous... hep-tam'ėr-us
heptarchy... hep'tar-ki
heptateuch... hep'ta-tūk
her... hėr

H

herald... he'rald
heraldic... he-rald'ik
heraldry... he'rald-ri
herb... hėrb
herbaceous... hėrb-ā'shus
herbage... hėrb'āj
herbal... hėrb'al
herbalist... hėrb'al-ist
herbarium... hėr-bā'ri-um
herbivorous... hėrb-iv'or-us
herculean... hėr-kū'lē-an
herd... hėrd
herdsman... hėrdz'man
here... hėr
hereafter... hėr-af'tėr
hereditable... he-red'i-ta-bl
hereditarily... he-red'it-a-ri-li
hereditary... he-red'it-a-ri
heredity... he-red'i-ti
herein... hėr-in'
hereinafter... hėr-in-af'tėr
hereof... hėr-of'
hereon... hėr-on'
heresy... he're-si
heretic... he're-tik
heretical... he-ret'ik-al
hereto... hėr-to'
heretofore... hėr-to-fōr'
hereupon... hėr-up-on'
herewith... hėr-with'
heritable... he'rit-a-bl
heritage... he'rit-āj
hermetically... hėr-met'ik-al-li
hermit... hėr'mit
hermitage... hėr'mit-āj
hernia... hėr'ni-a
hero... hē'rō
heroic... he-rō'ik
heroically... he-rō'ik-al-li
heroine... he'rō-in
heroism... he'rō-izm
heron... her'un
heronry... he'run-ri
hero-worship... hē'rō-wėr-ship
herpes... hėr'pez
herpetology... hėr-pe-tol'o-ji
herr... hār
herring... he'ring
herring-bone... he'ring-bōn
hers... hėrz
herse... hėrs
herself... hėr-self'
hesitancy... he'zi-tan-si
hesitate... he'zi-tāt

hesitation... he-zi-tā'shon
hesperian... hes-pē'ri-an
hest... hest
heteroclite... he'te-rō-klīt
heterodox... he'te-rō-doks
heterodoxy... he'te-rō-dok-si
hexagon... heks'a-gon
hexagonal... heks-ag'on-al
hexahedron... heks-a-hē'dron
hexangular... heks-ang'gū-lėr
hey... hā
heyday... hā'dā
hiatus... hī-ā'tus
hibernal... hī-bėr'nal
hibernate... hī-bėr'nāt
hibernation... hī-bėr-nā'shon
hibernian... hī-bėr'ni-an
hiccup... hik'up
hickory... hik'ō-ri
hid... hid, hid'n
hide... hīd
hideous... hid'ē-us
hideously... hid'ē-us-li
hiding... hī'd'ing
hie... hī
hiemal... hī-em'al
hiemation... hī-e-mā''shon
hierarch... hī-ėr-ark
hierarchy... hī'ėr-ar-ki
hieratic... hī-ėr-at'ik
hierology... hī'ėr-ol'o-ji
hierophant... hī'ėr-o-fant
high... hī
highbrow... hī'brou
high-flown... hī'flōn
high-flying... hī'flī-ing
high-handed... hī'hand-ed
highland... hī'land
highlander... hī'land-ėr
highly... hī'li
highness... hī'nes
high-pressure... hī'prē-shūr
high-priest... hī'prēst
highroad... hī'rōd
high-sounding... hī'sound-ing
high-spirited... hī'spi-rit-ed
high-strung... hī'strung
high-toned... hī'tōnd
highway... hī'wā
high-wrought... hī'rat
hike... hīk
hilarious... hi-lā'ri-us
hilarity... hi-la'ri-ti
hill... hil

hillock... *hil'ok*
hilly... *hil'i*
hilt... *hilt*
himself... *him-self'*
hind... *hīnd*
hinder... *hīnd'ėr*
hinder... *hin'dėr*
hindrance... *hin'drans*
hinge... *hinj*
hint... *hint*
hip... *hip*
hippocras... *hip'ō-kras*
hippodrome... *hip'ō-drōm*
hippophagy... *hip-pof'a-ji*
hip-shot... *hip'shot*
hire... *hīr*
hirsute... *hėr-sūt'*
his... *hiz*
hispid... *his'pid*
hiss... *his*
hist... *hist*
histology... *his-tol'o-ji*
historian... *his-tō'ri-an*
historic... *his-to'rik*
historically... *his-to'rik-al-li*
historiette... *his-tō'ri-et''*
history... *his'to-ri*
hit... *hit*
hitch... *hich*
hither... *hifH'ėr*
hithermost... *hifH'ėr-mōst*
hitherto... *hifH'ėr-to*
hitherward... *hifH'ėr-wėrd*
hitter... *hit'ėr*
hive... *hīv*
ho... *hō*
hoar... *hōr*
hoard... *hōrd*
hoarding... *hōrd'ing*
hoarse... *hōrs*
hoarsely... *hōrs'li*
hoary... *hōr'i*
hoax... *hōks*
hob... *hob*
hobble... *hob'l*
hobby... *hob'i*
hobby-horse... *hob'i-hors*
hobgoblin... *hob-gob'lin*
hock... *hok*
hock... *hok*
hockey... *hok'i*
hocus-pocus... *hō'kus-pō'kus*
hod... *hod*
hodge... *hoj*

hodge-podge... *hoj'poj*
hodometer... *ho-dom'et-ėr*
hoe... *hō*
hog... *hog*
hoggish... *hog'ish*
hogshead... *hogz'hed*
hog-wash... *hog'wosh*
hoiden... *hoi'den*
hoist... *hoist*
hold... *hōld*
holder... *hōld'ėr*
holdfast... *hōld'fast*
hole... *hōl*
holiday... *ho'li-dā*
holiness... *hō'li-nes*
holism... *hol'izm*
holland... *hol'land*
hollands... *hol'landz*
hollow... *hol'lō*
holly... *hol'i*
hollyhock... *hol'i-hok*
holocaust... *hol'o-kast*
holograph... *hol'o-g̈raf*
holster... *hōl'stėr*
holt... *hōlt*
holy... *hō'li*
homage... *hom'āj*
home... *hōm*
home-bred... *hōm'bred*
homefelt... *hōm'felt*
homeless... *hōm'les*
homely... *hōm'li*
homeric... *hō-me'rik*
home-rule... *hom'rol*
home-sick... *hōm'sik*
home-sickness... *hōm'sik-nes*
homespun... *hōm'spun*
homestead... *hōm'sted*
homeward... *hōm'wėrd*
homewards... *hōm'wėrdz*
homicidal... *ho-mi-sī'd'al*
homicide... *ho'mi-sī d*
homiletic... *ho-mi-let'ik*
homiletics... *ho-mi-let'iks*
homilist... *ho'mi-list*
homing... *hōm'ing*
hominy... *hom'i-ni*
homologate... *hō-mol'o-gāt*
homologous... *hō-mol'o-gus*
homonym... *ho'mō-nim*
honest... *on'est*
honestly... *on'est-li*
honesty... *on'est-i*
honey... *hun'i*

H

honey-comb... hun'i-kōm
honey-dew... hun'i-dū
honeyed... hun'id
honeymoon... hun'i-mōn
honeysuckle... hun'i-suk-l
honorarium... on-ėr-ā'ri-um
honorary... on'ėr-a-ri
honor... on'ėr
honorable... on'ėr-a-bl
honorably... on'ėr-a-bli
hood... hud
hooded... hud'ed
hoodwink... hud'wingk
hoof... hof
hook... hok
hooligan... hō'li-gan
hoop... hōp
hooping-cough... hop'ing-kof
hoot... hot
hop... hop
hope... hōp
hopeful... hōp'ful
hopeless... hōp'les
hopper... hop'ėr
horal... hor'al
horary... hōr'a-ri
horatian... ho-rā'shan
horde... hōrd
horizon... ho-rī'zon
horizontal... ho-ri-zon'tal
hormones... hor'mōnz
horn... horn
horned... hornd
hornet... horn'et
hornpipe... horn'pip
hornwork... horn'wėrk
horny... horn'i
horologe... ho'ro-lōj
horological... ho-ro-loj'ik-al
horoscope... hor'os-kōp
horrible... hor'ri-bl
horribly... hor'ri-bli
horrid... hor'rid
horridly... hor'rid-li
horrific... hor'rif-ik
horrify... hor'ri-fi
horror... hor'rėr
horse... hors
horseback... hors'bak
horse-cloth... hors'kloth
horse–guards... hors'gardz
horse-leech... hors'lēch
horseman... hors'man
horsemanship... hors'man-ship

horse-play... hors'plā
horse-power... hors'pou-ėr
horseradish... hors'rad-ish
horseshoe... hors'sho
horsewhip... hors'whip
horsy, Horsey... hor'si
hortation... hor-tā'shon
hortative... hort'at-iv
hortatory... hort'a-to-ri
horticulturist... hor-tik-ul'tūr-ist
hosanna... hō-zan'na
hose... hōz
hosier... hō'zhi-ėr
hosiery... hō'zhi-ė-ri
hospice... hos'pis
hospitable... hos'pit-a-bl
hospitably... hos'pit-a-bli
hospital... hos'pit-al
hospitality... hos-pit-al'i-ti
hospitaller... hos'pit-al-ėr
host... hōst
hostage... host'āj
hostel... hos'tel
hostess... hōst'es
hostile... hos'tīl
hostility... hos-til'i-ti
hostler... os'lėr
hot... hot
hot-bed... hot'bed
hot-blast... hot'blast
hot-blooded... hot'blud-ed
hotchpot... hoch'pot
hotch-potch... hoch'poch
hot-headed... hot'hed-ed
hot-house... hot'hous
hotly... hot'li
hot-press... hot'pres
hotspur... hot'spėr
hot-tempered... hot'tem-pėrd
hottentot... hot'n-tot
houdah... hou'da
hough... hok
hound... hound
hour... our
hour-glass... our'glas
houri... hou'ri or hō'ri
hourly... our'li
house... hous
house-boat... hous'bōt
housebreaker... hous'brāk-ėr
household... hous'hōld
householder... hous'hōld-ėr
housekeeper... hous'kēp-ėr
housekeeping... hous'kēp-ing

housel... *hou'zel*
housemaid... *hous'mād*
house-surgeon... *hous'sėr-jon*
housewifery... *hous'wif-ri*
housing... *houz'ing*
hovel... *ho'vel*
hover... *ho'vėr*
how... *hou*
howbeit... *hou-bē'it*
howdah... *hou'da*
however... *hou-ev'ėr*
howitzer... *hou'its-ėr*
howl... *houl*
howlet... *hou'let*
howling... *houl'ing*
howsoever... *hou-sō-ev'ėr*
hoyden... *hoi'dn*
hub... *hub*
hubbub... *hub'bub*
huckster... *huk'stėr*
huddle... *hud'l*
hue... *hū*
huff... *huf*
huffy... *huf'i*
hug... *hug*
huge... *hūj*
hugely... *hūj'li*
hulk... *hulk*
hulking... *hul'king*
hull... *hul*
hum... *hum*
human... *hū'man*
humane... *hū-mān'*
humanity... *hū-man'i-ti*
humanize... *hū'man-īz*
human-kind... *hū'man-kīnd*
humanly... *hū'man-li*
humble... *hum'bl*
humble-pie... *hum'bl-pī*
humbles... *hum'blz*
humbling... *hum'bl-ing*
humbly... *hum'bli*
humbug... *hum'bug*
humdrum... *hum'drum*
humid... *hū'mid*
humidity... *hū-mid'i-ti*
humiliate... *hū-mil'i-āt*
humiliating... *hū-mil'i-āt-ing*
humiliation... *hū-mil'i-ā''shun*
humility... *hū-mil'i-ti*
hummock... *hum'ok*
humorous... *hū'mėr-us or ū'*
humor... *hū'mėr*
hump... *hump*

humpback... *hump'bak*
humus... *hū'mus*
hunch... *hunsh*
hunchback... *hunsh'bak*
hundred... *hun'dred*
hungarian... *hung-gā'ri-an*
hunger... *hung'gėr*
hungry... *hung'gri*
hunk... *hungk*
hunks... *hungks*
hunt... *hunt*
hunter... *hunt'ėr*
hunting... *hunt'ing*
huntress... *hunt'res*
huntsman... *hunts'man*
hurdle... *hėr'dl*
hurdy-gurdy... *hėr'di-gėr-dl*
hurl... *hėrl*
hurly-burly... *hėr'li-bėr'li*
hurricane... *hu'ri-kān*
hurried... *hu'rid*
hurry... *hu'ri*
hurry-skurry... *hu'ri-sku-ri*
hurt... *hėrt*
hurtful... *hėrt'ful*
hurtle... *hėr'tl* ¨
husband... *huz'band*
husbandry... *huz'band-ri*
hush... *hush*
hush-money... *hush'mu-ni*
husk... *husk*
husky... *husk'i*
hussar... *hu-zar'*
hussif... *huž'lf*
hussy... *huz'i*
hustle... *hus'l*
hut... *hut*
hutch... *huch*
hyacinth... *hī'a-sinth*
hyacinthine... *hī-a-sinth'īn*
hyaline... *hī'al-in*
hyalography... *hī-al-og'ra-fi*
hybrid... *hīb'rid*
hydatid... *hīd'a-tid*
hydra... *hī'dra*
hydrant... *hī'drant*
hydrate... *hī'drāt*
hydraulic... *hī-dral'ik*
hydraulics... *hī-dral'iks*
hydrocarbon... *hī-dro-kar'bon*
hydrogen... *hī'drō-jen*
hydrogenous... *hī-dro'jen-us*
hydrography... *hī-drog'ra-fi*
hydrology... *hī-drol'o-ji*

H

hydrometer... *hī-drom'et-ėr*
hydropathy... *hī-dro'pa-thi*
hydrophobia... *hī-drō-fō'bi-a*
hydrophyte... *hī'drō-fīt*
hydroponics... *hī drō-pon'iks*
hydrostatic... *hī-drō-stat'ik*
hydrostatics... *hī-drō-stat'iks*
hyena... *hī-ē'na*
hygeian... *hī-jē'an*
hygiene... *hī'ji-ēn*
hygienic... *hī-ji-en'ik*
hygrometer... *hī-grom'et-ėr*
hygroscope... *hī'grō-skōp*
hymen... *hī'men*
hymn... *him*
hyoid... *hī'oid*
hyperbola... *hī-pėr'bō-la*
hyperbole... *hī-pėr'bō-lē*
hyperbolic... *hī-pėr-bol'ik,*
hypercritic... *hī-pėr-krit'ik*
hypercritical... *hī-pėr-krit'ik-al*
hyphen... *hī'fen*
hypnotic... *hip-not'ik*
hypnotism... *hip'no-tizm*
hypnotize... *hip'no-fīz*
hypocrisy... *hi-pok'ri-si*
hypocrite... *hi'pō-krit*
hypocritical... *hi-pō-krit'ik-al*
hypotenuse... *hī-pot'ē-nūs*
hypothec... *hī-poth'ek*
hypothecate... *hī-poth'e-kāt*
hypothesis... *hī-poth'e-sis*
hypsometer... *hip-som'et-ėr*
hyson... *hīs'on*
hyssop... *his'sop*
hysteria... *his-tē'ri-a*
hysteric... *his-te'rik*

I

iamb... *ī-amb'*
iambus... *ī-am'bus*
iatric... *ī-at'rik*
iberian... *ī-be'ri-an*
ibex... *ī'beks*
ibis... *ī'bis*
ice... *īs*
iceberg... *īs'bėrg*
ice-bound... *īs'bound*
ice-cream... *īs'krēm*
icheumon... *ik-nū'mon*
icicle... *īs'i-kl*

icy... *īs'i*
idea... *ī-dē'a*
ideal... *ī-dē'al*
idealism... *ī'dē'al-izm*
idealist... *ī-dē'al-ist*
ideality... *ī-dē-al'i-ti*
idealize... *ī-dē'al-iz*
ideation... *ī-dē-ā-shun*
identical... *ī-den'tik-al*
identifiable... *ī-den'ti-fī-a-bl*
identify... *ī-den'ti-fi*
identity... *ī-den'ti-ti*
ideology... *ī-dē-ol'o-ji*
idiograph... *id'ī-ō-graf*
idiom... *id'i-om*
idiomatic... *id'i-om-at''ik*
idiopathy... *id-i-op'a-thi*
idiosyncrasy... *id'i-o-sin''kra-si*
idiot... *i'di-ot*
idiotic... *id-i-ot'ik*
idleness... *ī'dl-nes*
idly... *ī'd'li*
idol... *ī'dol*
idolater... *ī-dol'at-ėr*
idolatrous... *ī-dol'at-rus*
idolatry... *ī-dol'at-ri*
idolize... *ī'dol-īz*
idyl... *id'il* or *ī'dil*
idyllic... *ī-dil'ik*
if... *if*
igloo... *ig'lo*
igneous... *ig'nē-us*
ignite... *ig-nīt'*
ignition... *ig-ni'shun*
ignominious... *ig-nō-mi'ni-us*
ignominy... *ig'nō-mi-ni*
ignoramus... *ig-nō-rā'mus*
ignorant... *ig'nō-rant*
ignore... *ig-nōr'*
iguana... *ig-wa'na*
ill... *il*
ill-bred... *il-bred'*
illegal... *il-lē'gal*
illegality... *il-lē-gal'i-ti*
illegible... *il-le'ji-bl*
illegitimacy... *il-lē-jit'i-ma-si*
illegitimate... *il-lē-jit'i-māt*
illiberal... *il-lib'ėr-al*
illicit... *il-lis'it*
illimitable... *il-lim'it-a-bl*
illiteracy... *il-lit'ėr-a-si*
illiterate... *il-lit'ėr-āt*
ill-mannered... *il-man'ėrd*
ill-nature... *il'nā-tūr*

illness... *il'nes*
illogical... *il-lo'jik-al*
ill-tempered... *il'tem-pėrd*
illude... *il-lūd'*
illuminate... *il-lūm'in-āt*
illuminati... *il-lū'mi-nā''fī*
illumination... *il-lūm'in-ā''shun*
illusion... *il-lū'zhon*
illusionist... *il-lū'zhon-ist*
illusive... *il-lū'siv*
illusory... *il-lū'so-ri*
illustrate... *il-lus'trāt*
illustrious... *il-lus'tri-us*
illwill... *il'wil*
image... *im'āj*
imagery... *im'āj-e-ri*
imaginable... *im-aj'in-a-bl*
imaginary... *im-aj'in-a-ri*
imagination... *im-aj'in-ā''shun*
imaginative... *im-aj'in-āt-iv*
imagine... *im-aj'in*
imbecile... *im'be-sil*
imbed... *im-bed'*
imbrication... *im-bri-kā'shun*
imitable... *im'i-ta-bl*
imitate... *im'i-tāt*
imitation... *im-i-tā'shun*
imitative... *im'i-tāt-iv*
imitator... *im'i-tāt-ėr*
immaculate... *im-ma'kū-lāt*
immanate... *im'ma-nāt*
immaterial... *im-ma-tē'ri-al*
immature... *im-ma-tūr'*
immaturity... *im-ma-tūr'i-ti*
immediate... *im-mē'di-āt*
immemorial... *im-me-mō'ri-al*
immense... *im-mens'*
immensity... *im-mens'i-ti*
immerge... *im-merj'*
immerse... *im-mėrs'*
immersion... *im-mėr'shun*
immigrant... *im'mi-grant*
immigrate... *im'mi-grāt*
immigration... *im-mi-grā'shun*
imminence... *im'mi-nens*
imminent... *im'mi-nent*
imminently... *im'mi-nent-li*
immobile... *im-mōb'il*
immobility... *im-mō-bil'i-ti*
immoderate... *im-mo'dėr-āt*
immodest... *im-mo'dest*
immodesty... *im-mo'des-ti*
immolate... *im'mō-lāt*
immoral... *im-mo'ral*

immorality... *im-mō-ral'i-ti*
immortality... *im-mor-tal'i-ti*
immortalize... *im-mor'tal-īz*
immovable... *im-mov'a-bl*
immovably... *im-mov'a-bli*
immunity... *im-mū'ni-ti*
immure... *im-mūr'*
immutable... *im-mū'ta-bl*
immutably... *im-mu'ta-bli*
imp... *imp*
impact... *im'pakt*
impair... *im-pār'*
impale... *im-pāl'*
impalpable... *im-pal'pa-bl*
imparity... *im-pa'ri-ti*
impart... *im-part'*
impartial... *im-par'shal*
impartiality... *im-par'shi-al''-ti*
impassable... *im-pas'a-bl*
impassibility... *im-pas'i-bil''i-ti*
impassible... *im-pas'i-bl*
impassion... *im-pa'shun*
impassive... *im-pas'iv*
impatience... *im-pā'shens*
impatient... *im-pā'shent*
impeach... *im-pēch'*
impeachable... *im-pēch'a-bl*
impeccable... *im-pek'a-bl*
impecunious... *im-pē-kū'ni-us*
impede... *im-pēd'*
impediment... *im-ped'i-ment*
impel... *im-pel'*
impend... *im-pend'*
impenitence... *im-pe'ni-tens*
impenitent... *im-pe'ni-tent*
imperative... *im-pe'rat-iv*
imperfect... *im-pėr'fekt*
imperfectly... *im-pėr'fekt-li*
imperforate... *im-pėr'fo-rāt*
imperial... *im-pē'ri-al*
imperialism... *im-pē'ri-al-izm*
imperialist... *im-pē'ri-al-ist*
imperil... *im-pe'ril*
imperious... *im-pē'ri-us*
imperishable... *im-pe'rish-a-bl*
impersonal... *im-pėr'son-al*
impersonally... *im-pėr'son-al-li*
impersonate... *im-pėr'son-āt*
impertinent... *im-pėr'ti-nent*
impetuosity... *im-pe'tū-os''i-ti*
impetuous... *im-pe'tū-us*
impetus... *im'pe-tus*
impinge... *im-pinj'*
impious... *im'pi-us*

impiously... *im'pi-us-li*
impish... *imp'ish*
implacable... *im-plā'ka-bl*
implacably... *im-plā'ka-bli*
implant... *im-plant'*
impleader... *im-plē d'ėr*
implicate... *im'pli-kāt*
implication... *im-pli-kā'shun*
implicit... *im-pli'sit*
implicitly... *im-pli'sit-li*
implore... *im-plōr*
imply... *im-plī'*
impolicy... *im-po'li-si*
impolite... *im-pō-līt'*
impolitic... *im-po'lit-ik*
import... *im-pōrt'*
importable... *im-pōrt'a-bl*
importance... *im-pōrt'ans*
important... *im-pōrt'ant*
importation... *im-pōrt-ā'shun*
importer... *im-pōrt'ėr*
importune... *im-por-tūn'*
importunity... *im-por-tūn'i-ti*
impose... *im-pōz'*
imposing... *im-pōz'ing*
imposition... *im-pō-zi'shun*
impossibility... *im-pos'i-bil'i-ti*
impossible... *im-pos'i-bl*
impost... *im'pōst*
imposter... *im-pos'tėr*
imposture... *im-pos'tūr*
impotent... *im'pō-tent*
impotently... *im'pō-tent-li*
impound... *im-pound'*
impoverish... *im-po'vėr-ish*
imprecate... *im'prē-kāt*
imprecation... *im-prē-kā'shun*
impregnable... *im-preg'na-bl*
impregnably... *im-preg'na-bli*
impregnate... *im-preg'nāt*
impress... *im-pres'*
impressible... *im-pres'i-bl*
impression... *im-pre'shun*
impressive... *im-pres'iv*
impressment... *im-pres'ment*
imprimatur... *im-pri-mā'tėr*
imprimis... *im-prī'mis*
imprint... *im-print'*
imprison... *im-pri'zn*
improbable... *im-pro'ba-bl*
improbably... *im-pro'ba-bli*
impromptu... *im-promp'tū*
improper... *im-pro'pėr*
improperly... *im-pro'pėr-li*

impropriety... *im-prō-prī'e-ti*
improvable... *im-prov'a-bl*
improve... *im-prov'*
improvement... *im-prov'ment*
improvident... *im-pro'vi-dent*
improving... *im-prov'ing*
imprudence... *im-pro'dens*
imprudent... *im-pro'dent*
impudence... *im'pū-dens*
impudent... *im'pū-dent*
impugn... *im-pūn'*
impulse... *im'puls*
impulsive... *im-puls'iv*
impunity... *im-pū'ni-ti*
impure... *im-pūr'*
impurely... *im-pūr'li*
impurity... *im-pūr'i-ti*
imputable... *im-pūt'a-bl*
imputation... *im-pū-tā'shun*
impute... *im-pūt'*
in... *in*
inability... *in-a-bil'i-ti*
inaccessible... *in-ak-ses'i-bl*
inaccuracy... *in-ak'kū-ra-si*
inaccurate... *in-ak'kū-rāt*
inaccurately... *in-ak'kū-rāt-li*
inaction... *in-ak'shun*
inactive... *in-ak'tiv*
inactivity... *in-ak-tiv'i-ti*
inadequacy... *in-ad'ē-kwā-si*
inadequate... *in-ad'ē-kwāt*
inadmissible... *in-ad-mis'i-bl*
inadvertent... *in-ad-vėrt'ent*
inalienable... *in-āl'yen-a-bl*
inalterable... *in-al'tėr-a-bl*
inamorata... *in-ā'mō-ra''ta*
inamorato... *in-ā'mō-ra''tō*
inanimate... *in-an'i-māt*
inapplicable... *in-ap'pli-ka-bl*
inapt... *in-apt'*
inaptitude... *in-apt'ti-tūd*
inarch... *in-arch'*
inarticulate... *in-ar-tik'ū-lāt*
inarticulately... *in-ar-tik'ū-lāt-li*
inartificial... *in-ar'ti-fi''shal*
inartificially... *in-ar'ti-fi''shal-li*
inasmuch... *in-az-much'*
inattention... *in-at-ten'shun*
inattentive... *in-at-tent'iv*
inattentively... *in-at-tent'iv-li*
inaudibility... *in-a'di-bil''i-ti*
inaudible... *in-a'di-bl*
inaudibly... *in-a'di-bli*
inaugural... *in-ā'gū-ral*

inaugurate... in-a'gū-rāt
inauspicious... in-a-spi'shus
inboard... in'bōrd
inborn... in'born
inbreathe... in-brēŦH'
inbred... in'bred
incage... in-kāj'
incalculably... in-kal'kū-la-bli
incantation... in-kan-tā'shun
incapability... in-kā'pa-bil'i-ti
incapable... in-kā'pa-bl
incapably... in-kā'pa-bli
incapacitate... in-ka-pa'si-tāt
incapacity... in-ka-pa'si-ti
incarcerate... in-kar'sė-rāt
incarnadine... in-kar'na-dīn
incarnate... in-kar'nāt
incarnation... in-kar-nā'shun
incase... in-kās'
incaution... in-ka'shun
incautious... in-ka'shus
incautiously... in-ka'shus-li
incendiarism... in-sėn'di-a-rizm
incendiary... in-sen'di-a-ri
incense... in'sens
incense... in-sens'
incentive... in-sen'tiv
inception... in-sep'shun
inceptive... in-sep'tiv
inceptor... in-sep'tėr
incertitude... in-sėr'ti-tūd
incessantly... in-ses'ant-li
incest... in'sest
incestuous... in-sest'ū-us
inch... insh
incidence... in'si-dens
incident... in'si-dent
incidental... in-si-dent'al
incinerate... in-sin'ė-rāt
incipient... in-si'pi-ent
incise... in-sīz'
incision... in-si'zhon
incisive... in-sī'siv
incisor... in-sīz'ėr
incite... in-sīt'
incitement... in-sīt'ment
inclement... in-kle'ment
inclination... in-klin-ā'shun
incline... in-klīn'
inclined... in-klīnd'
inclose... in-klōz'
inclosure... in-klō'zhūr
include... in-klod'
inclusion... in-klo'zhon

inclusive... in-klo'siv
incoherent... in-kō-hēr'ent
income... in'kum
income-tax... in'kum-taks
incoming... in'kum-ing
incomplete... in-kom-plēt'
inconclusive... in-kon-klos'iv
incongruity... in-kong-gru'i-ti
incongruous... in-kong'gru-us
inconsistent... in-kon-sist'ent
inconsolable... in-kon-sōl'a-bl
inconstancy... in-kon'stan-si
inconstant... in-kon'stant
incontinent... in-kon'ti-nent
inconvertible... in-kon-vėrt'i-bl
incorporate... in-kor'pō-rāt
incorporeal... in-kor-pō'rē-al
incorrect... in-ko-rekt'
incorrectly... in-ko-rekt'li
incorrigible... in-ko'ri-ji-bl
incorrigibly... in-ko'ri-ji-bli
incorrodible... in-ko-rō'd'i-bl
incorrupt... in-ko-rupt'
incorruptible... in-ko-rupt'i-bl
incorruption... in-ko-rup'shun
increasingly... in-krēs'ing-li
incredibility... in-kred'i-bil'i-ti
incredible... in-kred'i-bl
incredibly... in-kred'i-bli
incredulous... in-kred'ū-lus
increment... in'krē-ment
incriminate... in-krim'in-āt
incrust... in-krust'
incrustation... in-krust-ā'shun
incubate... in'kū-bāt
incubation... in-kū-bā'shun
incubator... in'kū-bāt-ėr
incubus... in'kū-bus
inculcate... in-kul'kāt
inculcation... in-kul-kā'shun
inculpate... in-kul'pāt
incumbency... in-kum'ben-si
incumbent... in-kum'bent
incur... in-kėr'
incurable... in-kūr'a-bl
incurious... in-kū'ri-us
incursion... in-kėr'shun
incursive... in-kėr'siv
incurvate... in-kėrv'āt
indebted... in-det'ed
indebtedness... in-det'ed-nes
indecency... in-dē'sen-si
indecent... in-dē'sent
indecision... in-dē-si'zhon

I

indecisive... *in-dē-sis'iv*
indeclinable... *in-dē-klīn'a-bl*
indeed... *in-dēd'*
indefensible... *in-dē-fens'i-bl*
indefinable... *in-dē-fīn'a-bl*
indefinite... *in-def'i-nit*
indelible... *in-de'li-bl*
indelicate... *in-de'li-kāt*
indemnify... *in-dem'ni-fī*
indemnity... *in-dem'ni-ti*
indent... *in-dent'*
indentation... *in-dent-ā'shun*
indenture... *in-den'tūr*
index... *in'deks*
indian... *in'di-an*
indicate... *in'di-kāt*
indication... *in-di-kā'shun*
indicative... *in-dik'a-tiv*
indicator... *in'di-kāt-ėr*
indict... *in-dīt'*
indictable... *in-dīt'a-bl*
indiction... *in-dik'shun*
indictment... *in-dīt'ment*
indifference... *in-dif'ėr-ens*
indifferent... *in-dif'ėr-ent*
indifferently... *in-dif'ėr-ent-li*
indigence... *in'di-jens*
indigene... *in'di-jēn*
indigenous... *in-di'jen-us*
indigent... *in'di-jent*
indigested... *in-di-jest'ed*
indigestible... *in-di-jest'i-bl*
indigestion... *in-di-jest'yon*
indignant... *in-dig'nant*
indignantly... *in-dig'nant-li*
indignation... *in-dig-nā'shun*
indignity... *in-dig'ni-ti*
indirect... *in-di-rekt'*
indirectly... *in-di-rekt'li*
indiscreet... *in-dis-krēt'*
indiscretion... *in-dis-kre'shun*
indispose... *in-dis-pōz'*
indisputable... *in-dis'pūt-a-bl*
indissolvable... *in-dīz-zolv'a-bl*
indistinct... *in-dis-tingkt'*
indite... *in-dīt'*
inditement... *in-dīt'ment*
individual... *in-di-vid'ū-al*
individualize... *in-di-vid'ū-al-īz*
indivisibility... *in-di-viz'i-bil'i-ti*
indivisible... *in-di-viz'i-bl*
indocile... *in-dō'sīl or in-dos'il*
indoctrinate... *in-dok'trin-āt*
indolence... *in'dō-lens*

indolent... *in'dō-lent*
indomitable... *in-dom'it-a-bl*
indoor... *in'dōr*
indubitable... *in-dū'bit-a-bl*
induce... *in-dūs'*
inducement... *in-dūs'ment*
inducible... *in-dūs'i-bl*
induct... *in-dukt'*
inductile... *in-duk'tīl*
induction... *in-duk'shun*
inductive... *in-dukt'iv*
indulge... *in-dulj'*
indulgence... *in-dulj'ens*
indurate... *in'dū-rāt*
induration... *in-dū-rā'shun*
industrial... *in-dus'tri-al*
industrious... *in-dus'tri-us*
industry... *in'dus-tri*
inebriate... *in-ē'bri-āt*
inebriation... *in'ē-bri-ā''shun*
ineffective... *in-ef-fekt'iv*
ineffectual... *in-ef-fek'tū-al*
inefficacious... *in-ef'fi-kā''shus*
inefficacy... *in-ef'fi-ka-si*
inefficiency... *in-ef-fi'shen-si*
inefficient... *in-ef-fi'shent*
inelegant... *in-el'ē-gant*
ineligibility... *in-el'i-ji-bil''i-ti*
ineligible... *in-el'i-ji-bl*
ineloquent... *in-el'ō-kwent*
inept... *in-ept'*
ineptitude... *in-ept'i-tūd*
inequable... *in-ē'kwa-bl*
inequality... *in-ė-kwol'i-ti*
inequitable... *in-ke'wit-a-bl*
inert... *in-ėrt'*
inertia... *in-ėr'shi-a*
inestimable... *in-es'tim-a-bl*
inestimably... *in-es'tim-a-bli*
inevitable... *in-ev'it-a-bl*
inevitably... *in-ev'it-a-bli*
inexact... *in-egz-akt'*
inexcusable... *in-eks-kūz'a-bl*
inexcusably... *in-eks-kūz'a-bli*
inexhaustible... *in-egz-ast'i-bl*
inexorable... *in-eks'ōr-ä-bl*
inexorably... *in-eks'ōr-a-bli*
inexpedient... *in-eks-pē'di-ent*
inexpensive... *in-eks-pen'siv*
inexplicable... *in-eks'pli-ka-bl*
inexplicably... *in-eks'pli''ka-bli*
inexplicit... *in-eks-plis'it*
inexplosive... *in-eks-plō'siv*
inexpressible... *in-eks-pres'i-bl*

inexpressibly... *in-eks-pres'i-bli*
inexpressive... *in-eks-pres'iv*
inextricable... *in-eks'tri-ka-bl*
infallibility... *in-fal'i-bil''i-ti*
infallible... *in-fal'i-bl*
infallibly... *in-fal'i-bli*
infamously... *in'fa-mus-li*
infancy... *in'fan-si*
infant... *in'fant*
infantry... *in'fant-ri*
infatuate... *in-fa'tū-āt*
infatuated... *in-fa'tū-āt-ed*
infatuation... *in-fa'tū-ā''shun*
infect... *in-fekt'*
infection... *in-fek'shun*
infectious... *in-fek'shus*
infelicitous... *in-fē-lis'it-us*
infelicity... *in-fē-lis'i-ti*
infer... *in-fėr'*
inferable... *in-fėr'a-bl*
inference... *in'fėr-ens*
inferential... *in-fėr-en'shal*
inferior... *in-fē'ri-ėr*
inferiority... *in-fē'ri-or''i-ti*
infernal... *in-fėr'nal*
infernally... *in-fėr'nal-li*
infertile... *in-fėr'fīl*
infertility... *in-fėr-til'i-ti*
infest... *in-fest'*
infidel... *in'fi-del*
infidelity... *in-fi-del'i-ti*
infiltration... *in-fil-trā'shun*
infinite... *in'fi-nit*
infinitesimal... *in'fi-ni-tes''i-mal*
infinitive... *in-fin'it-iv*
infinity... *in-fin'i-ti*
infirm... *in-fėrm'*
infirmary... *in-fėrm'a-ri*
infirmity... *in-fėrm'i-ti*
inflame... *in-flām'*
inflammation... *in-flam-ā'shun*
inflammatory... *in-flam'a-to-ri*
inflate... *in-flāt'*
inflation... *in-flā'shun*
inflatus... *in-flā'tus*
inflect... *in-flekt'*
inflection... *in-flek'shun*
inflective... *in-flekt'iv*
inflexed... *in-flekst'*
inflexibility... *in-fleks'i-bil''i-ti*
inflexible... *in-fleks'i-bl*
inflexibly... *in-fleks'i-bli*
inflict... *in-flikt'*
infliction... *in-flik'shun*

inflow... *in'flō*
influent... *in-flu-ent*
influential... *in-flu-en'shal*
influenza... *in-flu-en'za*
influx... *in'fluks*
infold... *in-fōld'*
inform... *in-form'*
informal... *in-form'al*
informality... *in-form-al'i-ti*
informally... *in-form'al-li*
informant... *in-form'ant*
information... *in-form-ā'shun*
informer... *in-form'ėr*
infraction... *in-frak'shun*
infrangible... *in-fran'ji-bl*
infra-red... *in'fra-red*
infrequency... *in-frē'kwen-si*
infrequent... *in-frē'kwent*
infringe... *in-frinj'*
infringement... *in-frinj'ment*
infuriate... *in-fū'ri-āt*
infuse... *in-fūz'*
infusible... *in-fūz'i-bl*
infusible... *in-fūz'i-bl*
infusion... *in-fū'zhon*
ingenuity... *in-jen-ū'i-ti*
ingenuous... *in-jen'ū-us*
ingest... *in-jest'*
ingoing... *in'gō-ing*
ingot... *in'got*
ingrate... *in'grāt*
ingratiate... *in-grā'shi-āt*
ingratitude... *in-grat'i-tūd*
ingredient... *in-grē'di-ent*
ingress... *in'gres*
ingulf... *in-gulf'*
inhabit... *in-ha'bit*
inhalation... *in-ha-lā'shun*
inhale... *in-hāl'*
inhaler... *in-hāl'ėr*
inherent... *in-hēr'ent*
inherit... *in-he'rit*
inheritable... *in-he'rit-a-bl*
inheritance... *in-he'rit-ans*
inheritor... *in-he'rit-ėr*
inhibit... *in-hib'it*
inhibition... *in-hi-bis'hon*
inhospitable... *in-hos'pit-a-bl*
inhospitality... *in-hos'pit-al''i-ti*
inhumanity... *in-hū-man'i-ti*
inhumanly... *in-hū'man-li*
inhumation... *in-hūm-ā'shun*
inimical... *in-im'ik-al*
inimitable... *in-im'it-a-bl*

inimitably... *in-im'it-a-bli*
iniquitous... *in-ik'wit-us*
iniquity... *in-ik'wi-ti*
initial... *in-i'shal*
initiate... *in-i'shi-āt*
initiation... *in-i'shi-ā''shun*
initiative... *in-i'shi-āt-iv*
initiatory... *in-i'shi-a-to-ri*
inject... *in-jekt'*
injection... *in-jek'shun*
injector... *in-jekt'ėr*
injudicial... *in-jū-di'shal*
injudicious... *in-jū-di'shus*
injudiciously... *in-jū-di'shus-li*
injunction... *in-jungk'shun*
injure... *in'jėr*
injurious... *in-jū'ri-us*
injuriously... *in-jū'ri-us-li*
injury... *in'jū-ri*
ink... *ingk*
inkling... *ingk'ling*
inland... *in'land*
inlay... *in-lā'*
inlet... *in'let*
inmate... *in'māt*
inmost... *in'mōst*
inn... *in*
innate... *in-nāt'*
innately... *in-nāt'li*
innavigable... *in-na'vig-a-bl*
inner... *in'ėr*
innermost... *in'ėr-mōst*
innervate... *in-nėr'vāt*
innervation... *in-nėr-vā'shun*
inning... *in'ing*
innkeeper... *in'kēp-ėr*
innocent... *in'nō-sent*
innocently... *in'nō-sent-li*
innocuous... *in-nok'ū-us*
innominate... *in-nom'i-nāt*
innovate... *in'nō-vāt*
innovation... *in-nō-vā'shun*
innoxious... *in-nok'shus*
innumerable... *in-nū'mėr-a-bl*
innumerably... *in-nū'mėr-a-bli*
innutrition... *in-nū-tri'shun*
innutritious... *in-nū-tri'shus*
inobservant... *in-ob-zėrv'ant*
inobtrusive... *in-ob-tro'siv*
inoculate... *in-ok'ū-lāt*
inoculation... *in-ok'ū-lā''shun*
inoffensive... *in-of-fens'iv*
inoffensively... *in-of-fens'iv-li*
inofficial... *in-of-fi'shal*

inoperative... *in-o'pe-rāt-iv*
inopportune... *in-op'por-tūn*
inordinacy... *in-or'din-a-si*
inordinate... *in-or'din-āt*
inordinately... *in-or'din-āt-li*
inorganic... *in-or-gan'ik*
inosculate... *in-os'kū-lāt*
in-patient... *in'pā'shent*
inquest... *in'kwest*
inquietude... *in-kwī'et-ūd*
inquire... *in-kwīr'*
inquirer... *in-kwīr'ėr*
inquiring... *in-kwīr'ing*
inquisition... *in-kwi-zi'shun*
inquisitive... *in-kwiz'i-tiv*
inquisitor... *in-kwiz'i-tėr*
inroad... *in'rōd*
insalubrious... *in-sa-lū'bri-us*
insalubrity... *in-sa-lū'bri-ti*
insalutary... *in-sal'ū-ta-ri*
insane... *in-sān'*
insanely... *in-sān'li*
insanity... *in-san'i-ti*
insatiability... *in-sā'shi-a-bil''i-ti*
insatiable... *in-sā'shi-a-bl*
insatiate... *in-sā'shi-āt*
inscribe... *in-skrīb'*
inscription... *in-skrip'shun*
inscriptive... *in-skript'iv*
inscrutability... *in-skro'ta-bil''i-ti*
inscrutable... *in-skro'ta-bl*
insect... *in'sekt*
insecticide... *in-sek'ti-sīd*
insecure... *in-sē-kūr'*
insecurity... *in-sē-kū'ri-ti*
insensate... *in-sens'āt*
insensibility... *in-sens'i-bil''i-ti*
insensibly... *in-sens'i-bli*
insensitive... *in-sens'i-tiv*
insentient... *in-sen'shi-ent*
inseparable... *in-sep'a-ra-bl*
insert... *in-sėrt'*
insertion... *in-sėr'shun*
insessorial... *in-ses-sō'ri-al*
inset... *in-set'*
inshore... *in'shōr*
inside... *in'sīd*
insidious... *in-sid'i-us*
insight... *in'sit*
insignia... *in-sig'ni-a*
insignificant... *in-sig-ni'fi-kant*
insincere... *in-sin-sėr'*
insincerity... *in-sin-ser'i-ti*
insinuate... *in-sin'ū-āt*

insinuating... *in-sin′ū-āt-ing*
insinuation... *in-sin′ū-ā″shun*
insipid... *in-sip′id*
insipidity... *in-si-pid′i-ti*
insist... *in-sist′*
insistence... *in-sis′tens*
insobriety... *in-sō-brī′e-ti*
insolence... *in′sō-lens*
insolent... *in′sō-lent*
insolubility... *in-sol′ū-bil″i-ti*
insoluble... *in-sol′ū-bl*
insolvable... *in-sol′va-bl*
insolvency... *in-sol′ven-si*
insolvent... *in-sol′vent*
insomnia... *in-som′ni-a*
insomuch... *in-sō-much′*
inspect... *in-spekt′*
inspection... *in-spek′shun*
inspector... *in-spekt′ér*
inspiration... *in-spi-rā′shun*
inspire... *in-spīr′*
instability... *in-sta-bil′i-ti*
install... *in-stal′*
installation... *in-stal-ā′shun*
installment... *in-stäl′ment*
instance... *in′stans̈*
instant... *in′stant*
instantly... *in′stant-li*
instate... *in-stāt′*
instead... *in-sted′*
instep... *in′step*
instigation... *in-sti-gā′shun*
instigator... *in′sti-gāt-ér*
instil... *in-stil′*
instillation... *in-stil-ā′shun*
instilment... *in-stil′ment*
instinct... *in′stingkt*
instinctive... *in-stingk′tiv*
institute... *in′sti-tūt*
institution... *in-sti-tū′shun*
institutional... *in-sti-tū′shun-al*
instruct... *in-strukt′*
instruction... *in-struk′shun*
instructive... *in-struk′tiv*
instructor... *in-strukt′ér*
instructress... *in-strukt′res*
instrument... *in′stru-ment*
instrumental... *in-stru-ment′al*
insufferable... *in-suf′ér-a-bl*
insufferably... *in-suf′ér-a-bli*
insufficiency... *in-suf-fi′shen-si*
insufficient... *in-suf-fi′shent*
insular... *in′sū-lér*
insularity... *in-sū-la′ri-ti*

insulate... *in′sū-lāt*
insulator... *in′sū-lāt-ér*
insulin... *ins′ū-lin*
insult... *in′sult*
insulting... *in-sult′ing*
insuperable... *in-sū′pér-a-bl*
insuperably... *in-sū′pér-a-bli*
insurable... *in-shor′a-bl*
insurance... *in-shor′ans*
insure... *in-shor′*
insurer... *in-shor′ér*
insurrection... *in-sér-rek′shun*
insusceptible... *in-sus-sept′i-bl*
intact... *in-takt′*
intangible... *in-tan′ji-bl*
integral... *in′ti-gral*
integrate... *in′ti-grāt*
integration... *in-ti-grā′shun*
integrity... *in-teg′ri-ti*
intellect... *in′tel-lekt*
intellection... *in-tel-lek′shun*
intellectual... *in-tel-lek′tū-al*
intelligence... *in-tel′i-jens*
intelligent... *in-tel′i-jent*
intelligibility... *in-tel′i-ji-bil″i-ti*
intemperate... *in-tem′pér-ēt*
intend... *in-tend′*
intended... *in-tend′ed*
intense... *in-tens′*
intensify... *in-ten′si-fī*
intension... *in-ten′shun*
intensity... *in-ten′si-ti*
intensive... *in-ten′siv*
intent... *in-tent′*
intention... *in-ten′shun*
intentional... *in-ten′shun-al*
intently... *in-tent′li*
inter... *in-tér′*
interact... *in′tér-akt*
interaction... *in-tér-ak′shun*
intercede... *in-tér-sēd′*
intercept... *in-tér-sept′*
intercession... *in-tér-se′shun*
intercessor... *in′tér-ses-ér*
interchange... *in-tér-chänj′*
intercourse... *in′tér-kōrs*
interdict... *in-tér-dikt′*
interdiction... *in-tér-dik′shun*
interdictory... *in-tér-dik′to-ri*
interested... *in′tér-est-ed*
interesting... *in′tér-est-ing*
interfere... *in-ter-fēr′*
interference... *in-tér-fēr′ens*
interim... *in′tér-im*

interior . . . *in-tē'ri-ér*
interject . . . *in-tér-jekt'*
interjection . . . *in-tér-jek'shun*
interlace . . . *in-tér-lās'*
interlock . . . *in-tér-lok'*
interlocutor . . . *in-tér-lo'kūt-ér*
interlope . . . *in-tér-lōp'*
interloper . . . *in-tér-lōp'ér*
interlude . . . *in'tér-lūd*
intermarriage . . . *in-tér-ma'rij*
intermarry . . . *in-tér-ma'ri*
intermeddle . . . *in-tér-med'l*
intermeddler . . . *in-tér-med'lér*
interment . . . *in-tér'ment*
interminable . . . *in-tér'min-a-bl*
interminate . . . *in-tér'min-āt*
intermingle . . . *in-tér-ming'gl*
intermission . . . *in-tér-mi'shun*
intermit . . . *in-tér-mit'*
intermix . . . *in-tér-miks'*
intermixture . . . *in-tér-miks'tūr*
intern . . . *in-térn'*
internal . . . *in-térn'al*
interpellate . . . *in-tér'pel-lāt*
interposal . . . *in-tér-pōs'al*
interpose . . . *in-tér-pōz'*
interpret . . . *in-tér'pret*
interpretable . . . *in-tér'pret-a-bl*
interpreter . . . *in-tér'pret-ér*
interrogate . . . *in-te'rō-gāt*
interrogative . . . *in-te-rog'at-iv*
interrogator . . . *in-te'rō-gāt'ér*
interrogatory . . . *in-te-rog'a-to-ri*
interrupt . . . *in-tér-rupt'*
interrupted . . . *in-tér-rupt'ed*
interruption . . . *in-tér-rup'shun*
intersect . . . *in-tér-sekt'*
intersection . . . *in-tér-sek'shun*
intersperse . . . *in-tér-spérs'*
intertwine . . . *in-tér-twīn'*
interval . . . *in'tér-val*
intervene . . . *in-tér-vēn'*
intervention . . . *in-tér-ven'shun*
intestable . . . *in-test'a-bl*
intestacy . . . *in-test'a-si*
intestate . . . *in-test'āt*
intestinal . . . *in-tes'tin-al*
intestine . . . *in-tes'tīn*
intimacy . . . *in'ti-ma-si*
intimate . . . *in'ti-māt*
intimation . . . *in-ti-mā'shun*
intimidate . . . *in-tim'id-āt*
into . . . *in'to*
intolerable . . . *in-tol'ér-a-bl*

intolerably . . . *in-tol'ér-a-bli*
intolerance . . . *in-tol'ér-ans*
intolerant . . . *in-tol'ér-ant*
intonate . . . *in'tōn-āt*
intonation . . . *in-tōn-ā'shun*
intoxicant . . . *in-toks'i-kant*
intoxicate . . . *in-toks'i-kāt*
intoxicating . . . *in-toks'i-kāt-ing*
intractable . . . *in-trakt'a-bl*
intransigent . . . *in-tran'si-jent*
intransitive . . . *in-trans'it-iv*
intrench . . . *in-trensh'*
intrenchment . . . *in-trensh'ment*
intrepidity . . . *in-tre-pid'i-ti*
intricacy . . . *in'tri-ka-si*
intricate . . . *in'tri-kāt*
intrigue . . . *in-trēg'*
introduce . . . *in-trō-dūs'*
introduction . . . *in-trō-duk'shun*
introductory . . . *in-trō-duk'to-ri*
introspect . . . *in-trō-spekt'*
introvert . . . *in-trō-vért'*
intrude . . . *in-trod'*
intrusion . . . *in-tro'zhon*
intrusive . . . *in-tro'siv*
intrust . . . *in-trust'*
intuition . . . *in-tū-i'shun*
intuitive . . . *in-tū'it-iv*
intuitively . . . *in-tū'it-iv-li*
inundate . . . *in-un'dāt* or *in'-*
inundation . . . *in-un-dā'shun*
invade . . . *in-vād'*
invader . . . *in-vād'ér*
invalid . . . *in-va'lid*
invalid . . . *in'va-lēd*
invalidate . . . *in-va'li-dāt*
invalidation . . . *in-va'li-dā"shun*
invaluable . . . *in-va'lū-a-bl*
invaluably . . . *in-va'lū-a-bli*
invariable . . . *in-vā'ri-a-bl*
invariably . . . *in-vā'ri-a-bli*
invasion . . . *in-vā'zhon*
invasive . . . *in-vā'siv*
invent . . . *in-vent'*
invention . . . *in-ven'shun*
inventive . . . *in-vent'iv*
inventor . . . *in-vent'ér*
inventory . . . *in'ven-to-ri*
inverse . . . *in'vérs* or *in-vérs'*
inversely . . . *in-vérs'li*
inversion . . . *in-vér'shun*
invert . . . *in-vért'*
invertebrate . . . *in-vér'tē-brāt*
inverted . . . *in-vért'ed*

invest... *in-vest'*
investigate... *in-ves'ti-gāt*
investigator... *in-ves'ti-gāt-ėr*
investiture... *in-ves'ti-tūr*
investment... *in-vest'ment*
investor... *in-vest'ėr*
inveterate... *in-vet'ėr-āt*
invidiously... *in-vid'i-us-li*
invigorate... *in-vi'gor-āt*
invincible... *in-vin'si-bl*
invincibly... *in-vin'si-bli*
inviolable... *in-vī'ō-la-bl*
inviolably... *in-vī'ō-la-bli*
inviolate... *in-vī'ō-lāt*
invisibility... *in-vi'zi-bil''i-ti*
invisible... *in-vi'zi-bl*
invisibly... *in-vi'zi-bli*
invitation... *in-vi-tā'shun*
invite... *in-vīt'*
inviting... *in-vīt'ing*
invocate... *invō-kāt*
invocation... *in-vō-kā'shun*
invoice... *in'vois*
invoke... *in-vōk'*
involuntarily... *in-vo'lun-ta-ri-li*
involuntary... *in-vo'lun-ta-ri*
involution... *in-vō-lū'shun*
involve... *in-volv'*
invulnerable... *in-vul'nėr-a-bl*
inward... *in'wėrd*
iodine... *T'ō-dīn, T'ō-dēn*
iranian... *i-rā'ni-an*
irascibility... *T-ras'i-bil''i-ti*
irascible... *T-ras'i-bl*
irascibly... *T-ras'i-bli*
irate... *T-rāt'*
iridescence... *T-rid-es'ens*
iridescent... *T-rid-es'ent*
iris... *T'ris*
irish... *T'rish*
irk... *ėrk*
irksome... *ėrk'sum*
irksomely... *ėrk'sum-li*
iron... *T'ėrn*
iron-clad... *T'ėrn-klad*
ironical... *T-ron'ik-al*
ironically... *T-ron'ik-al-li*
irony... *T'ėrn-i*
irony... *T'ron-i*
irrradiant... *ir-rā'di-ant*
irradiate... *ir-rā'di-āt*
irradiation... *ir-rā'di-ā''shun*
irrational... *ir-ra'shun-al*
irrationally... *ir-ra'shun-al-li*

irreducible... *ir-rē-dūs'i-bl*
irregularity... *ir-re'gū-la''ri-ti*
irregularly... *ir-re'gū-lėr-li*
irrelevant... *ir-rē'lė-vant*
irreligion... *ir-rē-li'jon*
irremediable... *ir-rē-mē'di-a-bl*
irremissible... *ir-rē-mis'i-bl*
irremovable... *ir-rē-mov'a-bl*
irreparable... *ir-rē'pa-ra-bl*
irrepressible... *ir-rē-pres'i-bl*
irreprovable... *ir-rē-prov'a-bl*
irresistance... *ir-rē-zis'tans*
irresistible... *ir-rē-zist'i-bl*
irresolute... *ir-re'zō-lūt*
irresolvable... *ir-rē-zolv'a-bl*
irrespective... *ir-rē-spekt'iv*
irresponsible... *ir-rē-spons'i-bl*
irresponsible... *ir-rēspons'iv*
irretrievable... *ir-rē-trēv'a-bl*
irreverence... *ir-rev'er-ens*
irreverent... *ir-rev'er-ent*
irreversible... *ir-rē-vėr'si-bl*
irrevocable... *ir-rev'vōk-a-bl*
irrigate... *ir'ri-gāt*
irrigation... *ir-ri-gā'shun*
irritable... *ir'rit-a-bl*
irritant... *ir'rit-ant*
irritate... *ir'rit-āt*
irritating... *ir'rit-āt-ing*
irritation... *ir-rit-ā'shun*
irruption... *ir-rup'shun*
irruptive... *ir-rup'tiv*
islamism... *is'lam-izm*
island... *T'land*
islander... *T'land-ėr*
isle... *Tl*
isolate... *T'sō-lāt*
isolation... *Ts-ō-lā'shun*
isolationist... *Ts-ō-lā'shun-ist*
isosceles... *T-sos'e-lēz*
israelite... *iz'ra-el-Tt*
issuable... *ish'ū-a-bl*
issue... *ish'ū*
it... *it*
italian... *i-ta'i-an*
italic... *i-ta'lik*
italicize... *i-ta'li-sīz*
itch... *ich*
itchy... *ich'i*
iterate... *it'ėr-āt*
iteration... *it-ėr-ā'shun*
itinerancy... *i- or T-tin'ėr-an-si*
itinerant... *i- or T-tin'ėr-ant*
itinerary... *i- or T-tin'ėr-a-ri*

I

itinerate . . . i- or ī-tin'ėr-āt
its . . . its
itself . . . it-self'
ivory . . . ī'vo-ri
ivy . . . ī'vi

J

jabber . . . jab'ėr
jackass . . . jak'as
jacket . . . jak'et
jacobean . . . ja-kō-bē'an
jacobin . . . ja'kō-bin
jade . . . jād
jag . . . jag
jagged . . . jag'ed
jaggy . . . jag'i
jaguar . . . ja-gwar'
jail . . . jāl
jailer . . . jāl'ėr
jam . . . jam
janitor . . . ja'ni-tor
january . . . ja'nū-a-ri
japan . . . ja-pan'
jar . . . jar
jargon . . . jar'gon
jasmine . . . jas'min
jasper . . . jas'pėr
jaundice . . . jan'dis
jaunt . . . janẗ
jauntily . . . jan-ti-li
jaunty . . . jan'ti
javelin . . . jav'lin
jaw . . . ja
jay . . . jā
jazz . . . jaz
jealous . . . je'lus
jealously . . . je'lus-li
jealousy . . . je'lus-i
jean . . . jān
jeep . . . jēp
jeer . . . jēr
jeeringly . . . jēr'ing-li
jehovah . . . jē-hō'va
jelly . . . je'li
jeopardize . . . je'pėrd-īz
jeopardous . . . je'pėrd-us
jeopardy . . . je'pėrd-i
jerk . . . jėrk
jerked . . . jėrkt
jerkin . . . jėr'kin
jersey . . . jėr'zi

jessamine . . . jes'a-min
jest . . . jest
jester . . . jest'ėr
jesuit . . . je'zū-it
jesuitism . . . je'zū-it-izm
jesus . . . jē'zus
jet . . . jet
jet-black . . . jet'blak
jettison . . . jet'i-son
jetty . . . jet'i
jew . . . jū
jewel . . . jū'el
jeweller . . . jū'el-ėr
jewelry . . . jū-el-ėr-i
jewess . . . jū'es
jewish . . . jū'ish
jewry . . . jū'ri
jiffy . . . jif'i
jig . . . jig
jilt . . . jilt
jingle . . . jing'gl
jingo . . . jing'go
job . . . job
jobber . . . job'ėr
jockey . . . jok'i
jocular . . . jok'ū-lėr
jocularity . . . jok-ū-la'ri-ti
jog . . . jog
joggle . . . jog'l
jog-trot . . . jog'trot
join . . . join
joiner . . . join'ėr
joinery . . . join'ėr-i
joining . . . join'ing
joint . . . joint
jointed . . . joint'ed
jointly . . . joint'li
joint-stock . . . joint'stok
jointure . . . joint'ūr
joist . . . joist
joke . . . jōk
jokingly . . . jōk'ing-li
jolly . . . jol'i
jolt . . . jōlt
jonquil . . . jon'kwil
joss . . . jos
jostle . . . jos'l
jot . . . jot
jotting . . . jot'ing
journal . . . jėr'nal
journalism . . . jėr'nal-izm
journalist . . . jėr'nal-ist
journey . . . jėr'ni
journeyman . . . jėr'ni-man

joust... *jost*
jovial... *jō'vi-al*
joviality... *jō-vi-al'i-ti*
jovially... *jō'vi-al-li*
joy... *joi*
joyful... *joi'ful*
joyfully... *joi'ful-li*
jubilant... *jū'bĭ-lant*
jubilation... *jū-bi-lā'shun*
jubilee... *jū'bi-lē*
judaism... *jū'dā-izm*
judge... *juj*
judgeship... *juj'ship*
judgment... *juj'ment*
judicative... *jū'di-kā-tiv*
judicatory... *jū'di-kā-to-ri*
judicature... *jū'di-kā-tūr*
judicial... *jū-di'shal*
judicially... *jū-di'shal-li*
judiciary... *jū-di'shi-a-ri*
judicious... *jū-di'shus*
judiciously... *jū-di'shus-li*
jug... *jug*
juggle... *jug'l*
juggler... *jug'lèr*
jugular... *ju'gū-lèr*
juice... *jūs*
juicy... *jūs'i*
jujitsu... *jo-jit'so*
julep... *jū'lep*
july... *jū-lī'*
jumble... *jum'bl*
jump... *jump*
jumper... *jump'èr*
junction... *jungk'shun*
june... *jūn*
jungle... *jung'gl*
junior... *jū'ni-èr*
juniper... *jū'ni-pèr*
junk... *jungk*
jupiter... *jū'pi-tèr*
jurassic... *jū-ras'ik*
juridical... *jū-rid'ik-al*
jurisdiction... *jū-ris-dik'shun*
jurisprudence... *jū-ris-pro'dens*
jurist... *jū'rist*
juror... *jū'rèr*
jury... *jū'ri*
just... *just*
justice... *jus'tis*
justifiable... *just'i-fī-a-bl*
justifiably... *just'i-fī-a-bli*
justification... *just'i-fi-kā''shun*
justificatory... *just-it'i-kā-to-ri*

justify... *just'i-fī*
justly... *just'li*
justness... *just'nes*
jut... *jut*
jute... *jūt*

K

kaftan... *kaf'tan*
kaiser... *kī'zèr*
kaleidoscope... *ka-lī'dos-kōp*
kangaroo... *kang'ga-ro*
keel... *kēl*
keen... *kēn*
keenly... *kēn'li*
keep... *kēp*
keeper... *kēp'èr*
keeping... *kēp'ing*
keepsake... *kēp'sāk*
keg... *keg*
kelp... *kelp*
kelt... *kelt*
kennel... *ken'el*
kerchief... *kèr'chif*
kernel... *kèr'nel*
kerosene... *ke'ro-sēn*
ketchup... *kech'up*
kettle... *ket'l*
key-board... *kē'bōrd*
keyed... *kēd*
khaki... *ka'ki*
kibe... *kīb*
kick... *kik*
kid... *kid*
kidnap... *kid'nap*
kidney... *kid'ni*
kill... *kil*
kiln... *kil*
kilogram... *kil'ō-gram*
kilometer... *kil'ō-mā-tr*
kilt... *kilt*
kimono... *kim-ō'nō*
kin... *kin*
kind... *kīnd*
kindergarten... *kin'dèr-gar-tn*
kindle... *kin'dl*
kindly... *kīnd'li*
kindness... *kind'nes*
kindred... *kin'dred*
kinematics... *ki-nē-mat'iks*
kinetic... *ki-net'ik*
king... *king*
kingdom... *king'dum*

kingship... *king'ship*
kink... *kingk*
kinsman... *kinz'man*
kismet... *kis'met*
kiss... *kis*
kit... *kit*
kitchen... *ki'chen*
kitchen-range... *ki'chen-rānj*
kite... *kīt*
kitten... *kit'n*
knack... *nak*
knap... *nap*
knapsack... *nap'sak*
knave... *nāv*
knavery... *nāv'ė-ri*
knavish... *nāv'ish*
knead... *nēd*
knee... *nē*
knee-cap... *nē'kap*
kneed... *nēd*
kneel... *nēl*
knell... *nel*
knick-knack... *nik'nak*
knife... *nīf*
knight... *nīt*
knighthood... *nīt'hụd*
knit... *nit*
knitting... *nit'ing*
knob... *nob*
knobby... *nob'i*
knock... *nok*
knocker... *nok'ėr*
knoll... *nōl*
knot... *not*
knotted... *not'ed*
knotty... *not'i*
knout... *nout*
know... *nō*
knowable... *nō'a-bl*
knowing... *nō'ing*
knowledge... *nol'ej*
known... *nōn*
knuckle... *nuk'l*
koran... *kō'ran*
kudos... *kū'dos*
kyanize... *kī'an-īz*

L

laager... *la'ger*
label... *lā'bel*
laboratory... *lab-or'a-to-ri*

labored... *lā'bėrd*
laborer... *lā'bėr-ėr*
laborious... *la-bō'ri-us*
labrum... *lā'brum*
laburnum... *la-bėr'num*
labyrinth... *lab'i-rinth*
lac... *lak*
lace... *lās*
lacerate... *la'sėr-āt*
laceration... *la-sėr-ā'shun*
lachrymatory... *lak'rim-a-to-ri*
lachrymose... *lak'rim-ōs*
lacing... *lās'ing*
lack... *lak*
lackadaisical... *lak-a-dā'zik-al*
lackey... *lak'i*
lacquer... *lak'ėr*
lacros... *la-kros'*
lactation... *lak-tā'shun*
lacteal... *lak'tē-al*
lactescent... *lak-tes'ent*
lactic... *lak'tik*
lactometer... *lak-tom'et-ėr*
lacuna... *la-kū'na*
lad... *lad*
ladanum... *lad'a-num*
ladder... *lad'ėr*
lade... *lād*
laden... *lād'n*
lading... *lād'ing*
ladle... *lā'dl*
lady... *lā'di*
lady-like... *lā'di-līk*
lag... *lag*
lager-beer... *la'gėr-bēr*
lagoon... *la-gon'*
lair... *lār*
laird... *lārd*
laity... *lā'i-ti*
lake... *lāk*
lama... *lā'ma*
lame... *lām*
lamely... *lām'li*
lament... *la-ment'*
lamentable... *la'ment-a-bl*
lamentably... *la'ment-a-bli*
lamentation... *la-ment-ā'shun*
lamina... *la'mi-na*
lamination... *la-mi-nā'shun*
lammas... *lam'mas*
lamp... *lamp*
lampoon... *lam-pon'*
lamprey... *lam'prā*
lance... *lans*

lanceolate... *lan'sē-o-lāt*
lancer... *lans'ėr*
lancinating... *lan'si-nāt-ing*
land... *land*
landau... *lan-da'*
land-breeze... *lånd'brēz*
landed... *land'ed*
landholder... *land'hōld-ėr*
landing... *land'ing*
landlady... *land'lā-di*
landlord... *land'lord*
landlubber... *land'lub-ėr*
landmark... *land'mark*
land-mine... *land'mīn*
land-owner... *land'ōn-ėr*
landscape... *land'skāp*
lane... *lān*
language... *lang'gwāj*
languidly... *lang'gwid li*
languish... *lang'gwish*
languishing... *lang'gwėsh-ing*
languorous... *lang'gwėr-us*
lanky... *lang'ki*
lanoline... *lan'ō-lin*
lantern... *lan'tėrn*
lap... *lap*
lapel... *la-pel'*
lapidary... *lap'i-da-ri*
lapse... *laps*
larceny... *lar'se-ni*
lard... *lard*
larder... *lard'ėr*
large... *larj*
largely... *larj'li*
largess... *larj-es'*
largo... *lar'go*
lariat... *la'ri-at*
lark... *lark*
larva... *lar'va*
larval... *lar'val*
larynx... *la'ringks*
lascivious... *las-si'vi-us*
lass... *las*
lassitude... *las'i-tū d*
lasso... *las'sō*
last... *last*
lasting... *last'ing*
lastingly... *last'ing-li*
lastly... *last'li*
latch... *lach*
latchet... *lach'et*
late... *lāt*
lately... *lāt'li*
latency... *lā'ten-si*

latent... *lā'tent*
lateral... *lat'ėr-al*
lathe... *lāŦH*
lather... *laŦH'ėr*
lathing... *lath'ing*
latin... *laī tin*
latinist... *la'tin-ist*
latinity... *la-tin'i-ti*
latitude... *la'ti-tū d*
latrine... *la-trēn'*
latter... *lat'ėr*
latterly... *lat'ėr-li*
laud... *la d*
laudable... *la d'a-bl*
laudation... *la-dā'shun*
laudatory... *läd'a-to-ri*
laugh... *laf*
laughable... *laf'a-bl*
laughably... *laf'a-bli*
laughingly... *laf'ing-li*
laughing-stock... *laf'ing-stok*
laughter... *laf'tėr*
launch... *lansh or lansh*
laundry... *lan'dri or lan'dri*
laureate... *la'rē-āt*
lava... *la'va*
lavatory... *lav'a-to-ri*
lavender... *lav'en-dėr*
lavish... *lav'ish*
lavishly... *lav'ish-li*
law... *la*
lawful... *la'ful*
lawfully... *la'ful-li*
lawgiver... *la'giv-ėr*
lawless... *la'les*
lawn... *lan*
lawyer... *la'yėr*
lax... *laks*
laxative... *laks'at-iv*
laxity... *laks'i-ti*
lay... *lā*
layer... *lā'ėr*
layman... *lā'man*
lazily... *lā'zi-li*
laziness... *lā'zi-nes*
lazy... *lā'zi*
lea... *lē*
lead... *led*
lead... *lēd*
leaded... *led'ed*
leaden... *led'n*
leader... *lēd'ėr*
leadership... *lēd'ėr-ship*
leading... *lēd'ing*

L

leaf... *lēf*
league... *lēg*
leagued... *lēgd*
leaguer... *lēg'ėr*
leak... *lēk*
leakage... *lēk'āj*
lean... *lēn*
lean... *lēn*
leanly... *lēn'li*
leap... *lēp*
leap-frog... *lēp'frog*
leap-year... *lēp'yēr*
learn... *lėrn*
learned... *lėrn'ed*
learnedly... *lėrn'ed-li*
learner... *lėrn'ėr*
learning... *lėrn'ing*
lease... *lēs*
leash... *lēsh*
leasing... *lēz'ing*
least... *lēst*
leather... *leŦH'ėr*
leathery... *leŦH'ėr-i*
leave... *lēv*
leave... *lēv*
leaven... *lev'n*
leavings... *lēv'ingz*
leavy... *lēv'i*
lecher... *lech'ėr*
lecherous... *lech'ėr-us*
lectern... *lek'tėrn*
lection... *lek'shun*
lecture... *lek'tūr*
lecturer... *lek'tūr-ėr*
lectureship... *lek'tūr-ship*
ledge... *lej*
ledger... *lej'ėr*
leech... *lēch*
leek... *lēk*
leer... *lēr*
leeway... *lē'wā*
left... *left*
left-hand... *left'hand*
left-off... *left'of*
leg... *leg*
legacy... *leg'a-si*
legal... *lē'gal*
legality... *lē-gal'i-ti*
legalize... *lē'gal-īz*
legally... *lē'gal-li*
legate... *le'gāt*
legation... *lē-gā'shun*
legator... *le-ga'tō*
legend... *le'jend*

legibility... *le-ji-bil'i-ti*
legible... *le'ji-bl*
legibly... *le'ji-bli*
legion... *lē'jon*
legionary... *lē'jon-a-ri*
legislate... *le'jis-lāt*
legislation... *le-jis-lā'shun*
legislative... *le'jis-lāt-iv*
legislator... *le'jis-lāt-ėr*
legislature... *le'jis-lāt-ūr*
legitimacy... *lē-jit'i-ma-si*
legitimate... *lē-jit'i-māt*
legitimation... *lē-jit'i-mā-shun*
legitimist... *lē-jit'i-mist*
legitimize... *lē-jit'i-mīz*
legume... *leg'ūm, le-gūm'*
leguminous... *le-gū'min-us*
leisure... *lē'zhūr*
leisurely... *lē'zhūr-li*
lemon... *le'mon*
lemonade... *le-mon-ād'*
lemur... *lē'mėr*
lend... *lend*
lender... *lend'ėr*
lengthen... *length'n*
lengthily... *length'i-li*
lengthwise... *length'wīz*
lengthy... *length'i*
lenient... *lē'ni-ent*
leniently... *lē'ni-ent-li*
lenity... *le'ni-ti*
lens... *lenz*
lent... *lent*
lenten... *lent'en*
lentil... *len'til*
leper... *lep'ėr*
leporine... *lep'or-īn*
leprosy... *lep'rō-si*
leprous... *lep'rus*
lesion... *lē'zhon*
less... *les*
lessee... *les-sē'*
lessen... *les'n*
lesser... *les'ėr*
lesson... *les'n*
lest... *lest*
let... *let*
let... *let*
lethargic... *le-thar'jik*
lethargy... *le'thar-ji*
letter... *let'ėr*
lettered... *let'ėrd*
lettering... *let'ėr-ing*
lettuce... *let'is*

leucoma . . . lū-kō'ma
leucopathy . . . lū-kop'a-thi
levant . . . le-vant'
levanter . . . lē-vant'ėr
levantine . . . lē-vant'īn
levee . . . lev'ā or lev'ē
level . . . le'vel
leveller . . . le'vel-ėr
levelling . . . le'vel-ing
lever . . . lē've̊r
leverage . . . lē've̊r-āj
leviable . . . le'vi-a-bl
leviathan . . . lē-vī'a-than
levigate . . . le'vi-gāt
levite . . . lē'vīt
levitical . . . lē-vit'ik-al
levity . . . le'vi-ti
levy . . . le'vi
lewdly . . . lūd'li
lexicon . . . leks'i-kon
liability . . . lī-a-bil'i-ti
liable . . . lī'a-bl
liaison . . . lē-ā-zōng
liar . . . lī'e̊r
lias . . . lī'as
libation . . . lī-bā'shun
libel . . . lī'bel
libeller . . . lī'bel-ėr
libellous . . . kī'bel-us
liberal . . . li'bėr-al
liberalism . . . li'bėr-al-izm
liberality . . . li-bėr-al'i-ti
liberalize . . . li'bėr-al-īz
liberally . . . li'bėr-al-li
liberate . . . li'bėr-āt
liberation . . . li-bėr-ā'shun
liberator . . . li'bėr-āt-ėr
libertine . . . li'bėr-tīn
libertinism . . . li'bėr-tin-izm
liberty . . . li'bėr-ti
libidinous . . . li-bid'i-nus
libra . . . lī'bra
library . . . lī'bra-ri
librate . . . lī'brāt
libration . . . lī-brā'shun
lice . . . līs
license . . . lī'sens
licenser . . . lī'sens-ėr
licentiate . . . lī-sen'shi-āt
licentious . . . lī-sen'shus
lick . . . lik
licorice . . . lik'or-is
lid . . . lid
lie . . . lī

lie . . . lī
lien . . . lī'en
lieu . . . lū
lieutenancy . . . lū-ten'an-si
lieutenant . . . lū-ten'ant
life . . . līf
life-boat . . . līf'bōt
life-giving . . . līf'giv-ing
life-guard . . . līf'gard
lifeless . . . līf'les
lifelike . . . līf'līk
lifelong . . . līf'long
lifetime . . . līf'tīm
lift . . . lift
ligament . . . li'ga-ment
ligation . . . lī-gā'shun
ligature . . . li'ga-tūr
light . . . līt
lighten . . . līt'n
lighter . . . līt'ėr
light-footed . . . līt'fut-ed
light-headed . . . līt'hed-ed
light-hearted . . . līt'hart-ed
lighthouse . . . līt'hous
lightly . . . līt'li
lightning . . . līt'ning
lightning-rod . . . līt'ning-rod
lights . . . līts
ligneous . . . lig'nē-us
lignify . . . lig'ni-fī
like . . . līk
likeable . . . līk'a-bl
likelihood . . . līk'li-hu̇d
likely . . . līk'li
liken . . . līk'en
likeness . . . līk'nes
liking . . . līk'ing
lilac . . . lī'lak
lilliputian . . . lil-i-pū'shan
lilt . . . lilt
lily . . . lil'i
limb . . . lim
limber . . . lim'bėr
limbo . . . lim'bo
lime . . . līm
lime-juice . . . līm'jūs
limerick . . . lim'er-ik
limestone . . . līm'stōn
limit . . . lim'it
limitable . . . lim'it-a-bl
limitation . . . lim-it-ā'shun
limited . . . lim'it-ed
limp . . . limp
limpid . . . lim'pid

L

line... līn
lineage... lin'ē-āj
lineal... lin'ē-al
linear... lin'ē-ėr
linen... lin'en
liner... līn'ėr
linger... ling'gėr
lingering... ling'gėr-ing
lingual... ling'gwal
linguist... ling'gwist
linguistic... ling-gwist'ik
linguistics... ling-gwist'iks
liniment... lin'i-ment
lining... līn'ing
link... lingk
links... lingks
linseed... lin'sē d
linstock... lin'stok
lint... lint
lion... lī'on
lioness... lī'on-es
lion-hearted... lī'on-hart-ed
lionize... lī'on-īz
lip... lip
lipstick... lip-stik
liquate... lī'kwāt
liquefier... lik'wē-fi-ėr
liquefy... lik'wē-fi
liqueur... li-kūr'
liquid... lik'wid
liquidation... lik-wid-ā'shun
liquidity... lik-wid'i-ti
liquor... lik'ėr
liquorice... lik'ėr-is
lira... lē'ra
lisp... lisp
list... list
listen... lis'n
listless... list'les
listlessly... list'les-li
litany... li'ta-ni
liter... lē'tr
literal... li'tėr-al
literally... li'tėr-al-li
literary... li'tėr-a-ri
literature... li'tėr-a-tūr
lith... lith
litharge... lith'arj
lithe... līŦH
lithesome... līŦH'sum
lithia... lith'i-a
lithium... lith'i-um
lithograph... lith'ō-graf
lithographer... li-tho'graf-ėr

lithography... li-tho'gra-fi
lithology... li-thol'o-ji
lithotomy... li-thot'ō-mi
litigant... li'ti-gant
litigate... li'ti-gāt
litigation... li-ti-gā'shun
litigious... li-tij'us
litter... lit'ėr
little... lit'l
littoral... lit'ō-ral
liturgist... li'tėr-jist
liturgy... li'tėr-ji
live... liv
live... līv
lived... livd or līvd
livelihood... līv'li-hu̇d
lively... līv'li
liver... liv'ėr
livery... liv'ėr-i
livid... liv'id
living... liv'ing
lixivium... lik-siv'i-um
lizard... li'zėrd
llama... lā'ma
load... lōd
loading... lōd'ing
loadstar... lōd'star
loaf... lōf
loafer... lōf'ėr
loam... lōm
loamy... lōm'i
loan... lōn
loath... lōth
loathe... lōŦH
loathing... lōŦH'ing
loathness... lōŦH'nes
loathness... lōŦH'sum
lob... lob
lobar... lō'bar
lobby... lob'i
lobe... lōb
lobster... lob'stėr
lobular... lob'ū-lėr
lobule... lob'ūl
local... lō'kal
locale... lō-kal'
localism... lō'kal-izm
locality... lō-kal'i-ti
locally... lō'kal-li
locate... lō'kāt
location... lō-kā'shun
loch... loch
lock... lok
lockage... lok'āj

locker... *lok'ėr*
locket... *lok'et*
lock-jaw... *lok'ja*
locksmith... *lok'smith*
lock-up... *lok'up*
locomotion... *lō-kō-mō'shun*
locomotive... *lō-kō-mō'tiv*
locust... *lō'kust*
locution... *lō-kū'shun*
lode... *lōd*
lodge... *loj*
lodger... *loj'ėr*
lodging... *loj'ing*
lodgment... *loj'ment*
loft... *loft*
loftily... *loft'i-li*
lofty... *loft'i*
log... *log*
loggerhead... *log'ėr-hed*
logic... *lo'jik*
logical... *lo'jik-al*
logically... *lo'jik-al-li*
logician... *lō-ji'shan*
logistic... *lō-jis'tik*
logogram... *log'ō-gram*
log-rolling... *log'rōl-ing*
logwood... *log'wụd*
loin... *loin*
loiter... *loi'tėr*
loiterer... *loi'tėr-ėr*
loll... *lol*
lollipop... *lol'i-pop*
lone... *lōn*
lonely... *lōn'li*
lonesome... *lōn'sum*
long... *long*
longevity... *lon-jev'i-ti*
longhand... *long'hand*
longing... *long'ing*
longingly... *long'ing-li*
longitude... *lon'ji-tūd*
longitudinal... *lon-ji-tūd'in-al*
longsome... *long'sum*
longways... *long'wāz*
long-winded... *long'wind-ed*
loofah... *lo'fa*
look... *luk*
looking-glass... *luk'ing-glas*
look-out... *luk-ọūt'*
loom... *lom¨*
loon... *lon*
loop... *lop*
loophole... *lop'hōl*
loose... *los*

loosely... *los'li*
loosen... *los'n*
loot... *lot*
lop... *lop*
lopping... *lop'ing*
lop-sided... *lop'sīd-ed*
loquacious... *lo-kwā'shus*
loquacity... *lo-kwas'i-ti*
lorcha... *lōr'cha*
lord... *lord*
lordling... *lord'ling*
lordly... *lord'li*
lore... *lōr*
lorgnette... *lor-nyet'*
lorgnon... *lor-nyōng*
loricate... *lo'ri-kāt*
lose... *loz*
losing... *loz'ing*
loss... *los*
lost... *lost*
lot... *lot*
lothario... *lō-thā'ri-ō*
lotion... *lō'shun*
lottery... *lot'ė-ri*
lotus... *lō'tus*
loud... *loud*
loudly... *loud'li*
loudspeaker... *loud-spē'kėr*
lounge... *lounj*
lounger... *lounj'ėr*
louse... *lous*
lousy... *louz'i*
lout... *lout*
loutish... *lout'ish*
lovable... *luv'a-bl*
love... *luv*
loveless... *luv'les*
love-lorn... *luv'lorn*
lovely... *luv'li*
lover... *luv'ėr*
loving... *luv'ing*
lovingly... *luv'ing-li*
low... *lō*
low... *lō*
lower... *lō'ėr*
lower... *lou'ėr*
lowering... *lou'ėr-ing*
lowing... *lō'ing*
lowland... *lō'land*
lowly... *lō'li*
low-water... *lō'wạ-tėr*
loyal... *loi'al*
loyalist... *loi'al-ist*
loyally... *loi'al-li*

L

loyalty... *loi'al-ti*
lozenge... *lo'zenj*
lubricant... *lū'brik-ant*
lubricate... *lū-brik-āt*
lubrication... *lū-brik-ā'shun*
lubricator... *lū-brik-āt-ėr*
lucent... *lū'sent*
lucid... *lū'sid*
lucidity... *lū-sid'i-ti*
lucifer... *lū'si-fėr*
luck... *luk*
luckily... *luk'i-li*
lucky... *luk'i*
lucrative... *lū'krat-iv*
lucre... *lū'kėr*
luculent... *lū'kū-lent*
ludicrous... *lū'di-krus*
luff... *luf*
lug... *lug*
luggage... *lug'āj*
lugger... *lug'ėr*
lugubrious... *lū-gū'bri-us*
lugworm... *lug'wėrm*
lukewarm... *lūk'warm*
lull... *lul*
lullaby... *lul'a-bī*
lumbago... *lum-bā'gō*
lumbar... *lum'bar*
lumber... *lum'bėr*
luminary... *lū'min-a-ri*
luminous... *lū'min-us*
lump... *lump*
lumping... *lump'ing*
lumpish... *lump'ish*
lumpy... *lump'i*
lunacy... *lū'na-si*
lunar... *lū'nar*
lunatic... *lū'nat-ik*
lunation... *lū-nā'shun*
lune... *lūn*
lunette... *lū-net'*
lung... *lung*
lunge... *lunj*
lunged... *lungd*
lunular... *lū'nū-lėr*
lupine... *lū'pin*
lupus... *lū'pus*
lurch... *lėrch*
lure... *lūr*
lurid... *lū'rid*
lurk... *lėrk*
luscious... *lu'shus*
lush... *lush*
lust... *lust*

lustful... *lust'ful*
lustily... *lust'i-lī*
lustral... *lus'tral*
lustrate... *lus'trāt*
lustration... *lus-trā'shun*
lustring... *lūs'tring*
lustrous... *lus'trus*
lustrum... *lus'trum*
lusty... *lust'i*
lute... *lūt*
lutheran... *lū'thėr-an*
lutheranism... *lū'thėr-an-izm*
luxate... *luks'āt*
luxation... *luks-ā'shun*
luxuriance... *luks-ū'ri-ans*
luxuriant... *luks-ū'ri-ant*
luxuriate... *luks-ū'ri-āt*
luxurious... *luks-ū'ri-us*
luxuriously... *luks-ū'ri-us-li*
luxury... *luks'ū-ri*
lycanthropy... *lī-kan'thro-pi*
lyceum... *lī-sē'um*
lycopod... *lī'kō-pod*
lyddite... *lid'īt*
lyingly... *lī'ing-li*
lymph... *limf*
lymphatic... *lim-fat'ik*
lynch... *linsh*
lynx... *lingks*
lyre... *līr*
lyric... *li'rik*
lyrist... *līr'ist*

M

macabre... *mak-a'br*
macaroni... *ma-ka-rō'ni*
macaroon... *ma-ka-ron'*
macaw... *ma-ka'*
mace... *mās*
macerate... *ma'se-rāt*
maceration... *ma-se-rā'shun*
machinate... *mak'i-nāt*
machination... *mak'i-nā''shun*
machine... *ma-shēn'*
machine-gun... *ma-shēn'gun*
machinery... *ma-shēn'e-ri*
machinist... *ma-shēn'ist*
mackerel... *mak'ėr-el*
mackintosh... *mak'in-tosh*
maculate... *ma'kū-lāt*
mad... *mad*
madam... *ma'dam*

madden... *mad'n*
madder... *mad'ĕr*
madly... *mad'li*
madman... *mad'man*
madness... *mad'nes*
madonna... *ma-don'na*
madrepore... *ma'dre-pōr*
maestro... *ma-es'trō*
magazine... *mag'a-zēn*
magenta... *ma-jen'ta*
maggot... *ma'got*
magic... *ma'jik*
magical... *ma'jik-al*
magically... *ma'jik-al-li*
magician... *ma-ji'shan*
magisterial... *ma-jis-tē'ri-al*
magistracy... *ma'jis-tra-si*
magistrate... *ma'jis-trāt*
magnate... *mag'nāt*
magnesia... *mag-nē'si-a*
magnesian... *mag-nē'si-an*
magnet... *mag'net*
magnetic... *mag-net'ik*
magnetism... *mag'net-izm*
magnetize... *mag'net-īz*
magnific... *mag-nik'ik*
magnificence... *mag-nif'i-sens*
magnificent... *mag-nif'i-sent*
magnifier... *mag'ni-fī-ĕr*
magnify... *mag'ni-fī*
magnitude... *mag'ni-tūd*
magnum... *mag'num*
mahogany... *ma-hog'a-ni*
maid... *mād*
maiden... *mād'n*
maidenhood... *mād'n-hụd*
maidenly... *mād'n-li*
mail... *māl*
maim... *mām*
main... *mān*
mainland... *mān'land*
mainly... *mān'li*
main-stay... *mān'stā*
maintain... *mān-tān'*
maintainable... *mān-tān'a-bl*
maize... *māz*
majestic... *ma-jes'tik*
majestically... *ma-jes'tik-al-li*
majesty... *ma'jes-ti*
major... *mā'jĕr*
majority... *ma-jo'ri-ti*
make... *māk*
make-believe... *māk'bē-lēv*
maker... *māk'ĕr*

make-shift... *māk'shift*
make-up... *māk'up*
making... *māk'ing*
malachite... *mal'a-kit*
malacology... *mal-a-kol'o-ji*
malady... *mal'a-di*
malaria... *ma-lā'ri-a*
malcontent... *mal'kon-tent*
male... *māl*
malefactor... *mal-e-fak'tĕr*
malevolence... *ma-lev'ō-lens*
malevolent... *ma-lev'ō-lent*
malic... *mā'lik*
malice... *mal'is*
malicious... *ma-li'shus*
malignance... *ma-lig'nans*
malignant... *ma-lig'nant*
malignity... *ma-lig'ni-ti*
malinger... *ma-ling'gĕr*
malingerer... *ma-ling'gĕr-ĕr*
malison... *mal'i-zn*
mall... *mal*
mallard... *mal'ard*
malleability... *mal'lē-a-bil'i'ti*
malleable... *mal'lē-a-bl*
mallet... *mal'et*
mallow... *mal'ō*
malnutrition... *mal-nū-tri'shun*
malpractice... *mcl-prak'tis*
malt... *malt*
maltese... *mal-tēz'*
malting... *mält'ing*
malt-liquor... *malt'lik-ĕr*
maltreat... *mal-frēt*
maltreatment... *mal-trēt'ment*
mamma... *mam'ma*
mammal... *mam'mal*
mammalia... *mam-mā'li-a*
mammilla... *mam-mil'la*
mammoth... *mam'oth*
man... *man*
manacle... *man'a-kl*
manage... *man'āj*
manageable... *man'āj-a-bl*
management... *man'āj-ment*
manager... *man'āj-ĕr*
manakin... *man'a-kin*
manatee... *man-a-tē'*
manchet... *man'shet*
manciple... *man'si-pl*
mandamus... *man-dā'mus*
mandarin... *man-da-rēn'*
mandatary... *man'da-ta-ri*
mandate... *man'dāt*

M

mandatory... *man'da-to-ri*
mandible... *man'di-bl*
mandibular... *man-dib'ū-lėr*
mandrake... *man'drāk*
mandrill... *man'dril*
mane... *mān*
manequin... *man'i-kin*
maneuver... *ma-nū'vėr*
manes... *mā'nēz*
manganite... *man'gan-īt*
mange... *mānj*
manger... *mān'jėr*
mangle... *mang'gl*
mango... *mang'gō*
mangrove... *man'grōv*
mangy... *mān'ji*
manhole... *man'hōl*
manhood... *man'hụd*
mania... *mā'ni-a*
maniac... *mā'ni-ak*
maniacal... *ma-nī'ak-al*
manicure... *man'i-kūr*
manifest... *man'i-fest*
manifestly... *man'i-fest-li*
manifesto... *man-i-fest'ō*
manifold... *man'i-fōld*
manikin... *man'i-kin*
manilla... *ma-nil'a*
manipulate... *ma-nip'ū-lāt*
manipulator... *ma-nip'ū-lāt-ėr*
manis... *mā'nis*
mankind... *man-kind'*
manlike... *man'lik*
manly... *man'li*
mannequin... *man'ē-kin*
manner... *man'ėr*
mannered... *man'ėrd*
mannerism... *man'ėr-izm*
mannerly... *man'ėr-li*
mannish... *man'ish*
man-of-war... *man'ov-war*
manor... *ma'nor*
mansion... *man'shun*
manslaughter... *man'sla-tėr*
mantilla... *man-til'la*
mantle... *man'tl*
manual... *man'ū-al*
manufactory... *man-ū-fak'to-ri*
manufacture... *man-ū-fak'tūr*
manure... *man-ūr'*
manuscript... *man'ū-skript*
manx... *mangks*
many... *me'ni*
map... *map*

maple... *mā'pl*
mar... *mar*
marabou... *ma'ra-bo*
maraud... *ma-rad'*
marauder... *mā-rad'ėr*
marble... *mar'bl*
marbling... *mar'bl-ing*
mare... *mār*
margarine... *mar'ga-rin*
margin... *mar'jin*
marginal... *mar'jin-al*
marigold... *ma'ri-gōld*
marine... *ma-rēn'*
mariner... *ma'rin-ėr*
marionette... *ma'ri-o-net''*
marital... *ma'ri-tal*
maritime... *ma'ri-fīm*
marjoram... *mar'jō-ram*
mark... *mark*
marked... *markt*
marker... *mark'ėr*
market... *mar'ket*
marketable... *mar'ket-a-bl*
marketing... *mar'ket-ing*
marking-ink... *mark'ing-ingk*
marksman... *marks'man*
marl... *mārl*
marline... *mar'lin*
marly... *marl'i*
marmalade... *mar'ma-lād*
marmorate... *mar'mo-rāt*
marmoreal... *mar-mō'rē-al*
marmot... *mar'mot*
maroon... *ma-ron*
marque... *mark*
marquee... *mar-kē'*
marquetry... *mar'ket-ri*
marriage... *ma'rij*
marriageable... *ma'rij-a-bl*
married... *ma'rid*
marrow... *ma'rō*
marrow-bone... *ma'rō-bōn*
marry... *ma'ri*
mars... *marz*
marsh... *marsh*
marshal... *mar'shal*
marshalling... *mar'shal-ing*
marsh-mallow... *marsh'mal-ō*
marshy... *marsh'i*
marsupial... *mar-sū'pi-al*
mart... *mart*
martin... *mar'tin*
martinet... *mar'ti-net*
martingale... *mar'tin-gāl*

martyr... *mar'tėr*
martyrdom... *mar'tėr-dom*
marvel... *mar'vel*
marvellous... *mar'vel-us*
marvellously... *mar'vel-us-li*
mascot... *mas'kot*
masculine... *mas'kū-lin*
mash... *mash*
mask... *mask*
masked... *maskt*
masochism... *mas'ō-kism*
mason... *mā'sn*
masonic... *ma-son'ik*
masonry... *mā'sn-ri*
masquerade... *mas-kėr-ād'*
mass... *mas*
massacre... *mas'sa-kėr*
massage... *ma-sazh'*
masseuse... *mas'oz*
masseur... *mas-or*
masseter... *mas-sē'tėr*
massy... *mas'i*
mast... *mast*
masted... *mast'ed*
master... *mas'tėr*
masterful... *mas'tėr-ful*
master-key... *mas'tėr-kē*
masterly... *mas'tėr-li*
masterpiece... *mas'tėr-pēs*
mastery... *mas'tė-ri*
mast-head... *mast'hed*
masticate... *mas'ti-kāt*
mastication... *mas-ti-kā'shun*
masticatory... *mas'ti-kā-to-ri*
mastiff... *mas'tif*
mastodon... *mas'to-don*
mat... *mat*
matador... *ma-ta-dōr'*
match... *mach*
matchless... *mach'les*
mate... *māt*
mate... *ma'tā*
material... *ma-tē'ri-al*
materialism... *ma-tē'ri-al-izm*
materialist... *ma-tē'ri-al-ist*
materialize... *ma-tē'ri-al-īz*
materially... *ma-tē'ri-al-li*
maternal... *ma-tėr'nal*
maternity... *ma-tėr'ni-ti*
math... *math*
matinee... *mat'i-nā*
matricide... *mat'ri-sīd*
matriculate... *ma-trik'ū-lāt*
matrimonial... *mat-ri-mō'ni-al*

matrimony... *mat'ri-mō-ni*
matrix... *mā'triks*
matron... *mā'tron*
matronly... *mā'tron-li*
matted... *mat'ed*
matter... *mat'ėr*
matting... *mat'ing*
mattock... *mat'ok*
mattress... *mat'res*
maturation... *ma-tur-ā'shun*
maturative... *ma-tū'ra-tiv*
mature... *ma-tūr'*
maturely... *ma-tūr'li*
maturity... *ma-tūr'i-ti*
matutinal... *ma-tū-tīn'al*
maugre... *ma'gėr*
maul... *mal*
maunder... *man'dėr*
mausoleum... *ma-sō-lē'um*
mauve... *mōv*
mavis... *mā'vis*
maxilla... *mak-sil'la*
maxillar... *mak-sil'lar*
maxim... *mak'sim*
maximum... *mak'sim-um*
may... *mā*
may-day... *mā'dā*
mayonnaise... *mā-on-āz*
mayor... *mā'ėr*
mayoral... *mā'ėr-al*
mayoralty... *mā'ėr-al-ti*
may-pole... *mā'pōl*
mazarine... *maz-a-rēn'*
maze... *māz*
me... *mē*
mead... *mēd*
meadow... *me'dō*
meager... *mē'gėr*
meagerly... *mē'gėr-li*
mealy... *mēl'i*
mean... *mēn*
meander... *mē-an'dėr*
meaning... *mēn'ing*
meaningless... *mēn'ing-les*
meaningly... *mēn'ing-li*
meanly... *mēn'li*
meantime... *mēn'tīm*
meanwhile... *mēn'whīl*
measles... *mē'zlz*
measly... *mēz'li*
measurable... *me'zhūr-a-bl*
measure... *me'zhūr*
measured... *me'zhūrd*
meat... *mēt*

M

mechanic... *me-kan'ik*
mechanical... *me-kan'ik-al*
mechanically... *me-kan'ik-al-li*
mechanics... *me-kan'iks*
mechanism... *mek'an-izm*
medal... *med'al*
medallion... *me-dal'yon*
medalist... *med'al-ist*
meddle... *med'l*
meddlesome... *med'l-sum*
meddling... *med'ling*
medial... *mē'di-al*
median... *mē'di-an*
mediate... *mē'di-āt*
mediately... *mē'di-āt-li*
mediation... *mē-di-ā'shun*
mediative... *mē'di-āt-iv*
mediator... *mē'di-āt-ėr*
mediatorial... *mē'di-a-tō''ri-al*
medicable... *med'ik-a-bl*
medical... *med'i-kal*
medically... *med'i-kal-li*
medicate... *med'i-kāt*
medicative... *med'i-kā-tiv*
medicinal... *me-dis'in-al*
medicinally... *me-dis'in-al-li*
medicine... *med'sin*
medieval... *mē-di-ē'val*
mediocre... *mē'di-ō-kėr*
mediocrity... *mē-di-ok'ri-ti*
meditate... *med'i-tāt*
meditation... *med-i-tā'shun*
meditative... *med'i-tāt-iv*
medlar... *med'lėr*
medley... *med'li*
medoc... *me-dok'*
medulla... *me-dul'la*
medullary... *me-dul'la-ri*
medusa... *me-dū'sa*
meed... *mēd*
meek... *mēk*
meekly... *mēk'li*
meet... *mēt*
meeting... *mēt'ing*
meetly... *mēt'li*
megaphone... *meg'a-fōn*
melancholia... *mel-an-kō'li-a*
melancholic... *mel'an-kol-ik*
melancholy... *mel'an-ko-li*
melanic... *me-lan'ik*
meliorate... *mē'lyor-āt*
mellow... *mel'ō*
melodeon... *me-lō'de-on*
melodic... *me-lod'ik*

melodious... *me-lō'di-us*
melodiously... *me-lō'di-us-li*
melodist... *me'lō-dist*
melody... *me'lō-di*
melon... *me'lon*
melt... *melt*
melting... *melt'ing*
member... *mem'bėr*
membership... *mem'bėr-ship*
membrane... *mem'brān*
membranous... *mem'bra-nus*
memento... *mē-men'tō*
memoir... *mem'oir, mem'war*
memorable... *mem'or-a-bl*
memorably... *mem'or-a-bil*
memorial... *mē-mō'ri-al*
memoralist... *mē-mō'ri-al-ist*
memorialize... *mē-mō'ri-al-īz*
memorize... *mem'or-īz*
memory... *mem'ō-ri*
menace... *men'ās*
menacingly... *men'ās-ing-li*
menage... *men-azh'*
menagerie... *me-naj'ėr-i*
mend... *mend*
mendacious... *men-dā'shus*
mendacity... *men-das'i-ti*
mendicancy... *men'di-kan-si*
mendicant... *men'di-kant*
mendicity... *men-dis'i-ti*
menhaden... *men-hā'den*
menial... *mē'ni-al*
meningitis... *men-in-jī'tis*
menses... *men'sēz*
menstrual... *men'stru-al*
menstruate... *men'stru-āt*
mensurable... *men'sūr-a-bl*
mental... *men'tal*
mentally... *men'tal-li*
menthol... *men'thol*
mention... *men'shun*
mentionable... *men'shun-a-bl*
mentor... *men'tor*
menu... *men'o*
mephitis... *me-fī'tis*
mercantile... *mėr'kan-til*
mercenary... *mėr'se-na-ri*
mercer... *mėr'sėr*
mercery... *mėr'sė-ri*
merchandise... *mėr'chand-īz*
merchant... *mėr'chant*
mercifully... *mėr'si-ful-li*
merciless... *mėr'si-lės*
mercilessly... *mėr'si-les-li*

mercurial... *mėr-kū'ri-al*
mercurialize... *mėr-kū'ri-al-īz*
mercury... *mėr'kū-ri*
mercy... *mėr'si*
mere... *mēr*
merely... *mēr'li*
meretricious... *me-rē-tri'shus*
merge... *mėrj*
meridian... *mē-rid'i-an*
meridional... *mē-rid'i-on-al*
meringue... *mer-ang'*
merino... *me-rē'no*
merit... *me'rit*
meritorious... *me-rit-ō'ri-us*
mermaid... *mėr'mād*
merrily... *me'ri-li*
merriment... *me'ri-ment*
merry... *me'ri*
mesh... *mesh*
meshy... *mesh'i*
mesmerism... *mez'mėr-izm*
mesmerize... *mez'mėr-īz*
mesne... *mēn*
mess... *mes*
message... *mes'āj*
messenger... *mes'en-jėr*
messiah... *mes-sī'a*
messieurs... *mes'yėrz*
metabolic... *me-ta-bol'ik*
metabolism... *me-tab'ol-izm*
metacenter... *me-ta-sen'tėr*
metal... *me'tal*
metallic... *me-tal'ik*
metalline... *me'tal'īn*
metallist... *me'tal-ist*
metallurgic... *me-tal-ėr'jik*
metallurgy... *me'tal-ėr-ji*
metamorphic... *me-ta-mor'fik*
metaphor... *me'ta-for*
metaphrase... *me'ta-frāz*
metaphrastic... *me-ta-frast'ik*
metaphysic... *me-ta-fi'zik*
metaphysical... *me-ta-fi'zik-al*
metaphysics... *me-ta-fi'ziks*
metathesis... *me-ta'the-sis*
meteoric... *mē-tē-or'ik*
meteorite... *mē'tē-ėr-īt*
meterolite... *mē'tē-ėr-ō-līt*
meter... *mē'tėr*
method... *me'thod*
methodic... *me-thod'ik*
methodism... *me'thod-izm*
methodist... *me'thod-ist*
methodize... *me'thod-īz*

methyl... *meth'il*
methylated... *meth'i-lāt-ed*
metonymy... *me-ton'i-mi*
meter... *mē'tėr*
meter... *mē'tėr*
metric... *met'rik*
metric... *met'rik*
mettle... *met'l*
mettled... *met'ld*
mettlesome... *met'l-sum*
mew... *mū*
mezzo... *med'zō*
mezzotint... *mez'ō-tint*
miasma... *mī-az'ma*
mica... *mī'ka*
mice... *mīs*
microbe... *mī'krōb*
microcosm... *mī'krō-kozm*
micrography... *mī-krog'ra-fi*
micrology... *mī-krol'o-ji*
micrometer... *mī-krom'et-ėr*
microphone... *mī'krō-fōn*
microphyte... *mī'krō-fīt*
microscope... *mī'krō-skōp*
mid... *mid*
mid-air... *mid'ār*
mid-day... *mid'dā*
middle... *mid'l*
middle-aged... *mid'l-ājd*
middle-class... *mid'l-klas*
middleman... *mid'l-man*
middlemost... *mid'l-mōst*
midnight... *mid'nīt*
midriff... *mid'rif*
midshipman... *mid'ship-man*
midst... *midst*
midsummer... *mid'sum-ėr*
midway... *mid'wā*
midwife... *mid'wīf*
might... *mīt*
mightily... *mīt'i-li*
mighty... *mīt'i*
migrant... *mī'grant*
migrate... *mī'grāt*
migration... *mī'grā-shun*
migratory... *mī'grā-to-ri*
mild... *mīld*
mildew... *mil'dū*
mildly... *mīld'li*
mildness... *mīld'nes*
mile... *mīl*
mileage... *mīl'āj*
milestone... *mīl'stōn*
milfoil... *mil'foil*

M

militancy ... *mil'i-tan-si*
militant ... *mil'i-tant*
militarism ... *mil'i-ta-rizm*
military ... *mil'i-ta-ri*
militate ... *mil'i-tāt*
militia ... *mi-li'sha*
militiaman ... *mi-li'sha-man*
milk ... *milk*
milkman ... *milk'man*
mill ... *mil*
milled ... *mild*
millenarian ... *mil-le-nā'ri-an*
millennial ... *mil-len'i-al*
millennium ... *mil-len'i-um*
miller ... *mil'ėr*
millesimal ... *mil-les'im-al*
millet ... *mil'et*
milliard ... *mil-yard'*
milliner ... *mil'in-ėr*
millinery ... *mil'in-ė-ri*
milling ... *mil'ing*
million ... *mil'yon*
millionaire ... *mil'yon-ār*
millionth ... *mil'yonth*
mill-pond ... *mil'pond*
millstone ... *mil'stōn*
milt ... *milt*
mime ... *mīm*
mimic ... *mim'ik*
mimicry ... *mim'ik-ri*
mimosa ... *mī-mō'sa*
minaret ... *min'a-ret*
minatory ... *min'a-to-ri*
mince-meat ... *mins'mēt*
mince-pie ... *mins'pī*
mincing ... *mins'ing*
mind ... *mīnd*
minded ... *mīnd'ed*
mindful ... *mīnd'ful*
mindless ... *mīnd'les*
mine ... *mīn*
miner ... *mīn'ėr*
mineral ... *mi'ne-ral*
mineralogist ... *mi-ne-ral'o-jist*
mineralogy ... *mi-ne-ral'o-ji*
mingle ... *ming'gl*
miniature ... *min'i-a-tūr*
minify ... *min'i-fī*
minikin ... *min'i-kin*
minim ... *min'im*
minimize ... *min'i-mīz*
minimum ... *min'i-mum*
mining ... *mīn'ing*
minion ... *min'yon*

minister ... *min'is-tėr*
ministerial ... *min-is-tē'ri-al*
ministerialist ... *min-is-tē'ri-al-ist*
ministrant ... *min'is-trant*
ministration ... *min-is-trā'shun*
ministrative ... *min'is-trāt-iv*
ministry ... *min'is-tri*
minium ... *min'i-um*
mink ... *mingk*
minnesinger ... *min'ne-sing-ėr*
minnow ... *min'ō*
minor ... *mī'nor*
minorite ... *mī'nor-īt*
minority ... *mi-no'ri-ti*
minster ... *min'stėr*
minstrel ... *min'strel*
mint ... *mint*
mintage ... *mint'āj*
minuet ... *mi'nū-et*
minus ... *mī'nus*
minuscule ... *mi-nus'kūl*
minute ... *mi-nūt'*
minute ... *mi'nit*
minutely ... *mi-nūt'li*
minutiae ... *mi-nū'shi-ē*
miocene ... *mī'ō-sēn*
miracle ... *mi'ra-kl*
miraculous ... *mi-ra'kū-lus*
miraculously ... *mi-ra'kū-lus-li*
mirage ... *mi-razh'*
mire ... *mīr*
mirror ... *mi'rėr*
mirth ... *mėrth*
mirthful ... *mėrth'ful*
mirthless ... *mėrth'les*
misadvised ... *mis-ad-vīzd'*
misalliance ... *mis-al-lī'ans*
misapply ... *mis-ap-plī'*
misarrange ... *mis-a-rānj'*
misbecome ... *mis-bē-kum'*
misbegotten ... *mis-bē-got'n*
misbehave ... *mis-bē-hāv'*
misbehavior ... *mis-bē-hāv'yėr*
misbelief ... *mis-bē-lēf'*
misbelieve ... *mis-bē-lev'*
miscalculate ... *mis-kal'kū-lāt*
miscarriage ... *mis-ka'rij*
miscellany ... *mis'sel-la-ni*
mischief ... *mis'chif*
mischievous ... *mis'chiv-us*
misconceive ... *mis-kon-sēv'*
misconstrue ... *mis-kon'stro*
miscount ... *mis-kount'*
misdate ... *mis-dāt'*

misdeed... *mis-dēd'*	**misty**... *mist'i*
misdemean... *mis-dē-mēn'*	**misuse**... *mis-ūz'*
misdirect... *mis-di-rekt'*	**mite**... *mīt*
misdirection... *mis-di-rek'shun*	**mitigant**... *mi'ti-gant*
misdoubt... *mis-dout'*	**mitigate**... *mi'ti-gāt*
miser... *mī'zėr*	**mitigation**... *mi-ti-gā'shun*
miserable... *miz'ėr-a-bl*	**miter**... *mī'tėr*
miserably... *miz'ėr-a-bli*	**mitered**... *mī'tėrd*
miserly... *mī'zėr-li*	**mitten**... *mit'n*
misery... *miz'ėr-i*	**mittimus**... *mit'i-mus*
misfit... *mis-fit'*	**mix**... *miks*
misfortune... *mis-for'tūn*	**mixable**... *miks'a-bl*
misgive... *mis-giv'*	**mixed**... *mikst*
misgiving... *mis-giv'ing*	**mixen**... *mik'sn*
misgovern... *mis-guv'ėrn*	**mixture**... *miks'tūr*
misguide... *mis-gī d'*	**moanful**... *mōn'fu̇l*
mishap... *mis-hap'*	**mob**... *mob*
misinform... *mis-in-form'*	**mobile**... *mō'bil*
misinterpret... *mis-in-tėr'pret*	**mobility**... *mō-bil'i-ti*
misjudge... *mis-juj'*	**mobilize**... *mob'il-īz*
mislay... *mis-lā'*	**moccasin**... *mok'a-sin*
mismanage... *mis-man'āj*	**mock**... *mok*
misname... *mis-nām'*	**mocker**... *mok'ėr*
misogamist... *mi-sog'am-ist*	**mockery**... *mok'ė-ri*
misogamy... *mi-sog'a-mi*	**mocking-bird**... *mok'ing-bėrd*
misplace... *mis-plās*	**mode**... *mōd*
misprint... *mis-print'*	**model**... *mo'del*
misquote... *mis-kwōt*	**modelling**... *mo'del-ing*
misreport... *mis-rē-pōrt'*	**moderate**... *mo'de-rāt*
misrule... *mis-rol'*	**moderation**... *mo-de-rā'shun*
miss... *mis*	**moderator**... *mo'de-rāt-ėr*
missal... *mis'al*	**modern**... *mod'ėrn*
misshape... *mis-shāp'*	**modernism**... *mod'ėrn-izm*
missile... *mis'īl*	**modernize**... *mod'ėrn-īz*
missing... *mis'ing*	**modest**... *mod'est*
mission... *mi'shun*	**modesty**... *mod'es-ti*
missionary... *mi'shun-a-ri*	**modify**... *mod'i-fī*
missive... *mis'iv*	**modish**... *mōd'ish*
misspell... *mis-spel'*	**modulate**... *mod'ū-lāt*
misspelling... *mis-spel'ing*	**modulator**... *mod'ū-lāt-ėr*
misspend... *mis-spend'*	**module**... *mod'ūl*
misspent... *mis-spent'*	**modulus**... *mod'ū-lus*
misstate... *mis-stāt'*	**modus**... *mō'dus*
misstatement... *mis-stāt'ment*	**mogul**... *mō-gul'*
mist... *mist*	**mohair**... *mō'hār*
mistake... *mis-tāk'*	**moist**... *moist*
mistaken... *mis-tāk'n*	**moisten**... *mois'n*
mister... *mis'tėr*	**moisture**... *mois'tūr*
mistime... *mis-fīm'*	**molar**... *mō'lėr*
mistletoe... *mis'l-tō*	**molasses**... *mō-las'ez*
mistranslate... *mis-trans-lāt'*	**mold**... *mōld*
mistress... *mis'tres*	**molder**... *mōld'ėr*
mistrust... *mis-trust'*	**molding**... *mōld'ing*
mistrustful... *mis-trust'fu̇l*	**moldy**... *mōld'i*

M

mole... *mōl*
molecular... *mō-lek'ū-lėr*
molecule... *mo'le-kūl*
molest... *mō-lest'*
molestation... *mō-lest-ā'shun*
mollifier... *mol'i-fī-ėr*
mollify... *mol'i-fī*
molluscous... *mol-lus'kus*
moment... *mō'ment*
momentary... *mō-ment-a-ri*
momentous... *mō-ment'us*
momentum... *mō-ment'um*
monachism... *mon'ak-izm*
monad... *mon'ad*
monadic... *mon-ad'ik*
monarch... *mon'ark*
monarchist... *mon'ark-ist*
monarchy... *mon'ar-ki*
monastery... *mon'as-te-ri*
monastic... *mon-as'tik*
monatomic... *mon-a-tom'ik*
monetary... *mo'ne-ta-ri*
monetize... *mon-et-īz'*
money... *mun'i*
monger... *mung'gėr*
mongol... *mon'gol*
mongoose... *mung'gos*
mongrel... *mung'grel*
monied... *mun'id*
monitor... *mo'ni-tėr*
monitorial... *mo-ni-tō'ri-al*
monitory... *mo'ni-to-ri*
monk... *mungk*
monochrome... *mon'ō-krōm*
monodrama... *mon'ō-dra-ma*
monogamist... *mon-og'a-mist*
monogamy... *mon-og'a-mi*
monogram... *mon'ō-gram*
monograph... *mon'ō-graf*
monolith... *mon'ō-lith*
monologue... *mon'ō-log*
monopolist... *mo-nop'o-list*
monopolize... *mo-nop'o-līz*
monopoly... *mo-nop'o-li*
monosyllable... *mon'ō-sil-la-bl*
monotone... *mon'ō-tōn*
monotonous... *mon-ot'on-us*
monotony... *mon-ot'o-ni*
monsoon... *mon-son'*
monster... *mon'stėr*
monstrance... *mon'strans*
monstrosity... *mon-stros'i-ti*
monstrous... *mon'strus*
monstrously... *mon'strus-li*

month... *munth*
monthly... *munth'li*
monument... *mon'ū-ment*
moody... *mod'i*
moon... *mon*
moonbeam... *mon'bēm*
moonlight... *mon'līt*
moonlighter... *mon'līt-ėr*
moonshine... *mon'shīn*
moonstruck... *mon'struk*
moor... *mor*
moorish... *mor'ish*
moorland... *mor'land*
moose... *mos*
moot... *mot*
mop... *mop*
mope... *mōp*
mopet... *mop'et*
mopish, mop... *mōp'ish*
moral... *mo'ral*
morale... *mō-ral'*
moralist... *mo'ral-ist*
morality... *mō-ral'i-ti*
moralize... *mo'ral-īz*
morbid... *mor'bid*
morbidly... *mor'bid-li*
morbific... *mor-bif'ik*
mordacity... *mor-das'i-ti*
more... *mōr*
morganatic... *mor-ga-nat'ik*
mormon... *mor'mon*
morn... *morn*
morning... *morn'ing*
morocco... *mōrok'ō*
moron... *mo'ron*
morose... *mō-rōs'*
morrow... *mo'rō*
morsel... *mor'sel*
mortal... *mor'tal*
mortality... *mor-tal'i-ti*
mortally... *mor'tal-li*
mortar... *mor'tar*
mortgage... *mor'gāj*
mortgagee... *mor-ga-jē'*
mortgager... *mor'gāj-ėr*
mortify... *mor'ti-fī*
mortifying... *mor'ti-fī-ing*
mortise... *mor'tis*
mortuary... *mor'tū-a-ri*
mosaic... *mō-zā'ik*
moslem... *moz'lem*
mosquito... *mos-kē'tō*
moss... *mos*
most... *mōst*

mostly... *mōst'li*
mote... *mōt*
moth... *moth*
mother... *muͬH'er*
motherhood... *muͬH'er-hud*
motherly... *muͬH'ūer-li*
motion... *mō'shun*
motionless... *mō'shun-les*
motive... *mō'tiv*
motivity... *mō-tiv'i-ti*
motley... *mot'li*
motor... *mō'tor*
motto... *mot'tō*
moult... *mōlt*
mound... *mound*
mount... *mount*
mountain... *moun'tin*
mountaineer... *moun-tin-ēr'*
mountainous... *moun'tin-us*
mounting... *mount'ing*
mourn... *mōrn*
mournful... *mōrn'ful*
mournfully... *mōrn'ful-li*
mourning... *mōrn'ing*
mouse... *mous*
moustache... *mus-tash'*
mouth... *mouth*
mouthful... *mouth'ful*
mouth-piece... *mouth'pēs*
movable... *mov'a-bl*
movably... *mov'a-bli*
move... *mov*
movement... *mov'ment*
mover... *mo'vėr*
moving
mow... *mou or mō*
mow... *mō*
mower... *mō'ėr*
much... *much*
muck... *muk*
mucus... *mū'kus*
mud... *mud*
muddle... *mud'l*
muddy... *mud'i*
muff... *muf*
muffle... *muf'l*
muffled... *muf'ld*
muffler... *muf'lėr*
mug... *mug*
muggy... *mug'i*
mulatto... *mū-lat'tō*
mulberry... *mul'be-ri*
mulch... *mulsh*
mule... *mūl*

mulish... *mūl'ish*
mull... *mul*
mullet... *mul'et*
multangular... *mul-tang'gū-lėr*
multifarious... *mul-ti-fā'ri-us*
multiform... *mul'ti-form*
multilateral... *mul-ti-lat'ėr-al*
multilineal... *mul-ti-lin'ē-al*
multiped... *mul'ti-ped*
multiple... *mul'ti-pl*
multiplex... *mul'ti-pleks*
multiplicative... *mul'ti-pli-kāt-iv*
multiplier... *mul-ti-plī'-ėr*
multiply... *mul'ti-plī*
mumble... *mum'bl*
mumbler... *mum'blėr*
mummify... *mum'i-fi*
mummy... *mum'i*
mump... *mump*
mumps... *mumps*
munch... *munsh*
mundane... *mun'dān*
municipality... *mū-ni'si-pal'i-ti*
munificence... *mū-ni'fi-sens*
munificently... *mū-ni'fi-sent-li*
mural... *mū'ral*
murder... *mėr'dėr*
murderer... *mėr'dėr-ėr*
murderess... *mėr'dėr-es*
murderous... *mėr'dėr-us*
murk... *mėrk*
murky... *mėr'ki*
murmur... *mėr'mėr*
murmurer... *mėr'mėr-ėr*
murmuring... *mėr'mėr-ing*
muscat... *mus'kat*
muscled... *mus'ld*
muscular... *mus'kū-lėr*
muse... *mūz*
museum... *mū-zē'um*
mushroom... *mush'rom*
music... *mū'zik*
musical... *mū'zik-al*
musically... *mu'zik-al-li*
music-hall... *mū'zik-hal*
musician... *mū-zi'shan*
musing... *mūz'ing*
musk... *musk*
musket... *mus'ket*
musketeer... *mus-ket-ēr'*
musky... *musk'i*
muslin... *muz'lin*
mussel... *mus'el*
must... *must*

M

mustard... *mus'tèrd*
muster... *mus'tèr*
musty... *mus'ti*
mutability... *mū-ta-bil'i-ti*
mutable... *mūta-bl*
mutation... *mū-tā'shun*
mute... *mūt*
mutely... *mūt'li*
mutilation... *mū'ti-lā'shun*
mutinous... *mū-ti-nus*
mutiny... *muti-ni*
mutter... *müt'èr*
muttering... *mut'èr-ing*
mutton... *mut'n*
mutual... *mū'tū-al*
mutually... *mū'tū-al-li*
muzzle... *muz'l*
my... *mī*
mycology... *mī-kol'o-ji*
myology... *mī-ol'o-ji*
myriad... *mi'ri-ad*
myrrh... *mèr*
myrtle... *mèr'tl*
myself... *mī-self'*
mysterious... *mis-tē'ri-us*
mysteriously... *mis-tē'ri-us-li*
mystery... *mis'tèr-i*
mystic... *mis'tik*
mysticism... *mis'ti-sizm*
mystify... *mis'ti-fi*
myth... *mith*
mythic... *mith'ik*

N

nab... *nab*
nacre... *nā'kèr*
nacreous... *nā'krē-us*
nadir... *nā'dèr*
nag... *nag*
naiad... *nā'yad*
nail... *nāl*
naked... *nā'ked*
nakedly... *nā'ked-li*
nakedness... *nā'ked-nes*
name... *nām*
nameless... *nām'les*
namely... *nām'li*
namesake... *nam'sāk*
nap... *nap*
nape... *nāp*
napery... *nā'pèr-i*

napkin... *nap'kin*
narcissus... *nar-sis'us*
narcotic... *nar-kot'ik*
nard... *nard*
nardine... *nard'in*
narrate... *na-rāt'* or *nar'*
narrative... *nar'a-tiv*
narrow... *na'rō*
narrowly... *na'rō-li*
nasal... *nā'zal*
nasturtium... *nas-tèr'shi-um*
nasty... *nas'ti*
natal... *nā'tal*
natatory... *nā'ta-to-ri*
nation... *nā'shun*
nationality... *na-shun-al'i-ti*
nationalize... *na'shun-al-īz*
nationally... *na'shun-al-li*
native... *nā'tiv*
natively... *nā'tiv-li*
nativity... *na-tiv'i-ti*
natural... *na'tūr-al*
naturalism... *na'tūr-al-izm*
naturalist... *na'tūr-al-ist*
naturalize... *na'tūr-al-iz*
naturally... *na'tūr-al-li*
nature... *nā'tūr*
naught... *nat*
naughtily... *na'ti-li*
naughty... *na'ti*
nauseate... *ña'she-āt*
nauseous... *nä'shus*
nautical... *na'tik-al*
naval... *nā'val*
nave... *nāv*
navel... *nā'vl*
navigate... *na'vi-gāt*
navigation... *na-vi-gā'shun*
navigator... *na'vi-gāt-èr*
navy... *nā'vi*
nay... *nā*
nazi... *na'tsi*
near... *nēr*
nearly... *nēr'li*
near-sighted... *nēr'sīted*
neat... *nēt*
neatly... *nēt'li*
nebular... *neb'ū-lèr*
nebulous... *neb'ū-lus*
necessarily... *ne'ses-sa-ri-li*
necessary... *ne'ses-sa-ri*
necessitate... *nē-ses'si-tāt*
necessitous... *nē-ses'sit-us*
necessity... *nē-ses'si-ti*

neckerchief... *nek'ėr-chif*
necklace... *nek'kās*
necrology... *nek-rol'o-ji*
necromancy... *nek'rō-man-si*
necropolis... *nek-rō'po-lis*
necrosis... *nek-rō'sis*
nectar... *nek'tar*
nectarine... *nek'ta-rīn*
nectary... *nek'ta-ri*
need... *nēd*
needful... *nēd'ful*
needle... *nē'dl* ¨
needless... *nēd'les*
needlessly... *nēd'les-li*
needle-work... *nē'dl-wėrk*
needly... *nē'dl-i*
needs... *nēdz*
negation... *nē-gā'shun*
negative... *neg'at-iv*
negatively... *neg'at-iv-li*
neglect... *neg-lekt'*
neglectful... *neg-lekt'ful*
neglige... *neg'lē-zhā* ¨
negligence... *neg'li-jens*
negligently... *neg'li-jent-li*
negotiable... *nē-gō'shi-a-bl*
negotiate... *nē-gō'shi-āt*
negotiator... *nē-gō'shi-āt-ėr*
neighbor... *nā'bėr*
neighborhood... *nā'bėr-hud*
neighboring... *nā'bėr-ing*
neighborly... *nā'bėr-li*
neither... *nēᵗHėr or nī'ᵗHėr*
nematoid... *nem'a-toid*
nemesis... *nem'e-sis*
neologist... *nē-ol'o-jist*
neology... *nē-ol'o-ji*
neon... *nē'on*
neophyte... *nē'ō-fīt*
neoteric... *nē-ō-te'rik*
nephritic... *ne-frit'ik*
nephritis... *nē-frī'tis*
nepotism... *nē'pot-izm*
nerve... *nėrv*
nerveless... *nėrv'les*
nervous... *nėrv'us*
nervously... *nėrv'us-li*
nest... *nest*
nestle... *nes'l*
nestling... *nes'ling*
net... *net*
net... *net*
nethermost... *ne'ᵗHėr-mōst*
netting... *net'ing*

nettle... *net'l*
net-work... *net'wėrk*
neural... *nū'ral*
neuralgia... *nū-ral'ji-a*
neuralgic... *nū-ral'jik*
neurology... *nū-rol'o-ji*
neurotic... *nū-rot'ik*
neuter... *nū'tėr*
neutral... *nū'tral*
neutrality... *nū-tral'i-ti*
neutralize... *nū'tral-īz*
neutron... *nū'tron*
never... *nev'ėr*
nevermore... *nev'ėr-mōr*
new... *nū*
new-fangled... *nū'fang'gld*
news... *nūz*
newspaper... *nūz'pā-pėr*
newt... *nūt*
next... *nekst*
nexus... *nek'sus*
nib... *nib*
nibble... *nib'l*
nibbler... *nib'lėr*
nice... *nīs*
nicely... *nīs'li*
nicety... *nīs'e-ti*
nickel... *nik'el*
nick-nack... *nik'nak*
nicotine... *nik'ō-tin*
nictate... *nik'tāt*
niece... *nēs*
nigh... *nī*
night... *nīt*
nightfall... *nīt'fal*
nightingale... *nīt'in-gāl*
nightly... *nīt'li*
nightmare... *nīt'mār*
night-walker... *nīt'wak-ėr*
nightward... *nīt'wėrd*
night-watch... *nīt'woch*
nimble... *nim'bl*
nimbly... *nim'bli*
nimbus... *nim'bus*
nine... *nīn*
nineteenth... *nīn'tēnth*
ninetieth... *nīn'ti-eth*
ninety... *nīn'ti*
ninth... *nīnth*
ninthly... *nīnth'li*
nip... *nip*
nippers... *nip'ėrz*
nipple... *nip'l*
nit... *nit*

N

niter... $n\bar{\imath}$'*tèr*
nitrate... $n\bar{\imath}$'*trāt*
nitric... $n\bar{\imath}$'*trik*
nitrify... $n\bar{\imath}$'*tri-fī*
nitrogen... $n\bar{\imath}$'*tro-jen*
nitrogenous... $n\bar{\imath}$-*troj'e-nus*
nitrous... $n\bar{\imath}$'*trus*
nitwit... *nit'wit*
no... $n\bar{o}$
nobility... $n\bar{o}$'*bil'i-ti*
noble... $n\bar{o}$'*bl*
nobly... $n\bar{o}$'*bli*
nobody... $n\bar{o}$'*bo-di*
nocturnal... *nok'tèrn'āl*
nod... *nod*
node... $n\bar{o}$*d*
nodular... *nod'ū-lèr*
nodule... *nod'ūl*
noggin... *nog'in*
noise... *noiz*
noiseless... *noiz'les*
noisily... *noiz'i-li*
noisy... *noiz'i*
nomad... $n\bar{o}$'*mad*
nomadic... $n\bar{o}$-*mad'ik*
nominal... *no'mi-nal*
nominate... *no'mi-nāt*
nominative... *no'mi-nāt-iv*
nominator... *no'mi-nāt-èr*
nominee... *no-mi-nē'*
nonage... *non'āj*
nonagon... *non'a-gon*
nonchalant... *non'sha-lant*
non-content... *non-kon-tent'*
nondescript... *non'dē-skript*
nonentity... *non-en'ti-ti*
nones... $n\bar{o}$*nz*
non-juror... *non-jūr'èr*
nonpareil... *non-pa-rel'*
nonplus... *non'plus*
nonsense... *non'sens*
nonsensical... *non-sens'ik-al*
noodle... *no'dl*
nook... *nok*
noon... *non*
noose... *nos or noz*
nordic... *nor'dik*
norm... *norm*
normal... *nor'mal*
norse... *nors*
north... *north*
north-east... *north-ēst'*
north-easter... *north-ēst'èr*
north-eastern... *north-ēst'èrn*

northerly... *norŦH'èr-li*
northern... *norŦH'èrn*
northerner... *norŦH'èr-nèr*
northwardly... *north'wèrd-li*
nose... $n\bar{o}$*z*
nosegay... $n\bar{o}$*z'gā*
nostalgia... *nos-tal'ji-a*
nostril... *nos'tril*
not... *not*
notability... $n\bar{o}$*t-a-bil'i-ti*
notable... $n\bar{o}$*t'a-bl*
notably... $n\bar{o}$*t'a-bli*
notary... $n\bar{o}$*t'a-ri*
notation... $n\bar{o}$*t-ā'shun*
notch... *noch*
note... $n\bar{o}$*t*
note-book... $n\bar{o}$*t'buk*
noteworthy... $n\bar{o}$*t'wèr-ŦHi*
nothing... *nu'thing*
notice... $n\bar{o}$*t'is*
noticeable... $n\bar{o}$*t'is-a-bl*
notification... $n\bar{o}$*t'i-fi-kā''shun*
notify... $n\bar{o}$*t'i-fī*
notion... $n\bar{o}$'*shun*
notoriety... $n\bar{o}$-*tō-rī'e-ti*
notorious... $n\bar{o}$-*tō'ri-us*
nought... *nat*
noun... *noun*
nourisher... *nu'rish-èr*
nourishing... *nu'rish-ing*
nourishment... *nu'rish-ment*
nous... *nous*
novel... *no'vel*
novelist... *no'vel-ist*
novelty... *no'vel-ti*
november... $n\bar{o}$-*vem'bèr*
novice... *no'vis*
novitiate... $n\bar{o}$-*vi'shi-āt*
now... *nou*
nowadays... *nou'a-dāz*
nowhere... $n\bar{o}$'*whār*
noxious... *nok'shus*
nozzle... *noz'l*
nuance... *nu-angs*
nubile... *nū'bīl*
nuciferous... *nū-sif'èr-us*
nucleus... *nū'klē-us*
nude... *nūd*
nudge... *nuj*
nudity... *nūd'i-ti*
nugatory... *nū'ga-to-ri*
nugget... *nug'et*
null... *nul*
nullify... *nul'i-fī*

nullity... *nul'i-ti*
numb... *num*
number... *num'bèr*
numberless... *num'bèr-les*
numbles... *num'blz*
numerable... *nū'mèr-a-bl*
numeral... *nū'mèr-al*
numerate... *nū'mèr-āt*
numeration... *nū-mèr-ā'shun*
numerator... *nū'mèr-āt-èr*
numerical... *nū-me'rik-al*
numerically... *nū-me'rik-al-li*
numerous... *nū'mèr-us*
numismatic... *nū-mis-mat'ik*
numismatics... *nū-mis-mat'iks*
numismatist... *nū-mis'mat-ist*
numskull... *num'skul*
nun... *nun*
nunnery... *nun'è-ri*
nuptials... *nup'shalz*
nuptial... *nup'shal*
nurse... *nèrs*
nurture... *nèr'tūr*
nut... *nut*
nut-cracker... *nut'krak-èr*
nutmeg... *nut'meg*
nutrient... *nū'tri-ent*
nutriment... *nū'tri-ment*
nutrition... *nū-tri'shun*
nutritious... *nū-tri'shus*
nutritive... *nū'tri-tiv*
nut-shell... *nut'shel*
nutty... *nut'i*
nuzzle... *nuz'l*
nylon... *nī'lon*
nymph... *nimf*

O

oaf... *ōf*
oafish... *ōf'ish*
oak... *ōk*
oaken... *ōk'n*
oar... *ōr*
oared... *ōrd*
oarsman... *ōrz'man*
oasis... *ō-ā'sis*
oast... *ōst*
oath... *ōth*
oat-meal... *ōt'mēl*
obduracy... *ob'dū-ra-si*
obdurate... *ob'dū-rāt*

obdurately... *ob'dū-rāt-li*
obedience... *ō-bē'di-ens*
obedient... *ō-bē'di-ent*
obediently... *ō-bē'di-ent-li*
obeisance... *ō-bā'sans*
obese... *ō-bēs'*
obesity... *ō-bēs'i-ti*
obey... *ō-bā'*
obfuscate... *ob-fus'kāt*
obituary... *ō-bit'ū-a-ri*
object... *ob'jekt*
objection... *ob-jek'shun*
objective... *ob-jek'tiv*
objectivity... *ob-jek-tiv'i-ti*
objector... *ob-jekt'èr*
objuration... *ob-jū-rā'shun*
objurgate... *ob-jèr'gāt*
objurgation... *ob-jèr-gā'shun*
oblate... *ob-lāt'*
oblation... *ob-lā'shun*
obligation... *ob-li-gā'shun*
obligatory... *ob'li-ga-to-ri*
oblige... *ō-blīj'*
obliging... *ō-blīj'ing*
oblique... *ob-lēk'*
obliterate... *ob-lit'è-rāt*
obliteration... *ob-lit'è-rā''shun*
oblivion... *ob-li'vi-on*
oblivious... *ob-li'vi-us*
oblong... *ob'long*
obnoxious... *ob-nok'shus*
obscene... *ob-sēn'*
obscenely... *ob-sēn'li*
obscenity... *ob-sen'i-ti*
obscure... *ob-skūr'*
obscurely... *ob-skūr'li*
obscurity... *ob-skū'ri-ti*
obsequies... *ob'se-kwiz*
obsequious... *ob-sē'kwi-us*
observable... *ob-zèrv'a-bl*
observably... *ob-zèrv'a-bli*
observance... *ob-zèrv'ans*
observant... *ob-zèrv'ant*
observantly... *ob-zèrv'ant-li*
observatory... *ob-zèr'va-to-ri*
observe... *ob-zèrv'*
observer... *ob-zèrv'er*
observing... *ob-zèrv'ing*
observingly... *ob-zèrv'ing-li*
obsession... *ob-sesh'on*
obsolescent... *ob-sō-les'ent*
obsolete... *ob'sō-lēt*
obstacle... *ob'sta-kl*
obstetric... *ob-stet'rik*

obstetrician... ob-stet-rish'an
obstetrics... ob-stet'riks
obstinacy... ob'sti-na-si
obstinate... ob'sti-nāt
obstinately... ob'sti-nāt-li
obstruct... ob-strukt'
obstruction... ob-struk'shun
obstructive... ob-strukt'iv
obtain... ob-tān'
obtainable... ob-tān'a-bl
obtest... ob-test'
obtestation... ob-test'ā-shun
obtrusion... ob-tro'zhon
obtrusive... ob-tro'siv
obturate... ob'tū-rāt
obtuse... ob-tūs'
obverse... ob'vėrs
obvious... ob'vi-us
obviously... ob'vi-us-li
obvolute... ob'vo-lūt
occasion... ok-kā'zhon
occasional... ok-kā'zhon-al
occasionally... ok-kā'zhon-al-li
occident... ok'si-dent
occidental... ok-si-dent'al
occipital... ok'si'pit-al
occult... ok-kult'
occupancy... ok'kū-pan-si
occupant... ok'kū-pant
occupation... ok-kū-pā'shun
occupy... ok'kū-pī
occur... ok-kėr'
occurrence... ok-ku'rens
ocean... ō'shan
oceanic... ō-shē-an'ik
ochre... ō'kėr
ochry... ō'kėr-i
octagon... ok'ta-gon
octahedron... ok-ta-hed'ron
octangular... ok-tang'gū-lėr
octave... ok'tāv
octennial... ok-ten'i-al
octopus... ok'tō-pus
octosyllabic... ok'tō-sil-lab''ik
ocular... ok'ū-lėr
ocularly... ok'ū-lėr-li
oculist... ok'ū-list
odd... od
oddity... od'i-ti
oddly... od'li
odds... odz
ode... ōd
odious... ō'di-us
odiously... ō'di-us-li

odium... ō'di-um
odontology... ō-don-tol'o-ji
odoriferous... ō-dor-if'ėr-us
odorous... ō'dor-us
odor... ō'dor
odorless... ō'dor-les
of... ov
off... of
offend... of-fend'
offender... of-fend'ėr
offensive... of-fens'iv
offensively... of-fens'iv-li
offer... of'ėr
offering... of'ėr-ing
offertory... of'ėr-to-ri
off-hand... of'hand
office... of'is
officer... of'is-ėr
official... of-fi'shal
officially... of-fi'shal-li
officiate... of-fi'shi-āt
officinal... of-fi'si-nal
officious... of-fi'shus
officiously... of-fi'shus-li
offing... of'ing
offset... of'set
offshoot... of'shot
offspring... of'spring
oft... oft
often... of'n
oftentimes... of'n-tīmz
ofttimes... oft'timz
ogler... ō'glėr
ogre... ō'gėr
ogress... ō'gres
oh... ō
oil... oil
oil-color... oil'kul-ėr
oiler... oil'ėr
oil-painting... oil'pānt-ing
oily... oil'i
ointment... oint'ment
old... ōld
old-fashioned... ōld-fa'shund
oleaginous... ō-lē-a'jin-us
oleander... o-lē-an'dėr
olfactory... ol-fak'to-ri
oligarch... o'li-gark
olio... ō'li-o
olive... o'liv
olympiad... ō-lim'pi-ad
olympian... ō-lim'pi-an
omega... ō'me-ga
omelet... o'me-let

omen... ō'men
ominous... o'min-us
omissible... ō-mis'i-bl
omission... ō-mi'shun
omissive... ō-mis'iv
omit... ō-mit'
omnibus... om'ni-bus
omnifarious... om-ni-fā'ri-us
omnipotence... om-nip'ō-tens
omnipotent... om-nip'ō-tent
omnipresent... om-ni-prez'ent
omniscient... om-ni'shi-ent
omnisciently... om-ni'shi-ent-li
omphalic... om-fal'ik
on... on
once... wuns
oncoming... on'kum-ing
one... wun
oneness... wun'nes
onerary... on'e-ra-ri
onerous... on'ē-rus
onerously... on'ē-rus-li
oneself... wun-self'
one-sided... wun-sī d'ed
ongoing... on'gō-ing
onion... un'yun
only... ōn'li
onrush... on'rush
onset... on'set
onslaught... on'slat
onus... ō'nus
onward... on'wėrd
onyx... o'niks
ooze... oz
oozy... oz'i
opacity... ō-pas'i-ti
opal... ō-pal
opalescent... ō-pal-es'ent
opaline... ō'pal-īn
opaque... ō-pāk'
open... ō'pn
open-hearted... ō'pn-hart-ed
opening... ō'pn-ing
openly... ō'pn-li
opera... o'pe-ra
operate... o'pe-rāt
operatic... o-pe-rat'ik
operation... o-pe-rā'shun
operative... o'pe-rāt-iv
operator... o'pe-rāt-ėr
operetta... op-e-ret'ta
ophidian... ō-fid'i-an
ophiology... of-i-ol'o-ji
ophthalmia... of-thal'mi-a

ophthalmic... of-thal'mik
ophthalmist... of-thal'mist
opiate... ō'pi-āt
opinion... ō-pin'yon
opinionative... ō-pin'yon-āt-iv
opium... ō'pi-um
opponent... op-pō'nent
opportune... op-or-tūn'
opportunely... op-or-tūn'li
opportunist... op-or-tūn'ist
opportunity... op-or-tūn'i-ti
oppose... op-pōz'
opposed... op-pōzd'
opposite... op'pō-zit
oppositely... op'pō-zit-li
opposition... op-pō-zi'shun
oppress... op-pres'
oppression... op-pres'shun
oppressive... op-pres'iv
oppressor... op-pres'ėr
oppugnant... op-pug'nant
optic... op'tik
optical... op'tik-al
optician... op-ti'shan
optics... op'tiks
optimism... op'tim-izm
optimist... op'tim-ist
optimistic... op-tim-ist'ik
option... op'shun
optional... op'shun-al
opulence... op'ū-lens
opulent... op'ū-lent
opulently... op'ū-lent-li
oracle... o'ra-kl
oracular... ō-rak'ū-lėr
oracularly... ō-rak'ū-lėr-li
oral... ō'ral
orally... ō'ral-li
orange... o'ranj
orange-peel... o'ranj-pēl
orate... ō'rāt
oration... ō-rā'shun
orator... o'ra-tėr
oratorical... o-ra-to'rik-al
oratory... o'ra-to-ri
orbicular... or-bik'ū-lėr
orbit... or'bit
orbital... or'bit-al
orchard... or'chėrd
orchestra... or'kes-tra
orchestral... or-kes'tral
orchestration... or-kes-trā'shun
orchid... or'kid
ordain... or-dān'

O

ordainment... or-dān'ment
ordeal... or'dē-al
order... or'dėr
orderly... or'dėr-li
ordinal... or'din-al
ordinance... or'din-ans
ordinarily... or'din-a-ri-li
ordinary... or'din-a-ri
ordinate... or'din-āt
ordination... or-din-ā'shun
ordnance... ord'nans
ore... ōr
organ... or'gan
organic... or-gan'ik
organism... or'gan-izm
organist... or'gan-ist
organize... or'gan-īz
orgasm... or'gazm
orgy... or'ji
oriel... ō'ri-el
orient... ō'ri-ent
oriental... ō-ri-ent'al
orientalism... ō-ri-ent'al-izm
orientalist... ō-ri-ent'al-ist
orientate... ō-ri-ent'āt
orientation... ōr'i-en-tā''shun
orifice... o'ri-fis
origin... o'ri-jin
original... ō-ri'jin-al
originate... ō-ri'jin-āt
origination... ō-ri'jin-ā''shun
originator... ō-ri'jin-āt-ėr
oriole... ō'ri-ōl
orion... ō-rī'on
ornament... or'na-ment
ornamental... or-na-ment'al
ornate... or'nāt
ornately... or'nāt-li
orphan... or'fan
orphanage... or'fan-āj
orphean... or-fē'an
orpiment... or'pi-ment
orris... o'ris
ort... ort
orthodox... or'thō-doks
orthodoxly... or'thō-doks-li
orthodoxy... or'thō-doks-i
orthoepist... or'thō-ep-ist
orthoepy... or'thō-e-pi
orthographer... or-thog'ra-fėr
orthography... or-thog'ra-fi
oscillate... os'sil-lāt
oscillation... os-sil-lā'shun
oscillatory... os'sil-la-to-ri

osculate... os'kū-lāt
osculation... o-skū-lā'shun
osmose... os'mōs
osprey... os'prā
osseous... os'ē-us
ossicle... os'i-kl
ossification... os'i-fi-kā''shun
ossifrage... os'i-frāj
ostensible... os-ten'si-bl
ostensibly... os-ten'si-bli
ostensive... os-ten'siv
ostentation... os-ten-tā'shun
ostentatious... os-ten-tā'shus
osteology... os-tē-ol'o-ji
osteopathy... os-tē-op'a-thi
ostracize... os'tra-sīz
ostrich... os'trich
other... uᵗH'ėr
otherwise... uᵗH'ėr-wīz
otology... ō-tol'o-ji
otter... ot'ėr
ottoman... ot'tō-man
ouch... ouch
ought... at
ounce... ouns
our... our
ourself... our-self'
ourselves... our-selvz'
oust... oust
out... out
outbid... out-bid'
outbreak... out'brāk
outcast... out'kast
outcome... out'kum
outcrop... out'krop
outcry... out'krī
outdistance... out-dis'tans
outdo... out-do'
outdoor... out'dōr
outdoors... out'dōrz
outer... out'ėr
outermost... out'ėr-mōst
outfall... out'fal
outfit... out'fit
outfitter... out'fit-ėr
outflank... out-flangk'
outflow... out'flō
outgo... out-gō'
outgoing... out-gō'ing
outgrow... out-grō'
outgrowth... out'grōth
outing... out'ing
outlandish... out-land'ish
outlast... out-last'

outlaw... *out'la*
outlawry... *out'la-ri*
outlet... *out'let*
outline... *out'līn*
outlive... *out-liv'*
outlook... *out'luk*
outlying... *out'lī-ing*
outmost... *out'mōst*
outnumber... *out-num'bėr*
out-patient... *out'pā-shent*
outpost... *out'pōst*
outpour... *out-pōr'*
outrage... *out'rāj*
outrageous... *out-rā'jus*
outrageously... *out-rā'jus-li*
outreach... *out-rēch'*
outride... *out-rīd'*
outrider... *out'rīd-ėr*
outrigger... *out'rig-ėr*
outright... *out'rīt*
outrun... *out-run'*
outset... *out'set*
outshine... *out-shīn'*
outside... *out'sīd*
outsider... *out'sīd-ėr*
outskirt... *out'skėrt*
outspoken... *out'spō-kn*
outspread... *out-spred'*
outstanding... *out-stand'ing*
outstrip... *out-strip'*
outvote... *out-vōt'*
outwalk... *out-wak'*
outward... *out'wėrd*
outwardly... *out'wėrd-li*
outwear... *out-wār'*
outweigh... *out-wā'*
outwit... *out-wit'*
outwork... *out'wėrk*
ova... *ō'va*
oval... *ō'val*
ovarian... *ō-vā'ri-an*
ovariotomy... *ō-vā'ri-ot''o-mi*
ovary... *ō'va-ri*
ovate... *ō'vāt*
ovation... *ō-vā'shun*
oven... *uv'n*
over... *ō'vėr*
overact... *ō-vėr-akt'*
overalls... *ō'vėr-alz*
overbalance... *ō-vėr-bal'ans*
overbearing... *ō-vėr-bār'ing*
overboard... *ō'vėr-bōrd*
overburden... *ō-vėr-ber'dn*
overcast... *ō-vėr-kast'*

overcharge... *ō-vėr-charj'*
overcloud... *ō-vėr-kloud'*
overcoat... *ō'vėr-kōt*
overcome... *ō-vėr-kum'*
overcrowd... *ō-vėr-kroud'*
overdo... *ō-vėr-do'*
overdose... *ō'vėr-dōs*
overdraw... *ō-vėr-dra'*
overdue... *ō'vėr-dū*
overflow... *ō-vėr-flō'*
overflowing... *ō-vėr-flō'ing*
overgrow... *ō-vėr-grō'*
overgrowth... *ō'vėr-grōth*
overhand... *ō'vėr-hand*
overhang... *ō-vėr-hang'*
overhaul... *ō-vėr-hal'*
overhead... *ō-vėr-hed'*
overhear... *ō-vėr-hēr'*
overheat... *ō-vėr-hēt'*
overhung... *ō-vėr-hung'*
overjoy... *ō-vėr-joi'*
overland... *ō'vėr-land*
overlap... *ō-vėr-lap'*
overlay... *ō-vėr-lā'*
overleap... *ō-vėr-lēp'*
overload... *ō-vėr-lōd'*
overlook... *ō-vėr-luk'*
overlord... *ō'vėr-lōrd*
overnight... *ō'vėr-nīt*
overpass... *ō-vėr-pas'*
overpower... *ō-vėr-pou'ėr*
overrate... *ō-vėr-rāt'*
overreach... *ō-vėr-rēch'*
override... *ō-vėr-rīd'*
overrule... *ō-vėr-rol'*
overrun... *ō-vėr-run'*
oversea... *ō'vėr-sē*
oversee... *ō-vėr-sē'*
overseer... *ō-vėr-sēr'*
overset... *ō-vėr-set'*
overshadow... *ō-vėr-sha'dō*
overshoe... *ō'vėr-sho*
overshoot... *ō-vėr-shot'*
overshot... *ō-vėr-shot'*
overstate... *ō-vėr-stāt'*
overstep... *ō-vėr-step'*
overstock... *ō-vėr-stok'*
overt... *ō-vėrt*
overtake... *ō-vėr-tāk'*
overtax... *ō-vėr-taks'*
overthrow... *ō-vėr-thrō'*
overtime... *ō-vėr-tīm*
overtly... *ō'vėrt-li*
overtop... *ō-vėr-top'*

O

overture... ō'vėr-tūr
overturn... ō-vėr-tėrn'
overvalue... ō-vėr-val'ū
overweigh... ō-vėr-wā'
overweight... ō-vėr-wāt'
overwhelm... ō-vėr-whelm'
overwise... ō'vėr-wīz
overwork... ō-vėr-wėrk'
overworn... ō'vėr-wōrn
overwrought... ō-vėr-rat'
ovine... ō'vīn
oviparous... ō-vip'a-rus
ovoid... ō'void
ovule... ō'vūl
owe... ō
owing... ō'ing
owl... oul
owlet... oul'et
owlish... oul'ish
own... ōn
owner... ōn'ėr
ownership... ōn'ėr-ship
ox... oks
oxidate... oks'id-āt
oxidation... oks-id-ā'shun
oxide... oks'īd
oxidize... oks'id-īz
oxonian... ok-sō'ni-an
oxygen... oks'i-jen
oxygenate... oks'i-jen-āt
oxygenize... oks'i-jen-īz
oxygenous... oks-ij'en-us
oyster... ois'tėr
oyster-bed... ois'tėr-bed
ozone... ō'zōn

P

pabulum... pab'ū-lum
pace... pās
pacific... pa-sif'ik
pacification... pa'si-fi-kā''shun
pacificator... pa-sif'i-kāt-ėr
pacificatory... pa-sif'i-ka-to-ri
pacifier... pa'si-fī-ėr
pacify... pa'si-fī
pack... pak
package... pak'āj
packer... pak'ėr
packet... pak'et
packing... pak'ing
pact... pakt

pad... pad
padding... pad'ing
paddle... pad'l
paddler... pad'l-ėr
paddock... pad'ok
padlock... pad'lok
padre... pad'rā
pagan... pā'gan
paganism... pā'gan-izm
paganize... pā'gan-īz
pageant... pa'jent
pageantry... pa'jent-ri
pagoda... pa-gō'da
pail... pāl
pailful... pāl'ful
pain... pān
painful... pān'ful
painless... pān'les
painstaking... pānz'tāk-ing
paint... pānt
painter... pānt'ėr
painting... pānt'ing
pair... pār
palace... pa'lās
palatable... pa'lat-a-bl
palatal... pa'lat-al
palate... pa'lāt
palatial... pa-lā'shal
palaver... pa-la'vėr
pale... pāl
palette... pa'let
palinode... pal'i-nōd
palisade... pa-li-sād'
palish... pāl'ish
palladium... pal-lā'di-um
pallet... pal'et
palliative... pal'i-āt-iv
pallid... pal'id
palm... pam
palmaceous... pal-mā'shus
palmer... pam'ėr
palpable... pal'pa-bl
palpably... pal'pa-bli
palpitate... pal'pi-tāt
palpitation... pal-pi-tā'shun
palsy... pal'zi
palter... pāl'tėr
paltry... pāl'tri
paludal... pal'ū-dal
pampas... pam'pas
pamper... pam'pėr
pamphlet... pam'flet
pan... pan
panacea... pan-a-sē'a

pancake... *pan'kāk*
pancreas... *pan'krē-as*
pancreatic... *pan-krē-at'ik*
pander... *pan'dėr*
pane... *pān*
panel... *pa'nel*
pang... *pang*
pangolin... *pan'gō-lin*
panic... *pan'ik*
panicle... *pan'i-kl*
pannier... *pa'ni-ėr*
panorama... *pan-ō-ra'ma*
panoramic... *pan-ō-ram'ik*
pansy... *pan'zi*
pant... *pant*
pantheism... *pan'thē-izm*
pantheist... *pan'thē-ist*
pantheistic... *pan-thē-ist'ik*
panther... *pan'thėr*
pantograph... *pan'tō-graf*
pantomime... *pan'tō-mīm*
pantry... *pan'tri*
papa... *pa-pa'*
papacy... *pā'pa-si*
papal... *pā'pal*
paper... *pā'pėr*
papery... *pā'pėr-i*
papillary... *pap'il-la-ri*
papist... *pā'pist*
papistry... *pā'pist-ri*
par... *par*
parable... *pa'ra-bl*
parachute... *pa'ra-shot*
paraclete... *pa'ra-klēt*
parade... *pa-rād'*
paradise... *pa'ra-dīs*
paradox... *pa'ra-doks*
paradoxical... *pa-ra-doks'ik-al*
paraffin... *pa'ra-fin*
paragon... *pa'ra-gon*
paragraph... *pa'ra-graf*
parakeet... *pa'ra-kēt*
parallax... *pa'ral-laks*
parallel... *pa'ral-lel*
parallelism... *pa'ral-lel-izm*
paralogism... *pa-ral'o-jism*
paralysis... *pa-ral'i-sis*
paralytic... *pa-ra-lit'ik*
paralyze... *pa'ra-līz*
paramount... *pa'ra-mount*
paramour... *pa'ra-mor*
parapet... *pa'ra-pet*
paraphrase... *pa'ra-frāz*
paraselene... *pa'ra-se-lē''nē*

parasol... *pa'ra-sol*
paratroops... *pa'ra-trops*
parboil... *par'boil*
parcel... *par'sel*
parcel-post... *par'sel-pōst*
parch... *parch*
parchment... *parch'ment*
pardon... *par'don*
pardonable... *par'dn-a-bl*
pare... *pār*
paregoric... *pa-re-go'rik*
parent... *pā'rent*
parentage... *pā'rent-āj*
parental... *pa-rent'al*
parenthesis... *pa-ren'the-sis*
parer... *pār'ėr*
parietal... *pa-rī'et-al*
paring... *pār'ing*
parish... *pa'rish*
parishioner... *pa-rish'on-ėr*
parisian... *pa-riz'i-an*
parity... *pa'ri-ti*
park... *park*
parka... *par'ka*
parley... *par'li*
parliament... *par'li-ment*
parlor... *par'lėr*
parnassian... *par-nas'i-an*
parochial... *pa-rō'ki-al*
parodist... *pa'rod-ist*
parody... *pa'rod-i*
parole... *pa-rōl'*
paroxysm... *pa'roks-izm*
parquetry... *par'ket-ri*
parr... *par*
parrakeet... *pa'ra-kēt*
parricide... *pa'ri-sīd*
parrot... *pa'rot*
parry... *pa'ri*
parsimonious... *par-si-mō'ni-us*
parsimony... *par'si-mō-ni*
parsley... *pars'li*
parsnip... *pars'nip*
parson... *par'sn*
parsonage... *par'sn-āj*
part... *part*
partake... *par-tāk'*
partaker... *par-tāk'ėr*
partiality... *par'shi-al''i-ti*
partially... *par'shal-li*
partible... *part'i-bl*
participate... *par-tis'i-pāt*
participator... *pār-tis'i-pāt-or*
participial... *par-ti-sip'i-al*

P

participle... *par'ti-si-pl*
particle... *par'ti-kl*
particular... *par-tik'ū-lėr*
particularity... *par'tik'ū-la''ri-ti*
particularize... *par-tik'ū-lėr-īz*
particularly... *par-tik'ū-lėr-li*
parting... *part'ing*
partisan... *par'ti-zan*
partition... *par-ti'shun*
partitive... *par'ti-tiv*
partly... *part'li*
partner... *part'nėr*
partnership... *part'nėr-ship*
partridge... *par'trij*
parturient... *par-tū'ri-ent*
parturition... *par-tū-ri'shun*
party... *par'ti*
parvenu... *par've-nū*
paschal... *pas'kal*
pass... *pas*
passable... *pas'a-bl*
passably... *pas'a-bli*
passage... *pas'āj*
pass-book... *pas'bok*
passenger... *pas'en-jėr*
passerine... *pas'ėr-īn*
passible... *pas'i-bl*
passim... *pas'im*
passing... *pas'ing*
passion... *pa'shun*
passionate... *pa'shun-āt*
passionately... *pa'shun-āt-li*
passionless... *pa'shun-les*
passion-play... *pa'shun-plā*
passive... *pas'iv*
passively... *pas'iv-li*
pass-key... *pas'kē*
passover... *pas'ō-vėr*
passport... *pas'pōrt*
pass-word... *pas'wėrd*
past... *past*
paste... *pāst*
pastel... *pas'tel*
pastime... *pas'fīm*
pastor... *pas'tor*
pastoral... *pas'tor-al*
pastorate... *pas'tor-āt*
pastry... *pās'tri*
pasturage... *pas'tūr-āj*
pasture... *pas'tūr*
pasty... *pās'ti*
patch... *pach*
patchwork... *pach'wėrk*
patchy... *pach'i*

pate... *pāt*
patent... *pā'tent or pa'tent*
paternal... *pa-tėr'nal*
paternity... *pa-tėr'ni-ti*
path... *path*
pathetic... *pa-thet'ik*
pathetically... *pa-thet'ik-al-li*
pathologist... *pa-thol'o-jist*
pathology... *pa-thol'o-ji*
pathos... *pā'thos*
patience... *pā'shens*
patient... *pā'shent*
patriarch... *pā'tri-ark*
patriarchal... *pā-tri-ark'al*
patrimonial... *pat-ri-mō'ni-al*
patrimony... *pat'ri-mo-ni*
patriot... *pā'tri-ot or pat'*
patriotic... *pā-tri-ot'ik or pat-*
patristic... *pa-tris'tik*
patrol... *pa-trōl'*
patron... *pā'tron*
patroness... *pā'tron-es*
patronize... *pat'ron-īz or pā'*
patter... *pat'ėr*
pattern... *pat'ėrn*
patty... *pat'i*
paucity... *pa'si-ti*
paunch... *pänsh*
paunchy... *pänsh'i*
pauper... *pa'pėr*
pauperism... *pa'pėr-izm*
pauperize... *pa''pėr-īz*
pause... *paz*
pave... *pāv*
pavement... *pāv'ment*
pavilion... *pa-vil'yon*
paw... *pa*
pawn... *pan*
pawnbroker... *pan'brōk-ėr*
pay... *pā*
payable... *pā'a-bl*
payee... *pā-ē'*
paymaster... *pā'mas-tėr*
payment... *pā'ment*
pea... *pē*
peace... *pēs*
peaceable... *pēs'a-bl*
peaceably... *pēs'a-bli*
peaceful... *pēs'ful*
peacefully... *pēs'ful-li*
peace-maker... *pēs'māk-ėr*
peach... *pēch*
peacock... *pē'kok*
peak... *pēk*

peaked... *pēkt*
peal... *pēl*
pear... *pãr*
pearl... *pèrl*
peasant... *pe'zant*
peasantry... *pe'zant-ri*
pebble... *peb'l*
pebbly... *peb'li*
pecan... *pē-kan'*
peccable... *pek'a-bl*
peccadillo.... *pek-a-dil'lō*
peccant... *pek'ant*
peck... *pek*
pecker... *pek'ėr*
peckish... *pek'ish*
pectic... *pek'tik*
pectinal... *pek'tin-al*
peculate... *pe'kū-lāt*
peculation... *pe-kū-lā'shun*
peculator... *pe'kū-lāt-ėr*
peculiar... *pē-kū'li-ėr*
peculiarity... *pē-kū'li-a''ri-ti*
peculiarly... *pē-kū'li-ėr-li*
pecuniary... *pē-kū'ni-a-ri*
pedagogic... *ped-a-goj'ik*
pedagogics... *ped-a-goj'iks*
pedagogue... *ped'a-gog*
pedagogy... *ped'a-go-ji*
pedal... *pēd'al*
pedant... *pe'dant*
pedantically... *pe-dant'ik-al-li*
pedantry... *pe'dant-ri*
peddle... *ped'l*
peddler... *ped'lėr*
pedestal... *pe'des-tal*
pedestrian... *pe-des'tri-an*
pedigree... *pe'di-grē*
pediment... *pe'di-ment*
pedlar... *ped'lėr*
peel... *pēl*
peep... *pēp*
peer... *pēr*
peerage... *pēr'āj*
peeress... *pēr'es*
peerless... *pēr'les*
peevish... *pē'vish*
peg... *peg*
pekoe... *pē'kō*
pelican... *pel'i-kan*
pell... *pel*
pellet... *pel'et*
pellucid... *pel-lū'sid*
pelt... *pelt*
pelvic... *pel'vik*

pen... *pen*
penal... *pē'nal*
penalty... *pen'al-ti*
penance... *pen'ans*
penates... *pē-nā'tēz*
penchant... *pan'shang*
pencil... *pen'sil*
pend... *pend*
pendant... *pen'dant*
pendent... *pen'dent*
pending... *pend'ing*
pendulate... *pen'dū-lāt*
pendulous... *pen'dū-lus*
pendulum... *pen'dū-lum*
penetrable... *pen'e-tra-bl*
penetrably... *pen'e-tra-bli*
penetralia... *pen'e-trā''li-a*
penetrate... *pen'e-trāt*
penetrating... *pen'e-trāt-ing*
penetration... *pen-e-trā'shun*
penetrative... *pe'ne-trāt-iv*
penguin... *pen'gwin*
penicillin... *pen-i-sil'in*
peninsula... *pen-in'sū-la*
penis... *pē'nis*
penitence... *pe'ni-tens*
penitent... *pe'ni-tent*
penitential... *pe-ni-ten'shal*
penitentiary... *pe-ni-ten'sha-ri*
penknife... *pen'nīf*
penman... *pen'man*
penmanship... *pen'man-ship*
pennant... *pen'ant*
penniless... *pen'i-les*
penny... *pen'i*
penny-wise... *pen'i-wīz*
pennyworth... *pen'i-wėrth*
pensil... *pen'sīl*
pension... *pen'shun*
pensionary... *pen'shun-a-ri*
pensioner... *pen'shun-ėr*
pensive... *pen'siv*
pent... *pent*
pentagon... *pen'ta-gon*
pentagonal... *pen-tag'on-al*
pentateuch... *pen'ta-tūk*
pentecost... *pen'tē-kost*
penthouse... *pent'hous*
penurious... *pe-nū'ri-us*
penury... *pe'nū-ri*
peon... *pē'on*
peony... *pē'o-ni*
people... *pē'pl*
pepper... *pep'ėr*

P

pepper-corn... *pep′ėr-korn*
peppermint... *pep′ėr-mint*
pepsin... *pep′sin*
peptic... *pep′tik*
per... *pėr*
perambulate... *pėr-am′bū-lāt*
perceivable... *pėr-sēv′a-bl*
perceive... *pėr-sēv′*
percentage... *pėr-sent′āj*
perceptible... *pėr-sep′ti-bl*
perception... *pėr-sep′shun*
perceptive... *pėr-sep′tiv*
perch... *pėrch*
percipient... *pėr-sip′i-ent*
percolate... *pėr′kō-lāt*
percuss... *pėr-kus′*
percussive... *pėr-kus′iv*
perdition... *pėr-di′shun*
peregrine... *pe′re-grin*
peremptorily... *p′remp-to-ri-li*
peremptory... *pe′remp-to-ri*
perennial... *pe-ren′i-al*
perfect... *pėr′fekt*
perfectibility... *pėr-fek′ti-bil′′i-ti*
perfection... *pėr-fek′shun*
perfidious... *pėr-fi′di-us*
perfidy... *pėr′fi-di*
perforate... *pėr′fo-rāt*
perforation... *pėr-fo-rā′shun*
perforator... *pėr′fo-rāt-ėr*
perforce... *pėr-fōrs′*
perform... *pėr-form′*
performable... *pėr-form′a-bl*
performance... *pėr-form′ans*
performer... *pėr-form′ėr*
perfume... *pėr′fūm*
perfumer... *pėr-fūm′ėr*
perfumery... *pėr-fūm′ėr-i*
perfunctory... *pėr-fungk′to-ri*
perhaps... *pėr-haps′*
peril... *pe′ril*
perilous... *pe′ril-us*
perimeter... *pe-rim′et-ėr*
period... *pē′ri-od*
periodic... *pē-ri-do′ik*
periodical... *pē-ri-oďik-al*
peripatetic... *pe′ri-pa-tet′′ik*
periphery... *pe-rif′ėr-i*
periphrasis... *pe-rif′ra-sis*
periphrastic... *pe-ri-fras′tik*
periscope... *pe′ri-skōp*
periscopic... *pe-ri-skop′ik*
perish... *pe′rish*
perishable... *pe′rish-a-bl*

periwinkle... *pe-ri-wing′kl*
perjure... *pėr′jūr*
perjurer... *pėr′jūr-ėr*
perjury... *pėr′jū-ri*
perk... *pėrk*
permanent... *pėr′ma-nent*
permeable... *pėr′mē-a-bl*
permeate... *pėr′mē-āt*
permeation... *pėr-mē-ā′shun*
permissible... *pėr-mis′i-bl*
permission... *pėr-mi′shun*
permissive... *pėr-mis′iv*
permute... *pėr-mūt′*
pernicious... *pėr-ni′shus*
perorate... *pe′rō-rāt*
peroxide... *pėr-ok′sid*
perpetrate... *pėr′pe-trāt*
perpetual... *pėr-pe′tū-al*
perpetuate... *pėr-pe′tū-āt*
perpetuity... *pėr-pe-tū′i-ti*
perplex... *pėr-pleks′*
perplexing... *pėr-pleks′ing*
perplexity... *pėr-pleks′i-ti*
perquisite... *pėr′kwi-zit*
persecute... *pėr′se-kūt*
persecution... *pėr-se-kū′shun*
persecutor... *pėr′se-kūt-ėr*
persevere... *pėr-se-vēr′*
persevering... *pėr-se-vēr′ing*
persiflage... *pėr′sē-flazh*
persist... *pėr-sist′*
persistent... *pėr-sist′ent*
persistently... *pėr-sist′ent-li*
person... *pėr′son*
personable... *pėr′son-a-bl*
personage... *pėr′son-āj*
personality... *pėr-son-al′i-ti*
personally... *pėr′son-al-li*
personalty... *pėr′son-al-ti*
personate... *pėr′son-āt*
personation... *pėr-son-ā′shun*
personify... *pėr-son′i-fī*
personnel... *pėr-son-el′*
perspective... *pėr-spek′tiv*
perspicuous... *pėr-spi′kū-us*
perspiration... *pėr-spi-rā′shun*
perspiratory... *pėr-spīr′a-to-ri*
perspire... *pėr-spīr′*
persuade... *pėr-swād′*
persuasion... *pėr-swā′zhon*
persuasive... *pėr-swā′siv*
pert... *pėrt*
pertain... *pėr-tān′*
pertinacious... *pėr-ti-nā′shus*

pertinacity... pėr-ti-nas'i-ti
pertinent... pėr'ti-nent
pertinently... pėr'ti-nent-li
perturb... pėr-tėrb'
perusal... pe-rūz'al
peruse... pe-rūz'
pervasive... pėr-vā'siv
perverse... pėr-vėrs'
perversion... pėr-vėr'shun
perversity... pėr-vėr'si-ti
pervert... pėr-vert'
pervious... pėr'vi-us
pessimism... pes'im-izm
pessimist... pes'im-ist
pessimistic... pes-im-is'tik
pest... pest
pester... pes'tėr
pestilence... pes'ti-lens
pestilent... pes'ti-lent
pet... pet
petal... pe'tal
petite... pė-tēt'
petition... pē-ti'shun
petitionary... pē-ti'shun-a-ri
petitioner... pē-ti'shun-ėr
petrify... pet-ri-fī
petrol... pet'rol
petroleum... pe-trō'lē-um
petticoat... pet'i-kōt
petty... pet'i
pew... pū
pewter... pū'tėr
pewterer... pū'tėr-ėr
phallic... fal'lik
phantasm... fan'tazm
phantom... fan'tom
pharisaism... fa'ri-sā-izm
pharisee... fa'ri-sē
pharmacy... far'ma-si
pharos... fa'ros
pharynx... fā'ringks
phase... fāz
phasis... fā'sis
pheasant... fe'zant
pheasantry... fe'zant-ri
phenomenal... fē-no'men-al
phenomenon... fē-no'me-non
phial... fī'al
philander... fi-lan'dėr
philanthropist... fī-lan'throp-ist
philanthropy... fī-lan'thro-pi
philatelist... fi-lat'e-list
philately... fi-lat'e-li
philharmonic... fil-har-mon'ik

philistine... fi-lis'tīn or fil'is-tin
philistinism... fil'is-tin-izm
philology... fi-lol'o-ji
philosopher... fi-los'o-fėr
philosophize... fi-los'o-fīz'
philosophy... fi-los'o-fi
philter... fil'tėr
phlebitis... flē-bī'tis
phlegm... flem
phlegmatic... fleg-mat'ik
phoenix... fē-niks
phonetic... fō-net'ik
phonetics... fō-net'iks
phonograph... fō'nō-graf
phosphate... fos'fāt
phosphorate... fos'for-āt
phosphoresce... fos-for-es'
phosphoric... fos-fo'rik
photograph... fō-'tō-graf
photographer... fō-tog'raf-ėr
photography... fō-tog'ra-fi
photogravure... fō'tō-grav-ūr
phrase... frāz
phraseology... frā-zē-ol'o-ji
phrenic... fren'ik
phrenologist... fre-nol'o-jist
physic... fi'zik
physical... fi'zik-al
physically... fi'zik-al-li
physician... fi-zi'shan
physicist... fi'zi-sist
physics... fi'ziks
physiography... fi-zi-og'ra-fi
physiologist... fi-zi-ol'o-jist
physiology... fi-zi-ol'o-ji
physique... fī-zēk'
piacular... pī-ak'ū-lar
pianist... pi'an-ist
piano... pi-a'nō
piano... pi-an'ō
pica... pī'ka
piccolo... pik'ko-lō
pick... pik
pickaxe... pik'aks
picked... pikt
picker... pik'ėr
picket... pik'et
picking... pik'ing
pickpocket... pik'pok-et
picnic... pik'nik
pictorial... pik-tō'ri-al
pictorially... pik-tō'ri-al-li
picture... pik'tūr
picturesque... pik-tūr-esk'

pie... *pī*
piece... *pēs*
piecemeal... *pēs'mēl*
piecer... *pēs'ėr*
piece-work... *pēs'wėrk*
pied... *pī d*
pier... *pēr*
pierce... *pērs*
piercer... *pērs'ėr*
piercing... *pērs'ing*
piety... *pī'e-ti*
pig... *pig*
pigeon... *pi'jon*
pig-headed... *pig'hed-ed*
pigment... *pig'ment*
pig-tail... *pig'tāl*
pike... *pīk*
pikeman... *pīk'man*
piles... *pīlz*
pilfer... *pil'fėr*
pilferer... *pil'fėr-ėr*
pilgrim... *pil'grim*
pilgrimage... *pil'grim-āj*
pill... *pil*
pillage... *pil'āj*
pillager... *pil'āj-ėr*
pillar... *pil'ėr*
pill-box... *pil-boks*
pillow... *pil'ō*
pilot... *pī'lot*
pimp... *pimp*
pimple... *pim'pl*
pimpled... *pim'pld*
pin... *pin*
pinafore... *pin'a-fōr*
pincers... *pin'sėrz*
pinch... *pinsh*
pincher... *pinsh'ėr*
pin-cushion... *pin'ku̇-shun*
pine... *pīn*
pineapple... *pīn'ap-l*
pinery... *pīn'ėr-i*
pink... *pingk*
pink-eye... *pingk'ī*
pin-money... *pin'mun-i*
pint... *pīnt*
pioneer... *pī-on-ēr'*
pious... *pī'us*
pipe... *pīp*
piper... *pīp'ėr*
piping... *pīp'ing*
pipy... *pīp'i*
piquancy... *pē'kan-si*
piquant... *pē'kant*

pique... *pēk*
piracy... *pī'ra-si*
pirate... *pī'rāt*
piratical... *pī-rat'ik-al*
pirouette... *pi'ro-et*
pismire... *pis'mīr*
piss... *pis*
pistachio... *pis-tā'shi-ō*
pistil... *pis'til*
pistillate... *pis'til-lāt*
pistol... *pis'tol*
pistole... *pis-tōl'*
piston-rod... *pis'ton-rod*
pit... *pit*
pitch... *pich*
pitch-dark... *pich'dark*
pitcher... *pich'ėr*
pitchfork... *pīch'fork*
piteous... *pi'tē-us*
pitfall... *pit'fal*
pith... *pith*
pithily... *pith'i-li*
pithy... *pith'i*
pitiable... *pi'ti-a-bl*
pitiably... *pi'ti-a-bli*
pitiful... *pi'ti-ful*
pitiless... *pi'ti-les*
pitman... *pit'man*
pittance... *pit'ans*
pity... *pi'ti*
pivot... *pi'vot*
placable... *pla'ka-bl*
placard... *plak'ėrd*
place... *plās*
placenta... *pla-sen'ta*
placid... *pla'sid*
plagiarism... *plā'ji-a-rizm*
plagiarist... *plā'ji-a-rist*
plagiarize... *plā'ji-a-rīz*
plagiary... *plā'ji-a-ri*
plague... *plāg*
plaid... *plād*
plain... *plān*
plainly... *plān'li*
plain-spoken... *plān'spōk-n*
plaintiff... *plānt'if*
plaintive... *plānt'iv*
plait... *plāt*
plaited... *plāt'ed*
plan... *plan*
plane... *plān*
planet... *pla'net*
planetary... *pla'net-a-ri*
plangent... *plan'gent*

planish... *pla'nish*
planisphere... *pla'ni-sfēr*
plank... *plangk*
plant... *plant*
plantain... *plan'tān*
plantar... *plan'tar*
planter... *plant'ér*
plantigrade... *plan'ti-grād*
plaque... *plak*
plasma... *plas'ma*
plasmic... *plaz'mik*
plaster... *plas'tér*
plasterer... *plas'tér-ér*
plastering... *plas'tér-ing*
plastic... *plas'tik*
plasticity... *plas-tis'i-ti*
plastron... *plas'tron*
plat... *plat*
plate... *plāt*
plate-armor... *plāt'ar-mér*
plateau... *pla-tō'*
plate-glass... *plāt'glas*
platform... *plat'form*
plating... *plāt'ing*
platinum... *pla'tin-um*
platitude... *pla'ti-tūd*
platitudinous... *pla-ti-tūd'i-nus*
platonic... *plā-ton'ik*
platoon... *pla-ton'*
platter... *plat'ér*
plaudit... *pla'dit*
plauditory... *pla'di-to-ri*
plausibility... *plaz-i-bil'i-ti*
plausible... *plaz'i-bl*
plausibly... *plaz'i-bli*
play... *plā*
play-bill... *plā'bil*
player... *plā'ér*
playful... *plā'ful*
playground... *plā'ground*
playmate... *plā'māt*
plaything... *plā'thing*
playwright... *plā'rīt*
plea... *plē*
plead... *plēd*
pleader... *plēd'ér*
pleading... *plēd'ing*
pleasance... *ple'zans*
pleasant... *ple'zant*
pleasantly... *ple'zant-li*
pleasantry... *ple'zant-ri*
please... *plēz*
pleasing... *plēz'ing*
pleasurable... *ple'zhūr-a-bl*

pleasure... *ple'zhūr*
plectrum... *plek'trum*
pledge... *plej*
plenary... *plē'na-ri*
plenipotent... *ple-nip'o-tent*
plentiful... *plen'ti-ful*
plentifully... *plen'ti-ful-li*
plenty... *plen'ti*
pleonasm... *plē'on-azm*
pleonastic... *plē'on-as'tik*
plethora... *pleth'o-ra*
plethoric... *ple-thor'ik*
pleural... *plū'ral*
pleuritic... *plū-rit'ik*
pliability... *plī-a-bil'i-ti*
pliable... *plī'a-bl*
pliancy... *plī'an-si*
pliant... *plī'ant*
plicate... *plī'kāt*
pliers... *plī'érz*
plight... *plīt*
plighter... *plīt'ér*
plod... *plod*
plodder... *plod'ér*
plot... *plot*
plotter... *plot'ér*
plover... *pluv'ér*
plow... *plou*
pluck... *pluk*
pluckily... *pluk'i-li*
plucky... *pluk'i*
plug... *plug*
plum... *plum*
plumage... *plom'āj*
plumb... *plum*
plumber... *plum'ér*
plumbing... *plum'ing*
plume... *plom*
plummet... *plum'et*
plump... *plump*
plumply... *plump'li*
plunder... *plun'dér*
plunderer... *plun'dér-ér*
plunge... *plunj*
plunger... *plunj'ér*
pluperfect... *plo'pér-fekt*
plural... *plo'ral*
pluralist... *plo'ral-ist*
plurally... *plo'ral-li*
plus... *plus*
plush... *plush*
plutocracy... *plo-tok'ra-si*
plutocrat... *plo'to-krat*
plutonic... *plo-ton'ik*

P

plutonium... *plo-tōn'i-um*
pluvial... *plo'vi-al*
pluviometer... *plo-vi-om'et-ėr*
ply... *plī*
plyer... *plī'ėr*
pneumatic... *nū-mat'ik*
pneumatics... *nū-mat'iks*
pneumonia... *nū-mō'ni-a*
poacher... *pōch'ėr*
pocket... *pok'et*
pocket-book... *pok'et-buk*
pocky... *pok'i*
pod... *pod*
podagra... *pod-ag'ra*
podgy... *poj'i*
poem... *pō'em*
poesy... *pō'e-si*
poet... *pō'et*
poetess... *pō'et-es*
poetic... *pō-et'ik*
poetically... *pō-et'ik-al-li*
poetics... *pō-et'iks*
poetry... *pō'et-ri*
poignancy... *poin'an-si*
poignant... *poin'ant*
poilu... *pwa-lu*
point... *point*
point-blank... *point-blangk*
pointed... *point'ed*
pointedly... *point'ed-li*
pointer... *point'ėr*
point-lace... *point'lās*
pointless... *point'les*
pointsman... *points'man*
poise... *poiz*
poison... *poi'zn*
poisonous... *poi'zn-us*
poke... *pōk*
poker... *pōk'ėr*
polar... *pō'lėr*
polarity... *pō-la'ri-ti*
polarize... *pō-lėr-īz*
pole-axe... *pōl'aks*
pole-cat... *pōl'kat*
polemic... *pō-lem'ik*
polemical... *pō-lem'ik-al*
polemics... *pō'lem'iks*
police... *pō-lēs'*
policy... *po'li-si*
polish... *po'lish*
polished... *po'lisht*
polite... *pō-līt'*
politely... *pō-līt-li*
politic... *po'li-tik*

political... *pō-lit'ik-al*
politically... *pō-lit'ik-al-li*
politician... *po-li-ti'shan*
politics... *po'li-tiks*
polity... *po'li-ti*
polka... *pōl'ka*
poll... *pōl*
polled... *pōld*
pollen... *pol'en*
pollenize... *pol'en-īz*
pollinate... *pol'i-nāt*
pollute... *pol-lūt'*
polo... *pō'lō*
polyandry... *po-li-an'dri*
polygamist... *po-lig'a-mist*
polygamy... *po-lig'a-mi*
polyglot... *po'li-glot*
polygraphy... *po-lig'ra-fi*
polygyny... *po-lij'i-ni*
polypus... *po'li-pus*
polysyllabic... *po'li-sil-lab''ik*
polysyllable... *po-li-sil'la-bl*
polysynthesis... *po-li-sin'the-sis*
polytechnic... *po-li-tek'nik*
polytheism... *po'li-thē-izm*
polytheist... *po'li-thē-ist*
pomace... *pom'ās*
pomaceous... *pō-mā'shus*
pomade... *pō-'mad'*
pomander... *pom'an-dėr*
pomatum... *pō-mā'tum*
pome... *pōm*
pomegranate... *pōm'gran-āt*
pommel... *pum'el*
pomology... *pō-mol'o-ji*
pomp... *pomp*
pompous... *pomp'us*
pompously... *pomp'us-li*
pond... *pond*
ponder... *pon'dėr*
ponderable... *pon'dėr-a-bl*
ponderous... *pon'dėr-us*
pontiff... *pon'tif*
pontifical... *pon-tif'ik-al*
pontificate... *pon-tif'i-kāt*
pontoon... *pon-ton*
pony... *pō'ni*
poodle... *pō'dl*
pooh... *po*
pooh-pooh... *po-po'*
pool... *pol*
poop... *pop*
poor... *por*
poorly... *por'li*

pop... *pop*
pop-corn... *pop'korn*
pope... *pōp*
popedom... *pōp'dum*
popery... *pōp'ē-ri*
popinjay... *pop'in-jā*
poplar... *pop'lėr*
poplin... *pop'lin*
poppy... *pop'i*
populace... *po'pū-lās*
popular... *po'pū-lėr*
popularity... *po-pū-la'ri-ti*
popularize... *po'pū-lėr-īz*
popularly... *po'pū'lėr-li*
populate... *po'pū-lāt*
population... *po-pū-lā'shun*
populous... *po'pū-lus*
porbeagle... *por'bē'gl*
porcelain... *pōr'se-lān*
porch... *pōrch*
porcine... *pōr'sīn*
porcupine... *por'kū-pīn*
pore... *pōr*
porgie, Porgy... *por'gi*
pork... *pōrk*
porker... *pōrk'ėr*
pornography... *por-nog'ra-fi*
porosity... *pōr-os'i-ti*
porous... *pōr'us*
porphyry... *por'fi-ri*
porridge... *po'rij*
porringer... *po'rin-jėr*
port... *pōrt*
portable... *pōrt'a-bl*
portage... *pōrt'āj*
portal... *pōrt'al*
portcullis... *pōrt-kul'is*
porte... *pōrt*
portend... *por-tend'*
portent... *pōr'tent*
portentous... *por-tent'us*
porter... *pōr'tėr*
porterage... *pōr'tėr-āj*
portfolio... *pōrt-fō'li-ō*
port-hole... *port'hōl*
portico... *pōr'ti-kō*
portion... *pōr'shun*
portioner... *pōr'shun-ėr*
portly... *pōrt'li*
portmanteau... *pōrt-man'tō*
portrait... *pōr'trāt*
portraiture... *pōr'trā-tūr*
portray... *pōr-trā'*
portrayal... *pōr-trā'al*

pory... *pō'ri*
pose... *pōz*
poser... *pōz'ėr*
posit... *poz'it*
position... *pō-zi'shun*
positive... *poz'it-iv*
positively... *poz'it-iv-li*
positivism... *poz'it-iv-izm*
positivist... *poz'it-iv-ist*
posse... *pos'se*
possess... *po-zes'*
possession... *po-ze'shun*
possessive... *po-zes'iv*
possessor... *po-zes'ėr*
posset... *pos'et*
possibility... *pos-i-bil'i-ti*
possible... *pos'i-bl*
possibly... *pos'i-bli*
post... *pōst*
postage... *pōst'āj*
postal... *pōst'al*
post-card... *pōst'kard*
post-date... *pōst-dāt'*
poster... *pōst'ėr*
posterity... *pos-te'ri-ti*
postern... *post'ern*
post-haste... *pōst-hāst'*
posthumous... *post'ū-mus*
postman... *pōst'man*
postmaster... *pōst'mas-tėr*
post-mortem... *pōst-mor'tem*
post-obit... *pōst-ob'it*
post-office... *pōst'of-is*
postpone... *pōst-pōn*
postscript... *pōst'skript*
postulate... *pos'tū-lāt*
posture... *pos'tūr*
posy... *pō'zi*
pot... *pot*
potable... *pō'ta-bl*
potash... *pot'ash*
potassic... *pō-tas'ik*
potassium... *pō-tas'si-um*
potation... *pō-tā'shun*
potato... *pō-tā'tō*
pot-boiler... *pot'boil-ėr*
poteen... *po-tēn'*
potency... *pō'ten-si*
potentate... *pō'ten-tāt*
potential... *pō-ten'shal*
potentiality... *pō-ten'shi-al''i-ti*
potentially... *pō-ten'shal-li*
potently... *pō'tent-li*
pother... *poŦH'ėr*

P

potion... pō'shun	**precedent**... prē-sēd'ent
pot-luck... pot'luk	**precentor**... prē-sen'tor
pot-pourri... pō-po-rē	**precept**... prē'sept
potsherd... pot'sherd	**preceptive**... prē-sep'tiv
pottage... pot'āj	**preceptor**... prē-sep'tor
potter... pot'er	**precession**... prē-se'shun
pottery... pot'e-ri	**precinct**... prē'singt
pottle... pot'l	**precious**... pre'shus
pouch... pouch	**preciously**... pre'shus-li
poult... pōlt	**preciousness**... pre'shus-nes
poulterer... pōl'ter-er	**precipice**... pre'si-pis
poultice... pōl'tis	**precipitant**... prē-si'pi-tant
poultry... pōl'tri	**precipitately**... prē-si'pi-tāt-li
pounce... pouns	**precipitous**... prē-si'pi-tus
pound... pound	**precise**... prē-sīs'
poundage... pound'āj	**precisely**... prē-sīs'li
pounder... pound'er	**precisian**... prē-si'zhan
pour... pōr	**precision**... prē-si'zhon
pouter... pout'er	**preclude**... prē-klod'
poverty... po'ver-ti	**preclusive**... prē-klo'siv
powder... pou'der	**precocious**... prē-kō'shus
powdery... pou'der-i	**precocity**... prē-kos'i-ti
power... pou'er	**preconceive**... prē-kon-sēv'
powerful... pou'er-ful	**preconcert**... prē-kon-sert'
powerfully... pou'er-fu-li	**precursive**... prē-ker'siv
powerless... pou'er-les	**precursor**... prē-ker'ser
pox... poks	**precursory**... prē-ker'so-ri
practicable... prak'ti-ka-bl	**predaceous**... prē-dā'shus
practicably... prak'ti-ka-bli	**predatory**... pred'a-to-ri
practical... prak'ti-kal	**predecease**... prē-dē-sēs'
practically... prak'ti-kal-li	**predecessor**... prē-dē-ses'er
practice... prak'tis	**predestinate**... prē-des'ti-nāt
practice... prak'tis	**predial**... prē-di-al
praetor... pē'tor	**predicable**... pre'di-ka-bl
praetorian... prē-tō'ri-an	**predicant**... pre'di-kant
prairie... prā'ri	**predicate**... pre'di-kāt
praise... prāz	**predicative**... pre'di-kāt-iv
prance... prans	**predict**... prē-dikt'
prank... prangk	**prediction**... prē-dik'shun
prate... prāt	**predictive**... prē-dik'tiv
prating... prāt'ing	**predictor**... prē-dik'tor
prattle... prat'l	**predilection**... prē-di-lek'shun
pray... prā	**predispose**... prē-dis-pōz'
prayer... prā'er	**predominate**... prē-dom'i-nāt
prayer-book... prā'er-buk	**pre-eminent**... prē-em'i-nent
prayerful... prā'er-ful	**pre-emption**... prē-em'shun
praying... prā'ing	**preen**... prēn
preach... prēch	**pre-engage**... prē-en-gāj'
preacher... prēch'er	**pre-establish**... prē-es-tab'lish
preaching... prēch'ing	**pre-exist**... prē-egz-ist'
preamble... prē-am'bl or prē'	**prefabricate**... prē-fab'ri-kāt
precarious... prē-kā'ri-us	**preface**... pre'fās
precaution... prē-ka'shun	**prefatory**... pre'fā-to-ri
precede... prē-sēd'	**prefect**... prē'fekt

prefecture... *prē'fekt-ūr*
prefer... *prē-fèr'*
preferable... *pre'fèr-a-bl*
preferably... *pre'fèr-a-bli*
preference... *pre'fèr-ens*
preferential... *pre-fèr-en'shal*
prefigure... *prē-fig'ūr*
prefix... *prē-fiks'*
pregnancy... *preg'nan-si*
pregnant... *preg'nant*
prehensible... *prē-hen'si-bl*
prehensile... *prē-hen'sīl*
prehension... *prē-hen'shun*
prehistoric... *prē-his-tor'ik*
prejudge... *prē-juj'*
prejudgment... *prē-juj'ment*
prejudicate... *prē-jū'di-kāt*
prejudice... *pre'jū-dis*
prejudicial... *pre-jū-di'shal*
preliminary... *prē-lim'in-a-ri*
prelude... *prel'ūd or prē-lūd'*
prelusive... *prē-lū'siv*
premature... *pre'ma-tūr*
premeditate... *prē-me'di-tāt*
premier... *pre'mi-èr*
premise... *prē-mīz'*
premise, Premiss... *pre'mis*
premium... *prē'mi-um*
premonish... *prē-mon'ish*
premonition... *prē-mō-ni'shun*
preoccupied... *prē-ok'kū-pīd*
preoccupy... *prē-ok'kū-pī*
preordain... *prē-or-dān'*
preparation... *pre-pa-rā'shun*
preparative... *prē-pa'rat-iv*
preparatory... *prē-pa'ra-to-ri*
prepare... *prē-pār'*
prepay... *prē-pā'*
prepayment... *prē-pā'ment*
prepense... *prē-pens'*
preposition... *pre-pō-zi'shun*
prepossess... *prē-po-zes'*
preposterous... *prē-pos'tèr-us*
prerogative... *prē-ro'ga-tiv*
presage... *prē'sāj or pres'āj*
presbyterian... *pres-bi-tē'ri-an*
prescience... *prē'shi-ens*
prescient... *prē'shi-ent*
prescind... *prē-sind'*
prescribe... *prē-skrīb'*
prescription... *prē-skrip'shun*
prescriptive... *prē-skrip'tiv*
presence... *pre'zens*
present... *pre'zent*

presentable... *prē-zent'a-bl*
presently... *pre'zent-li*
presentment... *prē-zent'ment*
preservative... *prē-zèrv'at-iv*
preserve... *prē-zèrv'*
preside... *prē-zīd'*
presidency... *pre'zi-den-si*
president... *pre'zi-dent*
presidential... *pre-zi-den'shal*
press... *pres*
pressing... *pres'ing*
pressman... *pres'man*
pressure... *pre'shūr*
prestige... *pres'tij*
presto... *pres'tō*
presumable... *prē-zūm'a-bl*
presumably... *prē-zūm'a-bli*
presume... *prē-zūm'*
presumption... *prē-zum'shun*
presumptive... *prē-zum'tiv*
presuppose... *prē-sup-pōz'*
pretend... *prē-tend'*
pretended... *prē-tend'ed*
pretender... *prē-tend'èr*
pretension... *prē-ten'shun*
pretentious... *prē-ten'shus*
pretermit... *prē-tèr-mit'*
pretext... *prē'tekst*
prettily... *prit'i-li*
pretty... *prit'i*
prevail... *prē-vāl'*
prevailing... *prē-vāl'ing*
prevalent... *pre'va-lent*
prevaricate... *prē-va'ri-kāt*
prevaricator... *prē-va'ri-kāt-or*
prevenient... *prē-vē'ni-ent*
prevent... *prē-vent'*
prevention... *prē-ven'shun*
preventive... *prē-vent'iv*
previous... *prē'vi-us*
previously... *prē'vi-us-li*
prevision... *prē-vi'zhon*
price... *prīs*
priceless... *prīs'les*
prick... *prik*
pricking... *prik'ing*
prickle... *prik'l*
prickly... *prik'li*
priest... *prēst*
priestess... *prēst'es*
priesthood... *prēt'hud*
priestly... *prēst'li*
prig... *prig*
prim... *prim*

P

primacy... prī'ma-si
primal... prī'mal
primarily... prī'ma-ri-li
primary... prī'ma-ri
primate... prī'māt
prime... prīm
primer... prim'ėr
primeval... prīm-ē'val
priming... prīm'ing
primitive... prim'it-iv
primitively... prim'it-iv-li
primordial... prīm-or'di-al
primrose... prim'rōz
prince... prins
princely... prins'li
princess... prin'ses
principal... prin'si-pal
principality... prin-si-pal'i-ti
principle... prin'si-pl
principled... prin'si-pld
print... print
printer... print'ėr
printing... print'ing
printing-press... print'ing-pres
prior... prī'or
prioress... prī'or-es
priority... prī-or'i-ti
priory... prī'o-ri
prise... prīz
prism... prizm
prismatic... priz-mat'ik
prismoid... priz'moid
prison... pri'zn
prisoner... pri'zn-ėr
pristine... pris'fīn
privacy... priv'a-si
private... prī'vat
privateer... prī-va-tēr'
privately... prī'vat-li
privation... prī-vā'shun
privative... pri'va-tiv
privet... priv'et
privily... pri'vi-li
privity... pri'vi-ti
privy... pri'vi
prize... prīz
prize-fight... prīz'fīt
probability... pro-ba-bil'i-ti
probable... pro'bab-l
probably... pro'ba-bli
probate... pro'bāt
probation... prō-bā'shun
probationer... prō-bā'shun-ėr
probe... prōb

problem... prob'lem
proboscis... prō-bos'is
procedure... prō-sē'd'ūr
proceed... prō-sēd,'
proceeding... prō-sēd'ing
proceeds... prō'sēdz
process... prō'ses
procession... prō-se'shun
processional... prō-se'shun-al
proclaim... prō-klām'
proclivity... prō-kliv'i-ti
proclivous... prō-kliv'us
procrastinate... prō-kras'ti-nāt
procreate... prō'krē-āt
procreation... prō-krē-ā'shun
proctor... prok'tor
procumbent... prō-kum'bent
procurable... prō-kūr'a-bl
procuration... pro-kūr-ā'shun
procurator... pro-kūr'āt-or
procure... prō-kūr'
procurement... prō-kūr'ment
procurer... prō-kūr'ėr
procuress... prō-kū'res
prod... prod
prodigal... prod'i-gal
prodigality... prod-i-gal'i-ti
prodigally... prod'i-gal-li
prodigious... prō-dij'us
prodigiously... prō-dij'us-li
prodigy... prod'i-ji
produce... prō-dūs'v
producer... prō-dūs'ėr
producible... prō-dūs'i-bl
product... pro'dukt
production... prō-duk'shun
productivity... prō-duk-tiv'i-ti
profane... prō-fān'
profanely... prō-fān'li
profanity... prō-fan'i-ti
profess... prō-fes'
professedly... prō-fes'ed-li
profession... prō-fe'shun
professional... prō-fe'shun-al
professor... prō-fes'or
professorial... prō-fes'sō'ri-al
professoriate... prō-fes-sō'ri-āt
professorship... prō-fes'or-ship
proffer... prof'ėr
proficient... prō-fi'shent
proficiently... prō-fi'shent-li
profile... prō'fīl
profit... pro'fit'
profitable... pro'fit-a-bl

profitably... pro'fit-a-bli
profitless... pro'fit-les
profligacy... pro'fli-ga-si
profligate... pro'fli-gāt
profound... prō-found'
profoundly... prō-found'li
profuse... prō-fūs'
profusely... prō-fūs'li
profusion... prō-fū'zhon
progeny... pro'je-ni
prognosis... prog-nō'sis
prognostic... prog-nos'tik
program... prō'gram
progress... prō'gres
progression... prō-gre'shun
progressive... prō-gres'iv
prohibit... prō-hib'it
prohibition... prō-hi-bi'shun
project... prō-jekt'
projectile... prō-jek'tīl
projection... prō-jek'shun
projector... prō-jek'tor
prolate... prō'lat
prolepsis... prō-lep'sis
proletarian... prō-le-tā'ri-an
prolific... prō-lif'ik
prolix... prō'liks
prolixity... prō-liks'i-ti
prologue... prō'log
prolusion... prō-lū'zhon
prominence... pro'mi-nens
prominent... pro'mi-nent
promiscuous... prō-mis'kū-us
promise... pro'mis
promising... pro'mis-ing
promissory... pro'mis-o-ri
promontory... pro'mon-to-ri
promote... prō-mōt'
promotion... prō-mō'shun
prompt... promt
prompter... promt'ėr
promptly... promt'li
promulgate... prō-mul'gāt
promulgator... prō'mul-gāt-or
prone... prōn
prong... prong
pronominal... prō-nom'in-al
pronoun... prō'noun
pronounce... prō-nouns'
proof... prof
prop... prop
propaganda... pro-pa-gan'da
propagate... pro'pa-gāt
propel... prō-pel'

propense... prō-pens'
propensity... prō-pens'i-ti
proper... pro'pėr
properly... pro'pėr-li
property... pro'pėr-ti
prophecy... pro'fe-si
prophesy... pro'fe-sī
prophet... pro'fet
prophetess... pro'fet-es
prophylactic... prō-fi-lak'tik
propinquity... prō-pin'kwi-ti
propitiate... prō-pi'shi-āt
propitiatory... prō-pi'shi-a-to-ri
propitious... prō-pi'shus
propitiously... prō-pi'shus-li
proportion... pro-pōr'shun
proportional... pro-pōr'shun-al
proposal... prō-pōz'al
propose... prō-pōz'
proposer... prō-pōz'ėr
proposition... pro-pō-zi'shun
propound... prō-pound'
proprietary... prō-prī'e-ta-ri
proprietor... pro-prī'e-tor
propulsion... prō-pul'shun
proscribe... prō-skrīb'
proscription... prō-skrip'shun
proscriptive... prō-skrip'tiv
prose... prōz
prosecute... pro'se-kūt
prosecution... pro-se-kū'shun
prosecutor... pro'se-kūt-or
prosecutrix... pro'sē-kūt-riks
proselyte... pro'se-līt
proselytism... pro'se-līt-izm
proselytize... pro'se-līt-īz
prospect... pros'pekt
prospective... pros-pek'tiv
prospectus... pros-pek'tus
prosper... pros'pėr
prosperity... pros-pe'ri-ti
prosperous... pros'pėr-us
prostitute... pros'ti-tūt
prostitution... pros-ti-tū'shun
prostrate... pros'trāt
prostration... pros-trā'shun
prosy... prōz'i
protean... prō'tē-an
protection... prō-tek'shun
protectionist... prō-tek'shun-ist
protective... prō-tekt'iv
protector... prō-tekt'or
protectorate... prō-tekt'or-āt
proteid... prō'tē-id

P

protect... prō-test'
protestant... pro'test-ant
protestation... prō-test'-ā'shun
protocol... prō'tō-kol
proton... prō'ton
protoplasm... prō'tō-plazm
prototype... prō'tō-fīp
protract... prō-trakt'
protraction... prō-trak'shun
protractive... prō-trakt'iv
protractor... prō-trakt'or
protrude... prō-trod'
protrusion... prō-tro'zhon
protrusive... prō-tro'siv
protuberant... prō-tū'bèr-ant
protuberate... prō-tū'bèr-āt
proud... proud
proudly... proud'li
prove... prov
proven... pro'vn
provenance... prov'e-nans
provender... prov'en-dèr
proverb... pro'vèrb
proverbial... prō-vèrb'i-al
proverbially... prō-vèrb'i-al-li
provide... prō-vīd'
provided... prō-vīd'ed
providence... pro'vi-dens
provident... pro'vi-dent
providential... pro-vi-den'shal
providently... pro'vi-dent-li
province... pro'vins
provincial... prō-vin'shal
provision... prō-vi'zhon
provisional... prō-vi'zhon-al
provisionally... prō-vi'zhon-al-li
provisory... prō-vī'zo-ri
provocation... pro-vō-kā'shun
provocative... prō-vok'a-tiv
provost... pro'vost
prow... prou
prowess... prou'es
proximity... proks-im'i-ti
proxy... proks'i
prude... prod
prudence... pro'dens
prudent... pro'dent
prudential... pro-den'shal
prudery... prod'è-ri
prudish... prod'ish
prune... pron
prurient... pro'ri-ent
pry... prī
prying... prī'ing

psalm... sam
psalmist... sam'ist
psalter... sal'tèr
psaltery... sal'te-ri
pseudonym... sū'dō-nim
psychiatry... sī'ki-at-ri
psychic... sī'kik
psychologist... sī-kol'o-jist
psychology... sī-kol'o-ji
ptarmigan... tar'mi-gan
ptolemaic... to-lē-mā'ik
ptomaine... tō'mān
puberty... pū'bèr-tl
pubescence... pū-bes'ens
pubescent... pū-bes'ent
public... pub'lik
publican... pub'li-kan
publication... pub-li-kā'shun
public-house... pub'lik-hous
publicist... pub'li-sist
publicity... pub-lis'i-ti
publicly... pub'lik-li
publish... pub'lish
publisher... pub'lish-èr
pucker... puk'èr
pudding... pud'ing
puddle... pud'l
puddling... pud'ling
pudgy... puj'i
puerperal... pū-èr'pèr-al
puff... puf
puffin... puf'in
puffy... puf'i
pug... pug
pugilistic... pū-jil-ist'ik
pugnacious... pug-nā'shus
pug-nose... pug'nōz
puisne... pū'ni
puissance... pū'is-ans
puissant... pū'is-ant
puke... pūke
pulchritude... pul'kri-tūd
pule... pūl
pulkha... pul'ka
pull... pul
pullet... pul'et
pull-over... pul'ō-vèr
pull-through... pul'thro
pulmonary... pul'mon-a-ri
pulp... pulp
pulpit... pul'pit
pulpy... pul'pi
pulsate... pul'sāt
pulsation... pul-sā'shun

pulse... *puls*
pulverize... *pul'vėr-īz*
pulverulent... *pul-ver'ū-lent*
puma... *pū'ma*
pumice... *pū'mis or pum'is*
pumisceous... *pū-mi'shus*
pumpkin... *pump'kin*
pun... *pun*
punch... *punsh*
puncheon... *pun'shun*
punchy... *punsh'i*
punctual... *pungk'tū-al*
punctuality... *pungk-tū-al'i-ti*
punctuate... *pungk'tū-āt*
puncture... *pungk'tūr*
pundit... *pun'dit*
pungency... *pun'jen-si*
pungent... *pun'jent*
punic... *pū'nik*
punish... *pun'ish*
punishable... *pun'ish-a-bl*
punishment... *pun'ish-ment*
punitive... *pū'ni-tiv*
punitory... *pū'ni-to-ri*
punning... *pun'ing*
punster... *pun'stėr*
punt... *punt*
puny... *pūn'i*
pup... *pup*
pupa... *pū'pa*
puppet... *pup'et*
puppy... *pup'i*
purchasable... *pėr'chās-a-bl*
purchase... *pėr'chās*
purchaser... *pėr'chās-ėr*
pure... *pūr*
purely... *pūr'li*
purgation... *pėr-gā'shun*
purgative... *pėr'ga-tiv*
purgatory... *pėr'ga-to-ri*
purge... *pėrj*
purification... *pū'ri-fi-kā''shun*
purifier... *pū'ri-fī-ėr*
purify... *pū'ri-fī*
purism... *pūr'izm*
purist... *pūr'ist*
puritan... *pūr'i-tan*
purity... *pūr'i-ti*
purl... *pėrl*
purlieu... *pėr'lū*
purloin... *pėr-loin'*
purple... *pėr'pl*
purport... *pėr'pōrt*
purpose... *pėr'pos*

purr... *pėr*
purse... *pėrs*
purser... *pėrs'ėr*
purslane... *pėrs'lān*
pursuance... *pėr-sū'ans*
pursuant... *pėr-sū'ant*
pursue... *pėr-sū'*
pursuer... *pėr-sū'ėr*
pursuit... *pėr-sūt'*
pursuivant... *pėr'swi-vant*
pursy... *pėr'si*
purtenance... *pėr'te-nans*
purulent... *pū'ru-lent*
purvey... *pėr-vā'*
purveyance... *pėr-vā'ans*
purveyor... *pėr-vā'or*
purview... *pėr'vū*
pus... *pus*
puseyism... *pū'zi-izm*
push... *push*
pushing... *push'ing*
pusillanimity... *pū'sil-la-nim''i-ti*
puss... *pus*
pussy... *pus'i*
pustule... *pus'tūl*
put... *put*
putrefaction... *pū-trē-fak'shun*
putrefactive... *pū-trē-fak'tiv*
putrefy... *pū'trē-fī*
putrescence... *pū-tres'ens*
putrescent... *pū-tres'ent*
putrid... *pū'trid*
putridity... *pū-trid'i-ti*
putter... *put'ėr*
putting-green... *put'ing-grēn*
puttock... *put'ok*
putty... *put'i*
puzzle... *puz'l*
puzzlement... *puz'l-ment*
puzzler... *puz'l-ėr*
puzzling... *puz'ling*
pyemia... *pī-ē'mi-a*
pygmy... *pig'mi*
pylorus... *pī-lō'rus*
pyramid... *pi'ra-mid*
pyramidal... *pi-ram'id-al*
pyre... *pīr*
pyrethrum... *pi-reth'rum*
pyrites... *pi-rī'tēz*
pyrolatry... *pī-rol'a-tri*
pyroligneous... *pī-rō-lig'nē-us*
pyrology... *pī-rol'o-ji*
pyrometer... *pī-rom'et-ėr*
pyrotechnic... *pī-rō-tek'nik*

P

pyrotechnist... _pī-rō-tek'nist_
pyrrhic... _pi'rik_
python... _pī'thon_
pythoness... _pī'thon-es_
pyx... _piks_

Q

quack... _kwak_
quackery... _kwak'ė-ri_
quackish... _kwak'ish_
quad... _kwod_
quadrangle... _kwod-rang-gl_
quadrant... _kwod'rant_
quadrate... _kwod'rāt_
quadratic... _kwod-rat'ik_
quadrennial... _kwod-ren'ni-al_
quadripartite... _kwod-ri-par'tī t_
quadroon... _kwod-ron'_
quadruped... _kwod'ru-ped_
quagmire... _kwag'mīr_
quail... _kwāl_
quaint... _kwānt_
quaintly... _kwānt'li_
quake... _kwāk_
qualified... _kwo'li-fī d_
qualify... _kwo'li-fī_
qualitative... _kwo'li-tā-tiv_
quality... _kwo'li-ti_
qualm... _kwam_
quandary... _kwon-dā'ri_
quantify... _kwon'ti-fī_
quantitative... _kwon'ti-tā-tiv_
quantity... _kwon'ti-ti_
quantum... _kwan'tum_
quarantine... _kwo'ran-fī n_
quarrel... _kwo'rel_
quarrelsome... _kwo'rel-sum_
quarry... _kwo'ri_
quart... _kwart_
quarter... _kẅar'tėr_
quartering... _kẅar'tėr-ing_
quarterly... _kwar̈'tėr-li_
quartet... _kwar̈-tet'_
quatrain... _kẅot'rān_
quaver... _kwā'vėr_
quayage... _kē'āj_
quean... _kwēn_
queasy... _kwē'zi_
queen... _kwēn_
queer... _kwēr_
quell... _kwel_

quench... _kwensh_
quenchable... _kwensh'a-bl_
quern... _kwėrn_
query... _kwē'ri_
quest... _kwest_
question... _kwest'yon_
questionable... _kwest'yon-a-bl_
queue... _kū_
quibble... _kwib'l_
quick... _kwik_
quicken... _kwik'n_
quickline... _kwik'līn m_
quickly... _kwik'li_
quicksand... _kwik'sand_
quid... _kwid_
quiescence... _kwī-es'ens_
quiet... _kwī'et_
quietly... _kwī'et-li_
quill... _kwil_
quilt... _kwilt_
quilting... _kwilt'ing_
quince... _kwins_
quinine... _kwin'ēn_
quintet... _kwin-tet'_
quintuple... _kwin'tu̯-pl_
quirk... _kwėrk_
quit... _kwit_
quite... _kwī t_
quiver... _kwi'vėr_
quiz... _kwiz_
quizzical... _kwiz'i-kal_
quoit... _koit_
quondam... _kwon'dam_
quorum... _kwō'rum_
quota... _kwō'ta_
quotable... _kwōt'a-bl_
quotation... _kwōt-ā'shun_
quote... _kwōt_
quotient... _kwō'shent_

R

rabbi... _rab'bī_
rabbit... _rab'it_
rabble... _rab'l_
rabid... _ra'bid_
rabidly... _ra'bid-li_
rabies... _rā'bi-ēs_
raccoon... _ra-kon'_
race... _rās_
race-horse... _rās'hors_
racial... _rā'si-al_
racing... _rās'ing_

rack... *rak*
racket... *rak'et*
racy... *rā'si*
radar... *rā'dar*
radial... *rā'di-al*
radiance... *rā'di-ans*
radiant... *rā'di-ant*
radiate... *rā'di-āt*
radical... *ra'di-kal*
radicalism... *ra'di-kal-izm*
radicle... *ra'di-kl*
radio... *rā'di-ō*
radish... *ra'dish*
radius... *rā'di-us*
raffle... *raf'l*
raft... *raft*
rafter... *raf'tėr*
rag... *rag*
ragamuffin... *rag-a-muf'in*
rage... *rāj*
ragged... *rag'ed*
ragout... *ra-go'*
raid... *rād*
raider... *rād'ėr*
rail... *rāl*
railing... *rāl'ing*
raillery... *rāl'ė-ri*
railroad... *rāl'rōd*
railway... *rāl'wā*
raiment... *rā'ment*
rain... *rān*
rainbow... *rān'bō*
rainfall... *rān'fal*
rainy... *rān'i*
raise... *rāz*
raisin... *rā'zn*
rake... *rāk*
rally... *ral'i*
ram... *ram*
ramble... *ram'bl*
rambler... *ram'blėr*
rambling... *ram'bling*
ramify... *ra'mi-fī*
rammer... *ram'ėr*
ramp... *ramp*
rampage... *ram'pāj*
rampant... *ram'pant*
rampart... *ram'part*
ramrod... *ram'rod*
ramson... *ram'zon*
ranch... *ranch*
rancid... *ran'sid*
rancor... *rang'kor*
rancorous... *rang'kor-us*

random... *ran'dum*
range... *rānj*
ranger... *rānj'ėr*
rank... *rangk*
rankle... *rang'kl*
rankly... *rangk'li*
ransack... *ran'sak*
rant... *rant*
ranter... *rant'ėr*
rap... *rap*
rapacious... *ra-pā'shus*
rapacity... *ra-pa'si-ti*
rape... *rāp*
rapid... *ra'pid*
rapidity... *ra-pid'i-ti*
rapidly... *ra'pid-li*
rapine... *ra'pīn*
rapt... *rapt*
raptorial... *rap-tō'ri-al*
rapture... *rap'tūr*
rare... *rār*
rarefaction... *rā-rē-fak'shun*
rarefy... *rā'rē-fī*
rarely... *rār'li*
rarity... *ra'ri-ti*
rascal... *ras'kal*
rash... *rash*
rashly... *rash'li*
rasorial... *ra-sō'ri-al*
rasp... *rasp*
raspberry... *raz'be-ri*
rat... *rat*
ratafia... *rat-a-fē'a*
ratchet... *rach'et*
rate... *rāt*
rath... *rath*
rather... *raͭH'ėr*
ratification... *ra'ti-fi-kā''shun*
ratify... *ra'ti-fī*
ratio... *rā'shi-ō*
ration... *ra'shun*
rational... *ra'shun-al*
rationale... *ra-shun-ā'lē*
rationalism... *ra'shun-al-izm*
rationalist... *ra'shun-a-list*
rationality... *ra-shun-al'i-ti*
rationally... *ra'shun-al-li*
rattan... *rat'an or rat-tan'*
rattle... *rat'l*
rattlesnake... *rat'l-snāk*
raucous... *ra'kus*
ravage... *ra'vāj*
rave... *rāv*
ravel... *ra'vel*

R

raven... *rā'vn*
ravenously... *rav'en-us-li*
ravine... *ra-vēn'*
raving... *rāv'ing*
ravish... *ra'vish*
ravishing... *ra'vish-ing*
ravishment... *ra'vish-ment*
raw... *ra*
rayon... *rā'on*
razor... *rā'zor*
reach... *rēch*
react... *rē-akt'*
reaction... *rē-ak'shun*
reactionary... *rē-ak'shun-a-ri*
read... *rēd*
readable... *rēd'a-bl*
reader... *rēd'ėr*
readily... *re'di-li*
readiness... *re'di-nes*
reading... *rēd'ing*
ready... *re'di*
ready-made... *re'di-mād*
reaffirm... *rē-af-fėrm'*
reagent... *rē-ā'jent*
real... *rē'al*
realist... *rē'al-ist*
reality... *rē-al'i-ti*
realize... *rē'al-īz*
really... *rē'al-li*
realm... *relm*
realty... *rē'al-ti*
ream... *rēm*
reanimate... *rē-an'i-māt*
reap... *rēp*
reaper... *rēp'ėr*
reappear... *rē-ap-pēr'*
reappoint... *rē-ap-point'*
rear... *rēr*
rearrange... *rē'a-rānj*
reason... *rē'zn*
reasonable... *rē'zn-a-bl*
reasonably... *rē'zn-a-bli*
reasoning... *rē'zn-ing*
reassemble... *rē-as-sem'bl*
reassert... *rē-as-sėrt'*
reassurance... *rē-a-shor'ans*
reassure... *rē-a-shor'*
rebate... *rē-bāt'*
rebel... *re'bel*
rebellious... *rē-bel'yus*
rebound... *rē-bound'*
rebuff... *rē-buf'*
rebuild... *rē-bild'*
rebuke... *rē-būk'*

rebukingly... *rē-būk'ing-li*
rebut... *rē-but'*
rebuttal... *rē-but'al*
recalcitrate... *rē-kal'si-trāt*
recall... *rē-kal'*
recant... *rē-kant'*
recantation... *rē-kant-ā'shun*
recapitulate... *rē-ka-pit'ū-lāt*
recapture... *rē-kap'tūr*
recast... *rē-kast'*
recede... *rē-sēd'*
receipt... *rē-sēt'*
receivable... *rē-sēv'a-bl*
receive... *rē-sēv'*
recent... *rē'sent*
recently... *rē'sent-li*
receptacle... *rē-sep'ta-kl*
reception... *rē-sep'shun*
receptionist... *rē-sep'shun-ist*
recess... *rē-ses'*
recession... *rē-se'shun*
recherche... *rė-sher'shā*
recipe... *re'si-pē*
recipient... *rē-si'pi-ent*
reciprocal... *rē-sip'rō-kal*
reciprocity... *re-si-pros'i-ti*
recital... *rē-sīt'al*
recitation... *re-si-tā'shun*
recitative... *re'si-ta-tēv*
recite... *rē-sīt'*
reciter... *rē-sīt'ėr*
reck... *rek*
reckless... *rek'les*
recklessly... *rek'les-li*
reckon... *rek'n*
reckoning... *rek'n-ing*
reclaim... *rē-klām'*
reclaimable... *rē-klām'a-bl*
reclamation... *re-kla-mā'shun*
recline... *rē-klīn'*
recluse... *rē-klos'*
reclusion... *rē-klo'zhon*
recognition... *re-kog-ni'shun*
recognize... *re'kog-nīz*
recoil... *rē-koil'*
recollect... *re'kol-lekt*
recollect... *rē-kol-lekt'*
recollection... *re-kol-lek'shun*
recommence... *rē-kom-mens'*
recommend... *re-kom-mend'*
recommit... *rē-kom-mit'*
recompense... *re'kom-pens*
reconcile... *re'kon-sīl*
reconsider... *rē-kon-si'dėr*

reconstruct... *rē-kon-strukt'*
record... *rē-kord'*
recorder... *rē-kord'ėr*
recount... *rē-kount'*
recoup... *rē-kop'*
recourse... *rē-kōrs'*
recover... *rē-kuv'ėr*
recoverable... *rē-kuv'ėr-a-bl*
recreate... *re'krē-āt*
re-create... *rē-krē-āt'*
recreation... *re-krē-a'shun*
recreative... *re'krē-āt-iv*
recrement... *re'krē-ment*
recruit... *rē-krot'*
rectangle... *rek'tang-gl*
rectification... *rek'ti-fi-kā''shun*
rectifier... *rek'ti-fī-ėr*
rectify... *rek'ti-fī*
rector... *rek'tor*
rectorial... *rek-tō'ri-al*
rectory... *rek'to-ri*
rectum... *rek'tum*
recumbent... *rē-kum'bent*
recuperate... *rē-kū'pėr-āt*
recuperative... *rē-kū'pėr-ā-tiv*
recur... *rē-kėr'*
recurrence... *rē-ku'rens*
recurrent... *rē-ku'rent*
red... *red*
redact... *rē-dakt'*
redaction... *rē-dak'shun*
redactor... *rē-dakt'ėr*
redden... *red'n*
reddish... *red'ish*
reeddition... *red-di'shun*
reddle... *red'l*
redeem... *rē-dēm'*
redeemer... *rē-dēm'ėr*
redeliver... *rē-dē-liv'ėr*
redemption... *rē-dem'shun*
red-handed... *red'hand-ed*
red-hot... *red'hot*
redintegrate... *re-din'ti-grāt*
red-letter... *red'let-ėr*
redolence... *re'dō-lens*
redolent... *re'dō-lent*
redouble... *rē-du'bl*
redoubt... *rē-dout'*
redoubtable... *rē-dout'a-bl*
redoubted... *rē-dout'ed*
redound... *rē-dound'*
redraft... *rē-dräft'*
redraw... *rē-dra'*
redress... *rē-drės'*

redstart... *red'start*
red-tape... *red'tāp*
reduce... *rē-dūs'*
reducible... *rē-dūs'i-bl*
reduction... *rē-duk'shun*
redundant... *rē-dun'dant*
redwood... *red'wud*
reedy... *rēd'i*
reef... *rēf*
reefer... *rēf'ėr*
reek... *rēk*
reel... *rēl*
re-elect... *rē-ē-lekt'*
re-embark... *rē-em-bark'*
re-enact... *rē-en-akt'*
re-enforce... *rē-en-fōrs'*
re-engage... *rē-en-gāj'*
re-enter... *rē-en'tėr*
re-establish... *rē-es-tab'lish*
reeve... *rēv*
re-examine... *rē-eg-zam'in*
re-export... *rē-eks-pōrt'*
re-fashion... *rē-fa'shun*
refection... *rē-fek'shun*
refectory... *rē-fek'to-ri*
refer... *rē-fėr'*
referable... *ref'ėr-a-bl*
referee... *ref-ėr-ē'*
reference... *re'fėr-ens*
referendum... *ref-ėr-en'dum*
refill... *rē-fil'*
refinement... *rē-fīn'ment*
refiner... *rē-fīn'ėr*
refinery... *rē-fīn'ėr-i*
refit... *rē-fit'*
reflect... *rē-flekt'*
reflection... *rē-flek'shun*
reflective... *rē-flekt'iv*
reflector... *rē-flekt'or*
reflex... *rē'fleks*
reflexible... *rē-fleks'i-bl*
refluent... *ref'lu-ent*
reflux... *rē'fluks*
reform... *rē-form'*
reformation... *re-for-mā'shun*
re-formation... *rē-for-mā'shun*
reformatory... *rē-for'ma-to-ri*
reformed... *rē-formd'*
reformer... *rē-form'ėr*
refract... *rē-frakt'*
refraction... *rē-frak'shun*
refractor... *rē-frakt'ėr*
refrain... *rē-frān'*
refresh... *rē-fresh'*

R

refresher... rē-fresh'ér
refreshment... rē-fresh'ment
refrigerate... rē-frij'jė-rāt
refrigerator... rē-frij'ė-rāt-ér
refuge... re'fūj
refugee... re-fū-jē'
refund... rē-fund'
refurnish... rē-fér'nish
refuse... rē-fūz'
refuse... re'fūz
refutable... rē-fūt'a-bl
refute... rē-fūt'
regain... rē-gān'
regal... rē'gal
regale... rē-gāl'
regality... rē-gal'i-ti
regally... rē'gal-li
regard... rē-gard'
regardful... rē-gard'ful
regarding... rē-gard'īng
regardless... rē-gard'les
regelation... rē-je-lā'shun
regency... rē'jen-si
regenerate... rē-jen'ė-rāt
regent... rē'jent
regimen... re'ji-men
regiment... re'ji-ment
regimentals... re-ji-ment'alz
region... rē'jun
register... re'jis-tér
registrar... re'jis-trar
registration... re-jis-trā'shun
registry... re'jis-tri
regress... rē'gres
regression... rē-gre'shun
regret... rē-gret'
regretful... rē-gret'ful
regular... re'gū-lér
regularity... re-gū-la'ri-ti
regularly... re'gū-lér-li
regulate... re'gū-lāt
regurgitate... rē-gér'jit-tāt
rehabilitate... rē-ha-bil'i-tāt
rehearsal... rē-hérs'al
rehearse... rē-hérs'
reign... rān
reimburse... rē-im-bérs'
reindeer... rān'dēr
reinforce... rē-in-fōrs'
reinstate... rē-in-stāt'
reissue... rē-ish'ū
reiterate... rē-it'ér-āt
reject... rē-jekt'
rejoice... rē-jois'

rejoicing... rē-jois'ing
rejuvenate... rē-jū'ven-āt
relapse... rē-laps'
relate... rē-lāt'
relation... rē-lā'shun
relationship... rē-lā'shun-ship
relative... re'lat-iv
relatively... re'lat-iv-li
relator... rē-lāt'ér
relax... rē-laks'
relaxation... re-laks-ā'shun
relay... rē-lā'
release... rē-lēs'
re-lease... rē-lēs'
relent... rē-lent'
relentless... rē-lent'les
relevance... re'le-vans
relevant... re'le-vant
reliable... rē-lī'a-bl
reliance... rē-lī'ans
reliant... rē-lī'ant
relic... re'lik
relief... rē-lēf'
relieve... rē-lēv'
religion... rē-li'jon
religious... rē-li'jus
religiously... rē-li'jus-li
relinquish... rē-ling'kwish
relish... re'lish
relive... rē-liv'
reluctant... rē-luk'tant
rely... rē-lī'
remain... rē-mān'
remainder... rē-mān'dér
remake... rē-māk'
remand... rē-mand'
remanent... rem'a-nent
remark... rē-mark'
remarkable... rē-mark'a-bl
remarkably... rē-mark'a-bli
remarry... rē-ma'ri
remediable... re-mē'di-a-bl
remedial... re-mē'di-al
remember... rē-mem'bér
remind... rē-mīnd'
reminder... rē-mīnd'ér
reminiscence... re-mi-nis'ens
reminiscent... re-mi-nis'ent
remiss... rē-mis'
remission... rē-mi'shun
remit... rē-mit'
remittance... rē-mit'ans
remittent... rē-mit'ent
remnant... rem'nant

remonstrance...rē-mon'strans
remonstrant...rē-mon'strant
remonstrate...rē-mon'strāt
remora...rem'o-ra
remorse...rē-mors'
remorseful...rē-mors'ful
remorseless...rē-mors'les
remote...rē-mōt'
remotely...rē-mōt'li
remount...rē-mount'
removable...rē-mov'a-bl
removal...rē-mov'al
remove...rē-mov'
renaissance...re-nā'sans
renal...rē'nal
renascence...rē-nas'ens
renascent...rē-nas'ent
rencounter...ren-koun'tèr
rend...rend
render...ren'dèr
rendering...ren'dèr-ing
rendezvous...ren'de-vo
rendition...ren-di'shun
renegade...re'nē-gād
renew...rē-nū'
renewal...rē-nū'al
renitent...rē-nī'tent
renounce...rē-nouns'
renovate...re'nō-vāt
renovation...re-nō-vā'shun
renown...rē-noun'
renowned...rē-nound'
rent...rent
rental...rent'al
renter...rent'èr
reoccupy...rē-ok'kū-pī
reopen...rē-ō'pen
repair...rē-pār'
reparable...re'pa-ra-bl
reparation...re-pa-rā'shun
reparative...re-pa'ra-tiv
repast...rē-past'
repatriate...rē-pā'tri-āt
repay...rē-pā'
repayable...rē-pā-a-bl
repayment...rē-pā'ment
repeal...rē-pēl'
repeat...rē-pēt'
repeatedly...rē-pēt'ed-li
repeater...rē-pēt'èr
repeating...rē-pēt'ing
repel...rē-pel'
repellent...rē-pel'ent
repent...rē-pent'

repent...rē'pent
repentance...rē-pent'ans
repercussion...rē-pèr-ku'shun
repercussive...rē-pèr-kus'iv
repertoire...rep'èr-twar
repertory...re'pèr-to-ri
repetition...re-pē-ti'shun
replenish...rē-plen'ish
replete...rē-plēt'
replica...rep'li-ka
replication...re-pli-kā'shun
reply...rē-plī'
report...rē-pōrt'
reporter...rē-pōrt'èr
reposal...rē-pōz'al
repose...rē-pōz'
reposeful...rē-pōz'ful
reprehend...re-prē-hend'
reprehensive...re-prē-hen'siv
represent...re-prē-zent'
repress...rē-pres'
repression...rē-pre'shun
repressive...rē-pres'iv
reprieve...rē-prēv'
reprimand...rep'ri-mand
reprint...rē-print'
reprisal...rē-prīz'al
reproach...rē-prōch'
reproachable...rē-prōch'a-bl
reprobate...re'prō-bāt
reproduce...rē-prō-dūs'
reproval...rē-prōv'al
reprove...rē-prov'
reptile...rep'til
republic...rē-pub'lik
republican...rē-pub'lik-an
repudiate...rē-pū'di-āt
repugnance...rē-pug'nans
repugnant...rē-pug'nant
repulse...rē-puls'
repulsive...rē-puls'iv
repurchase...rē-pèr'chās
reputable...re'pūt-a-bl
reputation...re-pūt-ā'shun
repute...rē-pūt'
request...rē-kwest'
require...rē-kwīr'
requirement...rē-kwīr'ment
requisite...re'kwi-zit
requisition...re-kwi-zi'shun
requital...rē-kwīt'al
requite...rē-kwīt'
rescind...rē-sind'
rescue...res'kū

R

rescuer . . . res'kū-ėr
reseize . . . rē-sēz'
resemblance . . . rē-zem'blans
resemble . . . rē-zem'bl
resent . . . rē-zent'
resentful . . . rē-zent'ful
resentment . . . rē-zent'ment
reservation . . . re-zėrv-ā'shun
reserve . . . rė-zėrv'
reservoir . . . re'zėr-vwar
reset . . . rē-set'
reside . . . rē-zī d'
residence . . . re'zi-dens
resident . . . re'zi-dent
residential . . . re-zi-den'shal
residual . . . rē-zid'ū-al
residuary . . . rē-zid'ū-a-ri
residue . . . re'zi-dū
resign . . . rē-zī n'
resignation . . . re-zig-nā'shun
resilient . . . rē-si'li-ent
resin . . . re'zin
resist . . . rē-zist'
resistance . . . rē-zist'ans
resistible . . . rē-zist'i-bl
resolute . . . re'zō-lūt
resolution . . . re-zō-lū'shun
resolvable . . . rē-zolv'a-bl
resolve . . . rē-zolv'
resolver . . . rē-zolv'ėr
resonance . . . re'zo-nans
resonant . . . re'zo-nant
resort . . . rē-zort'
resound . . . rē-zound'
resource . . . rē-sōrs'
respect . . . rē-spekt'
respectable . . . rē-spekt'a-bl
respectably . . . rē-spekt'a-bli
respectful . . . rē-spekt'ful
respective . . . rē-spekt'ĭv
respiration . . . re-spi-rā'shun
respirator . . . re'spi-rāt-ėr
respiratory . . . re'spī-ra''to-ri
respite . . . res'pit
respond . . . rē-spond'
respondent . . . rē-spond'ent
response . . . rē-spons'
responsible . . . rē-spons'i-bl
responsive . . . rē-spons'iv
restaurant . . . res'tō-rong
restaurateur . . . res-tō'ra-tėr
restful . . . rest'ful
restitution . . . rēs-ti-tū'shun
restless . . . rest'les

restorable . . . rē-stor'a-bl
restoration . . . re-stō-rā'shun
restore . . . rē-stōr'
restrain . . . rē-strān'
restraint . . . rē-strānt'
restrict . . . rē-strikt'
restriction . . . rē-strik'shun
restrictive . . . rē-strikt'iv
result . . . rē-zult'
resumable . . . rē-zūm'a-bl
resume . . . rē-zūm'
resurgent . . . rē-sėr'jent
resurrection . . . re-zėr-rek'shun
resuscitate . . . rē-sus'i-tāt
retail . . . rē-tāl'
retailer . . . rē-tāl'ėr
retain . . . rē-tān'
retainer . . . rē-tān'ėr
retake . . . rē-tāk'
retaliation . . . rē-ta'li-ā''shun
retard . . . rē-tard'
retardation . . . rē-tard-ā'shun
retention . . . rē-ten'shun
retentive . . . rē-ten'tiv
reticence . . . re'ti-sens
reticent . . . re'ti-sent
retina . . . re'ti-na
retinue . . . re'ti-nū
retire . . . rē-fīr'
retired . . . rē-fīrd'
retirement . . . rē-fīr'ment
retiring . . . rē-fīr'ing
retort . . . rē-tort'
retouch . . . rē-tuch'
retrace . . . rē-trās'
retract . . . rē-trakt'
retractable . . . rē-trakt'a-bl
retractation . . . rē-trak-tā'shun
retraction . . . rē-trak'shun
retractive . . . rē-trakt'iv
retractor . . . rē-trakt'ėr
retranslate . . . rē-trans-lāt'
retreat . . . rē-trēt'
retribution . . . re-tri-bū'shun
retrievable . . . rē-trēv'a-bl
retrieval . . . rē-trēv'al
retrieve . . . rē-trēv'
retriever . . . rē-trēv'ėr
retroact . . . rē-trō-akt'
retrorse . . . rē-trors'
retrospect . . . ret'rō-spekt
return . . . rē-tėrn'
reunion . . . rē-ūn'yon
reunite . . . rē-ū-nī t'

reveal . . . rē-vēl′
revel . . . re′vel
revelation . . . re-ve-lā′shun
revenge . . . rē-venj′
revengeful . . . rē-venj′ful
revenue . . . re′ve-nū
reverberate . . . rē-vėr′bė-rāt
revere . . . rē-vēr′
reverence . . . rev′er-ens
reverend . . . rev′er-end
reverent . . . rev′er-ent
reverie . . . re′ver-i
reverse . . . rē-vėrs′
revert . . . rē-vėrt′
revertible . . . rē-vėrt′i-bl
review . . . rē-vū′
reviewer . . . rē-vū′ėr
revile . . . rē-vīl′
revisal . . . rē-vīz′al
revise . . . rē-vīz′
revision . . . rē-vi′zhon
revisit . . . rē-vi′zit
revival . . . rē-vīv′al
revive . . . rē-vīv′
revocable . . . re′vōk-a-bl
revocation . . . re-vōk-ā′shun
revoke . . . rē-vōk′
revolt . . . rē-vōlt′
revolution . . . re-vō-lū′shun
revolutionist . . . re-vō-lū′shun-ist
revolve . . . rē-volv′
revolver . . . rē-volv′ėr
revue . . . rē-vū′
revulsion . . . rē-vul′shun
reward . . . rē-ward′
rhapsody . . . rap′so-di
rhetoric . . . re′to-rik
rheum . . . rūm
rheumatic . . . rū-mat′ik
rheumatism . . . rū′mat-izm
rheumy . . . rūm′i
rhinal . . . rī′nal
rhinoceros . . . ri-nos′e-ros
rhubarb . . . ro′barb
rhyme . . . rīm
rhythm . . . rithm
rhythmic . . . rith′mik
rib . . . rib
ribbon . . . ri′bon
rice . . . rīs
rich . . . rich
riches . . . rich′ez
richness . . . rich′nes
rickets . . . rik′ets

rickety . . . rik′et-i
ricochet . . . rik′o-shet
rid . . . rid
riddance . . . rid′ans
riddle . . . rid′l
ride . . . rīd
rider . . . rīd′ėr
ridicule . . . ri′di-kūl
ridiculous . . . ri-dik′ū-lus
riding . . . rīd′ing
rife . . . rīf
rifle . . . rī′fl
rifleman . . . rī′fl-man
rig . . . rig
rigger . . . rig′ėr
rigging . . . rig′ing
right . . . rīt
righteous . . . rīt′yus
righteously . . . rīt′yus-li
righteousness . . . rīt′yus-nes
right-hand . . . rīt′hand
right-handed . . . rīt′hand-ed
rightly . . . rīt′li
rigid . . . ri′jid
rigidity . . . ri-jid′i-ti
rigidly . . . ri′jid-li
rigmarole . . . rig′ma-rōl
rigor . . . rī′gor
rigor . . . rig′or
rigorous . . . rig′or-us
rigorously . . . rig′or-us-li
rime . . . rīm
rind . . . rīnd
ring . . . ring
ringleader . . . ring′lēd-ėr
ringlet . . . ring′let
ringworm . . . ring′wėrm
rink . . . ringk
rinse . . . rins
riot . . . rī′ot
rioter . . . rī′ot-ėr
riotous . . . rī′ot-us
rip . . . rip
ripe . . . rīp
ripen . . . rīp′n
ripple . . . rip′l
rise . . . rīz
rising . . . rīz′ing
risk . . . risk
risky . . . risk′i
ritual . . . rit′ū-al
ritualism . . . rit′ū-al-izm
rival . . . rī′val
rivalry . . . rī′val-ri

R

rivel... *riv'l*
rivet... *ri'vet*
riveter... *ri'vet-ẻr*
rivulet... *ri'vū-let*
roach... *rōch*
road... *rōd*
roadway... *rōd'wā*
roam... *rōm*
roar... *rōr*
roaring... *rōr'ing*
roast... *rōst*
rob... *rob*
robber... *rob'ẻr*
robbery... *rob'ẻr-i*
robe... *rōb*
robin... *rob'in*
robot... *rōb'ot*
robust... *rō-bust'*
rock... *rok*
rocker... *rok'ẻr*
rockery... *rok'ẻr-i*
rocket... *rok'et*
rocking-horse... *rok'ing-hors*
rock-salt... *rok'salt*
rocky... *rok'i*
rodent... *rō'dent*
rodeo... *rōd-ā'o*
roe... *rō*
rogation... *rō-gā'shun*
rogue... *rōg*
roguery... *rōg'ẻr-i*
roguish... *rōg'ish*
roil... *roil*
roister... *rois'tẻr*
roll... *rōl*
roll-call... *rōl'kal*
roller... *rōl'ẻr*
roller-skate... *rōl'ẻr-skāt*
rollick... *rol'ik*
rolling... *rōl'ing*
rolling-pin... *rōl'ing-pin*
rollock... *rol'ok*
romaic... *rō-mā'ik*
roman... *rō'man*
romance... *rō-mans'*
romancer... *rō'mans'ẻr*
romancist... *rō-mans'ist*
romanesque... *rō-man-esk'*
romanism... *rō'man-izm*
romanticism... *rō-man'ti-sizm*
romanticist... *rō-man'ti-sist*
romany, Rommany... *rom'a-ni*
romp... *romp*
rondeau... *ron'dō*

rohdel... *ron'del*
rood... *rod*
roof... *rof*
roofing... *rof'ing*
rook... *ruk*
rookery... *ruk'ẻr-i*
rooky... *ruk''i*
room... *rōm*
roomy... *rom'i*
roost... *rost*
rooster... *rost'ẻr*
root... *rot*
rooted... *rot'ed*
rope... *rōp*
rosaceous... *rōz-ā'shus*
rosary... *rōz'a-ri*
rose... *rōz*
roseate... *rōz'ē-āt*
rosemary... *rōz'ma-ri*
rosette... *rō-zet'*
rose-water... *rōz'wa-tẻr*
rosewood... *rōz'wüd*
roster... *ros'tẻr*
rosy... *rōz'i*
rot... *rot*
rotary... *rō'ta-ri*
rotate... *rō'tāt*
rotation... *rō-tā'shun*
rotatory... *rō'ta-to-ri*
rote... *rōt*
rotten... *rot'n*
rotund... *rō-tund'*
rotunda... *rō-tun'da*
rouble... *ro'bl*
roue... *ro-ā*
rouge... *rozh*
rough... *ruf*
rough-cast... *ruf'kast*
roughen... *ruf'n*
roughly... *ruf'li*
roulade... *ro-lad*
rouleau... *ro-lō'*
roulette... *ro-let'*
roundabout... *round'a-bout*
roundelay... *round'ē-lā*
rounder... *roun'dẻr*
roundhead... *round'hed*
roundish... *round'ish*
roundly... *round'li*
round-robin... *round-rob'in*
rouse... *rouz*
rousing... *rouz'ing*
rout... *rout*
route... *rot*

routine...ro-tēn'
rove...rōv
rover...rōv'ėr
row...rō
row...rou
rowdy...rou'di
rowel...rou'el
rowlock...rō'lok
royal...roi'al
royalist...roi'al-ist
royally...roi'al-li
royalty...roi'al-ti
rub...rub
rubbish...rub'ish
rubble...rub'l
rubescent...ro-bes'ent
rubric...ro'brik
ruby...ro'bi
rudd...rud
rudder...rud'ėr
ruddy...rud'i
rude...rod
rudely...rod'li
rudiment...ro'di-ment
rudimentary...ro-di-ment'a-ri
rue...ro
rueful...ro'ful
ruff...ruf
ruffian...ruf'i-an
ruffle...ruf'l
rufous...ro'fus
rug...rug
ruga...ro'ga
rugby...rug'bi
rugged...rug'ed
ruin...ro'in
ruination...ro'i-nā'shun
rule...rol
ruler...rol'ėr
ruling...rol'ing
rum...rum
rumble...rum'bl
ruminant...ro'min-ant
ruminate...ro'min-āt
rumination...ro-min-ā'shun
rummage...rum'āj
rumor...ro'mėr
rump...rump
rumpus...rum'pus
run...run
runaway...run'a-wā
rung...rung
runnel...run'l
runner...run'ėr

running...run'ing
runt...runt
rupture...rup'tūr
rural...ro'ral
ruse...roz
rush...rush
rusk...rusk
russian...ru'shi-an
rust...rust
rustic...rus'tik
rustle...rus'l
rusty...rust'i
rut...rut
ruthless...roth'les
ruttish...rut'ish
rye...rī

S

sabaism...sa-bā'izm
sabaoth...sa-bā'oth
sabbatarian...sa-ba-tā'ri-an
sabbath...sa'bath
sabbatic...sa-bat'ik
saber...sā'bėr
sable...sā'bl
sabot...sa-bō'
sabotage...sa-bō-tazh
sac...sak
saccharin...sak'a-rin
saccharine...sak'ka-rīn
saccharose...sak'a-rōs
sachem...sā'chem
sack...sak
sacking...sak'ing
sacrament...sa'kra-ment
sacramental...sa-kra-ment'al
sacred...sā'kred
sacredly...sā'kred-li
sacrifice...sa'kri-fīs
sacrificial...sa-kri-ti'shal
sacrilege...sa'kri-lej
sacrilegious...sa-kri-lē'jus
sacristan...sa'krist-an
sacristy...sa'krist-i
sacrum...sā'krum
sad...sad
sadden...sad'n
saddle...sad'l
saddler...sad'lėr
sadism...sād'ism
safe...sāf
safeguard...sāf'gard

S

safely... sāf'li
safety... sāf'ti
safety-valve... sāf'ti-valv
saffron... saf'ron
saga... sa'ga
sagacious... sa-gā'shus
sagaciously... sa-gā'shus-li
sagacity... sa-gas'i-ti
sage... sāj
sagely... sāj'li
sagittate... sa'ji-tāt
sago... sā'gō
sail... sāl
sail-cloth... sāl'kloth
sailor... sāl'or
saint... sānt
sainted... sānt'ed
salacious... sa-lā'shus
salacity... sa-las'i-ti
salad... sa'lad
salamander... sa-la-man'dėr
salaried... sa'la-rid
salary... sa'la-ri
sale... sāl
saleable... sāl'a-bl
salesman... sālz'man
salic... sal'ik
salicin... sal'i-sin
salience... sā'li-ens
salient... sā'li-ent
salina... sa-lī'na
saline... sa-līn'
saliva... sa-lī'va
salivant... sa'li-vant
salivate... sa'li-vāt
salivation... sa-li-vā'shun
sallow... sal'ō
salmon... sa'mun
salmon-trout... sa'mun-trout
salon... sa-long
saloon... sa-lon'
salse... sals
salsify... sal'si-fi
saltant... sal'tant
saltation... sal-tā'shun
saltatory... sal'ta-to-ri
saltern... salt'ėrn
saltire... sal'tēr
saltish... salt'ish
salt-mine... salt'mīn
saltpeter... sȧlt'pē-tėr
salts... salts
salubrious... sa-lū'bri-us
salutary... sa'lū-ta-ri

salutation... sa-lū-tā'shun
salute... sa-lūt'
salvable... sal'va-bl
salvage... sal'vāj
salvation... sal-vā'shun
salve... salv
salve... salv or sav
salver... sal'vėr
salvor... sal'vor
same... sām
sameness... sām'nes
samite... sā'mīt
samphire... sam'fīr
sanable... san'a-bl
sanative... san'a-tiv
sanatorium... san-a-tō'ri-um
sanatory... san'a-to-ri
sanctified... sangk'ti-fī d
sanctify... sangk'ti-fī
sanction... sangk'shun
sanctity... sangk'ti-ti
sanctuary... sangk'tū-a-ri
sand... sand
sandal... san'dal
sandal-wood... san'dal-wụd
sand-blast... sand'blast
sandiver... san'di-vėr
sand-paper... sand'pā-pėr
sandpiper... sand'pī-pėr
sandstone... sand'stōn
sandwich... sand'wich
sandy... sand'i
sane... sān
sanguinary... sang'gwin-a-ri
sanguine... sang'gwin
sanguineous... sang-gwin'ē-us
sancile... san'i-kl
sanitary... san'i-ta-ri
sanitation... san-i-tā'shun
sanity... san'i-ti
sap... sap
sapient... sā'pi-ent
sapless... sap'les
saponaceous... sa-pon-ā'shus
sapor... sā'por
sapper... sap'ėr
sappy... sap'i
saracen... sa'ra-sen
sarcasm... sar'kazm
sarcastic... sar-kas'tik
sarcoid... sar'koid
sardine... sar'dēn
sardonic... sar-don'ik
sardonyx... sar'dō-niks

sark... *sark*
sarmentum... *sar-men'tum*
sarsaparilla... *sar'sa-pa-ril'la*
sartorial... *sar-tō'ri-al*
sash... *sash*
sassafras... *sas'a-fras*
satan... *sā'tan*
satanic... *sā-tan'ik*
satchel... *sa'chel*
satiate... *sā'shi-āt*
satiety... *sa-fī'e-tl*
satin... *sa'tin*
satin-wood... *sa'tin-wụd*
satiny... *sa'tin-i*
satire... *sa'tīr*
satiric... *sa-ti'rik*
satisfaction... *sa-tis-fak'shun*
satisfactorily... *sa-tis-fak'to-ri-li*
satisfy... *sa'tis-fī*
saturable... *sa'tūr-a-bl*
saturate... *sa'tūr-āt*
saturation... *sa-tūr-ā'shun*
saturn... *sa'tėrn*
satyr... *sa'tėr*
sauce... *sạs*
sauce-pan... *sạs'pan*
saucer... *sạ'sėr*
saucy... *sạs'i*
saunter... *sän'tėr*
saurian... *sä'ri-an*
sausage... *sạ'sāj*
savage... *sa'vāj*
savagely... *sa'vāj-li*
save... *sāv*
saving... *sāv'ing*
savior... *sāv'yėr*
savor... *sā'vor*
savory... *sā'vo-ri*
savory... *sā'vėr-i*
saw... *sạ*
saw-mill... *sạ'mil*
saxon... *saks'on*
saxophone... *saks'ō-fōn*
say... *sā*
saying... *sā'ing*
scab... *skab*
scabbard... *skab'ard*
scabby... *skab'i*
scabious... *skā'bi-us*
scaffold... *skaf'old*
scaffolding... *skaf'old-ing*
scagliola... *skal-yō-'la*
scald... *skald*
scald... *skäld or skạld*

scale... *skāl*
scall... *skạl*
scallion... *skal'yun*
scallop... *skal'op*
scalp... *skalp*
scamp... *skamp*
scamper... *skam'pėr*
scan... *skan*
scandal... *skan'dal*
scandalize... *skan'dal-īz*
scandent... *skan'dent*
scansorial... *skan-sō'ri-al*
scant... *skant*
scantily... *skant'i-li*
scanty... *skant'i*
scape... *skāp*
scape-goat... *skāp'gōt*
scapula... *skap'ū-la*
scapular... *skap'ū-lėr*
scar... *skar*
scarab... *skaāab*
scarce... *skārs*
scarce... *skārs*
scarcity... *skārs'i-tl*
scare... *skār*
scarecrow... *skār'krō*
scarf... *skarf*
scarlet... *skar'let*
scarlet-fever... *skar'let-fē-vėr*
scarp... *skarp*
scatter... *skat'ėr*
scatter-brain... *skat'ėr-brān*
scattered... *skat'ėrd*
scavenger... *ska'ven-jėr*
scenery... *sēn'ė-ri*
scenic... *sēn'ik*
scent... *sent*
scentless... *sent'les*
sceptic... *skep'tik*
sceptical... *skep'tik-al*
scepticism... *skep'ti-sizm*
scepter... *sep'tėr*
schedule... *shed'ūl*
scheme... *skēm*
schemer... *skēm'ėr*
scheming... *skēm'ing*
schism... *sizm*
schismatic... *siz-mat'ik*
scholar... *skol'ėr*
scholarly... *skol'ėr-li*
scholarship... *skol'ėr-ship*
scholastic... *skō-las'tik*
scholasticism... *skō-las'ti-sizm*
school... *skol*

S

school-house... skol'hous
sciatic... sī-at'ik
sciatica... sī-at'i-ka
science... sī'ens
scientist... sī'ent-ist
scimitar... sī'mi-tėr
sciolism... sī'ol-izm
sciolist... sī'ol-ist
scion... sī'on
scission... sī'zhon
scissors... siz'ėrz
scoff... skof
scoffer... skof'ėr
scoffingly... skof'ing-li
scold... skōld
scolding... skōld'ing
scolecida... skō-lē'si-da
scollop... skol'op
sconce... skons
scoop... skop
scope... skōp
scorch... skorch
score... skōr
scorer... skōr'ėr
scoria... skō'ri-a
scorn... skorn
scorner... skorn'ėr
scornfully... skorn'ful-li
scotch... skoch
scotch... skoch
scotchman... skoch'man
scot-free... skot'frē
scottice... skot'ti-sē
scotticism... skot'i-sizm
scottish... skot'ish
scoundrel... skoun'drel
scour... skour
scourer... skour'ėr
scourge... skėrj
scout... skout
scout-master... skout-mas'tėr
scowl... skoul
scrabble... skrab'l
scrag... skrag
scraggy... skrag'i
scramble... skram'bl
scrambling... skram'bling
scrap... skrap
scrap-book... skrap'buk
scrape... skrāp
scraper... skrāp'ėr
scraping... skrāp'ing
scratcher... skrach'ėr
scrawl... skral

screak... skrēk
scream... skrēm
screamer... skrēm'ėr
screaming... skrēm'ing
screech... skrēch
screech-owl... skrēch-oul
screen... skrēn
screenings... skren'ingz
screes... skrēz
screw... skro
screw-driver... skro'drīv-ėr
scribble... skrib'l
scribbler... skrib'lėr
scribe... skrīb
scrimmage... skrim'āj
scrimp... skrimp
scrip... skrip
script... skript
scriptorium... skrip-tō'ri-um
scriptural... skrip'tūr-al
scripture... skrip'tūr
scrivener... skri'ven-ėr
scrotum... skrō'tum
scrub... skrub
scrubby... skrub'i
scruple... skro'pl
scrupulosity... skro-pū-los'i-ti
scrupulous... skro'pū-lus
scrutineer... skro'ti-nēr
scrutinize... skro'ti-nīz
scrutinous... skro'tin-us
scrutiny... skro'ti-ni
scuffle... skuf'l
scull... skul
sculler... skul'ėr
scullery... skul'ė-ri
sculptor... skulp'tor
sculptural... skulp'tūr-al
sculpture... skulp'tūr
scum... skum
scummy... skum'i
scurf... skėrf
scurfy... skėrf'l
scurrility... sku-ril'i-ti
scurrilous... sku'ril-us
scurry... sku'ri
scurvy... skėr'vi
scutage... skū'tāj
scye... sī
scythe... sīŦH
sea... sē
sea-board... sē'bōrd
sea-breeze... sē'brēz
sea-coast... sē'kōst

sea-going... sē'gō-ing
sea-horse... sē'hors
seal... sēl
sealer... sēl'ėr
sea-level... sē'le-vel
sealing... sēl'ing
seam... sēm
seaman... sē'man
seamanship... sē'man-ship
seamstress... sēm'stres
seamy... sēm'i
seaplane... sē'plān
sea-port... sē'pōrt
sear... sēr
sear... sēr
search... sėrch
searcher... sėrch'ėr
searching... sėrch'ing
searchless... sėrch'les
sea-scape... sē'skāp
sea-serpent... sē'sėr-pent
sea-shore... sē'shōr
sea-sick... sē'sik
season... sē'zn
seasonable... sē'zn-a-bl
seasoning... sē'zn-ing
seat... sēt
seaward... sē'wėrd
sea-weed... sē'wēd
sea-worthy... sē'wėr-ᴛHi
sebaceous... sē-bā'shus
secede... sē-sēd'
seceder... sē-sēd'ėr
secern... sē-sėrn'
secernent... sē-sėr'nent
secession... sē-se'shun
seclude... sē-klod'
seclusive... sē-klo'sive
second... se'kund
secret... sē'kret
secrete... sē-krēt'
sect... sekt
sectarian... sek-tā'ri-an
sectarianism... sek-tā'ri-an-izm
sectary... sek'ta-ri
sectile... sek'fīl
section... sek'shun
sectional... sek'shun-al
sector... sek'tor
secular... se'kū-lėr
secularism... sek'ū-lėr-izm
secularist... sek'ū-lėr-ist
securable... sē-kūr'a-bl
secure... sē-kūr'

securely... sē-kūr'li
security... sē-kū'ri-ti
sedan... sē-dan'
sedate... sē-dāt'
sedative... se'da-tiv
sedentary... se'den-ta-ri
sedge... sej
sediment... se'di-ment
sedimentary... se-di-ment'a-ri
seduce... sē-dūs'
seducible... sē-dūs'i-bl
seduction... sē-duk'shun
seductive... sē-duk'tiv
sedulity... se-dū'li-ti
sedulous... se'dū-lus
see... sē
seed... sēd
seedling... sēd'ling
seeing... sē'ing
seek... sēk
seem... sēm
seemingly... sēm'ing-li
seemly... sēm'li
seer... sēr
see-saw... sē'sa
seethe... sēᴛH
segment... seg'ment
segregate... se'grē-gāt
segregation... se-grē-gā'shun
seismology... sīs-mol'o-ji
seizable... sēz'a-bl
seize... sēz
seizure... sēz'ūr
seldom... sel'dom
selection... sē-lek'shun
selective... sē-lek'tiv
selenite... sel'en-īt
selenium... se-lē'ni-um
self... self
self-conceit... self-kon-sēt'
self-conscious... self-kon'shus
self-control... self-kon-trōl'
self-denial... self-dē-nī'al
self-denying... self-dē-nī'ing
self-esteem... self-es-tēm'
self-evident... self-ev'i-dent
self-imposed... self'im-pōzd
selfish... self'ish
self-made... self'mād
self-respect... self're-spekt
self-righteous... self-rī t'yus
self-seeking... self'sēk-ing
self-sufficient... self-suf-fi'shent
sell... sel

S

seller... sel'ẻr
selvedge... sel'vej
semblance... sem'blans
semen... sē'men
semicircular... se-mi-sẻr'kū-lẻr
semicolon... se'mi-kō-lon
seminal... se'min-al
seminary... se'min-a-ri
semination... se-min-ā'shun
semite... sem'īt
semitic... sem-it'ik
semitone... se'mi-tō
semolina... se-mō-lī'na
senary... sē'na-ri
senate... se'nāt
senator... se'nat-or
senatorial... se-na-tō'ri-al
send... send
senescence... sē-nes'ens
seneschal... se'ne-shal
senile... sē'nīl
senility... sē-nil'i-ti
senior... sē'ni-or, sēn'yor
seniority... sē-ni-or'i-ti
sensation... sen-sā'shun
sense... sens
sensibility... sens-i-bil'i-tl
sensible... sens'i-bl
sensitive... sens'i-tiv
sensitize... sens'i-tīz
sensorial... sen-sō'ri-al
sensorium... sen-sō'ri-um
sensory... sen'so-ri
sensual... sens'ū-al
sensualism... sens'ū-al-izm
sensualist... sens'ū-al-ist
sensuality... sens-ū-al'i-ti
sensuous... sens'ū-us
sentence... sen'tens
sentential... sen-ten'shal
sententious... sen-ten'shus
sentiment... sen'ti-ment
sentimental... sen-ti-men'tal
sentinel... sen'ti-nel
sentry... sen'tri
separable... se'pa-ra-bl
separate... se'pa-rāt
separately... se'pa-rāt-li
separation... se-pa-rā'shun
separator... se'pa-rāt-ẻr
sepia... sē'pi-a
septenary... sep'ten-a-ri
septic... sep'tik
septum... sep'tum

sepulcher... se'pul-kẻr
sepulture... se'pul-tūr
sequacious... sē-kwā'shus
sequel... sē'kwel
sequence... sē'kwens
sequestered... se-kwes'tẻrd
serai... se-rī'
seraph... se'raf
seraphic... se-raf'ik
serenade... se-rē-nād'
serene... sē-rēn'
serenely... sē-rēn'li
serenity... sē-ren'i-ti
serge... sẻrj
sergeant... sar'jant
serial... sē'ri-al
sericeous... sē-ri'shus
sericulture... sē'ri-kul-tūr
series... sē'ri-ēz
serious... sē'ri-us
seriously... sē'ri-us-li
sermon... sẻr'mon
serrate... ser'rāt
serration... ser-rā'shun
serrature... ser'ra-tūr
serum... sē'rum
serval... sẻr'val
servant... sẻrv'ant
serve... sẻrv
service... sẻrv'is
serviceable... sẻrv'is-a-bl
servile... sẻr'vīl
servility... sẻr-vil'i-ti
servitor... sẻrv'i-tor
servitude... sẻrv'i-tūd
sesame... ses'a-me
sessile... ses'īl
session... se'shun
sessional... se'shun-al
set... set
setaceous... se-tā'shus
set-off... set'of
seton... sē'ton
settee... set-tē'
setter... set'ẻr
setting... set'ing
settled... set'ld
settlement... set'l-ment
settler... set'lẻr
settling... set'ling
seven... se'ven
seventeen... se'ven-tēn
seventh... se'venth
seventieth... se'ven-ti-eth

seventy... se'ven-ti
sever... se'vėr
severable... se'vėr-a-bl
several... se'vėr-al
severally... se'vėr-al-li
severalty... se'vėr-al-ti
severance... se'vėr-ans
severe... sē-vēr'
severely... sē-vēr'li
severity... sē-ve'ri-ti
sew... sō
sewage... sū'āj
sewer... sū'ėr
sewer... sō'ėr
sewerage... sū'ėr-āj
sewing... sō'ing
sexennial... seks-en'ni-al
sexual... seks'ū-al
sexuality... seks'ū-al'i-ti
sexually... seks'ū-al-li
shabbily... shab'i-li
shabby... shab'i
shackle... shak'l
shade... shād
shadow... sha'dō
shadowy... sha'dō-i
shady... shād'i
shaft... shaft
shafting... shaft'ing
shag... shag
shaggy... shag'i
shah... sha
shake... shāk
shake-down... skāk'doun
shaky... shāk'i
shale... shāl
shall... shal
shallop... shal'op
shallot... sha-lot'
shallow... shal'ō
sham... sham
shamanism... shā'man-izm
shamble... sham'bl
shambles... sham'blz
shambling... sham'bling
shame... shām
shameful... shām'ful
shameless... shām'les
shampoo... sham-po'
shamrock... sham'rok
shank... shangk
shanty... shan'ti
shape... shāp
shapeless... shāp'les

shapely... shāp'li
shard... shard
share... shār
shareholder... shār'hōld-ėr
sharer... shār'ėr
shark... shark
sharp... sharp
sharpen... sharp'n
sharpener... sharp'nėr
sharper... sharp'ėr
sharpness... sharp'nes
shatter... shat'ėr
shave... shāv
shaw... sha
shawl... shạl
she... shē
shea... shē'a
sheaf... shēf
shealing... shēl'ing
shear... shēr
shearer... shēr-ėr
shears... shērz
sheath... shēth
sheathe... shēŦH
sheathing... shēŦH'ing
sheave... shēv
shed... shed
sheen... shēn
sheep... shēp
sheepish... shēp'ish
sheep-skin... shēp'skin
sheer... shēr
sheers... shērz
sheet... shēt
shelf... shelf
shell... shel
shellac... shel-lak'
shell-fish... shel'fish
shell-shock... shel'shok
shelter... shel'tėr
shelve... shelv
shelving... shelv'ing
shepherd... shep'ėrd
sherbet... sher'bet
sherd... shėrd
sheriff... she'rif
sherry... she'ri
shield... shēld
shift... shift
shiftless... shift'les
shifty... shift'i
shilling... shil'ing
shimmer... shim'ėr
shin... shin

S

shine... shīn
shingle... shing'gl
shingling... shing'gling
shining... shīn'ing
ship... ship
shipboard... ship'bōrd
ship-builder... ship'bild-ėr
shipmate... ship'māt
shipment... ship'ment
ship-shape... ship'shāp
shipwreck... ship'rek
ship-yard... ship'yard
shirk... shėrk
shirt... shėrt
shirting... shėrt'ing
shive... shīv
shiver... shi'vėr
shivery... shi'vėr-i
shoal... shōl
shock... shok
shocking... shok'ing
shoddy... shod'i
shoe... sho
shoemaker... sho'māk-ėr
shoot... shot
shooting... shot'ing
shop... shop
shopkeeper... shop'kēp-ėr
shore... shōr
short... short
shortage... short'āj
shortcoming... short'kum-ing
shorten... short'n
shorthand... short'hand
short-handed... short'hand-ed
short-lived... short'līvd
shortly... short'li
short-sighted... short'sīt-ed
short-winded... short'wind-ed
shot... shot
shoulder... shōl'dėr
shout... shout
shove... shuv
shovel... shu'vel
shovelful... shu'vel-fu̇l
show... shō
shower... shō'ėr
showery... shou'ėr-i
showily... shō'i-li
show-room... shō'rom
shrapnel... shrap'nel
shred... shred
shrewd... shrod
shrewdly... shrod'li

shriek... shrēk
shrift... shrift
shrill... shril
shrimp... shrimp
shrimper... shrimp'ėr
shrine... shrīn
shrinkage... shringk'āj
shrive... shrīv
shrivel... shri'vel
shroud... shroud
shrub... shrub
shrubbery... shrub'ėr-i
shrubby... shrub'i
shrug... shrug
shrunken... shrungk'n
shuck... shuk
shudder... shud'ėr
shuffle... shuf'l
shuffler... shuf'lėr
shut... shut
shutter... shut'ėr
shuttle... shut'l
shyly... shī'li
shyness... shī'nes
siamese... sī-a-mēz'
sibilant... si'bi-lant
sibilate... si'bi-lāt
sibilation... si-bi-lā'shun
sic... sik
siccate... sik'āt
siccative... sik'a-tiv
sick... sik
sicken... sik'n
sickening... sik'n-ing
sickish... sik'ish
sickle... sik'l
sickly... sik'li
sickness... sik'nes
sick-room... sik'rom
side... sīd
side-arms... sīd'armz
sided... sīd'ed
side-saddle... sīd'sad-l
sidewalk... sīd'wak
siding... sīd'ing
siege... sēj
siesta... sē-es'ta
sieve... siv
sift... sift
sifter... sift'ėr
sigh... sī
sight... sīt
sighted... sīt'ed
sightless... sīt'les

sightly... *sīt'li*
sight-seeing... *sīt'sē-ing*
sign... *sīn*
signalize... *sig'nal-īz*
signally... *sig'nal-li*
signatory... *sig'na-to-ri*
signature... *sig'na-tūr*
signer... *sīn'er*
signet... *sig'net*
signifiable... *sig-ni-fī'a-bl*
significant... *sig-ni'fi-kant*
significantly... *sig-ni'fi-kant-li*
signification... *sig'ni-fi-kā''shun*
signify... *sig'ni-fī*
sign-post... *sīn'pōst*
silence... *sī'lens*
silently... *sī'lent-li*
silhouette... *sil'o-et*
silica... *sil'i-ka*
siliceous... *si-lish'us*
silicon... *sil'i-kon*
silk... *silk*
silken... *silk'en*
silk-worm... *silk'werm*
silky... *silk'i*
sill... *sil*
silly... *sil'li*
silo... *sī'lō*
silt... *silt*
silurian... *sī-lū'ri-an*
silver... *sil'ver*
silversmith... *sil'ver-smith*
silvery... *sil'ver-i*
similar... *si'mi-ler*
similarity... *si-mi-la'ri-ti*
similarly... *si'mi-ler-li*
simile... *si'mi-le*
similitude... *si-mil'i-tūd*
simmer... *si'mer*
simple... *sim'pl*
simplicity... *sim-plis'i-ti*
simplify... *sim'pli-fī*
simply... *sim'pli*
simulate... *sim'ū-lāt*
simulation... *sim-ū-lā'shun*
simulator... *sim'ū-lāt-or*
simultaneous... *si-mul-tā'nē-us*
sin... *sin*
since... *sins*
sincere... *sin-sēr'*
sincerely... *sin-sēr'li*
sincerity... *sin-se'ri-ti*
sine... *sīn*
sinew... *si'nū*

sing... *sing*
singe... *sinj*
singer... *sing'er*
single... *sing'gl*
single-entry... *sing'gl-en-tri*
singly... *sing'gli*
singular... *sing'gū-ler*
singularity... *sing-gū-la'ri-ti*
singularly... *sing'gū-ler-li*
sinister... *si'nis-ter*
sinistrorse... *si'nis-trors*
sink... *singk*
sinker... *singk'er*
sinking... *singk'ing*
sinless... *sin'les*
sinner... *sin'er*
sinuate... *sin'ū-āt*
sinuosity... *sin-ū-os'i-ti*
sinuous... *sin'ū-us*
sinus... *sī'nus*
sip... *sip*
siphon... *sī'fon*
sir... *ser*
sire... *sīr*
siren... *sī'ren*
sirloin... *ser'loin*
sirocco... *si-rok'kō*
siskin... *sis'kin*
sist... *sist*
sister... *sis'ter*
sisterhood... *sis'ter-hud*
sister-in-law... *sis'ter-in-la̤*
sisterly... *sis'ter-li*
sit... *sit*
sitter... *sit'er*
sitting... *sit'ing*
situate... *sit'ū-āt*
situated... *sit'ū-āt-ed*
situation... *sit-ū-ā'shun*
six... *siks*
sixteenth... *siks'tēnth*
sixth... *siksth*
sixtieth... *siks'ti-eth*
sixty... *siks'ti*
sizable... *sīz'a-bl*
size... *sīz*
sized... *sīzd*
sizer... *sīz'er*
sizing... *sīz'ing*
skate... *skāt*
skein... *skān*
skeleton... *ske'le-ton*
skeleton-key... *ske'le-ton-kē*
sketch... *skech*

S

sketcher... *skech'ėr*
sketchy... *skech'i*
skew... *skū*
skewer... *skū'ėr*
skid... *skid*
skilful... *skil'ful*
skilfully... *skil'ful-li*
skill... *skil*
skilled... *skild*
skillet... *skil'et*
skim... *skim*
skimmer... *skim'ėr*
skim-milk... *skim'milk*
skimming... *skim'ing*
skin... *skin*
skin-deep... *skin'dēp*
skink... *skingk*
skinner... *skin'ėr*
skinny... *skin'i*
skip... *skip*
skipper... *skip'ėr*
skipping... *skip'ing*
skipping-rope... *skip'ing-rōp*
skirmish... *skėr'mish*
skirt... *skėrt*
skit... *skit*
skittish... *skit'ish*
skittles... *skit'lz*
skulk... *skulk*
skull... *skul*
skunk... *skungk*
sky... *skī*
skylark... *skī'lark*
skyward... *skī'wėrd*
slab... *slab*
slack... *slak*
slacken... *slak'n*
slackly... *slak'li*
slag... *slag*
slaggy... *slag'i*
slam... *slam*
slander... *slan'dėr*
slanderer... *slan'dėr-ėr*
slanderous... *slan'dėr-us*
slang... *slang*
slant... *slant*
slap... *slap*
slashed... *slasht'*
slat... *slat*
slate... *slāt*
slattern... *slat'ėrn*
slatternly... *slat'ėrn-li*
slaughterous... *sla'tėr-us*
slave... *slāv*

slave-driver... *slāv'drīv-ėr*
slavery... *slāv'ė-ri*
slavish... *slāv'ish*
slavishly... *slāv'ish-li*
slay... *slā*
slayer... *slā'ėr*
sleazy... *slē'zi*
sled... *sled*
sledge... *slej*
sleek... *slēk*
sleeky... *slēk'i*
sleep... *slēp*
sleeper... *slēp'ėr*
sleeping... *slēp'ing*
sleepless... *slēp'les*
sleepy... *slēp'i*
sleet... *slēt*
sleety... *slēt'i*
sleeve... *slēv*
sleeveless... *slēv'les*
sleigh... *slā*
sleight... *slīt*
slew... *slo*
sley... *slā*
slice... *slīs*
slide... *slīd*
slider... *slīd'ėr*
sliding... *slīd'ing*
slight... *slīt*
slightly... *slīt'li*
slim... *slim*
slime... *slīm*
slimy... *slīm'i*
sling... *sling*
slinger... *sling'ėr*
slip... *slip*
slipper... *slip'ėr*
slippery... *slip'ėr-i*
slipshod... *slip'shod*
slit... *slit*
slitter... *slit'ėr*
sliver... *sli'vėr*
slobber... *slob'ėr*
slogan... *slō'gan*
slop... *slop*
slope... *slōp*
slopy... *slōp'i*
sloth... *slōth or sloth*
slothful... *slōth'ful*
slouch... *slouch*
slouching... *slouch'ing*
slough... *slou*
slough... *sluf*
sloughy... *sluf'i*

sloven... *slu'ven*
slovenly... *slu'ven-li*
slow... *slō*
slowly... *slō'll*
sludge... *sluj*
sludgy... *sluj'i*
slue... *slo*
slug... *slug*
sluggard... *slug'ard*
sluggish... *slug'ish*
slum... *slum*
slumber... *slum'bėr*
slumberous... *slum'bėr-us*
slump... *slump*
slur... *slėr*
slush... *slush*
slut... *slut*
sluttish... *slut'ish*
sly... *slī*
slyly... *slī'li*
slyness... *slī'nes*
smack... *smak*
small... *smal*
small-pox... *smal'poks*
smart... *smart*
smarten... *smart'n*
smartly... *smart'li*
smash... *smash*
smatter... *smat'ėr*
smatterer... *smat'ėr-ėr*
smattering... *smat'ėr-ing*
smear... *smēr*
smell... *smel*
smelling... *smel'ing*
smelling-salts... *smel'ing-saltz*
smelt... *smelt*
smelter... *smelt'ėr*
smeltery... *smelt'ė-ri*
smile... *smīl*
smiling... *smīl'ing*
smite... *smīt*
smith... *smith*
smithery... *smith'ė-ri*
smithy... *smith'i*
smock... *smok*
smocking... *smok'ing*
smoke... *smōk*
smokeless... *smōk'les*
smoker... *smōk'ėr*
smoking... *smōk'ing*
smoky... *smōk'i*
smolt... *smōlt*
smooth... *smōŦH*
smoothly... *smōŦH'li*

smother... *smuŦH'ėr*
smothery... *smuŦH'ėr-i*
smoulder... *smōl'dėr*
smudge... *smuj*
smug... *smug*
smuggle... *smug'l*
smuggler... *smug'lėr*
smuggling... *smug'ling*
smut... *smut*
smutch... *smuch*
snack... *snak*
snaffle... *snaf'l*
snag... *snag*
snail... *snāl*
snake... *snāk*
snaky... *snāk'i*
snap... *snap*
snap-shot... *snap'shot*
snare... *snār*
snarl... *snarl*
snarling... *snarl'ing*
snary... *snār'i*
snatch... *snach*
sneak... *snēk*
sneaking... *snēk'ing*
sneaky... *snēk'i*
sneer... *snēr*
sneeze... *snēz*
snick... *snik*
sniff... *snif*
snip... *snip*
snipe... *snīp*
snippet... *snip'et*
snivel... *sni'vel*
snivelly... *sni'vel-i*
snob... *snob*
snobbish... *snob'ish*
snobbism... *snob'izm*
snooze... *snoz*
snore... *snōr*
snort... *snort*
snout... *snout*
snow... *snō*
snow-ball... *snō'bal*
snow-plow... *snō'plou*
snow-shoe... *snō'sho*
snub... *snub*
snub-nose... *snub'nōz*
snuff... *snuf*
snuffer... *snuf'ėr*
snuffle... *snuf'l*
snuffy... *snuf'i*
snug... *snug*
snuggery... *snug'ė-ri*

S

snuggle... *snug'l*
snugly... *snug'li*
so... *sō*
soak... *sōk*
soaking... *sōk'ing*
soaky... *sōk'i*
so-and-so... *sō'and-sō*
soap... *sōp*
soapy... *sōp'i*
soar... *sōr*
sob... *sob*
sober... *sō'bèr*
soberly... *sō'bèr-li*
sobriety... *sō-brī'e-ti*
sobriquet... *so-brē-kā*
sociability... *sō'shi-a-bil''i-ti*
sociable... *sō'shi-a-bl*
sociably... *sō'shi-a-bli*
social... *sō'shal*
socialism... *sō'shal-izm*
socialist... *sō'shal-ist*
socialistic... *sō-shal-is'tik*
sociality... *sō-shal'i-ti*
socialize... *sō'shal-īz*
socially... *sō'shal-li*
society... *sō-sī'e-ti*
socinian... *sō-sin'i-an*
sociologist... *sō-shi-ol'o-jist*
sock... *sok*
socket... *sok'et*
sod... *sod*
soda... *sō'da*
soddy... *sod'i*
sodium... *sō'di-um*
sodomite... *sod'om-īt*
sodomy... *sod'om-i*
sofa... *sō'fa*
soffit... *sof'it*
soft... *soft*
soften... *sof'n*
softening... *sof'n-ing*
softly... *soft'li*
soft-spoken... *soft'spō-kn*
soil... *soil*
sojourn... *sō'jèrn*
sojourner... *sō'jèrn-èr*
solar... *sō'lèr*
solatium... *sō-lā'shi-um*
solder... *sol'dèr*
soldier... *sōl'jèr*
soldiering... *sōl'jèr-ing*
soldiery... *sōl'jė-ri*
solecism... *so'le-sizm*
solecize... *so'le-sīz*

solely... *sōl'li*
solemn... *so'lem*
solemnity... *so-lem'ni-ti*
solemnize... *so'lem-nīz*
solemnly... *so'lem-li*
solfeggio... *sol-fej'i-ō*
solicit... *sō-lis'it*
solicitant... *sō-lis'it-ant*
solicitation... *sō-lis'it-ā''shun*
solicitor... *sō-lis'it-èr*
solicitous... *sō-lis'it-us*
solicitude... *sō-lis'i-tūd*
solid... *so'lid*
solidarity... *so-li-dar'i-ti*
solidify... *so-lid'i-fī*
solidity... *so-lid'i-ti*
solidly... *so'lid-li*
soliloquize... *sō-lil'ō-kwīz*
soliloquy... *sō-lil'ō-kwi*
solitaire... *so'li-tār*
solitarily... *so'li-ta-ri-li*
solitary... *so'li-ta-ri*
solo... *sō'lō*
soloist... *sō'lō-ist*
solstice... *sol'stis*
solstitial... *sol-sti'shal*
solubility... *so-lū-bil'i-ti*
soluble... *so'lū-bl*
solution... *so-lū'shun*
solve... *solv*
solvency... *sol'ven-si*
solvent... *sol'vent*
somatic... *sō-mat'ik*
somatology... *sō-ma-tol'o-ji*
somber... *som'bèr*
sombrero... *som-brār'ō*
sombrous... *som'brus*
some... *sum*
somebody... *sum'bo-di*
somehow... *sum'hou*
something... *sum'thing*
sometime... *sum'fīm*
sometimes... *sum'fīmz*
somewhat... *sum'whot*
somewhere... *sum'whār*
somite... *sō'mīt*
somnific... *som-nif'ik*
somnolence... *som'nō-lens*
somnolent... *som'nō-lent*
son... *sun*
sonant... *sō'nant*
sonata... *sō-na'ta*
song... *song*
songstress... *song'stres*

son-in-law ... sun'in-la
sonnet ... son'et
sonneteer ... son-et-ēr'
sonorous ... sō-nō'rus
soon ... son
soot ... sot
sooth ... soth
soothe ... sōṭH
soothing ... sōṭH'ing
soothsayer ... soth'sā-ėr
soothsaying ... soth'sā-ing
sooty ... sot'i
sop ... sop
sophism ... sof'izm
sophist ... sof'ist
sophisticate ... sō-fist'ik-āt
soporiferous ... sō-pō-rif'ik
soppy ... sop'i
soprano ... sō-pra'nō
sorb ... sorb
sorcerer ... sōr'sėr-ėr
sorceress ... sōr'sėr-es
sorcery ... sōr'sėr-i
sordid ... sor'did
sordidly ... sor'did-li
sore ... sōr
sorghum ... sor'gum
sororal ... sō-rō'ral
sorrel ... so'rel
sorrily ... so'ri-li
sorrow ... so'rō
sorrowful ... so'rō-ful
sorry ... so'ri
sort ... sort
sorter ... sort'ėr
sortilege ... sor'ti-lej
sortment ... sort'ment
so-so ... sō'sō
sot ... sot
sottish ... sot'ish
soul ... sōl
souled ... sōld
soulless ... sōl'les
sound ... sound
sounding ... sound'ing
soundings ... sound'ingz
soundless ... sound'les
soundly ... sound'li
soundness ... sound'nes
soup ... sop
sour ... sour
source ... sōrs
sourly ... sour'li
souse ... sous

south ... south
southerner ... suṭH'ėr-nėr
souvenir ... so-ve-nēr'
sovereign ... so've-rin
sovereignty ... so've-rin-ti
soviet ... sov'i-et
sovran ... sov'ran
sow ... sou
sow ... sō
sowar ... sou'ar
soy ... soi
spa ... spa
space ... spās
spacious ... spā'shus
spade ... spād
spadeful ... spād'ful
span ... span
spandrel ... span'drel
spangle ... spang'gl
spangly ... spang'gli
spaniard ... Span'yėrd
spaniel ... span'yel
spank ... spangk
spanker ... spangk'ėr
spanking ... spangk'ing
spanner ... span'ėr
spar ... spar
sparable ... spar'a-bl
spare ... spār
sparely ... spār'li
sparing ... spār'ing
sparingly ... spār'ing-li
spark ... spark
sparkish ... spark'ish
sparrow ... spa'rō
sparse ... spars
spartan ... spar'tan
spasm ... spazm
spasmodic ... spaz-mod'ik
spastic ... spas'tik
spat ... spat
spatial ... spā'shal
spatter ... spat'ėr
spatula ... spat'ū-la
spawn ... span
spawner ... span'ėr
spay ... spā
speak ... spēk
speakable ... spēk'a-bl
speaker ... spēk'ėr
speaking ... spēk'ing
spear ... spēr
special ... spe'shal
specialism ... spe'shal-izm

S

specialist... *spe'shal-ist*
speciality... *spe-shi-al'i-ti*
specialize... *spe-shal-īz*
specially... *spe'shal-li*
specie... *spē'shi*
species... *spē'shēz*
specific... *spe-sif'ik*
specifically... *spe-sif'ik-al-li*
specify... *spe'si-fī*
specimen... *spe'si-men*
specious... *spē'shus*
speciously... *spē'shus-li*
speck... *spek*
speckle... *spek'l*
spectacle... *spek'ta-kl*
spectacular... *spek-tak'ū-lèr*
spectator... *spek-tā'tor*
spectral... *spek'tral*
specter... *spek'tèr*
specular... *spek'ū-lar*
speculate... *spek'ū-lāt*
speculator... *spek'ū-lāt-or*
speculum... *spek'ū-lum*
speech... *spēch*
speechify... *spēch'i-fī*
speechless... *spēch'les*
speed... *spēd*
speedily... *spēd'i-li*
spell... *spel*
spelling... *spel'ing*
spelter... *spel'tèr*
spend... *spend*
spendthrift... *spend'thrift*
spent... *spent*
sperm... *spèrm*
spermatic... *spèr-mat'ik*
sperm-whale... *spèrm'whāl*
spew... *spū*
sphenoid... *sfē'noid*
spheral... *sfēr'al*
sphere... *sfēr*
spherically... *sfe'rik-al-li*
spheroid... *sfēr'oid*
spheroidal... *sfēr-oid'al*
sphinx... *sfingks*
spicate... *spi'kāt*
spice... *spīs*
spicery... *spīs'è-ri*
spicily... *spīs'i-li*
spicule... *spik'ūl*
spicy... *spīs'i*
spider... *spī'dèr*
spike... *spīk*
spile... *spīl*

spill... *spil*
spin... *spin*
spinach... *spin'āj*
spinal... *spīn'al*
spindle... *spin'dl*
spine... *spīn*
spined... *spīnd*
spinel... *spi-nel'*
spinet... *spin'et*
spinner... *spin'èr*
spinney... *spin'i*
spinose... *spīn'ōs*
spinster... *spin'stèr*
spiny... *spīn'i*
spiracle... *spi'ra-kl or spī'ra-kl*
spirea... *spī-rē'a*
spirally... *spī'ral-li*
spire... *spīr*
spirit... *spi'rit*
spirited... *spi'rit-ed*
spiritless... *spi'rit-les*
spiritual... *spi'rit-ū-al*
spiritualist... *spi'rit-ū-al-ist*
spiritualistic... *spi'rit-ū-a-lis''tik*
spirituality... *spi'rit-ū-al'i-ti*
spiritualize... *spi'rit-ū-al-īz*
spiritually... *spi'rit-ū-al-li*
spirituous... *spi'rit-ū-us*
spirt... *spèrt*
spiry... *spīr'i*
spit... *spit*
spite... *spīt*
spiteful... *spīt'ful*
spitfire... *spit'fīr̈*
spittle... *spit'l*
spittoon... *spit-ton'*
splanchnic... *splangk'nik*
splash... *splash*
spleen... *splēn*
splendent... *splen'dent*
splendid... *splen'did*
splendidly... *splen'did-li*
splendor... *splen'dèr*
splice... *splīs*
splint... *splint*
splinter... *splint'èr*
splotch... *sploch*
splutter... *splut'èr*
spode... *spōd*
spoil... *spoil*
spoiler... *spoil'èr*
spoke... *spōk*
spoken... *spōk'n*
spokesman... *spōks'man*

spoliate... spō-li-āt
sponge... spunj
spongy... spunj'i
sponsor... spon'sor
spontaneity... spon-ta-nē'i-ti
spontaneous... spon-tā'nē-us
spook... spok
spool... spol
spoon... spon
spoonful... spon'ful
spoor... spor
sporadic... spō-rad'ik
spore... spōr
sport... spōrt
sportful... spōrt'ful
sporting... spōrt'ing
sportsman... spōrts'man
spot... spot
spotless... spot'les
spotted... spot'ed
spotty... spot'i
spousal... spouz'al
spouse... spouz
spout... spout
spouter... spout'er
sprain... sprān
sprat... sprat
sprawl... spral
spray... sprä
spread... spred
spread-eagle... spred'ē-gl
spree... sprē
sprig... sprig
sprightly... sprīt'li
spring... spring
springy... spring'i
sprinkle... spring'kl
sprint... sprint
sprit... sprit
sprite... sprīt
spruce... spros
spry... sprī
spud... spud
spunk... spungk
spur... sper
spurious... spū'ri-us
spurn... spern
spurt... spert
sputter... sput'er
spy... spī
squab... skwob
squabble... skwob'l
squad... skwod
squadron... skwod'ron

squalid... skwo'lid
squall... skwal
squally... skwäl'i
squalor... skwöl'er
squama... skwä'ma
squamose... skwa-mōs'
squander... skwon'der
square... skwār
squarely... skwār'li
squash... skwosh
squaw... skwa
squawk... skwak
squeak... skwēk
squeal... skwēl
squeamish... skwēm'ish
squeeze... skwēz
squelch... skwelch
squib... skwib
squid... skwid
squinch... skwinsh
squint... skwint
squire... skwīr
squirm... skwerm
squirrel... skwi'rel
squirt... skwert
stab... stab
stability... sta-bil'i-ti
stable... stā'bl
staccato... stak-ka'tō
stack... stak
staddle... stad'l
stadium... stā'di-um
staff... staf
stag... stag
stager... stāj'er
stage-struck... stāj'struk
stagger... stag'er
staging... stāj'ing
stagnant... stag'nant
stagnate... stag'nāt
stagnation... stag-nā'shun
staid... stād
stain... stān
stainless... stān'les
stair... stār
staircase... stār'kās
stake... stāk
stalactite... sta-lak'fīt
stalagmite... sta-lag'mīt
stale... stāl
stalk... stak
stalker... stak'er
stall... stal
stallion... stal'yun

S

stamen... _stā'men._
stamina... _sta'mi-na_
stammer... _stam'ér_
stamp... _stamp_
stanch... _stansh_
standard... _stan'dard_
standing... _stand'ing_
standish... _stan'dish_
stand-point... _stand'point_
stand-still... _stand'stil_
stannary... _stan'a-ri_
stannic... _stan'ik_
stanniferous... _stan-if'ér-us_
stanza... _stan'za_
stanzaic... _stan-zā'ik_
staple... _stā'pl_
star... _star_
starch... _starch_
starched... _starcht_
starchy... _starch'i_
stare... _stār_
star-fish... _star'fish_
stark... _stark_
starling... _star'ling_
start... _stärt_
starter... _start'ér_
startle... _start'l_
startling... _start'ling_
starve... _starv_
state... _stāt_
stated... _stāt'ed_
stately... _stāt'li_
statement... _stāt'ment_
statesman... _stāts'man_
static... _stat'ik_
statical... _stat'ik-al_
station... _stā'shun_
stationary... _stā'shun-a-ri_
stationer... _stā'shun-ér_
stationery... _stā'shun-é-ri_
statist... _stat'ist_
statistician... _stat-is-ti'shan_
statistics... _sta-tist'iks_
statuary... _stat'ū-a-ri_
statue... _stat'ū_
statuesque... _stat-ū-esk'_
statuette... _stat-ū-et'_
stature... _stat'ūr_
status... _stā'tus_
statute... _stat'ūt_
statutory... _stat'ū-to-ri_
stave... _stāv_
stead... _sted_
steadfast... _sted'fast_

steadily... _sted'i-li_
steady... _sted'i_
steal... _stēl_
stealing... _stēl'ing_
stealth... _stelth_
steam... _stēm_
steamer... _stēm'ér_
steam-ship... _stēm'ship_
steed... _stēd_
steel... _stēl_
steely... _stēl'i_
steelyard... _stēl'yard_
steep... _stēp_
steeple... _stē'pl_
steeple-chase... _stē'pl-chās_
steer... _stēr_
steerage... _stēr'āj_
steeve... _stēv_
stela... _stē'la_
stellar... _stel'ér_
stellate... _stel'lāt_
stem... _stem_
stencil... _sten'sil_
stenograph... _sten'ō-graf_
stentorian... _sten-tō'ri-an_
step... _step_
step-ladder... _step'lad-ér_
steppe... _step_
stepping-stone... _step'ing-stōn_
stepson... _step'sun_
stereography... _ste-rō-og'ra-fi_
stereotype... _ste'rē-ō-tīp_
sterile... _ste'ril_
sterility... _ste-ril'i-ti_
sterlize... _ste'ril-īz_
sterling... _stér'ling_
stern... _stérn_
sternly... _stérn'li_
sternum... _stér'num_
stertorous... _stér'to-rus_
stethoscope... _ste'thō-skōp_
stevedore... _stē've-dōr_
stew... _stū_
steward... _stū'érd_
stewardess... _stū'ard-es_
stick... _stik_
stiff... _stif_
stiffly... _stif'li_
stiff-necked... _stif'nekt_
stiffness... _stif'nes_
stifle... _stī'fl_
stigma... _stig'ma_
stigmatize... _stig'mat-īz_
stile... _stīl_

stiletto... *sti-let′tō*
still... *stil*
stilt... *stilt*
stilted... *stilt′ed*
stimulant... *stim′ū-lant*
stimulate... *stim′ū-lāt*
stimulating... *stim′ū-lāt-ing*
stimulation... *stim-ū-lā′shun*
stimulus... *stim′ū-lus*
sting... *sting*
stingily... *stin′ji-li*
stinging... *sting′ing*
stingy... *stin′ji*
stink... *stingk*
stint... *stint*
stipe... *stīp*
stipendiary... *sti-pend′i-a-ri*
stipple... *stip′l*
stipulate... *stip′ū-lāt*
stipulaton... *stip-ū-lā′shun*
stir... *stėr*
stirrup... *sti′rup*
stitch... *stich*
stitching... *stich′ing*
stiver... *stī′vėr*
stoa... *stō′a*
stock... *stok*
stockade... *stok-ād′*
stockbroker... *stok′brō-kėr*
stockholder... *stok′hōld-ėr*
stocking... *stok′ing*
stodgy... *stoj′i*
stoic... *stō′ik*
stoical... *stō′ik-al*
stoicism... *stō′i-sizm*
stoke... *stōk*
stoker... *stōk′ėr*
stole... *stōl*
stolid... *stol′id*
stolidity... *sto-lid′i-ti*
stomach... *stum′ak*
stone... *stōn*
stony... *stōn′i*
stook... *stuk*
stool... *stōl*
stoop... *stop*
stooping... *stop′ing*
stop... *stop*
stop-watch... *stop′woch*
storage... *stōr′āj*
store... *stōr*
storehouse... *stōr′hous*
store-room... *stōr′rom*
storied... *stō′rid*

stork... *stork*
storm... *storm*
stormy... *storm′i*
story... *stō′ri*
story... *stō′ri*
stout... *stout*
stoutly... *stout′li*
stove... *stōv*
stow... *stō*
stowage... *stō′āj*
straddle... *strad′l*
straggle... *strag′l*
straight... *strāt*
straight-edge... *strāt′ej*
straighten... *strāt′n*
strain... *strān*
strained... *strānd*
strainer... *strān′ėr*
strait... *strāt*
straiten... *strāt′n*
strait-laced... *strāt′lāst*
straitly... *strāt′li*
strake... *strāk*
stramineous... *stra-min′ē-us*
stramonium... *stra-mō′ni-um*
strand... *strand*
strange... *strānj*
strangely... *strānj′li*
stranger... *strān′jėr*
strangle... *strang′gl*
strangulate... *strang′gū-lāt*
strangury... *strang′gū-ri*
strap... *strap*
strapper... *strap′ėr*
strass... *stras*
stratagem... *stra′ta-jem*
strategist... *stra′te-jist*
strategy... *stra′te-ji*
stratify... *stra′ti-fī*
stratosphere... *stra′tō-sfėr*
stratum... *strā′tum*
stratus... *strā′tus*
straw... *stra*
strawberry... *stra′be-ri*
stray... *strā*
stream... *strēm*
streamer... *strēm′ėr*
streamline... *strēm-līn′*
street... *strēt*
strength... *strength*
strengthen... *strength′en*
strenuous... *stren′ū-us*
stress... *stres*
stretch... *strech*

S

stretcher... *strech'ěr*
strew... *stro or strō*
strict... *strikt*
stricture... *strik'tūr*
strident... *strī'dent*
strife... *strīf*
strike... *strīk*
string... *string*
stringent... *strin'jent*
strip... *strip*
stripe... *strīp*
strive... *strīv*
stroke... *strōk*
stroll... *strōl*
strong... *strong*
stronghold... *strong'hōld*
strongly... *strong'li*
strontia... *stron'shi-a*
strontium... *stron'shi-um*
strop... *strop*
strophe... *strō'fē*
structural... *struk'tūr-al*
structure... *struk'tūr*
struggle... *strug'l*
strum... *strum*
struma... *stro'ma*
strumose... *stro'mōs*
strumpet... *strum'pet*
strychnia... *strik'ni-a*
stub... *stub*
stubble... *stub'l*
stubbly... *stub'li*
stubborn... *stub'orn*
stubby... *stub'i*
stucco... *stuk'kō*
stuck-up... *stuk'up*
stud... *stud*
student... *stū'dent*
studied... *stu'did*
studio... *stū'di-ō*
studious... *stū'di-us*
stuff... *stuf*
stultify... *stul'ti-fi*
stumble... *stum'bl*
stump... *stump*
stun... *stun*
stunning... *stun'ing*
stunt... *stunt*
stunted... *stunt'ed*
stupe... *stūp*
stupefy... *stū'pē-fī*
stupendous... *stū-pen'dus*
stupidity... *stū-pid'i-ti*
stupor... *stū'por*

stuprate... *stū'prāt*
sturdily... *stěr'di-li*
sturdy... *stěr'di*
sturgeon... *stěr'jon*
stutter... *stut'ěr*
sty... *stī*
stye... *stī*
stygian... *stij'i-an*
style... *stīl*
stylish... *stīl'ish*
stylist... *stīl'ist*
stylite... *stī'līt*
stylobate... *stī'lō-bāt*
stylus... *stī'lus*
styptic... *stip'tik*
suave... *swāv*
sub... *sub*
subclass... *sub'klas*
subdivide... *sub-di-vī'd'*
subdue... *sub-dū'*
subject... *sub'jekt*
subjoin... *sub-join'*
subjunctive... *sub-jungk'tiv*
sublease... *sub'lēs*
sublet... *sub-let'*
sublimate... *sub'li-māt*
sublime... *sub-līm'*
submarine... *sub-ma-rēn'*
submerge... *sub-měrj'*
submersion... *sub-měr'shun*
submission... *sub-mi'shun*
submissive... *sub-mis'iv*
submit... *sub-mit'*
subordinate... *sub-or'din-āt*
suborn... *sub-orn'*
subpoena... *sub-pē'na*
subscribe... *sub-skrīb'*
subsequence... *sub'sē-kwens*
subsequent... *sub'sē-kwent*
subside... *sub-sīd'*
subsidiary... *sub-si'di-a-ri*
subsidize... *sub-si-dīz*
subsidy... *sub'si-di*
subsist... *sub-sist'*
subsistence... *sub-sist'ens*
subsistent... *sub-sist'ent*
subspecies... *sub'spē-shēz*
substance... *sub'stans*
substantial... *sub-stan'shal*
substantiate... *sub-stan'shi-āt*
substantive... *sub'stan-tiv*
substitute... *sub'sti-tūt*
substitution... *sub-sti-tū'shun*
substructure... *sub'struk-tūr*

subsume... *sub-sūm'*
subtenant... *sub-te'nant*
subtend... *sub-tend'*
subterfuge... *sub'tér-fūj*
subtle... *sut'l*
subtlety... *sut'l-ti*
subtly... *sut'li*
subtract... *sub-trakt'*
subtraction... *sub-trak'shun*
subulate... *sū'bū-lāt*
suburb... *sub'ėrb*
suburban... *sub-ėrb'an*
subversion... *sub-vėr'shun*
subversive... *sub-vėrs'iv*
subvert... *sub-vėrt'*
subway... *sub'wā*
success... *suk-ses'*
succession... *suk-se'shun*
successional... *suk-se'shun-al*
successive... *suk-ses'iv*
successor... *suk-ses'or*
succinct... *suk-singkt'*
succinic... *suk-sin'ik*
succor... *suk'ėr*
succulent... *suk'kū-lent*
succumb... *suk-kum'*
such... *such*
suchwise... *such'wīz*
suck... *suk*
sucrose... *sū'krōs*
suction... *suk'shun*
suctorial... *suk'tō-ri-al*
sudden... *sud'en*
sudorific... *sū-do-rif'ik*
suds... *sudz*
sue... *sū*
suet... *sū'et*
suffer... *suf'ėr*
sufferance... *suf'ėr-ans*
sufferer... *suf'ėr-ėr*
sufficiency... *suf-fi'shen-si*
sufficient... *suf-fi'shent*
suffix... *suf'fiks*
suffocate... *suf'fō-kāt*
suffocative... *suf'fō-kāt-iv*
suffrage... *suf'frāj*
suffuse... *suf-fūz'*
suffusion... *suf-fū'zhon*
sugar... *shu'gėr*
sugary... *shu'gėr-i*
suggest... *sŭ-jest' or sug-jest'*
suggestion... *su-jest'yon*
suggestive... *su-jest'iv*
suicidal... *sū-i-sī'd'al*

suicide... *sū'i-sīd*
suit... *sūt*
suitability... *sūt-a-bil'i-ti*
suitable... *sūt'a-bl*
suitably... *sūt'a-bli*
suite... *swēt*
suitor... *sūt'or*
sulcate... *sul'kāt*
sulk... *sulk*
sulky... *sulk'i*
sullenly... *sul'en-li*
sully... *sul'i*
sulphate... *sul'fāt*
sulphide... *sul'fīd*
sulphite... *sul'fīt*
sulphur... *sul'fėr*
sulphurate... *sul'fū-rāt*
sulphuret... *sul'fū-ret*
sulphuric... *sul-fū'rik*
sulphurous... *sul'fėr-us*
sultan... *sul'tan*
sultry... *sul'tri*
sum... *sum*
sumac... *sū'mak*
summarily... *sum'a-ri-li*
summarize... *sum'a-rīz*
summary... *sum'a-ri*
summation... *sum-ā'shun*
summer... *sum'ėr*
summit... *sum'it*
sump... *sump*
sumptuary... *sump'tū-a-ri*
sumptuous... *sump'tū-us*
sumptuously... *sump'tū-us-li*
sunbeam... *sun'bēm*
sun-bonnet... *sun'bon-et*
sun-burn... *sun'bėrn*
sunder... *sun'dėr*
sundry... *sun'dri*
sunflower... *sun'flou-ėr*
sunken... *sungk'en*
sunlit... *sun'lit*
sunny... *sun'i*
sunrise... *sun'rīz*
sunset... *sun'set*
sunshine... *sun'shīn*
sunstroke... *sun'strōk*
sup... *sup*
superable... *sū'pėr-a-bl*
superb... *sū-pėrb'*
superciliary... *sū-pėr-sil'i-a-ri*
supercilious... *sū-pėr-sil'i-us*
superficial... *sū-pėr-fi'shal*
superficially... *sū-pėr-fi'shal-li*

S

superficies... sū-pėr-fi'shēz
superfine... sū-pėr-fīn'
superfluity... sū-pėr-flu'i-ti
superfluous... sū-pėr'flu-us
superinduce... sū'pėr-in-dūs''
superintend... sū'pėr-in-tend''
superior... sū-pē'ri-or
superiority... sū-pē'ri-o''ri-ti
superlative... sū-pėr'lat-iv
superlatively... sū-pėr'lat-iv-li
supernal... sū-pėr'nal
supernatant... sū-pėr-nā'tant
superscribe... sū-pėr-skrīb'
supersede... sū-pėr-sēd'
supersonic... sū-pėr-son'ik
superstition... sū-pėr-sti'shun
superstitious... sū-pėr-sti'shus
supervene... sū-pėr-vēn'
supervise... sū-pėr-vīz'
supine... sū-pīn'
supper... sup'ėr
supplant... sup-plant'
supple... sup'l
supplement... sup'lē-ment
suppliance... sup'li-ans
suppliant... sup'li-ant
support... sup-pōrt'
supposable... sup-pōz'a-bl
supposition... sup-po-zi'shun
suppress... sup-pres'
suppurate... sup'pū-rāt
suppuration... sup-pū-rā'shun
supremacy... sū-prem'a-si
supreme... sū-prēm'
surcharge... sėr-charj'
sure... shor
surely... shor'li
surety... shor'ti
surf... sėrf
surface... sėr'fās
surfeit... sėr'fit
surge... sėrj
surgeon... sėr'jon
surgery... sėr'je-ri
surgical... sėr'ji-kal
surly... sėr'li
surmise... sėr-mīz'
surmount... sėr-mount'
surname... sėr'nām
surpass... sėr-pas'
surplice... sėr'plis
surplus... sėr'plus
surprising... sėr-prīz'ing
surrealism... sėr-ē'al-izm

surrender... sėr-ren'dėr
surreptitious... sėr-rep-ti'shus
surrogate... su'rō-gāt
surround... sėr-round'
surrounding... sėr-round'ing
surtax... sėr'taks
surveillance... sėr-vāl'yans
survey... sėr-vā'
surveyor... sėr-vā'or
survive... sėr-vīv'
survivor... sėr-vīv'or
susceptibility... sus-sep'ti-bil''i-ti
susceptible... sus-sep'ti-bl
susceptive... sus-sep'tiv
suspect... sus-pekt'
suspend... sus-pend'
suspensive... sus-pen'siv
suspicion... sus-pi'shun
suspicious... sus-pi'shus
suspiciously... sus-pi'shus-li
sustain... sus-tān'
sustenance... sus'ten-ans
swab... swob
swaddle... swod'l
swag... swag
swaggering... swag'ėr-ing
swain... swān
swallow... swol'ō
swamp... swomp
swan... swon
swap... swop
sward... sward
swarm... swärm
swarthy... swärth'i
swash... swosh
swastika... swas'tik-a
swath... swath or swath
sway... swā
swear... swār
sweat... swet
sweater... swet'ėr
swedish... swēd'ish
sweep... swēp
sweet... swēt
sweetheart... swēt'hart
sweetly... swēt'li
sweet-pea... swēt'pē
sweet-william... swēt-wil'yam
swell... swel
swelter... swel'tėr
sweltry... swel'tri
swerve... swėrv
swift... swift
swiftly... swift'li

swig... *swig*
swill... *swil*
swim... *swim*
swindle... *swin'dl*
swindler... *swin'dlėr*
swine... *swīn*
swing... *swing*
swinge... *swingj*
swinish... *swīn'ish*
swink... *swingk*
swipe... *swīp*
swirl... *swėrl*
swish... *swish*
swiss... *swis*
switch... *swich*
switzer... *swit'zėr*
swollen... *swōln*
swoon... *swon*
swoop... *swop*
sword-fish... *sōrd'fish*
swordsman... *sōrdz'man*
sworn... *swōrn*
sybarite... *sib'a-rīt*
sycamore... *si'ka-mōr*
sycophancy... *si'kō-fan-si*
sycophant... *si'kō-fant*
sycophantic... *si-kō-fant'ik*
syenite... *sī'en-īt*
syllabary... *sil'a-ba-ri*
syllable... *sil'la-bi*
sylphid... *silf'id*
sylphine... *silf'in*
sylva... *sil'va*
sylvan... *sil'van*
sylviculture... *sil-vi-kul'tūr*
symbol... *sim'bol*
symbolic... *sim-bol'ik*
symmetry... *sim'me-tri*
sympathize... *sim'pa-thīz*
sympathy... *sim'pa-thi*
symposium... *sim-pō'zi-um*
symptom... *sim'tom*
symptomatic... *sim-tom-at'ik*
synagogue... *sin'a-gog*
synchronal... *sin'kron-al*
synchronism... *sin'kron-izm*
synchronize... *sin'kron-īz*
synchronous... *sin'kron-us*
synchrony... *sin'kron-i*
synclinal... *sin-klī'nal*
syncopate... *sin'ko-pāt*
syncopation... *sin-ko-pā'shun*
syncretism... *sin'krēt-izm*
syndic... *sin'dik*

syndicalism... *sin'dik-al-izm*
syndicate... *sin'di-kāt*
synecdoche... *sin-ek'do-kē*
syneresis... *si-nē're-sis*
synod... *sin'od*
synodic... *sin-od'ik*
synonym... *sin'ō-nim*
synopsis... *sin-op'sis*
synoptic... *sin-op'tik*
syntax... *sin'taks*
syphilis... *sif'i-lis*
syringe... *si'rinj*
syrinx... *sī'ringks*
syrup... *si'rup*
syrupy... *si'rup-i*
system... *sis'tem*
systemic... *sis-tem'ik*
systole... *sis'to-lē*
systolic... *sis-tol'ik*
sythe... *sifH*
syzygy... *siz'i-ji*

T

tab... *tab*
tabaret... *tab'a-ret*
tabby... *tab'i*
tabernacle... *tab'ėr-na-kl*
tabid... *ta'bid*
tabinet... *tab'i-net*
table... *tā'bl*
tableau... *tab-lō'*
table-cloth... *tā'bl-kloth*
tablet... *tab'let*
taboo... *ta-bo'*
tabor... *tā'bor*
tabular... *ta'bū-lėr*
tabulate... *ta'bū-lāt*
tacit... *ta'sit*
tacitly... *ta'sit-li*
tack... *tak*
tact... *takt*
tactic... *tak'tik*
tactician... *tak-ti'shan*
taction... *tak'shun*
tactless... *takt'les*
tactual... *tak'tu-al*
tadpole... *tad'pōl*
taffeta... *taf'e-ta*
tag... *tag*
tail... *tāl*
tailor... *tā'lor*
taint... *tānt*

take... tāk
taking... tāk'ing
talc... talk
tale... tāl
talent... ta'lent
talion... tā'li-on
talisman... ta'lis-man
talkative... tak'a-tiv
talker... tak'ẽr
tall... tal
tallow... tal'ō
tally... tal'i
talmud... tal'mud
talon... ta'lon
talus... tā'lus
tamable... tām'a-bl
tamarind... tam'a-rind
tamarisk... tam'a-risk
tambour... tam'bor
tambourine... tam-bo-rēn'
tame... tām
tameless... tām'les
tamely... tām'li
tamis... tam'i
tamp... tamp
tamper... tam'pẽr
tan... tan
tandem... tan'dem
tang... tang
tangent... tan'jent
tangential... tan-jen'shal
tangible... tan'ji-bl
tangle... tang'gl
tanist... tan'ist
tanistry... tan'ist-ri
tank... tangk
tankard... tang'kard
tanner... tan'ẽr
tannic... tan'ik
tannin... tan'in
tanning... tan'ing
tansy... tan'zi
tantalize... tan'ta-līz
tantamount... tan'ta-mount
tantivy... tan-ti'vi
tantrum... tan'trum
tap... tap
tape... tāp
taper... tā'pẽr
tapestry... ta'pes-tri
tape-worm... tāp'wẽrm
tapioca... tap-i-ō'ka
tapir... tā'pir
tapping... tap'ing

tap-root... tap'rot
tarantula... ta-ran'tū-la
tardy... tar'di
tare... tār
targe... tarj
target... tar'get
targum... tar'gum
tariff... ta'rif
tarlatan... tar'la-tan
tarn... tarn
tarnish... tar'nish
tarpan... tar'pan
tarpon... tar'pon
tarry... ta'ri
tarry... tar'i
tarsia... tar'si-a
tarsus... tar'sus
tart... tart
tartan... tar'tan
tartar... tar'tar
tartly... tart'li
task... task
tassel... tas'el
taste... tāst
tatter... tat'ẽr
tatting... tat'ing
tattle... tat'l
tattoo... tat-to'
taunt... tant
taurine... ta'rīn
taurus... ta'rus
taut... tat
tavern... ta'vẽrn
tawdry... ta'dri
tawery... tā'ē-ri
tawny... ta'ni
tax... taks
taxable... taks'a-bl
taxation... taks-ā'shun
taxicab... tak'si-kab
taxidermy... tak'si-dẽr-mi
taxology... tak-sol'o-ji
taxonomy... tak-son'o-mi
tea... tē
teach... tēch
teachable... tēch'a-bl
teacher... tēch'ẽr
teaching... tēch'ing
tea-cup... tē'kup
teal... tēl
team... tēm
teamster... tēm'stẽr
tea-pot... tē'pot
tear... tēr

tease... *tēz*
teat... *tēt*
technical... *tek'ni-kal*
technique... *tek-nēk'*
technology... *tek-nol'o-ji*
tectonic... *tek-ton'ik*
tectonics... *tek-ton'iks*
tedious... *tē'di-us*
tedium... *tē'di-um*
tee... *tē*
teem... *tēm*
teens... *tēnz*
teeth... *tēth*
teethe... *tēŦH*
teething... *tēŦH'ing*
teetotal... *tē'tō-tal*
tegument... *teg'ū-ment*
teil... *tēl*
telegram... *tel'e-gram*
telemeter... *te-lem'et-ėr*
teleology... *tel-ē-ol'o-ji*
teleostean... *tel-ē-os'tē-an*
telepathic... *tel-e-path'ik*
telephone... *tel'e-fōn*
telephonic... *tel-e-fon'ik*
telescope... *tel'e-skōp*
telescopic... *tel-e-skop'ik*
television... *tel'e-vizh''un*
telic... *tel'ik*
tell... *tel*
teller... *tel'ėr*
telling... *tel'ing*
tell-tale... *tel'tāl*
tellurian... *tel-ū'ri-an*
telluric... *tel-ū'rik*
tellurium... *tel-ū'ri-um*
temerarious... *tem-ē-rā'ri-us*
temerity... *tē-me'ri-ti*
temper... *tem'pėr*
tempera... *tem'pe-ra*
temperance... *tem'pėr-ans*
temperate... *tem'pėr-āt*
temperature... *tem'pėr-a-tūr*
tempest... *tem'pest*
templar... *tem'plėr*
temple... *tem'pl*
tempo... *tem'pō*
temporal... *tem'pō-ral*
temporality... *tem-pō-ral'i-ti*
temporize... *tem'pō-rīz*
tempt... *temt*
temptation... *tem-tā'shun*
temptress... *temt'res*
temulence... *tem'ū-lens*

temulent... *tem'ū-lent*
ten... *ten*
tenable... *te'na-bl*
tenacious... *te-nā'shus*
tenaciously... *te-nā'shus-li*
tenacity... *te-nas'i-ti*
tenancy... *te'nan-si*
tenant... *te'nant*
tenantable... *te'nant-a-bl*
tenantless... *te'nant-les*
tenantry... *te'nant-ri*
tend... *tend*
tendance... *ten'dans*
tender... *ten'dėr*
tendinous... *ten'din-us*
tendon... *ten'don*
tendril... *ten'dril*
tenebrosity... *te-nē-bros'i-ti*
tenement... *te'nē-ment*
tenet... *te'net*
tenfold... *ten'fōld*
tenia... *tē'ni-a*
tennis... *ten'is*
tenon... *ten'on*
tenor... *ten'or*
tense... *tens*
tensile... *tens'īl*
tension... *ten'shun*
tensity... *tens'i-ti*
tensor... *ten'sor*
tent... *tent*
tentacle... *ten'ta-kl*
tentative... *ten'ta-tiv*
tenter... *ten'tėr*
tenth... *tenth*
tenuity... *ten-ū'i-ti*
tenuous... *ten'ū-us*
tepid... *te'pid*
teratology... *ter-a-tol'o-ji*
terce... *tėrs*
tercentenary... *tėr-sen'ten-a-ri*
terebene... *ter'ē-bēn*
terebinth... *te'rē-binth*
teredo... *te-rē'dō*
terete... *te-rēt'*
tergal... *tėr'gal*
term... *tėrm*
terminal... *tėr'min-al*
terminate... *tėr'min-āt*
terminus... *tėr'mi-nus*
termite... *tėr'mīt*
termless... *tėrm'les*
termly... *tėrm'li*
tern... *tėrn*

ternary... *tėr'na-ri*
ternate... *tėr'nāt*
terra... *ter'ra*
terrace... *te'ras*
terra-cotta... *ter'ra-kot-a*
terrapin... *te'ra-pin*
terrene... *te-rēn'*
terrible... *te'ri-bl*
terrier... *te'ri-ėr*
terrific... *te-rif'ik*
terrigenous... *te-rij'en-us*
territorial... *te-ri-tō'ri-al*
territory... *te'ri-to-ri*
terror... *te'ror*
terse... *tėrs*
tessellar... *tes'se-lar*
tessera... *tes'e-ra*
test... *test*
testacean... *tes-tā'shē-an*
testaceous... *tes-tā'shus*
testacy... *tes'ta-si*
testament... *tes'ta-ment*
testate... *tes'tāt*
testator... *tes-tāt'or*
testatrix... *tes-tāt'riks*
testicle... *tes'ti-kl*
testify... *tes'ti-fī*
testily... *tes'ti-li*
testimonial... *tes-ti-m'ō'ni-al*
testimony... *tes'ti-mo-ni*
testy... *tes'ti*
tether... *teŦH'ėr*
tetragon... *tet'ra-gon*
tetralogy... *te-tral'o-ji*
tetrameter... *te-tram'et-ėr*
tetrarch... *tet'rark*
tetter... *tet'ėr*
teuton... *tū'ton*
teutonic... *tū-ton'ik*
text... *tekst*
textile... *teks'fīl*
textorial... *teks-tō'ri-al*
textual... *teks'tū-al*
textualist... *teks'tū-al-ist*
texture... *teks'tūr*
thalamus... *thal'a-mus*
thaler... *ta'lėr*
thallus... *thal'us*
than... *ŦHan*
thank... *thangk*
thankful... *thangk'ful*
thankfully... *thangk"ful-li*
thankless... *thangk'lės*
thanksgiving... *thangks'giv-ing*

that... *ŦHat*
thatcher... *thach'ėr*
thatching... *thach'ing*
thaw... *tha*
the... *ŦHē ̈ or ŦHi*
thearchy... *thē'ar-ki*
theater... *thē'a-tėr*
theatricals... *thē-at'rik-alz*
thee... *ŦHē*
theft... *theft*
their... *ŦHār*
theist... *thē'ist*
them... *ŦHem*
theme... *thēm*
then... *ŦHen*
thence... *ŦHens*
thenceforth... *ŦHens'fōrth*
theocracy... *thē-ok'ra-si*
theologian... *thē-o-lō'ji-an*
theologist... *thē-ol'o-jis*
theologize... *thē-ol'o-jīz*
theology... *thē-ol'o-ji*
theorem... *thē'ō-rem*
theorize... *thē'ō-rīz*
theory... *thē'ō-ri*
there... *ŦHār*
thereafter... *ŦHār-aft'ėr*
thereby... *ŦHār-bī'*
therefor... *ŦHār-for'*
therefore... *ŦHār'for*
therein... *ŦHār-in'*
thereof... *ŦHār-ov'*
thereon... *ŦHār-on'*
thereupon... *ŦHār-up-on'*
therewith... *ŦHar-with'*
theriotomy... *thē-ri-ot'o-mi*
thermotic... *thėr-mot'ik*
thesaurus... *the-sa'rus*
these... *ŦHēz ̈*
thesis... *thē'sis*
thespian... *thes'pi-an*
theurgy... *thē'ėr-ji*
they... *ŦHā*
thick... *thik*
thicken... *thik'n*
thicket... *thik'et*
thickset... *thik'set*
thick-skinned... *thik'skind*
thief... *thēf*
thimble... *thim'bl*
thin... *thin*
thine... *ŦHīn*
thing... *thing*
think... *thingk*

thinker... *thingk'ẻr*
thinking... *thingk'ing*
thinly... *thin'li*
thin-skinned... *thin'skind*
third... *thẻrd*
thirst... *thẻrst*
thirsty... *thẻrst'i*
thirteen... *thẻr'tēn*
thirty... *thẻr'ti*
this... *ŦHis*
thistle... *this'l*
thong... *thong*
thorax... *thōraks*
thorn... *thorn*
thorough... *thu'rō*
thorough-bred... *thu'rō-bred*
thoroughfare... *thu'rō-fär*
thoroughly... *thu'rō-li*
thorp... *thorp*
though... *ŦHō*
thought... *that*
thousand... *ŧhou'zand*
thrall... *thral*
thrasher... *ŧhrash'ẻr*
thread... *thred*
threadbare... *thred'bär*
threat... *thret*
threaten... *thret'n*
threatening... *thret'n-ing*
three... *thrē*
threefold... *thrē'fōld*
three-ply... *thrē'plī*
threescore... *thrē'skōr*
thresh... *thresh*
threshold... *Thresh'ōld*
thrice... *thrīs*
thrift... *thrift*
thrill... *thril*
thrilling... *thril'ing*
thrive... *thrīv*
throat... *thrōt*
thrombosis... *throm'bō-sis*
through... *thro*
throw... *thrō*
throw-back... *thrō'bak*
thrush... *thrush*
thrust... *thrust*
thumb... *thum*
thumb-screw... *thum'skro*
thump... *thump*
thumping... *thump'ing*
thunder... *thund'dẻr*
thus... *ŦHus*
thwack... *thwak*

thwart... *thwart*
thy... *ŦHĪ*
thyme... *tīm*
thymol... *tīm'ol*
thyrsus... *thẻr'sus*
thyself... *ŦHĪ-self'*
tiara... *ti-a'ra*
tibia... *tib'i-a*
tibial... *tib'i-al*
tic... *tik*
tick... *tik*
ticket... *tik'et*
ticking... *tik'ing*
tide... *tīd*
tidy... *tī'di*
tie... *tī*
tier... *tēr*
tiff... *tif*
tiffany... *tif'a-ni*
tiger... *tī'gẻr*
tight... *tīt*
tigress... *tī'gres*
tile... *tīl*
till... *til*
tillage... *til'āj*
tiller... *til'ẻr*
tilt... *tilt*
timber... *tim'bẻr*
timbering... *tim'bẻr-ing*
timbre... *tim'br or tam'br*
timbrel... *tim'brel*
time... *tīm*
timid... *ti'mid*
timorous... *ti'mor-us*
tin... *tin*
tincal... *ting'kal*
tincture... *tingk'tūr*
tin-foil... *tin'foil*
tinge... *tinj*
tingle... *ting'gl*
tinker... *ting'kẻr*
tinkle... *ting'kl*
tinning... *tin'ing*
tinplate... *tin'plāt*
tinsel... *tin'sel*
tinsmith... *tin'smith*
tint... *tint*
tinware... *tin'wār*
tiny... *tī'ni*
tip... *tip*
tippet... *tip'et*
tipple... *tip'l*
tipsy... *tip'si*
tirade... *ti-rād'*

tire . . . *fīr*
tiresome . . . *fīr'sum*
tissue . . . *ti'shū*
titan . . . *fī'tan*
titanium . . . *fī-tā'ni-um*
tithe . . . *fīŦH*
tithonic . . . *ti'thon'ik*
title . . . *fī'tl*
titrate . . . *fī'trāt*
titter . . . *tit'ėr*
tittle . . . *tit'l*
titular . . . *tit'ū-lėr*
to . . . *tu*
toad . . . *tōd*
toast . . . *tōst*
tobacco . . . *tō-bak'ō*
today . . . *tu-dā'*
toddle . . . *fŏd'l*
toddy . . . *tod'i*
to-do . . . *tu-do'*
toe . . . *tō*
toffy . . . *tof'i*
toga . . . *tō'ga*
together . . . *tu-geŦH'ėr*
toil . . . *toil*
toilet . . . *toi'let*
toilsome . . . *toil'sum*
token . . . *tō'kn*
tolerate . . . *tol'ė-rāt*
toll . . . *tōl*
tomahawk . . . *to'ma-hạk*
tomb . . . *tom*
tomboy . . . *tom'boi*
tombstone . . . *tom'stōn*
tome . . . *tōm*
tomorrow . . . *to-mo'rō*
ton . . . *tun*
tone . . . *tōn*
tongs . . . *tongz*
tongue . . . *tung*
tonic . . . *ton'ik*
tonight . . . *to-nīt'*
tonite . . . *tōn'it*
tonnage . . . *tun'āj*
tonsil . . . *ton'sil*
tonsile . . . *ton'sīl*
too . . . *to*
tool . . . *tol*
toot . . . *tot*
tooth . . . *toth*
toothache . . . *toth'āk*
top . . . *top*
topaz . . . *tō'paz*
tope . . . *tōp*

topiary . . . *tō'pi-a-ri*
topical . . . *to'pik-al*
topmast . . . *top'mast*
topography . . . *to-pog'ra-fi*
topple . . . *top'l*
topsy-turvy . . . *top'si-tėr-vi*
torch . . . *torch*
torment . . . *tor'ment*
tornado . . . *tor-nā'dō*
torpedo . . . *tor-pē'do*
torpid . . . *tor'pid*
torrent . . . *to'rent*
torrential . . . *to-ren'shal*
torrid . . . *to'rid*
torsion . . . *tor'shun*
tort . . . *tort*
tortive . . . *tor'tiv*
tortoise . . . *tor'tois or tor'tis*
tortuous . . . *tor'tū-us*
torture . . . *tor'tūr*
toss . . . *tos*
tot . . . *tot*
total . . . *tō'tal*
totalitarian . . . *tō-tal'it-ār''i-an*
totality . . . *tō'tal'i-ti*
totem . . . *tō'tem*
totter . . . *tot'ėr*
toucan . . . *to'kan*
touch . . . *tuch*
tough . . . *tuf*
toupee . . . *to-pē'*
tour . . . *tor*
tourist . . . *tor'ist*
tournament . . . *tor'na-ment*
tourniquet . . . *tor'ni-ket*
touse . . . *touz*
tousle . . . *tou'zl*
tout . . . *tout*
tow . . . *tō*
toward . . . *tō'ērd*
towel . . . *tou'el*
tower . . . *tou'ėr*
tow-line . . . *tō'līn*
town . . . *toun*
toxic . . . *tok'sik*
toxin . . . *toks'in*
toy . . . *toi*
trace . . . *trās*
trachea . . . *trā'kē-a*
track . . . *trak*
tract . . . *trakt*
traction . . . *trak'shun*
tractor . . . *trak'tor*
trade . . . *trād*

tradition... *tra-di'shun*
traduce... *tra-dūs'*
traffic... *traf'ik*
tragedian... *tra-jē'di-an*
tragedy... *tra'je-di*
tragic... *tra'jik*
tragopan... *trag'ō-pan*
trail... *trāl*
train... *trān*
traipse... *trāps*
trait... *trāt* or *trā*
trajectory... *tra-jek'to-ri*
tram... *tram*
trammel... *tram'el*
tramontane... *tra-mon'tān*
tramp... *tramp*
trample... *tram'pl*
tramway... *tram'wā*
trance... *trans*
transact... *trans-akt'*
transalpine... *trans-al'pīn*
transatlantic... *trans-at-lan'tik*
transcend... *trans-send'*
transcript... *tran'skript*
transept... *tran'sept*
transfer... *trans-fėr'*
transfigure... *trans-fig'ūr*
transfix... *trans-fiks'*
transfluent... *trans'flu-ent*
transform... *trans-form'*
transfuse... *trans-fūz'*
transgress... *trans-gres'*
transient... *tran'si-ent*
transit... *tran'sit*
transition... *tran-zi'shun*
translate... *trans-lātu'*
transliterate... *trans-lit'ėr-āt*
translucent... *trans-lū'sent*
transmigrate... *trans'mi-grāt*
transmission... *trans-mi'shun*
transmit... *trans-mit'*
transmogrify... *trans-mog'ri-fi*
transmutable... *trans-mūt'a-bl*
transom... *tran'sum*
transparence... *trans-pā'rens*
transpire... *trans-pīr*
transplant... *trans-plant'*
transport... *trans-pōrt'*
transportable... *trans-pōrt'abl*
transpose... *trans-pōz'*
transversal... *trans-vėrs'al*
trap... *trap*
trape... *trāp*
trapeze... *tra-pēz'*

trapezoid... *tra'pē-zoid*
trapper... *trap'ėr*
traps... *traps*
trash... *trash*
trass... *tras*
traumatic... *tra-mat'ik*
travail... *tra'vāl*
travel... *tra'vel*
traverse... *tra'vėrs*
travertin... *tra'vėr-tin*
travesty... *tra'ves-ti*
trawl... *tral*
tray... *trā̈*
tread... *tred*
treadmill... *tred'mil*
treadwheel... *tred'whēl*
treason... *trē'zon*
treasure... *tre'zhūr*
treat... *trēt*
treatise... *trē'tiz*
treatment... *trēt'ment*
treaty... *trē'ti*
treble... *tre'bl*
tree... *trē*
trefoil... *trē'foil*
trek... *trek*
trellis... *trel'is*
tremble... *trem'bl*
tremendous... *trē-men'dus*
tremor... *tre'mor*
tremulous... *tre'mū-lus*
trench... *trensh*
trenchant... *tren'shant*
trend... *trend*
trental... *tren'tal*
trepan... *trē-pan'*
trepidation... *tre-pid-ā'shun*
tress... *tres*
trestle... *tres'l*
tret... *tret*
trews... *troz*
triad... *trī'ad*
trial... *trī'al*
triangle... *trī-ang'gl*
triarchy... *trī'ark-i*
trias... *trī'as*
tribe... *trīb*
tribrach... *trī'brak*
tribulation... *tri-bū-lā'shun*
tribunal... *trī-bū'nal*
tribune... *trī'būn*
tributary... *tri'bū-ta-ri*
tribute... *tri'būt*
trice... *trīs*

tricennial... _trī-sen'ni-al_
tricentenary... _trī-sen'ten-a-ri_
trichina... _tri-kī'na_
trichord... _trī'kord_
trick... _trik_
tricolor... _trī'kul-ėr_
tricycle... _trī'si-kl_
tried... _trīd_
triennial... _trī-en'ni-al_
trifarious... _trī-fā'ri-us_
trifid... _trī-fid_
trifle... _trī'fl_
triform... _trī'form_
trig... _trig_
trigamist... _tri'ga-mist_
trigger... _trig'ėr_
trill... _tril_
trillion... _tril'yon_
trilobate... _trī-lō'bāt_
trilocular... _trī-lok'ū-lėr_
trilogy... _tril'o-ji_
trim... _trim_
trimester... _trī-mes'tėr_
trimeter... _trim'et-ėr_
trimly... _trim'li_
trine... _trīne_
tringle... _tring'gl_
trinket... _tring'ket_
trinomial... _trī-nō'mi-al_
trio... _trī'ō or trē'ō_
triolet... _trī'o-let or trē'o-let_
tripedal... _trī-ped-al_
triple... _tri'pl_
triplet... _trip'let_
tripod... _trī'pod_
tripper... _trip'ėr_
triptych... _trip'tik_
trisect... _trī-sekt'_
tristichous... _trī'stik-us_
trisulcate... _trī-sul'kāt_
trisyllable... _tri-sil'la-bl_
tritheism... _trī'thē-izm_
triturate... _tri'tū-rāt_
triumph... _trī'umf_
triumvirate... _trī-um'vėr-āt_
trivalve... _trī'valv_
trivial... _tri'vi-al_
triviality... _tri-vi-al'i-ti_
trivially... _tri'vi-al-li_
trochaic... _trō-kā'ik_
troche... _trōch or trosh_
troglodyte... _trō'glod-īt_
trogon... _trō'gon_
trojan... _trō'jan_

troll... _trōl_
trolling... _trōl'ing_
trollop... _trol'lop_
trombone... _trom'bōn_
tromp... _tromp_
troop... _trop_
tropaeolum... _trō-pē'o-lum_
trope... _trōp_
trophy... _trō'fi_
tropic... _tro'pik_
trotter... _trōt'ėr_
troubador... _tro'ba-dor_
trouble... _tru'bl_
trough... _trof_
trounce... _trouns_
troupe... _trop_
trousering... _trou'zėr-ing_
trousers... _trou'zėrz_
trousseau... _tro-sō_
trout... _trout_
trover... _trō'vėr_
trow... _trou or trō_
trowel... _trou'el_
truant... _tro'ant_
truce... _tros_
truckle... _truk'l_
truculent... _tru'kū-lent_
trudge... _truj_
true... _tro_
truffle... _truf'l_
truism... _tro'izm_
trull... _trul_
truly... _tro'li_
trump... _trump_
trumpet... _trum'pet_
truncate... _trung'kāt_
trundle... _trun'dl_
trunk... _trungk_
trunnion... _trun'yon_
truss... _trus_
trust... _trust_
trustee... _trus-tē'_
truth... _troth_
try... _trī_
trying... _trī'ing_
tryst... _trīst_
tsetse... _tset'se_
tub... _tub_
tuba... _tū'ba_
tube... _tūb_
tuber... _tū'bėr_
tubing... _tūb'ing_
tubular... _tūb'ū-lėr_
tubule... _tūb'ūl_

U

tuck . . . *tuk*
tuesday . . . *tūz′dā*
tug . . . *tug*
tuition . . . *tū-i′shun*
tulip . . . *tū′lip*
tulle . . . *tul*
tumble . . . *tum′bl*
tumid . . . *tū′mid*
tumult . . . *tū′mult*
tun . . . *tun*
tundra . . . *tun′dra*
tune . . . *tūn*
tungsten . . . *tung′sten*
tunic . . . *tū′nik*
tuning . . . *tūn′ing*
tunnel . . . *tun′el*
tunny . . . *tun′i*
tup . . . *tup*
turban . . . *tėr′ban*
turbine . . . *tėr′bīn*
turbot . . . *tėr′bot*
turbulent . . . *tėr′bū-lent*
turf . . . *tėrf*
turgent . . . *tėr′jent*
turgid . . . *tėr′jid*
turk . . . *tėrk*
turkey . . . *tėr′ki*
turmeric . . . *tėr′mer-ik*
turmoil . . . *tėr′moil*
turn . . . *tėrn*
turner . . . *tėrn′ėr*
turnip . . . *tėr′nip*
turnkey . . . *tėrn′kē*
turnpike . . . *tėrnpīk*
turnstile . . . *tėrn′sfīl*
turpentine . . . *tėr′pen-fīn*
turpitude . . . *tėr-pi-tūd*
turps . . . *tėrps*
turquoise . . . *tėr′koiz*
turret . . . *tu′ret*
turtle . . . *tėr′tl*
tuscan . . . *tus′kan*
tusk . . . *tusk*
tussle . . . *tus′l*
tussock . . . *tus′ok*
tutelage . . . *tū′tel-āj*
tutorial . . . *tū-tō′ri-al*
tuyere . . . *twi-yār′ or tu̯-yār′*
twaddle . . . *twod′l*
twain . . . *twān*
twang . . . *twang*
tweak . . . *twēk*
tweed . . . *twēd*
tweezers . . . *twē′zėrz*

twelfth . . . *twelfth*
twentieth . . . *twen′ti-eth*
twenty . . . *twen′ti*
twibill . . . *twī′bil*
twice . . . *twīs*
twiddle . . . *twid′l*
twig . . . *twig*
twilight . . . *twī′līt*
twill . . . *twil*
twin . . . *twin*
twine . . . *twīn*
twinge . . . *twinj*
twinkle . . . *twingk′l*
twirl . . . *twėrl*
twit . . . *twit*
twitch . . . *twich*
twitter . . . *twit′ėr*
two . . . *to*
tymbal . . . *tim′bal*
tympanum . . . *tim′pa-num*
type . . . *fīp*
typhoid . . . *fī′foid*
typhoon . . . *fī-fon′*
typhus . . . *fī′fus*
typical . . . *tip′ik-al*
typically . . . *tip′ik-al-li*
typify . . . *tip′i-fī*
typology . . . *fī-pol′o-ji*
tyranny . . . *ti′ran-i*
tyrant . . . *fī′rant*

U

ubiety . . . *ū-bī′e-ti*
ubiquity . . . *ū-bi′kwi-ti*
udder . . . *ud′ėr*
udometer . . . *ū-dom′et-ėr*
ugly . . . *ugh′li*
ulcer . . . *ul′sėr*
ulceration . . . *ul-sėr-ā′shun*
ulcerous . . . *ul′sėr-us*
ulster . . . *ul′stėr*
ulterior . . . *ul-tē′ri-or*
ultimate . . . *ul′ti-māt*
ulltimately . . . *ul′ti-māt-li*
ultimatum . . . *ul-ti-mā′tum*
ultimo . . . *ul′ti-mō*
ultra . . . *ul′tra*
ultra-violet . . . *ul′tra-vī′′ō-let*
ultroneous . . . *ul-trō′nē-us*
umbel . . . *um′bel*
umbellate . . . *um′bel-āt*
umber . . . *um′bėr*

umbilicus... *um-bi-li'kus*
umbra... *um'bra*
umbrageous... *um-brā'jus*
umbrella... *um-brel'la*
umpirage... *um'pīr-āj*
umpire... *um'pīr*
unable... *un-ā'bl*
unadorned... *un-a-dornd'*
unadvisable... *un-ad-vīz'a-bl*
unaided... *un-ād'ed*
unanimous... *ū-nan'i-mus*
unarmed... *un-armd'*
unaspiring... *un-as-pīr'ing*
unattractive... *un-at-trakt'iv*
unavoidable... *un-a-void'a-bl*
unaware... *un-a-wār'*
unawares... *un-a-wārz'*
unbearable... *un-bār'a-bl*
unbecoming... *un-bē-kum'ing*
unbefitting... *un-bē-fit'ing*
unbelief... *un-bē-lēf'*
unbroken... *un-brōk'n*
unbutton... *un-but'n*
uncalled... *un-kald'*
uncanny... *un-kän'i*
uncertain... *un-sėr'tān*
uncertainty... *un-sėr'tin-ti*
unchallenged... *un-chal'lenjd*
unchanging... *un-chānj'ing*
unchaste... *un-chāst'*
unchristian... *un-kris'ti-an*
uncivilized... *un-si'vil-īzd*
uncle... *ung'kl*
uncommon... *un-kom'mon*
unconfined... *un-kon-fīnd'*
unconscious... *un-kon'shus*
uncork... *un-kork'*
uncorrected... *un-ko-rekt'ed*
uncouple... *un-ku'pl*
uncourtly... *un-kōrt'li*
uncouth... *un-koth'*
uncover... *un-ku'vėr*
uncultivated... *un-kul'ti-vāt-ed*
uncut... *un-kut'*
undated... *un'dāt'ed*
undaunted... *un-dant'ed*
undecided... *un-dē-sī d'ed*
undefinable... *un-dē-fīn'a-bl*
undeniable... *un-dē-nī'a-bl*
under... *un'dėr*
undercarriage... *un'dėr-kar-ij*
undercharge... *un-dėr-charj'*
undercurrent... *un'dėr-ku-rent*
undergo... *un-dėr-gō*

underground... *un'dėr-ground*
undergrowth... *un'dėr-grō th*
underhand... *un'dėr-hand*
underlay... *un-dėr-lā'*
undermine... *un-dėr-mīn'*
underneath... *un-dėr-nēth'*
undershot... *un-dėr-shot'*
undershrub... *un'dėr-shrub*
undersized... *un'dėr-sīzd*
understand... *un-dėr-stand'*
understate... *un-dėr-stāt'*
undertake... *un'dėr-tāk*
undertaker... *un'dėr-tāk-ėr*
undertone... *un'dėr-tōn*
under-tow... *un'dėr-tō*
undervalue... *un-dėr-val'ū*
underwear... *un'dėr-wār*
underworld... *un'dėr-wėrld*
underwrite... *un-dėr-rīt*
underwriter... *un'dėr-rīt-ėr*
undesirable... *un-dē-zīr'a-bl*
undeterred... *un-dē-tėrd'*
undigested... *un-di-jest'ed*
undisguised... *un-dis-gīzd'*
undisposed... *un-dis-pōzd'*
undisputed... *un-dis-pūt'ed*
undisturbed... *un-dis-tėrbd'*
undivided... *un-di-vīd'ed*
undoing... *un-do'ing*
undone... *un-dun'*
undoubtedly... *un-dout'ed-li*
undress... *un-dres'*
undue... *un-dū'*
undulate... *un'dū-lāt*
undulatory... *un'dū-la-to-ri*
unduly... *un-dū'li*
undutiful... *un-dū'ti-ful*
undying... *un-dī'ing*
unearned... *un-ėrnd'*
unearth... *un-ėrth'*
uneasy... *un-ēz'i*
uneducated... *un-ed'ū-kāt-ed*
unemployed... *un-em-ploid'*
unending... *un-end'ing*
unendurable... *un-en-dūr'a-bl*
unengaged... *un-en-gājd'*
unenlightened... *un-en-līt'nd*
unenviable... *un-en'vi-a-bl*
unequalled... *un-ē'kwald*
unessential... *un-es-sen'shal*
uneven... *un-ē'vn*
unexcelled... *un-ek-seld'*
unexpired... *un-eks-pīrd'*
unexplored... *un-eks-plōrd'*

unfading... *un-fād'ing*
unfailing... *un-fāl'ing*
unfair... *un-fār'*
unfamiliar... *un-fa-mil'i-ėr*
unfasten... *un-fas'n*
unfavorable... *un-fā'vėr-a-bl*
unfeeling... *un-fēl'ing*
unfinished... *un-fin'isht*
unfit... *un-fit'*
unflinching... *un-flinsh'ing*
unfold... *un-fōld'*
unforeseen... *un-fōr-sēn'*
unforgiving... *un-for-giv'ing*
unformed... *un-formd'*
unfortunate... *un-for'tū-nāt*
unfortunately... *un-for'tū-nāt-li*
unfounded... *un-found'ed*
unfriendly... *un-frend'li*
unfruitful... *un-frot'ful*
unfunded... *un-fund'ed*
unfurl... *un-fėrl'*
unfurnished... *un-fėr'nisht*
unglazed... *un-glāzd'*
ungodly... *un-god'li*
ungracious... *un-grā'shus*
ungrateful... *un-grāt'ful*
ungrudging... *un-gruj'ing*
unhallowed... *un-hal'ō d*
unhand... *un-hand'*
unhappily... *un-hap'i-li*
unhappy... *un-hap'i*
unharmed... *un-harmd'*
unharness... *un-har'nes*
unhealthy... *un-helth'i*
unheard... *un-hėrd'*
unhesitating... *un-he'zi-tāt-ing*
unhinge... *un-hinj'*
unholy... *un-hō'li*
unicorn... *ū'ni-korn*
unicostate... *ū-ni-kos'tāt*
unification... *ū'ni-fi-kā''shun*
uniform... *ū'ni-form*
uniformity... *ū-ni-for'mi-ti*
uniformly... *ū'ni-form-li*
unify... *ū'ni-fī*
unigenous... *ū-ni'jen-us*
unimportant... *un-im-pōr'tant*
unimproved... *un-im-provd'*
uninhabited... *un-in-ha'bit-ed*
uninstructed... *un-in-strukt'ed*
unintelligible... *un-in-tel'i-ji-bl*
uninterested... *un-in'tėr-est-ed*
uninviting... *un-in-vīt'ing*
union... *ūn'yon*

unionist... *ūn'yon-ist*
uniparous... *ū-nip'a-rus*
unique... *ū-nēk'*
unison... *ū-ni-son*
unit... *ū'nit*
unitarian... *ū-ni-tā'ri-an*
unitarianism... *ū-ni-tā'ri-an-izm*
unitary... *ū'ni-ta-ri*
unite... *ū-nīt'*
united... *ū-nīt'ed*
unitedly... *ū-nīt'ed-li*
unity... *ū'ni-ti*
univalve... *ū'ni-valv*
universal... *ū-ni-vėrs'al*
universally... *ū-ni-vėrs'al-li*
universe... *ū'ni-vėrs*
univocal... *ū-ni'vō-kal*
unjust... *un-just'*
unjustifiable... *un-jus'ti-fī''a-bl*
unjustly... *un-just'li*
unkempt... *un-kempt'*
unkind... *un-kīnd'*
unkindly... *un-kind'li*
unknowingly... *un-nō'ing-li*
unknown... *un-nōn'*
unlace... *un-lās'*
unlawful... *un-la'ful*
unlearned... *un̈-lėr'ned*
unless... *un-les'*
unlicensed... *un-lī'senst*
unlike... *un-līk'*
unlikely... *un-līk'li*
unlimber... *un-lim'bėr*
unlimited... *un-lim'it-ed*
unload... *un-lōd'*
unlock... *un-lok'*
unlucky... *un-luk'i*
unmannerly... *un-man'ėr-li*
unmask... *un-mask'*
unmatched... *un-macht'*
unmeasured... *un-me'zhürd*
unmerciful... *un-mėr'si-ful*
unmerited... *un-mer'it-eä*
unmindful... *un-mīnd'ful*
unmitigated... *un-mi'ti-gāt-ed*
unmotherly... *un-muⱦH'ėr-li*
unmoved... *un-movd'*
unnamed... *un-nāmd'*
unnatural... *un-na'tūr-al*
unnavigable... *un-na'vi-ga-bl*
unnecessary... *un-ne'ses-sa-ri*
unneighborly... *un-nā'bėr-li*
unnerve... *un-nėrv'*
unnoticed... *un-nōt'ist*

unnumbered... *un-num'bėrd*
unobtrusive... *un-ob-tro'siv*
unoccupied... *un-ok'kū-pīd*
unoffending... *un-of-fend'ing*
unofficial... *un-of-fi'shal*
unopposed... *un-op-pōzd'*
unorthodox... *un-ōr'tho-doks*
unpack... *un-pak'*
unpaid... *un-pād'*
unpalatable... *un-pa'lat-a-bl*
unpatriotic... *un-pā'tri-ot''ik*
unpleasant... *un-ple'zant*
unpleasing... *un-plēz'ing*
unplumbed... *un-plumd'*
unpolished... *un-po'lisht*
unpopular... *un-po'pū-lėr*
unpractical... *un-prak'ti-kal*
unpracticed... *un-prak'tist*
unprejudiced... *un-pre'jū-dist*
unprepared... *un-prē-pārd'*
unprincipled... *un-prin'si-pld*
unproductive... *un-prō-duk'tiv*
unprofitable... *un-pro'fit-a-bl*
unpromising... *un-pro'mis-ing*
unproved... *un-provd'*
unpublished... *un-pub'lisht*
unpunctual... *un-pungk'tū-al*
unqualified... *un-kwo'li-fīd*
unquiet... *un-kwī'et*
unravel... *un-ra'vel*
unread... *un-red'*
unreadable... *un-rēd'a-bl*
unready... *un-re'di*
unreal... *un-rē'al*
unreason... *un-rē'zn*
unreasonable... *un-rē'zn-a-bl*
unrecorded... *un-rē-kord'ed*
unredeemed... *un-rē-dēmd'*
unrefined... *un-rē-find'*
unregistered... *un-re'jis-tėrd*
unrelated... *un-rē-lāt'ed*
unrelenting... *un-rē-lent'ing*
unreliable... *un-rē-lī'a-bl*
unrelieved... *un-rē-lēvd'*
unremitting... *un-rē-mit'ing*
unrequited... *un-rē-kwī't'ed*
unreserved... *un-rē-zėrvd'*
unrest... *un-rēst'*
unresting... *un-rest'ing*
unrestrained... *un-rē-strānd'*
unriddle... *un-rid'l*
unrighteous... *un-rī't'yus*
unripe... *un-rīp'*
unrivaled... *un-rī'vald*

unrobe... *un-rōb'*
unromantic... *un-rō-man'tik*
unruffled... *un-ruf'ld*
unruly... *un-ro'li*
unsaid... *un-sed'*
unsavory... *un-sā'vo-ri*
unscathed... *un-skāŦHd'*
unscrew... *un-skro'*
unscrupulous... *un-skro'pū-lus*
unseasonable... *un-sē'zn-a-bl*
unseat... *un-sēt'*
unseen... *un-sēn'*
unselfish... *un-sel'fish*
unsettle... *un-set'l*
unsettled... *un-set'ld*
unshaken... *un-shā'kn*
unshrinking... *un-shringk'ing*
unsightly... *un-sīt'li*
unsized... *un-sīzd'*
unskillful... *un-skil'ful*
unsociable... *un-sō''shi-a-bl*
unsocial... *un-sō'shal*
unsoiled... *un-soild'*
unsold... *un-sōld'*
unsolicited... *un-sō-lis'it-ed*
unsought... *un-sat'*
unsound... *un-soūnd'*
unsparing... *un-spār'ing*
unspoken... *un-spō'kn*
unspotted... *un-spōt'ed*
unstable... *un-stā'bl*
unstamped... *un-stampt'*
unsteady... *un-sted'i*
unstop... *un-stop'*
unstring... *un-string'*
unstrung... *un-strung'*
unsuccessful... *un-suk-ses'fụl*
unsuitable... *un-sūt'a-bl*
unsuited... *un-sūt'ed*
unsung... *un-sung'*
unsurpassed... *un-sėr-past'*
unsuspicious... *un-sus-pi'shus*
unswerving... *un-swėrv'ing*
untainted... *un-tānt-ed*
untamable... *un-tām'a-bl*
untasted... *un-tāst'ed*
untaught... *un-tat'*
unthanked... *un-̈thangkt'*
unthankful... *un-thangk'ful*
unthinkable... *un-thing'ǎ-bl*
unthinking... *un-thing'k'ing*
unthought... *un-that'*
unthrift... *un'thrift* ¨
unthrifty... *un-thrift'i*

U

untidy... *un-tī'di*
untie... *un-fī'*
until... *un-til'*
untimely... *un-tīm'li*
untiring... *un-tīr'ing*
untitled... *un-tī'tld*
unto... *un'to*
untold... *un-tōld'*
untouched... *un-tucht'*
untoward... *un-tō'wėrd*
untraceable... *un-trās'a-bl*
untractable... *un-trak'ta-bl*
untraveled... *un-tra'veld*
untried... *un-trīd'*
untroubled... *un-tru'bld*
untrue... *un-tro'*
untruth... *un-troth'*
untruthful... *un-troth'ful*
unused... *un-ūzd'*
unusual... *un-ū'zhū-al*
unutterable... *un-ut'ėr-a-bl*
unvarnished... *un-var'nisht*
unwarranted... *un-wo'rant-ed*
unwary... *un-wā'ri*
unwashed... *un-wosht'*
unwavering... *un-wā'vėr-ing*
unwearied... *un-wē'rid*
unwed... *un-wed'*
unwelcome... *un-wel'kum*
unwholesome... *un-hōl'sum*
unwieldy... *un-wēl'di*
unwilling... *un-wil'ing*
unwind... *un-wīnd'*
unwisdom... *un-wiz'dom*
unwise... *un-wīz'*
unwitting... *un-wit'ing*
unwomanly... *un-wu'man-li*
unworldly... *un-wėrld'li*
unworn... *un-wōrn'*
unworthy... *un-wėr'ŦHi*
unwrap... *un-rap'*
unwritten... *un-rit'n*
unyielding... *un-yēld'ing*
up... *up*
upbraid... *up-brād'*
upbringing... *up'bring-ing*
upheaval... *up-hēv'al*
upheave... *up-hēv'*
uphill... *up'hil*
uphold... *up-hōld'*
upholder... *up-hōld'ėr*
upholster... *up-hōl'stėr*
upholsterer... *up-hōl'stėr-ėr*
upholstery... *up-hōl'stė-ri*

upkeep... *up'kēp*
upland... *up'land*
uplift... *up-lift'*
up-line... *up'līn*
upmost... *up'mōst*
upon... *up-on'*
upper... *up'ėr*
upper-hand... *up'ėr-hand*
uppermost... *up'ėr-mōst*
uppish... *up'ish*
upraise... *up-rāz'*
uprear... *up-rēr'*
upright... *up'rīt*
uprise... *up-rīz'*
uprising... *up-rīz'ing*
uproar... *up'rōr*
uproot... *up-rot'*
upset... *up-set'*
upshot... *up'shot*
upside... *up'sīd*
upstairs... *up'stārz*
upstart... *up-start'*
upthrow... *up-thrō'*
upward... *up'wėrd*
upwards... *up'wėrdz*
uranium... *ū-rā'ni-um*
urban... *ėr'ban*
urbane... *ėr-bān'*
urbanity... *ėr-ban'i-ti*
urchin... *ėr'chin*
ureter... *ū-rē'tėr*
urethra... *ū-rē'thra*
urge... *ėrj*
urgency... *ėrj'en-si*
urgent... *ėrj'ent*
urgently... *ėrj'ent-li*
urinal... *ū-rin-al*
urinary... *ū'ri-na-ri*
urinate... *ū'ri-nāt*
urine... *ū'rin*
urticate... *ėr'ti-kāt*
urtication... *ėr-ti-kā'shun*
us... *us*
usable... *ūz'a-bl*
usage... *ūz'āj*
use... *ūs*
useful... *ūs'ful*
useless... *ūs'les*
user... *ūz'ėr*
usher... *ush'ėr*
usual... *ū'zhū-al*
usually... *ū'zhū-al-li*
usurer... *ū'zhūr-ėr*
usurious... *ū-zhū'ri-us*

usurp... _ū-zėrp'_
usurpation... _ū-zėrp-ā'zhon_
usurper... _ū-zėrp'ėr_
usury... _ū'zhū-ri_
utensil... _ū-ten'sil_
uterus... _ū'tėr-us_
utilitarian... _ū-til'i-tā''ri-an_
utility... _ū-til'i-ti_
utilize... _ū'til-īz_
utmost... _ut'mōst_
utter... _ut'ėr_
utterable... _ut'ėr-a-bl_
utterance... _ut'ėr-ans_
utterly... _ut'ėr-li_
uttermost... _ut'ėr-mōst_
uvula... _ū'vū-la_

V

vacancy... _vā'kan-si_
vacant... _vā'kant_
vacate... _va-kāt'_
vacation... _va-kā'shun_
vaccinate... _vak'si-nāt_
vaccination... _vak-si-nā'shun_
vaccine... _vak'sīn_
vacillate... _va'sil-lāt_
vacillating... _va'sil-lāt-ing_
vacillation... _va-sil-lā'shun_
vacuous... _va'kū-us_
vacuum... _va'kū-um_
vagabond... _va'ga-bond_
vagary... _va-gā'ri_
vagina... _va-jī'na_
vaginal... _va'ji-nal_
vagrant... _vā'grant_
vaguely... _vāg'li_
vail... _vāl_
vain... _vān_
vainly... _vān'li_
valance... _val'ans_
vale... _vāl_
valediction... _va-lē-dik'shun_
valedictory... _va-lē-dik'to-ri_
valence... _vā'lens_
valentine... _va'len-fīn_
valet... _va'let or va'lā_
valiant... _val'yant_
valiantly... _val'yant-li_
valid... _va'lid_
validate... _va'lid-āt_
validity... _va-lid'i-ti_

valise... _va-lēs'_
valley... _val'i_
valor... _va'lor_
valorous... _va'lor-us_
valuable... _va'lū-a-bl_
valuation... _va-lū-ā'shun_
valuator... _va'lū-āt-or_
value... _va'lū_
valve... _valv_
valvular... _valv'ū-lėr_
vamp... _vamp_
vampire... _vam'pīr_
van... _van_
vandal... _van'dal_
vandalism... _van'dal-izm_
vane... _vān_
vanguard... _van'gard_
vanilla... _va-nil'a_
vanish... _va'nish_
vanity... _va'ni-ti_
vanquish... _vang'kwish_
vanquisher... _vang'kwish-ėr_
vantage... _van'tāj_
vapidity... _va-pid'i-ti_
vaporize... _vā-por-īz_
vaporous... _vā'por-us_
vapor... _vā'por_
variability... _vā-ri-a-bil'i-ti_
variable... _vā'ri-a-bl_
variance... _vā'ri-ans_
variant... _vā'ri-ant_
variation... _vā-ri-ā'shun_
varied... _vā'rid_
variegate... _vā'ri-e-gāt_
variegation... _vā'ri-e-gā''shun_
variety... _va-rī'e-ti_
various... _vā'ri-us_
varnish... _var'nish_
vary... _vā'ri_
vascular... _vas'kū-lėr_
vasculum... _vas'kū-lum_
vase... _vaz_
vassal... _vas'al_
vast... _vast_
vastly... _vast'li_
vat... _vat_
vatican... _vat'i-kan_
vaticinate... _vā-tis'i-nāt_
vaudeville... _vōd'vēl_
vault... _valt_
vaulted... _valt'ed_
vaulting... _valt'ing_
veal... _vēl_
veer... _vēr_

V

vegetable... ve'je-ta-bl
vegetarian... ve-je-tā'ri-an
vegetation... ve-je-tā'shun
vegetative... ve'je-tāt-iv
vehement... vē'he-ment
vehemently... vē'he-ment-li
vehicle... vē'hi-kl
veil... vāl
vein... vān
veining... vān'ing
vellicate... vel'i-kāt
vellum... vel'um
velocipede... vē-los'i-pēd
velocity... vē-los'i-ti
velvet... vel'vet
velveteen... vel-vet-ēn'
venal... vē'nal
venality... vē-nal'i-ti
venation... vē-nā'shun
vend... vend
vender... ven'dėr
vendetta... ven-det'ta
vendor... ven'dor
veneer... ve-nēr'
venerable... ve'nė-ra-bl
venerate... ve'nė-rāt
venereal... ve-nē'rē-al
venetian... vē-nē'shi-an
vengeance... venj'ans
vengeful... venj'ful
venial... vē'ni-al
venison... ven'zn
venom... ve'nom
venomous... ve'nom-us
venous... vē'nus
vent... vent
ventage... vent'āj
venter... ven'tėr
ventilate... ven'ti-lāt
ventilation... ven-ti-lā'shun
ventilator... ven'ti-lāt-ėr
ventricle... ven'tri-kl
ventricular... ven-trik'ū-lėr
ventriloquist... ven-tri'lo-kwist
ventriloquize... ven-tri'lo-kwīz
venture... ven'tūr
venturesome... ven'tūr-sum
venturous... ven'tūr-us
venue... ven'ū
veracious... ve-rā'shus
veranda... ve-ran'da
verb... vėrb
verbal... vėrb'al
verbalism... vėrb'al-izm

verbalist... vėrb'al-ist
verbalize... vėrb'al-īz
verbally... vėrb'al-li
verbatim... vėr-bā'tim
verbiage... vėr'bi-āj
verbose... vėr-bōs'
verbosity... vėr-bos'i-ti
verdant... vėr'dant
verdict... vėr'dikt
verditer... vėr'di-tėr
verdurous... vėr'dūr-us
verge... vėrj
verger... vėrj'ėr
veridical... ve-rid'ik-al
verifiable... ve'ri-fī-a-bl
verification... ve'ri-fi-kā''shun
verify... ve'ri-fī
verily... ve'ri-li
veritable... ve'ri-ta-bl
verity... ve'ri-ti
vermicelli... vėr-mi-chel'li
vermicide... vėr'mi-sīd
vermicular... vėr-mik'ū-lėr
vermiculate... vėr-mik'ū-lāt
vermifuge... vėr'mi-fūj
vermilion... vėr-mil'yon
verminate... vėr'min-āt
verminous... vėr'min-us
vermivorous... vėr-miv'o-rus
vernacular... vėr-nak'ū-lėr
vernal... vėr'nal
vernation... vėr-nā'shun
versant... vėr'sant
versatile... vėrs'a-til
versatility... vėrs-a-til'i-ti
verse... vėrs
versed... vėrst
versifier... vėrs'i-fī-ėr
versify... vėrs'i-fī
version... vėr'shun
versus... vėr'sus
vertebra... vėr'te-bra
vertebral... vėr'te-bral
vertebrate... vėr'te-brāt
vertical... vėr'ti-kal
vertiginous... vėr-ti'jin-us
verve... verv
very... ve'ri
vesical... ve'si-kal
vesicant... ve'si-kant
vesicate... ve'si-kāt
vesication... ve-si-kā'shun
vesicle... ve'si-kl
vesicular... ve-sik'ū-lėr

vesper... *ves'pér*
vessel... *ves'el*
vest... *vest*
vestal... *ves'tal*
vested... *vest'ed*
vestibule... *ves'ti-būl*
vestige... *ves'tij*
vestment... *vest'ment*
vestry... *ves'tri*
vesture... *ves'tūr*
vesuvian... *ve-sū'vi-an*
veteran... *ve'te-ran*
veterinary... *ve'te-ri-na-ri*
veto... *vē'tō*
vexation... *veks-ā'shun*
vexatious... *veks-ā'shus*
vexed... *vekst*
via... *vī'a*
viable... *vī'a-bl*
viaduct... *vī'a-dukt*
vial... *vī'al*
viaticum... *vī-at'i-kum*
vibrant... *vī'brant*
vibrate... *vī'brāt*
vibration... *vī-brā'shun*
vibratory... *vī'bra-to-ri*
vicarial... *vī-kā'ri-al*
vicariate... *vī-kā'ri-āt*
vicarious... *vī-kā'ri-us*
vice... *vīs*
vice... *vī'sē*
vicegerent... *vīs-jē'rent*
vicenary... *vis'e-na-ri*
vicennial... *vi-sen'ni-al*
viceroy... *vīs'roi*
vicinage... *vi'sin-āj*
vicinity... *vi-sin'i-ti*
vicious... *vi'shus*
victimize... *vik'tim-īz*
victor... *vik'tor*
victorious... *vik-tō'ri-us*
victory... *vik'to-ri*
victress... *vik'tres*
victual... *vit'l*
vide... *vī'dē*
videlicet... *vī-del'i-set*
vidette... *vi-det'*
vidimus... *vī'di-mus or vid'*
viduity... *vi-dū'i-ti*
vie... *vī*
viennese... *vi-en-ēz'*
view... *vū*
viewer... *vū'ér*
viewless... *vū'les*

viewy... *vū'i*
vigil... *vi'jil*
vigilance... *vi'ji-lans*
vigilant... *vi'ji-lant*
vignette... *vin-yet' or vi-net'*
vigorous... *vi'gor-us*
vigor... *vi'gor*
viking... *vī'k'ing*
vilely... *vīl'li*
vilification... *vi'li-fi-kā''shun*
vilify... *vi'li-fī*
villa... *vil'a*
village... *vil'āj*
villager... *vil'āj-ér*
villain... *vil'an or vil'ān*
villainous... *vil'an-us*
villein... *vil'en*
villi... *vil'lī*
villosity... *vil-los'i-ti*
vim... *vim*
vinaceous... *vī-nā'shus*
vinaigrette... *vin-ā-gret*
vinaigrous... *vin'āg-rus*
vincible... *vin'si-bl*
vindicate... *vin'di-kāt*
vindication... *vin-di-kā'shun*
vindicative... *vin'di-kāt-iv*
vindicator... *vin'di-kāt-or*
vindicatory... *vin'di-ka-to-ri*
vindictive... *vin-dik'tiv*
vine... *vīn*
vinegar... *vi'nē-gér*
vinery... *vīn'ė-ri*
vineyard... *vin'yard*
vintage... *vint'āj*
vintager... *vint'āj-ér*
vintner... *vint'nér*
vintnery... *vint'nér-i*
viol... *vī'ol*
viola... *vī'ō-la*
viola... *vē-o'la*
violable... *vī'ō-la-bl*
violate... *vī'ō-lāt*
violation... *vī-ō-lā'shun*
violator... *vī'ō-lāt-or*
violence... *vī'ō-lens*
violent... *vī'ō-lent*
violently... *vī'ō-lent-li*
violet... *vī'ō-let*
violin... *vī-ō-lin'*
violinist... *vī-ō-lin'ist*
violist... *vī'ō-list*
violoncellist... *vī'ō-lon-sel''ist*
viper... *vī'pér*

viperine... *vī'pėr-īn*
viperish... *vī'pėr-ish*
virago... *vi-rā'gō*
virelay... *vi're-lā*
virgilian... *vėr-jil'i-an*
virgin... *vėr'jin*
virginal... *vėr'jin-al*
virginity... *vėr-jin'i-ti*
virgo... *vėr'gō*
viridity... *vi-rid'i-ti*
virile... *vi'rīl or vi'ril*
virility... *vi-ril'i-ti*
virose... *vī'rōs*
virtu... *vir-to'*
virtual... *vėr'tū-al*
virtually... *vėr'tū-al-li*
virtue... *vėr'tū*
virtuoso... *vėr-tū-ō'sō*
virtuous... *vėr'tū-us*
virtuously... *vėr'tū-us-li*
virulence... *vi'rū-lens*
virulent... *vi'rū-lent*
virulently... *vi'rū-lent-li*
virus... *vī'rus*
vis... *vis*
visage... *vi'zāj*
viscera... *vis'e-ra*
visceral... *vis'e-ral*
viscid... *vis'id*
viscidity... *vis-id'i-ti*
viscosity... *vis-kos'i-ti*
viscount... *vī'kount*
viscountess... *vī'kount-es*
viscous... *vis'kus*
visibility... *vi-zi-bil'i-ti*
visible... *vi'zi-bl*
visibly... *vi'zi-bli*
vision... *vi'zhon*
visionary... *vi'zhon-a-ri*
visit... *vi'zit*
visitant... *vi'zit-ant*
visitation... *vi-zit-ā'shun*
visitor... *vi'zit-or*
visiting... *vi'zit-ing*
visiting-card... *vi'zit-ing-kard*
visor... *vī'zor*
vista... *vis'ta*
visual... *vi'zhū-al*
vital... *vī'tal*
vitalism... *vī'tal-izm*
vitalize... *vī'tal-īz*
vitally... *vī'tal-li*
vitals... *vī'talz*
vitamin... *vī'ta-min*

vitiate... *vi'shi-āt*
vitiation... *vi-shi-ā'shun*
viticulture... *vit'i-kul-tūr*
vitreous... *vit'rē-us*
vitrescence... *vi-tres'ens*
vitrescent... *vi-tres'ent*
vitric... *vit'rik*
vitrifacture... *vit-ri-fak'tūr*
vitrify... *vit'ri-fī*
vitriol... *vit'ri-ol*
vitriolic... *vit'ri-ol'ik*
vitriolize... *vit'ri-ol-īz*
vitta... *vit'a*
vituline... *vit'ū-līn*
vituperate... *vī-tū'pe-rāt*
vituperative... *vī-tū'pe-rāt-iv*
vivacious... *vī-vā'shus or vi-*
vivacity... *vī-vas'i-ti or vi-*
vivid... *vi'vid*
vividly... *vi'vid-li*
viviparous... *vī-vip'a-rus*
vivisection... *vi-vi-sek'shun*
vivisector... *vi'vi-sek-tėr*
vixen... *viks'en*
vixenish... *viks'en-ish*
vizier... *vi-zēr' or vi'zi-ėr*
vocable... *vō'ka-bl*
vocabulary... *vō-kab'ū-la-ri*
vocal... *vō'kal*
vocalic... *vō-kal'ik*
vocalist... *vō'kal-ist*
vocalize... *vō'kal-īz*
vocally... *vō'kal-li*
vocation... *vō-kā'shun*
vocative... *vo'ka-tiv*
vociferate... *vō-sif'ė-rāt*
vociferous... *vō-sif'ėr-us*
vodka... *vod'ka*
vogue... *vōg*
voice... *vois*
voiceless... *vois'les*
void... *void*
voidance... *void'ans*
volant... *vō'lant*
volatility... *vo-la-til'i-ti*
volatilize... *vo'la-til-īz*
volcanic... *vol-kan'ik*
volcanism... *vol'kan-izm*
volcanist... *vol'kan-ist*
volcano... *vol-kā'no*
vole... *vōl*
volition... *vō-li'shun*
volley... *vol'i*
volt... *vōlt*

V

voltage... *vōlt'āj*
voltaic... *vol-tā'ik*
voltaism... *vol'ta-izm*
volubility... *vo-lū'bĭl'ĭ-tĭ*
voluble... *vo'lū-bl*
volubly... *vo'lū-blĭ*
volume... *vo'lūm*
volumeter... *vo-lū'me-tėr*
volumetric... *vo-lū-met'rik*
voluminous... *vō-lū'mĭn-us*
voluntarily... *vo'lun-ta-ri-lĭ*
voluntary... *vo'lun-ta-ri*
voluntaryism... *vo'lun-ta-ri-izm*
volunteer... *vo-lun-tēr'*
voluptuous... *vō-lup'tū-us*
voluptuously... *vō-lup'tū-us-lĭ*
volute... *vō-lūt'*
voluted... *vō-lūt'ed*
vomit... *vo'mit*
vomitory... *vo'mĭ-to-rĭ*
voodoo... *vo-do*
voracious... *vō-rā'shus*
voracity... *vō-ras'ĭ-tĭ*
vortex... *vor'teks*
vortical... *vor'tik-al*
votaress... *vō'ta-res*
votary... *vō'ta-rĭ*
vote... *vōt*
voter... *vōt'ėr*
votive... *vōt'iv*
vouch... *vouch*
voucher... *vouch'ėr*
vouchsafe... *vouch-sāf'*
voussoir... *vos'war*
vow... *vou*
vowel... *vou'el*
voyage... *voi'āj*
voyager... *voi'āj-ėr*
vulcanism... *vul'kan-izm*
vulcanite... *vul'kan-īt*
vulcanize... *vul'kan-īz*
vulgar... *vul'gėr*
vulgarian... *vul-gā'ri-an*
vulgarism... *vul'gėr-izm*
vulgarity... *vul-ga'ri-tĭ*
vulgarize... *vul'gėr-īz*
vulgarly... *vul'gėr-lĭ*
vulgate... *vul'gāt*
vulnerable... *vul'nėr-a-bl*
vulnerary... *vul'nėr-a-ri*
vulpine... *vul'pīn*
vulpinite... *vul'pin-īt*
vulture... *vul'tūr*
vulturine... *vul'tūr-īn*

W

wabble... *wob'l*
wacke... *wak'ē*
wad... *wod*
wadding... *wod'ing*
waddle... *wod'l*
wade... *wād*
wader... *wād'ėr*
waft... *waft*
wag... *wag*
wage... *wāj*
wager... *wā'jėr*
waggery... *wag'ė-rĭ*
waggle... *wag'l*
wagon... *wag'on*
wagoner... *wag'on-ėr*
waif... *wāf*
wail... *wāl*
wailing... *wāl'ing*
wain... *wān*
wainscot... *wān'skot*
waist... *wāst*
waistband... *wāst'band*
wait... *wāt*
waiter... *wāt'ėr*
waitress... *wāt'res*
waive... *wāv*
wake... *wāk*
wakeful... *wāk'ful*
waken... *wāk'n*
wale... *wāl*
walk... *wak*
walking... *wak'ing*
wall... *wal*
wallet... *wol'et*
wallop... *wol'op*
wallow... *wol'ō*
walnut... *wal'nut*
walrus... *wol'rus*
waltz... *walts*
waltzer... *walts'ėr*
wampum... *wom'pum*
wan... *won*
wand... *wond*
wander... *won'dėr*
wanderer... *won'dėr-ėr*
wandering... *won'dėr-ing*
wane... *wān*
wannish... *won'ish*
wanton... *won'ton*
war... *war*
warble... *war'bl*

warbler... war'bl-ėr
ward... ward
warden... war'den
wardrobe... ward'rōb
warehouse... wār'hous
warfare... war'fār
warily... wā'ri-li
warlike... wār'lik
warm... warm
warmer... warm'ėr
warmly... wärm'li
warmth... wärmth
warn... warn
warning... warn'ing
warp... warp
warped... warpt
warrant... wŏ'rant
warrantable... wo'rant-a-bl
warranter... wo'rant-ėr
warrantor... wo'rant-or
warranty... wo'ran-ti
warren... wo'ren
warrior... wa'ri-or
wart... wart
wary... wā'ri
was... woz
wash... wosh
washer... wosh'ėr
washy... wosh'i
wasp... wosp
waspish... wosp'ish
wassail... wos'el
waste... wāst
wasteful... wāst'ful
waster... wāst'ėr
wasting... wāst'ing
watch... woch
watch-dog... woch'dog
watcher... woch'ėr
watch-fire... woch'fir
watchful... woch'ful
watch-maker... wŏch'māk-ėr
watchman... woch'man
watch-tower... woch'tou-ėr
water... wa'tėr
water-bed... wa'tėr-bed
water-color... wä'tėr-kul-ėr
water-course... wa'tėr-kōrs
watered... wa'tėrd
waterfall... wä'tėr-fal
watering... wä'tėr-ing
water-line... wa'tėr-lin
water-logged... wa'tėr-logd
waterman... wa'tėr-man

water-mark... wa'tėr-mark
water-polo... wä'tėr-pō''lō
water-power... wa'tėr-pou-ėr
waterproof... wa'tėr-prof
watershed... wä'tėr-shed
water-spout... wa'tėr-spout
water-tight... wa'tėr-tīt
water-way... wä'tėr-wā
water-works... wa'tėr-wėrks
watery... wa'tėr-i
watt... wot
wave... wāv
waved... wāvd
waver... wā'vėr
waverer... wā'vėr-ėr
wavy... wāv'i
wax... waks
waxen... waks'en
waxy... waks'i
way... wā
wayfarer... wā'fār-ėr
wayside... wā'sid
wayward... wā'wėrd
waywardly... wā'wėrd-li
we... wē
weak... wēk
weaken... wēk'n
weakling... wēk'ling
weakly... wēk'li
weakness... wēk'nes
wealth... welth
wealthy... welth'i
wean... wēn
weanling... wēn'ling
weapon... we'pon
wear... wār
wearer... wār'ėr
wearily... wē'ri-li
wearing... wār'ing
wearisome... wē'ri-sum
weary... wē'ri
weasel... wē'zl
weather... weŦH'ėr
weatherly... weŦH'ėr-li
weathermost... weŦH'ėr-mōst
weave... wēv
weaver... wēv'ėr
weaving... wēv'ing
web... web
webbed... webd
webbing... web'ing
weber... vā'ber
web-foot... web'fut
wed... wed

W

wedded... *wed'ed*
wedding... *wed'ing*
wedge... *wej*
wedlock... *wed'lok*
wee... *wē*
weed... *wēd*
weeder... *wēd'ėr*
weedy... *wēd'i*
week... *wēk*
week-day... *wēk'dā*
weekly... *wēk'li*
weep... *wēp*
weeper... *wēp'ėr*
weeping... *wēp'ing*
weevil... *wē'vil*
weigh... *wā*
weight... *wāt*
weighty... *wāt'i*
weir... *wēr*
weird... *wērd*
welcome... *wel'kum*
weld... *weld*
welfare... *wel'fār*
well... *wel*
welsh... *welsh*
welt... *welt*
welter... *welt'ėr*
wen... *wen*
wench... *wensh*
were... *wer*
werewolf... *wēr'wulf*
wesleyan... *wes'li-än*
west... *west*
wet... *wet*
wether... *weŦH'ėr*
wettish... *wet'ish*
wey... *wā*
whack... *whak*
wharf... *wharf*
what... *whoṫ*
whatever... *whot-ev'ėr*
wheat... *whēt*
wheaten... *whēt'n*
wheedle... *whē'dl*
wheel... *whēl*
wheel-barrow... *whēl'ba-rō*
wheeled... *whēld*
wheeler... *whēl'ėr*
wheeze... *whēz*
wheezy... *whēz'i*
whelm... *whelm*
whelp... *whelp*
when... *when*
whence... *whens*

whensoever... *when-sō-ev'ėr*
where... *whār*
whereabouts... *whār'a-bouts*
whereat... *whār-at'*
whereby... *whār-bi'*
wherefore... *whār'for*
wherein... *whār-in'*
whereinto... *whār-in-to'*
whereon... *whār-on'*
whereto... *whār-to'*
whereupon... *whār-up-on'*
wherever... *whār-ev'ėr*
whether... *wheŦH'ėr*
whew... *whū*
whey... *whā*
which... *which*
whiff... *whif*
while... *whīl*
whilst... *whīlst*
whimper... *whim'pėr*
whimsical... *whim'zik-al*
whimsy... *whim'zi*
whin... *whin*
whine... *whīn*
whinny... *whin'i*
whip... *whip*
whipping... *whip'ing*
whirl... *whėrl*
whirlpool... *whėrl'pol*
whirlwind... *whėrl'wind*
whisk... *whisk*
whisker... *whis'kėr*
whisky... *whis'ki*
whisper... *whis'pėr*
whispering... *whis'pėr-ing*
whistle... *whis'l*
white... *whīt*
whiten... *whīt'n*
whitewash... *whīt'wosh*
whither... *whiŦH'ėr*
whiting... *whīt'ing*
whitish... *whīt'ish*
whitlow... *whit'lō*
whittle... *whit'l*
whiz... *whiz*
who... *ho*
whoever... *ho-ev'ėr*
whole... *hōl*
wholesale... *hōl'sāl*
wholesome... *hōl'sum*
wholly... *hōl'li*
whoop... *whop or hop*
whopper... *whop'ėr*
whore... *hōr*

whoredom... hōr'dum
whose... hoz
whosoever... ho-sō-ev'ėr
why... whī
wick... wik
wicked... wik'ed
wickedly... wik'ed-li
wickedness... wik'ed-nes
wide... wīd
wide-awake... wīd'a-wāk
widely... wīd'li
widen... wīd'n
widow... wi'dō
widower... wi'dō-ėr
widowhood... wi'dō-hu̇d
width... width
wield... wēld
wielder... wēld'ėr
wieldy... wēld'i
wife... wif
wifely... wīf'li
wig... wig
wigging... wig'ing
wight... wīt
wigwam... wig'wam
wild... wild
wilderness... wil'dėr-nes
wildfire... wīld'fir
wilding... wīld'ing
wildish... wīld'ish
wildly... wīld'li
wile... wīl
wileful... wīl'ful
wiliness... wī'li-nes
will... wil
willful... wil'ful
willfully... wil'ful-li
willing... wil'ing
willingly... wil'ing-li
willow... wil'ō
willowy... wil'o-i
wilt... wilt
wily... wi'li
wimble... wim'bl
wimple... wim'pl
win... win
wince... wins
wind... wīnd
windage... wind'āj
wind-bag... wind'bag
winder... wīnd'ėr
windfall... wind'fal
winding... wīnd'ing
windmill... wind'mil

window... win'dō
windpipe... wind'pip
windward... wind'wėrd
windy... wind'i
wine... wīn
wine-cellar... wīn'sel-ėr
wine-glass... wīn'glas
wine-press... wīn'pres
wine-taster... wīn'tāst-ėr
wing... wing
winged... wingd
winglet... wing'let
wink... wingk
winner... win'ėr
winning... win'ing
winnow... win'ō
winsey... win'si
winsome... win'sum
winter... win'tėr
winterly... win'tėr-li
winy... wīn'i
winze... winz
wipe... wīp
wire... wīr
wireless... wir'les
wire-puller... wīr'pu̇l-ėr
wiry... wīr'i
wisdom... wiz'dom
wise... wīz
wiseacre... wīz'ā-kėr
wisely... wīz'li
wish... wish
wishful... wish'ful
wishy-washy... wish'i-wosh'i
wisp... wisp
wistful... wist'ful
wistfully... wist'ful-li
wit... wit
witch... wich
witchcraft... wich'kraft
witchery... wich'ė-ri
witching... wich'ing
with... wifH
withe... with or wīth
withy... wi'thi
witness... wit'nes
witty... wit'i
wive... wīv
wizard... wiz'ard
wobble... wob'l
woebegone... wō'bē-gon
woefully... wō'ful-li
wold... wōld
wolf... wu̇lf

W

wolfish... *wulf'ish*
woman... *wu'man*
womb... *wom*
wombat... *wom'bat*
wonder... *wun'der*
wonderful... *wun'der-ful*
wondrous... *wun'drus*
wont... *wont*
woo... *wo*
wood... *wud*
woodbine... *wud'bin*
woodcock... *wud-kok*
wood-cut... *wud'kut*
wooded... *wud'ed*
woodland... *wud'land*
woodman... *wud'man*
woodpecker... *wud'pek-er*
wood-pigeon... *wud'pi-jon*
woodruff... *wud'ruf*
wood-sorrel... *wud'so-rel*
wood-work... *wud'werk*
woody... *wud'i*
wooer... *wo'er*
woof... *wof*
wool... *wul*
wool-grower... *wul'gro-er*
woollen... *wul'en*
woolly... *wul'i*
woolpack... *wul'pak*
woolsack... *wul'sak*
wootz... *wuts*
word... *werd*
word-book... *werd'buk*
wording... *werd'ing*
wordy... *werd'i*
work... *werk*
workable... *werk'a-bl*
worker... *werk'er*
workhouse... *werk'hous*
working... *werk'ing*
working-class... *werk'ing-klas*
workman... *werk'man*
workmanlike... *werk'man-lik*
workmanly... *werk'man-li*
workshop... *werk'shop*
world... *werld*
worldling... *werld'ling*
worldly... *werld'li*
world-wide... *werld'wid*
worm... *werm*
worm-eaten... *werm'et-n*
wormling... *werm'ling*
wormwood... *werm'wud*

wormy... *werm'i*
worn... *worn*
worn-out... *worn'out*
worry... *wu'ri*
worse... *wers*
worsen... *wer'sn*
worser... *wers'er*
worship... *wer'ship*
worshipper... *wer'ship-er*
worst... *werst*
worsted... *wust'ed*
wort... *wert*
worth... *werth*
would-be... *wud'be*
wound... *wond*
wrack... *rak*
wraith... *rath*
wrangle... *rang'gl*
wrangler... *rang'gler*
wrap... *rap*
wrapper... *rap'er*
wrapping... *rap'ing*
wrath... *rath or rath*
wrathful... *rath'ful*
wreak... *rek*
wreath... *reth*
wreathe... *reŦH*
wreathy... *reth'i*
wreck... *rek*
wreckage... *rek'aj*
wrecker... *rek'er*
wren... *ren*
wrest... *rest*
wrestle... *res'l*
wrestler... *res'ler*
wretch... *rech*
wretched... *rech'ed*
wretchedly... *rech'ed-li*
wriggle... *rig'l*
wright... *rit*
wring... *ring*
wringer... *ring'er*
wrinkle... *ring'kl*
wrist... *rist*
writ... *rit*
write... *rit*
writhe... *riŦH*
wrong... *rong*
wroth... *roth*
wry... *ri*
wryneck... *ri'nek*
wynd... *wind*
wyvern... *wi'vern*

X

xanthic... *zan'thik*
xebec... *zē'bek or ze-bek'*
xylograph... *zī'lo-graf*
xyloid... *zī'loid*
xylonite... *zī'lō-nīt*
xylophagous... *zī-lof'a-gus*
xylophone... *zī-lo-fōn*
xyst... *zist*
xyster... *zis'tér*

Y

yacht... *yot*
yachter... *yot'ér*
yachting... *yot'ing*
yachtsman... *yots'man*
yahoo... *ya'ho*
yam... *yam*
yankee... *yang'kē*
yap... *yap*
yard... *yard*
yard-stick... *yard'stik*
yarn... *yarn*
yataghan... *yat'a-gan*
yawn... *yan*
yean... *yēn*
yeanling... *yēn'ling*
year-book... *yēr-buk*
yearling... *yēr'ling*
yearly... *yér'li*
yearn... *yérn*
yearning... *yérn'ing*
yeast... *yēst*
yeasty... *yēst'i*
yell... *yel*
yellow... *yel'ō*
yellow-fever... *yel'ō-fē-vér*
yellowish... *yel'ō-ish*
yelp... *yelp*
yeoman... *yō'man*
yeomanly... *yō'man-li*
yeomanry... *yō'man-ri*
yes... *yes*
yesterday... *yes'tér-dā*
yet... *yet*

yew... *yū*
yield... *yēld*
yielding... *yēld'ing*
yodel, Yodle... *yō'dl*
yoke... *yōk*
yolk... *yōk*
young... *yung*
youngish... *yung'ish*
youngling... *yung'ling*
youngster... *yung'stér*
your... *yor*
yours... *yorz*
youthful... *yoth'ful*
yule... *yol*

Z

zany... *zā'ni*
zeal... *zēl*
zealot... *ze'lot*
zealous... *ze'lus*
zealously... *ze'lus-li*
zebra... *zē'bra*
zephyr... *zef'ér*
zeppelin... *zep'el-in*
zereba... *ze-rē'ba*
zero... *zē'rō*
zest... *zest*
zigzag... *zig'zag*
zigzaggy... *zig'zag-i*
zinc... *zingk*
zincode... *zingk'ōd*
zincoid... *zingk'oid*
zip-fastener... *zip-fas'n-ér*
zircon... *zér'kon*
zither... *zith'ér*
zodiac... *zō'di-ak*
zodiacal... *zō-dī'ak-al*
zone... *zōn*
zonule... *zōn'ūl*
zoogony... *zō-og'o-ni*
zoography... *zō-og'ra-fi*
zoological... *zō-o-loj'ik-al*
zoologist... *zō-ol'o-jist*
zoology... *zō-ol'o-ji*
zymic... *zim'ik*
zymology... *zi-mol'o-ji*
zymotic... *zi-mot'ik*

X
Y
Z

SPECIAL OFFER
Reference Library

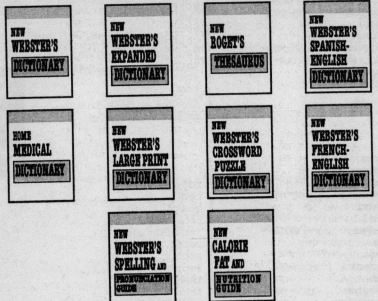

Special: Purchase any first book at regular price of $5.95 and choose any second book for $2.95 plus $1.50 for postage and handling. *For Canadian orders add $1.00 per book. All payments must be in U.S. Dollars.*

Please send me the following books:

_____ New Webster's Dictionary
_____ New Roget's Thesaurus
_____ Home Medical Dictionary
_____ New Webster's Crossword Dictionary
_____ Webster's Spelling & Pronunciation

_____ New Webster's Expanded Dictionary
_____ Webster's Spanish/English Dictionary
_____ New Webster's Large Print Dictionary
_____ Webster's French/English Dictionary
_____ Calorie Fat and Nutrition Guide

Name _____

Address _____

City _____ State _____ ZIP _____

I have enclosed $_____ for _____ books which includes all postage and handling costs. (No C.O.D.)

Send to: Paradise Press, Inc.
8551 Sunrise Blvd. #302
Plantation, FL 33322